Her Wicked Ways

USA TODAY
BESTSELLING AUTHOR

DARCY
BURKE

For my sweet Quinn and awesome Zane.
You make every day such a joy.

And for Steve. My partner in...everything.

HER WICKED WAYS

She was his savior

Banished from London for her reckless behavior, Lady Miranda Sinclair is robbed by a dashing highwayman en route to the country. By offering him a kiss in lieu of the jewels she had to leave behind, she commits the very type of act that caused her exile. When her dour guardians extend her punishment to performing charitable work at the local orphanage, she's further tempted by the home's owner, a provincial gentleman who stirs her passion.

He was her downfall

Desperate to save his orphanage from financial catastrophe, Montgomery "Fox" Foxcroft leads a double life as a highwayman. The arrival of wealthy, well-connected Miranda, whose kiss he can't forget, presents a lawful opportunity to increase his coffers. His problems seem solved—until she rejects his suit. Out of options and falling for the heiress, Fox must risk what principles he has left and take advantage of her wicked ways—even if it ruins them both.

Love romance? Have a free book (or two or three) on me!

Sign up at http://www.darcyburke.com/readerclub for members-only exclusives, including advance notice of pre-orders and insider scoop, as well as contests, give-aways, freebies, and 99 cent deals!

Want to share your love of my books with like-minded readers? Want to hang with me and get inside scoop? Then don't miss my exclusive Facebook groups!

Darcy's Duchesses for historical readers
Burke's Book Lovers for contemporary readers

HER WICKED WAYS

By Darcy Burke

Copyright © 2012 Darcy Burke
All rights reserved.
ISBN: 1939713889
ISBN-13: 9781939713889

Book design © Darcy Burke.
Cover design © Elizabeth Mackey.
Cover Image © Period Images.

❀ Created with Vellum

CHAPTER 1

"STAND and deliver!" Montgomery Foxcroft demanded a second time as he and the other four members of his band stepped out from the trees lining the rutted and muddy road. They'd scouted the two coaches for the last quarter mile. Each had a coachman at the reins and a footman on the back. The footman on the rear coach crouched low as both vehicles rumbled to a halt.

"You there, stand away!" Fox stalked toward the second coach, training his pistol on the man's chest. The servant stared, wide-eyed in the milky light offered by the half moon. Sweat trickled down Fox's back as he waited for the footman to obey. An eternity seemed to pass before the man jumped from the back of the dark blue lacquered coach, his arms spread. Fox let out his pent up breath.

They hadn't prepared for two coaches, but Fox's steward, Robert Knott, had come up with a plan to direct the four retainers to a single location. Rob came abreast of him and shouted, "Move between the coaches, and keep yer hands where I can see them!"

Fox resisted the urge to tug his mask further down his face. The rough, black fabric covered everything but his mouth. Surely that wouldn't be enough to spark recognition.

Hugh Carmody, landowner and retired MP, opened the door of the lead coach and thrust out his nearly bald head. "What is the meaning of this?"

Rob pointed his pistol at the man's face and was answered with a decidedly unmasculine shriek, followed by a thud.

"Wife!" Carmody retreated.

Rob murmured the question that had been plaguing Fox since they'd sighted their quarry. "Why two coaches?"

Carmody owned just one, and it wasn't the fancy, lacquered coach in the rear. He also didn't employ that many footmen. Someone had to be traveling with them. Someone wealthy.

The door of the expensive coach flew open. Pale hair glistened in the moonlight as a female head poked forth and glanced down at where the step would have been if the footman had pulled it out. She raised her face, and Fox's jaw loosened. He just managed to keep it from unhinging entirely. She was beautiful. No, that word didn't do her justice. She was incomparable.

Her heart-shaped countenance was perfectly proportioned with delicious bow lips set above a strong chin. A delicate nose turned up at the end in a rather saucy fashion. Softly angled cheekbones were accentuated by her annoyance. Eyes of an indiscernible color tilted at the outside. His heart took a decidedly different rhythm as his body reacted to her instead of the robbery.

"Are you here to steal our money or gape?" She jumped from the coach, scattering a spray of mud as she landed in the lane. The young woman looked down at the dark spots now marring the lower skirt of her dress. He'd no notion of its construction, but the rich fabric and sparkling decoration bespoke extravagance. She raised her gaze to Fox's once more and again, the impact of her beauty hit him like a bludgeon.

Rob coughed loudly.

Fox silently cursed his distraction. He nodded toward the first coach. "We're here to steal *his* money." He considered her gown again, the luxuriousness of her equipage, and the gold-trimmed livery worn by her retainers. "Though I'm happy to take yours as well."

A second chit stuck her head out of the window of the fancy coach. Fox recognized the young woman's dark hair and narrow face. "We don't have any money!" Beatrice Carmody squealed.

Fox found that hard to believe. He motioned toward the rich girl. "This one's got money to burn." He tightened his grip on the pistol. What he wouldn't give for a surplus of money. Hell, what he wouldn't give for just *enough* money.

The beauty pursed her lips. "Unfortunately, I do not."

Lying brat. He didn't believe her declaration of poverty for a trice. She had to possess something of value—that dress for instance. Christ, would he stoop to stripping a girl of her clothing to support the orphanage? He immediately imagined her pale flesh exposed to the moonlight, her radiant blond hair sweeping her shoulders, her breasts. *Dammit.* His first foray into criminal behavior, and he was already a blackguard.

An enigmatic smile lit her face, thankfully interrupting his thoughts. "Instead of coin, might I offer you something else?"

He relaxed a bit, glad she'd decided to be accommodating with whatever valuables she had in the coach. Perhaps this night's endeavor would reap a larger bounty than he'd anticipated. Feeling lighter than he had all evening, he waved Rob toward the first coach. "Get the money from the gent. I'll take care of these two."

Fox kept the pistol in his right hand as he moved toward the beauty, his boots squelching in the wet earth. She tried to shake the mud from her hem, clearly unaware Wiltshire dirt was a bloody, clinging nuisance. He considered offering assistance, but she raised her head and he judged such chivalry to be pointless. Her stare was direct, and she elevated her delightfully pert chin. Her regard all but dared him to come closer. And so he did.

Up close, she was even more stunning. Impossibly so. She smelled of orange and clove. Spicy. Completely feminine.

Fox wanted to knock his head against a tree. This wasn't like him. Mentally undressing hapless females whilst he stole their valuables. He had to keep his wits about him. Rob and so many others counted on his success tonight. "What do you have for me?"

She stepped toward him until they stood a mere hand's width apart. "I have nothing, save a kiss."

His jaw did drop then. *Brazen enchantress.* He willed his brain to think of his charges. Edward needed medicine. Dora needed shoes. They all needed a secure place to live that didn't leak.

He couldn't believe he was going to refuse her—his body certainly didn't agree. "I don't need a kiss. I need money."

She sighed, a sound of deep regret. "I told you, I have no money."

"You're lying. You reek of wealth." Fox sniffed loudly to punctuate his statement and got a nose full of her alluring scent for his trouble.

"I know." Her lips curved into a small, almost seductive smile. It stole his breath. Literally. When he finally remembered to take air, he did so quite audibly. Her mouth widened then, and her face shone like the sun on the brightest summer day.

What the hell kind of highwayman fixated on some chit like a cheap Byron impostor?

Fox reined in his wayward lust. "You must have something of value. A piece of jewelry? A quizzing glass?"

She arched a brow. "What do you take me for? A doddering dowager?"

Good God, no. Never that. If they'd been anywhere else, he would've laughed.

Instead, he called out to Rob, as much to distract himself from her as to determine his steward's progress. "How are you doing over there?" He was careful to lower his voice lest Carmody determine his identity. Highway robbery shouldn't be this bloody complicated.

"Coming along. Gent's being quite accommodating."

He returned his attention to the girl, disappointed she hadn't sprouted a wart in the last few seconds. "I don't have time to discuss the finer points of your doddering or lack thereof. Return to the carriage and retrieve whatever it is you have of value. I'd hate to have to use my pistol."

Her gaze flicked downward. "Your pistol?"

Hell's teeth, had she just looked at his crotch?

"You're not even pointing it at me."

She was quite maddeningly correct. The weapon hung from his fingers, forgotten amidst her beauty and the tormenting effect of her nearness.

Unwelcome desire charged through him despite his best efforts to keep it at bay. "Yes, my pistol. I'd prefer not to harm you, but if you do not procure your valuables immediately, I shall be forced to do so."

A pouch splattered in the mud near their feet. Both of them looked down.

"Here!" Beatrice called from the coach. "That's

everything we have. She's not lying to you. Her parents have exiled her to Wiltshire and gave her nothing of value as punishment. She doesn't even have her maid."

The beauty threw a glare at the coach.

Fox's lips quirked beneath his mask. A spoiled Society chit then. "Pick up the pouch and put it in my cloak." Perhaps it was foolish of him to invite her even closer, but he reasoned he couldn't very well pick up the pouch and leave himself vulnerable.

She contemplated him, her bow-shaped lips pressing together. He still couldn't detect the hue of her eyes, but imagined them to be the color of the sea—not blue, not green, but something just between.

With a huff, she bent and plucked the purse from the ground. She straightened and raised her right brow again. "Do you have a pocket?"

Fox held the left side of his black cloak open. "Here."

She reached inside and fumbled for a moment. The back of her hand—she wore no gloves—grazed the front of his waistcoat. Sensation leapt from the intimate contact. He was torn between rebuttal and encouragement.

Upon locating the pocket he'd had sewn solely for the purpose of this robbery, she deposited the purse. She pulled her hand back, but he grabbed her fingers, bare against the leather of his glove. Her gaze met his, and her lips parted in silent invitation.

Later he would chastise himself for his poor judgment, but now...now he would surrender.

Fox lowered his head and put his mouth on hers. The jolt of sensation flooded him with warmth, made him forget time and place and purpose. Soft lips moved beneath his in delicious response, as if this kiss were the reason for their meeting. With his free hand, he caressed her waist, pulling her closer. Her form fit against his with astonishing precision. His senses screamed for more.

Her tongue flicked against his mouth. *Her tongue?*

After her behavior thus far, he shouldn't have been surprised by her shocking display of experience. She was obviously not married, given her exile, but someone had taught her how to kiss. Someone he'd like to thrash.

Then her tongue slid into his mouth, and conscious thought evaded him completely. With a groan, he tugged her harder against his chest and wrapped his arms around her back. Her hands crept up and pulled his shoulders closer while her head angled beneath his.

He lost himself in the kiss, for once surrendering to his most primal needs, prioritizing them instead of everyone else's. He tipped his head to stroke deeper into her mouth, unable to get enough of her. This moment was for him, and he meant to indulge.

The swell of her breasts strained against him, echoing the insistent pressure of her palms driving him nearer. He was overwhelmed by her touch, her scent, her taste. He worked his free hand up to the back of her neck, his fingers caressing her warm flesh. Like silk...

"Christ! What're you doing out here?" Rob's booming voice crashed into their embrace like a pistol cocked against Fox's temple. Fox pulled away guiltily, feeling like a green lad instead of a grown man of eight and twenty.

She stared at him, her eyes wide. As if, like him, she couldn't quite believe what had just transpired. Despite the fact she'd been the instigator.

He smiled slowly, fixated on her kiss-reddened lips. "Siren."

She arched her brow again, and he couldn't tell if she was an innocent girl or an accomplished seductress. Not that it mattered. He hadn't the time for either complication.

Rob came to his side and elbowed him in the ribs.

Fox lowered his voice to barely above a whisper. "Did you get enough?"

The answering snort clearly said, *Is there ever enough?*

"Sorry, stupid question," Fox muttered.

Fox turned a wary eye on the beauty. She stood stock still, her chin thrust out, whether in pride or insubordination, he didn't know. The man foolish enough to court her was destined for agony.

He patted his cloak. "I got a bit of blunt from those two as well." He hoped it was enough for their immediate needs. He preferred not to play the highwayman again.

Rob called, "Let's go, lads." He led the other two members of their motley band into the trees where their horses waited. They'd meet up at the manor and tally the profit.

Fox should have followed directly on their heels, but he couldn't resist a final glance at the beauty who kissed too well. Her lips curved into that devastating smile, and for a brief moment, Fox pondered risking the hangman and sweeping her into his keeping. He shook the madness from his head and offered a slight wave.

She raised her hand in response. "Until next time, then?"

Fox chuckled. Incomparable. "Pray, my lady, there isn't a next time."

She dropped her fingers to her lips, touching them briefly before letting her arm swing down. "I shall do no such thing."

Beatrice gasped, drawing his attention. One of the footmen was reaching toward the back of the first coach, perhaps for a weapon. Fox refused to stay to find out. With a quick turn, he dashed into the trees. Out of sight but not out of hearing.

"What in God's name are you about, Miranda? Your

father won't be pleased to hear this!" Carmody wasted no time berating the lovely siren for her imprudent behavior.

Miranda.

After the man's tirade faded behind him, Fox approached his horse and mounted. The evening's tension drained from him under the pleasant memory of Miranda's kiss.

Before setting Icarus to a walk, he retrieved the velvet purse. With a tug, the drawstring came loose and he emptied the contents into his hand. Hairpins and a couple of biscuits. Biscuits?

The tension returned, with a shock of irritation. Why hadn't he checked the purse in the road? *Fool.*

Because he'd been too confounded. He cursed in self-recrimination.

He couldn't repair a leaky roof with biscuits and hairpins, which meant he'd likely have to do this again. For all his bravado, tonight's lawlessness hadn't come easy. Only the desperation of his tenants and his orphans had forced his hand. For them, he'd sell his soul.

*A*T Bassett Manor, Fox dumped the contents of Rob's bag on his two-hundred year-old desk. Coins clinked and rolled about, forming a not-too-impressive pile atop the scuffed and scratched mahogany.

Rob dropped his mask next to the money. "It's not as much as we'd hoped, but it's enough to start work on the orphanage roof."

Circling behind the desk, Fox sank into his rickety chair. One day the wood and leather would crumble to the floor in a worthless heap, but thankfully not tonight.

Rob held up an empty, chipped glass in question. Fox nodded in response. The brandy wasn't very good, but it was liquor and it was readily available.

After pouring, Rob handed him the glass while taking a drink from his own. His lips immediately puckered and his left eye squinted. "I can see why no one wanted that cask." Silence grew for a moment before Rob pierced it like a spade through soft earth. "That chit seems moneyed. And I reckon she's not married."

Really, Fox should have seen this coming. He'd no confusion as to whom Rob meant by 'that chit.' After seven years of working together and close friendship, Rob was the nearest thing to a brother Fox would ever have. "You're suggesting I leg-shackle myself to a bank?"

"A very comely bank." Rob tossed back another swallow, his face pinching less this time. "She'd be an easy answer to our money problems. And you could do worse."

Fox took a hearty drink, pretending the liquid was far smoother than it tasted. "So this is what it's come to? I have to trade myself for money?" He didn't want to marry a spoiled heiress, regardless of her stunning beauty. He didn't want to marry anyone. Not after Jane.

"That, or we find another mark. Makes no difference to me. I rather liked taking money from that skinny goat."

Carmody wasn't the richest gent in the district, but it didn't bother Fox to steal from him. He'd spent more money purchasing votes during his stint as MP than Fox could spend in a year on two estates. "I won't argue that, but it's a risk."

A soft rap on the door drew their attention. Fox called, "Come."

His housekeeper, Mrs. Afton, stepped inside. "Sorry to disturb you, Mr. Foxcroft. I've just received a note from Mrs. Gates." She handed Fox a piece of parchment. Before he could unfold it, she added, "Two children were left at Stipple's End earlier tonight. The vicar from Swindon brought them." Stipple's End had an excellent reputation throughout northern Wiltshire and as a result, there were always plenty of children to rescue.

Fox clenched the paper as tension rippled through his tired frame. New children at the orphanage always meant added expense. Clothing, extra rations, and usually medicine. "How old?"

"Wee things, I'm told. The older one's ill."

The parchment in his hand suddenly carried the weight of lead. "Thank you, Mrs. Afton."

The housekeeper bobbed and left, closing the door behind her.

"Methinks that heiress just got more attractive." Rob wriggled his eyebrows in the most annoying fashion.

Fox tossed the last of his wretched brandy back, hoping his selfish father was enjoying himself in hell. "You think I can lure a Society deb like her?" A hole had formed in Fox's shirt over his right elbow. The soles of his boots would need replacement come fall. He ran his thumb along the edge of his forefinger. The nail, ragged and worn, snagged his flesh. "Perhaps I can entice her with my extravagant estate?" He swept his arm about the study, bare of anything but the requisite items and even those were aged and worn. "Wait, maybe my title will induce her. Except 'mister' isn't as exciting as it used to be."

"Don't sell yourself short." Rob raised his glass and then drained it.

He wasn't. But he couldn't change who he was or what she appeared to be. "You have to admit my courting her would be tricky. I'm only trying to reason how it might work."

Rob snorted as he set his empty glass back on the sideboard. "Perhaps she's come to Wootton Bassett to find a kind-hearted husband."

"Ha! Perhaps." Fox drummed his fingers on the

desktop. Until the arrival of the new orphans, Fox had been prepared to argue against this idea, preferring to chance capture by the hangman's noose instead of the parson's trap. But that was a ludicrous notion anyway. A greater risk for a temporary windfall. Marriage to someone like Miranda—was she Lady Miranda?— would ensure their financial comfort indefinitely.

Fox's shoulders twitched as he looked at his steward and friend, happily married with two children. Yes, better to marry an heiress than risk Rob and the others. "I'll find out what I can about this rich girl."

Rob nodded. "A bit of fluff would do you good. You need more than Mrs. Danforth to keep you warm."

Christ. Polly. She'd invited him to visit tonight. It seemed the enchanting Miranda had obliterated any thought of his sometime lover. *Miranda*—just thinking her name filled his brain with the memory of spicy orange scent, soft curves, and delicious lips. She'd been interested in something, but marriage probably wasn't it.

Fox stood. He'd had enough of discussing marriage and thieving. "I'm for Stipple's End to see about these children." He scooped the coins back into the bag, mentally calculating how much of it he'd need to give Mrs. Gates for the new arrivals.

Rob plucked his mask off the desk and tucked it into his coat. "I'll be over early tomorrow. Bad weather or no, we need to get some vegetables into the ground. Thankfully the warmest months are still ahead of us." His hope hung in the air between them, as intangible and elusive as the money they needed to fix the orphanage roof.

Damn, but the edge of ruin was a desperate place, and unfortunately, the business of courting his heiress couldn't happen overnight. In the meantime, Fox would do what he could to increase their coffers without having to steal. "I'll attend the next vicarage tea.

Mayhap I can squeeze more money out of their self-important attendees." That probably wasn't the fairest assessment—they weren't all self-important—but the bi-weekly vicarage tea was the closest thing to a society event as Wootton Bassett ever came, and invitations meant you were *somebody*.

As Fox made his way back to the stable, his mind returned to Miranda. Her kiss had stirred something in him. Something that had died when Jane's father had forced her to marry Stratham instead of him.

He flinched, recalling Jane's tearful refusal of his proposal. Fox still couldn't look her father in the eye without wanting to punch it.

Would Miranda even accept his suit? Or, like Jane, would she be forced to spurn him in favor of someone with wealth or a title, or both?

CHAPTER 2

"*T*IME for breakfast, my lady."

Lady Miranda Sinclair roused from her dream, or perhaps nightmare, where she was once more caught in an intimate embrace on the Dark Walk at Vauxhall. The very event that had precipitated her banishment from London. And it hadn't even been a good kiss. Not like that of the highwayman.

"My lady, you must wake up," came the maid's plaintive tone.

"Fine." Miranda shivered in her narrow, lumpy bed, miserable without the benefit of a warming pan. Cracking one eye open, she didn't see the maid who'd only stuck her head into the room to awaken her. Couldn't she at least have stoked the fire before leaving? Miranda burrowed deeper into the covers.

Think of something warm. Something hot.

The highwayman's kiss.

Last night came back to her as if it had just happened. Heat rolled through her while she recalled his tongue in her mouth, his fingers stroking her neck. In the half dozen or so times she'd kissed Charles Darleigh, her body had never reacted so strongly. Her insides swirled like perfumed oil poured into a hot bath.

A chill pricked between her shoulders and she

twitched. She'd kissed a criminal. A man of indeterminate background and breeding. And she'd liked it. Quite a lot. Quite a bit more than she'd liked kissing Darleigh, the nephew of an earl with five thousand a year.

"My lady?" The maid had returned. "You're still abed."

Of course she was. She'd spent half the night tossing and turning trying to sleep in the infernally cold and quiet—too quiet—room. "What the devil time is it? Certainly too early for...breakfast, did you say?"

"Yes, breakfast is at half-eight. In ten minutes."

Couldn't she have just brought a cup of chocolate? Miranda always awakened to the tantalizing scent of chocolate. "I'll dine later. Civilized people don't rise this early."

"I'm sorry, my lady, but breakfast is at half-eight. Mr. Carmody expects everyone at table. He becomes quite cross if Mrs. Carmody is tardy—"

"Oh, for heaven's sake!" Miranda threw the covers off and gasped at the rush of cold air. She leapt to her feet, hugging herself. "And I suppose it's too much to expect you to stoke the fire?" At the maid's widened gaze and slackened jaw, Miranda regretted her tone. "Are you here to help me dress then?"

"Yes, if my lady requires my assistance."

Miranda glanced at a clock on the mantelpiece—one of few adornments in her tiny bedroom. "Ten minutes you say? This will be the fastest toilet of my twenty-two years."

Thirteen minutes later, Miranda picked her way down the creaking stairs to Birch House's pathetic excuse for an entry hall. The maid had given her the direction of the dining room—not that she'd needed it given the doll-size dimensions of Birch House. Upon reaching her destination, she stopped short in the doorway. Mr. and Mrs. Carmody and Beatrice were seated around a ridiculously small table. Goodness, it probably only sat eight at best. Fitchley—wasn't he the butler who'd greeted them last night?—attended the meal.

Miranda glanced around for the buffet table. Seeing none, she took the only remaining vacant seat. Presumably the other chairs—if there were other chairs—were located elsewhere. In fact, Miranda imagined they probably used them in other rooms. If their butler did double duty, perhaps their furniture did as well.

Mr. Carmody spread jam on a piece of toast. "Good of you to join us, Lady Miranda. You'll need to do better tomorrow."

Miranda repressed a scowl as Fitchley brought her a plate of food. Dark brown toast, probably cold, sat beside a parched slice of overcooked ham. At least the poached eggs looked sunny and appetizing. "Is there no fruit?"

Mrs. Carmody pursed her thin lips. "I'm sure you are accustomed to all manner of luxury, Lady Miranda, but here we do not enjoy the same level of comfort. The weather has made berry season late."

Miranda bit back her query regarding kippers.

After a few moments in which the gentle clink of silverware and the occasional rustle of Fitchley's footfalls were the only sounds, Mr. Carmody waved a forkful of ham in the air. "I've written to your father about your ghastly behavior last night." He darted a glare at her for good measure. Miranda purposefully pasted a placid smile on her face in response. "I also informed His Grace you will be working at the local orphanage starting today."

Miranda's mouth drooped. "What?"

Across the table, Beatrice said, "I work at Stipple's End several days a week. It's very rewarding and the children are…precocious. Truly, there is nothing better you can do with your time while you're here."

Miranda could think of at least a dozen things that would be better uses of her time. Reading, riding—she pressed her lips together. She couldn't do either of those because the Carmodys had neither books nor horses, and her parents had deprived her of both for the duration of her exile. So, ten things, perhaps. The first of which would be penning her own letter to Father detailing Mr. and Mrs. Carmody's stern and unwelcoming attitude.

Miranda's fingers clenched around her fork as she speared a piece of egg. "And just what does 'working' at the orphanage entail?"

Beatrice's silver clanked against her plate. "Any number of duties. Mrs. Gates, the headmistress, always has a need for extra hands."

"I hope it's nothing terribly taxing. I'm afraid I haven't the wardrobe for menial tasks." To take the sting from her words, Miranda summoned a smile she didn't think she could find. She couldn't afford not to. These people held her very livelihood in their pedestrian, judgmental hands. "I'm certain I can accomplish whatever service the orphanage needs."

"Lady Miranda," Mrs. Carmody began, her earth-brown eyes narrowing beneath thin, brutally arched brows, "You have not come to Wootton Bassett for a summer holiday. Your parents sent you here in order to better yourself and return to London a regretful and rehabilitated young woman."

Miranda set her fork beside her plate. "And I thought I came to help Beatrice acquire the attributes necessary to attract a husband." That wasn't precisely true. Miranda knew why she'd been exiled, but Mother had entreated upon her to view the summer as an opportunity instead of a punishment. Helping Beatrice would show Miranda's father that she was capable of creating good instead of mischief.

Mrs. Carmody's lips parted and she sucked in a breath.

Miranda cringed and hastily added, "I wish to help in whatever fashion I may, whether at the orphanage or with Beatrice." She folded her hands demurely in her lap, hoping she appeared appropriately dutiful.

Mr. Carmody dropped his hand to the table rather forcefully. The silver and plate clattered. "You'll do precisely what you're told and mind your smart tongue. And don't be worrying about your fine clothes. I doubt you'll be attending many functions."

Just what did he mean? This might be the edge of nowhere, but Miranda was fairly certain small villages had entertainments of some kind. And how could she aid Beatrice if she didn't attend those entertainments with her? Really, how *did* a woman find a husband out here?

"If you're finished, Miranda, we should be on our way to Stipple's End." Beatrice folded her napkin next to her plate. "May I be excused, Father?"

"Yes." Mr. Carmody turned an irritated eye on Miranda. She realized it didn't matter if she'd completed her meal or not.

Miranda half stood. Mr. Carmody's nostrils flared. Retaking her seat, she sought her faux smile once more. "May I be excused?"

"Go, then."

Such charm. Miranda followed Beatrice from the room, hoping against hope the orphanage would be a mite more pleasant than Birch House.

～

STIPPLE'S End looked to be an old medieval hall repeatedly enlarged over the ensuing centuries. The building rambled at the end of a long lane, surrounded by gardens that were obviously tended to, but devoid of order. In fact, it looked as if trees and shrubbery were allowed to bloom and grow wherever they seeded themselves.

A stone path led from the lane to the front entrance. Miranda followed Beatrice to the large oak door, her feet aching from the lengthy walk from Birch House. It opened before Beatrice could knock. A small, rather round woman greeted them with a wide, warm smile. "Beatrice! A delight to see you this morning."

Beatrice stepped inside. "Miranda, may I present Mrs. Gates, the headmistress here at Stipple's End. Mrs. Gates, Lady Miranda Sinclair, who is staying with us this summer and is eager to help."

Miranda flinched at the word "eager," but gave the portly Mrs. Gates her sunniest expression as she entered behind Beatrice. "A pleasure to make your acquaintance." Miranda eyed Beatrice's sturdy cotton dress and worried anew about the type of work she'd be assigned.

Her assumption the house had once been a medieval hall was verified in the interior. She shivered—everything about the country was perpetually cold. Especially this drafty old place. She studied the high ceiling, noting a water-stained hole in one corner. No wonder she was chilled. "You have a leak?"

Mrs. Gates folded her hands over her yellowed apron. "Yes. The orphanage is always in need, I'm afraid."

Miranda could see that quite clearly. The furniture looked as if it might collapse at any moment. The carpet beneath her feet was battered and moth-eaten. She itched to move away, wondering if anything *lived* in the dingy threads.

"I've brought some biscuits for the children." Beatrice handed a stuffed basket to Mrs. Gates. "How can we help you this morning?"

"Thank you, dear. We've two young boys who arrived last night. One's rather ill. Would you be up to nursing him for a bit? Annie's been tending him all night and could use a respite."

"Of course. I'll go at once." Beatrice departed toward a staircase against the right wall, leaving Miranda to fend for herself.

"It's nothing catching, is it? I'd hate for Beatrice to become ill." And in turn make *me* ill, Miranda mused.

"We can't often tell. I'm afraid we can't afford much in the way of a physician. Beatrice has nursed plenty of our charges and hasn't suffered even a sneeze. Don't you fret about her." The broad-bosomed headmistress touched Miranda's arm. It was a tiny gesture, but full of kindness. And completely outside of Miranda's experience. "Now tell me how you think you can help."

Miranda shifted and Mrs. Gates's hand fell away as if it had never breached the distance between them. "I don't suppose you need anything embroidered or water-colored?" Not that she had a particular talent for either, but she truly couldn't think of what she might offer.

Mrs. Gates's mouth puckered, as if she wasn't sure whether she should laugh or frown.

"I'm sure you'll find something suitable." Miranda only prayed it didn't involve chafed hands and broken fingernails.

"I appreciate your willingness to help, my lady. As it happens, I was just preparing for a task right here." Mrs. Gates gestured to a table in front of the wide windows facing the drive. On it were two bowls and a row of combs. Was she to style the children's hair? "Those are lice combs. This basin of water is for cleaning the combs as it becomes necessary."

Miranda clenched her teeth together, lest her jaw drop. "I see."

"Comb through each child's hair." Mrs. Gates picked up a comb and waved it about for a moment in demonstration. "Be sure to look for the eggs as well as the lice themselves. The eggs like to cling right to their little skulls."

The notion of lice and eggs "clinging" to these poor children's heads turned Miranda's stomach, but she refused to beg off. The Carmodys only needed another reason to disparage her to her parents.

"And if I should find any lice?" Miranda voiced the question even though the answer somewhat frightened her.

Mrs. Gates replaced the comb on the table. "I don't suppose you have any experience scrubbing them out?"

Miranda blinked at her. "My father is the Duke of Holborn. I wouldn't recognize a louse if it appeared at my mother's bi-weekly tea and engaged my father in a political debate."

Mrs. Gates chuckled. "Now, that would be a sight. My apologies. I should have realized someone of your station wouldn't have this sort of experience." Mrs. Gates smiled apologetically, and Miranda felt a trifle guilty. The woman was trying to give her the benefit of the doubt—no one ever did that. People made their assumptions based on her appearance and social status, and that was simply the way things were. "If you find an infestation, come find me in the kitchen, and we'll take the child to the bathing chamber."

Before Miranda could stall with further questions, two boys strode into the hall. "Ah, here are Philip and Bernard." Mrs. Gates beckoned for the children to come forward. They appeared to be about ten years old. "This is Lady Miranda. She is going to check your heads today. Don't give her any trouble, now."

The boys eyed Miranda and grinned.

"You're pretty," the taller of the two said.

Miranda had heard much lovelier praise, but was surprised at the nerve of a ten year-old country boy. "Thank you." Normally, she would turn the flirtation back on the instigator, but...what did one do out here? Since she knew nothing else, Miranda continued on as she would have done in London, giving the boy a slight curtsy. "You are a handsome lad yourself."

The other boy laughed while the first one turned the color of her favorite ruby necklace.

Mrs. Gates nodded approvingly at Miranda. "I shall leave them in your capable hands."

Miranda didn't want her to leave, but if she stayed what was the point of Miranda doing the task at all? The headmistress departed, and the boys stood rooted to the floor.

"All right then. Who's first?"

Each boy pointed at the other and said in unison, "Him."

"How about you?" She gestured to the taller boy, wondering if he was Philip or Bernard, whose color had faded to normal.

"Sure, Philip, you go." Bernard pointed to the chair positioned next to the table.

Philip's shoulders drooped, and he took his seat. Miranda stepped behind him and contemplated the top of his sandy brown head.

"Are you going to gawk at 'im all day then?" Bernard folded his arms across his chest.

"No." Miranda refused to be cowed by two young boys with a legion of bugs on their heads—God, she hoped they were lice-free. She turned to the table and studied the combs. They looked dirty. Swallowing her trepidation, she plucked one up using the very tips of her fingers. Upon closer scrutiny, she determined they were clean, just stained from age. Allowing her fingers to curl about the implement more securely, she thrust it into Philip's hair with a quick, jerky motion meant to minimize her contact with the boy and his potential lice.

"Ow!" Philip flinched as she caught a knot.

"Sorry." She recalled the brutal hair brushings from her nurse and didn't want to unduly torture the boy. She tried again, more gently, but with the same elevated concern for her cleanliness. After several moments, relief poured through her and she declared, "I don't see any lice."

Bernard took his turn in the chair. "My 'ead's been itching a bit."

"I'm sure it's, er, the cold weather." Miranda prayed it was so.

"I had lice last year. Felt the same."

He'd already had lice. Miranda swallowed against the bile rising in her throat. Best to be done with this.

Thrusting the comb into the boy's thick mop, she shrieked at the sight of a small creature leaping from his scalp. Dropping the comb, she jumped back and shook her hands furiously. At once, she felt a thousand tiny legs crawling over her body.

"That's quite a racket you're making. Am I infested again, then?" He turned in his chair and Miranda realized she was still squeaking.

"What's the matter?"

Miranda had no idea who had spoken. After a moment, hands grabbed her upper arms. "Are you all right, Lady Miranda?" Mrs. Gates studied her with grave concern.

Her body shaking, Miranda managed to stifle her screeching and nod. "There was a…thing…bug…louse." She pointed at Bernard, now vigorously scratching his head.

"I see. We'll have to cut your hair again, Bernard."

The boy sighed heavily, but nodded.

"And Philip, you'll need a good scrubbing. I bet you've got an egg or two since you and Bernard share a bed."

Miranda lifted her hands, raking them for a telltale

sign of anything moving. Or anything egg-like. One day in the country, and she was going to have lice.

"Come, boys." Mrs. Gates put an arm around each of them and stopped short. "Oh, Fox, maybe you can help Lady Miranda. She's had a fright with Bernard's lice."

Miranda spun toward the doorway leading to the back of the house. A tall man stood just inside the hall. Thick, too-long, brown hair swept back from his face. Garbed in simple brown woolen breeches and topcoat, he was utterly undistinguished.

"I wondered what the screaming was about." He came toward her, his gait and stature quite confident for a retainer. He passed the departing Mrs. Gates and assumed a stance before Miranda. "Lady Miranda, I presume? Montgomery Foxcroft at your service."

He offered a courteous bow and when he raised his gaze…she froze. Completely. Never had she seen such eyes. They were blue. Or green. Or maybe amber. All of them, she realized. Cobalt at the outside, they shaded to rich jade toward the middle and were flecked with gold just around the pupil. And upon closer inspection she couldn't exactly discount the rest of his face either. He was rather handsome, in a rugged sort of way, she supposed. His jaw was quite square and his lips—which she shouldn't be looking at, but that had never stopped her —were just full enough to provoke the notion of a kiss… She abruptly raised her gaze to his eyes again, noting the tiny lines that fanned out making him look as if he smiled often, something her family rarely did.

He looked at her hand, and she suddenly remembered she could be crawling with lice.

"Do I need a bath? That boy's head…"

"No, a simple hand-washing will suffice. I'll show you the washroom." He held out his arm.

"I, ah, you don't mind my touching your arm? I could be infested."

He laughed, the rich, dark timbre of his voice

warming her in the way she'd sought that very morning. "I doubt that. Have you no experience with lice?"

"No, I'm from London."

He laughed again. "And you expect me to believe there are no lice in London?"

"There aren't at Holborn House." Miranda wasn't wearing her finest gown, she had no jewels on her person, and her hair had been pulled into a rather severe style, but surely he recognized her station? "I'm Lady Miranda Sinclair. My father is Holborn. I'm visiting Birch House. Miss Carmody invited me to join her here this morning." Never mind this wasn't precisely the truth.

"Ah yes, Miss Carmody. She gives Stipple's End so much of her time. Come." He tucked her hand over his arm and led her from the hall. "You make time for charity work, then?"

Had he heard nothing she said? Or were pedigrees unimportant in the country? "Er, no. Though, I'm certain my father—the duke—donates to several charitable causes."

"Which ones?" Those unique eyes of his bored into her, the amber-flecked centers sizzling like burning embers. She felt strangely hot beneath his regard.

He steered her into a small room at the end of the back hallway.

"I don't know." Unless a topic pertained to her future marriage or her behavior, her father didn't discuss it with her.

He gestured to a large basin set into a long table beneath a small window overlooking the rear yard. "You can wash there."

A girl entered just then bearing a large bucket of steaming water. "Mrs. Gates thought you might need some hot water to clean up."

"Thank you, Flora." Mr. Foxcroft took the bucket

and poured the water into the basin beneath the window.

Flora gaped at Miranda. "Are you really a lady?"

"Yes."

"And you live in London?"

"Yes."

Mr. Foxcroft interrupted. "Flora, Lady Miranda would like to wash up. You can interrogate her later." He'd set the bucket on the table and now leaned against the edge.

"But, I just have a few—"

"Go." His tone was kind, yet firm.

The girl obeyed, but not without casting a longing glance over her shoulder at Miranda.

"I didn't mind answering her questions. The girl was positively charming." In fact, she'd given Miranda her nicest reception since arriving in this backwater.

"If you come back another day, you can do so. Forgive me for saying, but you don't seem the type to visit orphanages. In truth, you seem as if you belong in a ballroom."

How...expected. He saw her beauty and judged her a mindless ninny. She peeled back her sleeves from her wrists as she walked to the basin. Eagerly, she thrust her hands into the hot water, closing her eyes briefly as the heat seeped into her flesh and raced up her arms. The comfort banished the sensation that her skin crawled with lice. When she opened her eyes, she found Mr. Foxcroft staring at her. He was quite presumptuous for his station. Adopting her haughtiest tone, she endeavored to remind him of his place. "Have you worked at the orphanage long?"

He didn't flinch. "I own Stipple's End. My family founded this orphanage over four hundred years ago."

"Pardon, I assumed you were an employee." She cast him a glance, her gaze flicking down to his dirty fingernails. Now he reacted, quickly clasping his hands behind his back, and she felt a moment's regret. She'd judged him as certainly as he'd judged her.

"I do work here, but I also have my own estate to look after." He stood only a foot or so away, and from this distance she caught the scent of raw earth and something else. An herb. Rosemary, perhaps? His eyes glimmered in the gray light filtering through the window.

Miranda looked around for soap just as he handed it to her. The small cake felt greasier than she was used to and wasn't fragranced with roses or honeysuckle.

"The orphans make the soap. That's a special kind for lice, but the older girls make some flowery-smelling cakes which we sell at Mrs. Abernathy's in the village."

"How curious." Miranda couldn't imagine making soap, especially for the purpose of eradicating vermin. She scrubbed her hands and murmured her thanks when Mr. Foxcroft set a towel next to the basin. "Does everyone here have a specific job?"

He nodded. "I suppose so. Except the younger children. Although learning to read and figure is probably a job to them."

She dried her hands and turned, resting her hip against the table. "You teach these children to read?" What sort of lives could these orphans possibly aspire to? Miranda had no idea, but assumed they would end up as chimney sweeps or scullery maids.

He crossed his arms over his chest with a half-smile. It was the kind of smile that didn't readily expose his emotion. Amusement? Annoyance? "We teach them to do any number of things."

She was surprisingly interested in this conversation. "And where do they go from here?"

His shoulder lifted slightly. Still no clue as to what he thought behind those peculiar eyes. "Wherever they want."

"You pay for them to travel somewhere?" She found

this not only odd, but...charming. And that in itself was odd.

He dropped his arms, his left hand smacking down against the rim of the basin, crushing a large spider she hadn't seen crawling toward her. "Excuse me." He moved to take her place in front of the basin, and she barely jumped back before their bodies could occupy the same space.

He rinsed his palm in the water and then grabbed the towel she'd so recently discarded. "You misunderstand. We do our best to find a place for them, either here in Wootton Bassett or elsewhere in the district. Some leave and find their own way. It's entirely up to them what they make of themselves. We merely try to give them some useful skills and at least a rudimentary education."

"How kind of you." That seemed an inadequate observation, but she could think of nothing better. She'd never before met anyone who would invest such time and energy. "And what is it you provide?"

He blinked. "Everything."

"Well, if that's the case, you should repair the leak in the hall. It smells dank and the chill is pervasive. I've the impression it's been leaking for quite some time."

His eyes narrowed, and his lips pressed into a firm line. She caught herself staring at them again and shook her head at her fancy.

"It hasn't been leaking long, actually. And I *will* repair it. I'm certain things happen very quickly and perhaps without due consideration in your sphere. How fortunate you must be to have the benefit of time, wealth, and ability." Ice hung from his tone. He might be able to match her father in haughtiness. And she was right sick of being talked to that way, by her father, her mother, everyone.

Miranda turned toward him and propped her left

fist on her hip. "There is no call to be rude. You don't know anything about my 'sphere.'"

"I can well guess. Just look at the gown you wore to delouse orphans." His gaze flicked over her, further pricking her ire.

Miranda gritted her teeth. "I didn't know I would be *delousing* orphans." What else could she say? She'd no idea dressing for a tiny hamlet would be as complicated as dressing for London. "Don't you have a roof to fix?"

His eyes were ablaze with emotion. "I'll leave you to your chores." He turned away, and she wilted a little without the fervor of his stare.

What a disagreeable man! As he strode toward the door, she gave in to devilish impulse. "I'd be happy to give you a lesson in wardrobe selection and the latest fashion in men's hairstyles."

Mr. Foxcroft paused but didn't turn. Miranda waited, breathless, for his response. He left without another word.

Mrs. Gates appeared in the doorway. "Are you ready to continue? Neville is waiting for you in the hall."

Miranda's stomach knotted. She'd rather hoped she was finished. *No.* She could do this. She'd prove to all of them—her parents, the Carmodys, that insufferable Foxcroft—that she was made of the sternest stuff. She squared her shoulders. "Lead the way, Mrs. Gates."

The headmistress's eyes lit with appreciation. "Since Bernard's infested, you're like to find other cases. I've asked Beatrice to help. She's got enough experience with this for both of you."

Beatrice rounded the corner just then. "Are you coming, Lady Miranda?" Her sharp tone and pursed lips revealed her judgment: she found Miranda as empty as Mr. Foxcroft had.

Oh yes, she was ready to prove them all wrong. Miranda smiled sweetly. "Of course." Then she carried herself into the hall with all of the regal poise her three governesses had instilled. She'd conquered London. Wootton Bassett couldn't possibly be more difficult.

Resolved to show Beatrice she was no London ninny, she faced the young boy awaiting her on the chair then bit her cheek to keep from cringing. For he was quite earnestly and thoroughly scratching his scalp.

CHAPTER 3

*T*HE Thursday afternoon was far too cold for June. After scraping frost off the orphanage roof that morning, Fox and Rob had studied the hole and concluded the repair would be costlier than anticipated. In the meantime, they'd done what they could and managed to plug the leak, if not completely fix the damage. But now Fox's visit to the vicar's tea was suddenly quite necessary.

As was launching his courtship of Miranda. With luck, she would be here at the vicarage today. He hadn't exactly made a grand first impression last week at Stipple's End, but then she hadn't made things easy with her arrogance and presumption. Still, he had to make this work.

Fox handed his reins to the stable boy and turned toward a carriage rattling up the drive. He inwardly groaned at the sight of the scarlet coat of arms emblazoned on the ebony door.

Stratham.

Fox balled his hands into fists, the worn leather of his gloves pulling taut over his knuckles. Should he do the socially appropriate thing and await Stratham's arrival, for surely the man had seen him standing in the drive, or should he ignore the insufferable rotter and go into the vicarage? Fox turned and rapped on the large oak door. Social graces were for Society, and he wasn't Society.

The vicar's housekeeper, Mrs. Wren, greeted him. "Good afternoon, Mr. Foxcroft! We haven't seen you at tea in some time. Mrs. Johnson will be thrilled." Her gaze darted to the drive behind Fox. "I see Mr. Stratham is here and the Carmodys arrived with a special guest. Oh, this shall be the vicar's most illustrious tea ever."

She was here.

"I am pleased to be included in such an event." He stepped over the threshold and down the short corridor to the solar, where the vicar and his wife gave tea every other Thursday.

Perched on a settee in the center of the room, drawing the attention of probably every person there, Miranda—he simply couldn't think of her as Lady Miranda after having kissed her—held a teacup to her mouth. Fox watched as she puckered her pink lips and took a delicate sip. Sparkling aquamarine eyes peered at him over fine porcelain. He'd been right about their color—a fact he'd relished upon "meeting" her at the orphanage in the light of day.

"Fox!" The vicar, Samuel Johnson, jumped to his feet and clapped Fox on the back. "Pleased to see you. I've been meaning to stop by and discuss the planting…"

Fox listened to the vicar with one ear while the other picked up Mrs. Wren welcoming Donovan Stratham into the cottage. As Mr. Johnson droned on about which fields he ought to leave fallow, Fox covertly eyed Stratham. Of average height and build, with dark, wavy hair, and a ready smile, women generally found him attractive. He was also wealthy, well-dressed, and the hardest work his hands ever saw was extorting "tribute" money from his constituents. Fox looked to see Miranda's reaction to him.

She'd replaced her teacup on the table and perused Stratham with unguarded interest. For his part, Stratham walked straight toward her and immediately took her hand. Carmody introduced them.

"So, what do you think then?" The vicar leaned in close as he finished his monologue.

Fox tore his gaze from Miranda and Stratham. "I think you're right to plant potatoes in the south field. Pardon me for a moment, vicar. I'd like to speak with someone."

The vicar nodded, and Fox moved to stand near Miranda's settee. Stratham took a chair next to her and set his walking stick against its side.

Carmody came up beside Stratham and clapped him on the shoulder. "You're the MP. What have you heard about this highwayman? Has he struck again?"

Stratham accepted a cup of tea from Mrs. Wren. "I don't know anything other than the details of your unfortunate robbery." His lips parted in the familiar, condescending smirk he'd adopted since becoming MP... what, four years ago? When he turned back to Miranda, his face lost its superciliousness and he appeared earnest and sincere.

Weasel.

Carmody's chest puffed out, and his dark brows beetled over his small brown eyes. "I'm sure the blighter will strike again. He had gall, that one."

Miranda folded a napkin in her lap. "I found him rather dashing. Not at all what one might think of the criminal class."

Carmody narrowed his eyes at Miranda. "Careful, gel."

Fox couldn't keep himself from leaning toward her. "Dashing, really?"

Miranda turned her aqua gaze toward him. "He wasn't violent in the slightest. I doubt he'd have harmed any of us."

Stratham flicked a speck of something from his sleeve. "Doesn't sound like much of a highwayman." His tone held a wealth of disdain.

Carmody harrumphed. "Don't let her tale fool you. There was a band of them. We were outnumbered."

Fox wanted to hear more of Miranda's reaction, but it was enough to know she'd been as affected by the highwayman as he'd been by her.

Miranda reached for a biscuit from the tray on the table before her. "You are a member of Parliament, Mr. Stratham?"

"Indeed, my lady." He nodded. "My family has served the crown for generations. I consider it my duty and my honor." And so the conversation turned to Stratham. Fox refrained from rolling his eyes.

"How very noble of you, sir." She turned her head to look toward Fox. For the first time in his entire existence, he was glad he'd put up with having his cravat tied into a neck-clenching monstrosity. Christ, her vanity was contagious.

Stratham put his cup on the table and casually dangled an arm over the side of his chair so his hand rested within a few inches of Miranda's knee. "And how fortuitous you're visiting our humble village this summer."

Devil take it, the man was a menace to unmarried women everywhere. He'd used precisely the same tactics on Jane, not that she'd fallen prey. But her father had, and in the end Stratham had won her hand. Fox curbed his anger and tried to focus on soliciting money from the rest of this lot. There was an empty seat next to Mrs. Johnson, but he couldn't force himself to move away.

Miranda glanced toward the bank of windows. "Is it summer? I can scarcely credit the change in season given the abysmal weather."

Stratham waved his hand. "Oh, it's atrocious, isn't it?

I daresay a trip to Brighton this year would be a waste of time. Better that you are here, Lady Miranda."

Fox wanted to pound Stratham's face. The two of them spoke as if Fox wasn't standing right bloody next to them. "And when was the last time you were in Brighton, Stratham? I don't seem to recall you ever visiting there."

Stratham leveled a cool stare at Fox. "I'm not at all certain why you would presume to know my traveling habits, Foxcroft." His eyes slitted briefly before he turned a carefully manufactured look of delight toward Miranda. "Allow me to escort you on a tour of our charming village tomorrow."

She clapped her hands together. "I should like nothing more. It's been ever so long since I enjoyed a proper outing."

He leaned toward her, his fingers brushing the fabric of her blue dress. "Excellent. I shall call for you at two."

Oh, this was too much. Fox plucked a teacup from the tray and "tripped" on his way toward Mrs. Johnson. Pity the tea cascaded into Stratham's lap.

Stratham jumped to his feet, jostling the table and tea service with his movement. "Watch yourself, Foxcroft!"

"My sincerest apologies, Stratham. I do hope it doesn't stain." A dark spot spread over the front of his buff breeches.

Stratham dabbed at his clothing with a serviette. "I fear I must take my leave. Until tomorrow, Lady Miranda." He glared at Fox. "Foxcroft."

"Be sure and stop by the orphanage. It's been an age since you donated." Fox preferred highway robbery to asking Stratham for a handout, but the opportunity proved too ripe to ignore. Or, did he hope Stratham would show his true colors to Miranda and refuse?

Stratham's lip curled, but he contorted his mouth

into a pained smile. "I'm certain you are mistaken. I make quarterly donations to the orphanage. If the orphans are in need, it's likely due to your management."

Fox opened his mouth to call Stratham out, something he should have done when the rotter stole Jane away. But Miranda spoke. "Mr. Stratham, perhaps you aren't aware the hall is leaking quite badly at the orphanage. Surely you don't want the roof to collapse." She swept her lashes in overt flirtation. Fox would have laughed out loud if he didn't need her plea to work.

"No, I wouldn't." Stratham turned icy eyes on Fox. "I'll send some money over." The smug set of his mouth told Fox the orphanage could crumble to the ground before he did any such thing. Fox hadn't expected his help anyway.

Stratham nodded at Miranda and took his leave. She turned her head toward Fox. "That wasn't well done of you."

Fox released the tension from his shoulders with a flick of his wrists. He contemplated responding to her indirect question, but he needed to gain favor and so far he'd done a pathetic job. "Did you survive the delousing?" He cringed. *That* was not an improvement.

She blinked up at him, tilting her head to the side. "Evidently, since I am here."

He was a jackass. "Thank you for helping. Will you be coming again?"

She folded her hands demurely in her lap. "Yes." He couldn't tell if she looked forward to it or not. "I thought I might suggest augmenting the girls' lessons with some feminine skills they likely haven't developed. Penmanship, embroidery, dancing, that sort of thing."

"Embroidery?" Much as he wished things were different, these children would be servants. A lucky few would apprentice for a trade or make an advantageous marriage, as his steward's wife had done.

"Some women find it very soothing, and why

shouldn't they have something to do in their spare time?" She elevated her chin, daring him to find fault with the plan.

Spare time? These girls weren't going to spend what precious little time they might call their own practicing needlepoint. "You've discussed this folly with Mrs. Gates?"

Her eyes narrowed, their almond shape shrinking to a sliver. "You sound as if you don't wish for my help. I believed the orphanage to be in need."

"Of a new roof, not deportment!" Fox flexed his hands against his legs. This was *not* how to woo a lady. He took a deep breath and started anew. "I'm sure you and Mrs. Gates will agree on how you can best utilize your skills to help." He leaned a bit closer and caught a waft of her unique spicy citrus scent. The memory of their kiss hit him, and he willed himself to remember they were in the vicar's solar, not some moonlit lane. "Would you care to take a stroll in the garden?"

Her brow furrowed and she glanced outside. "Thank you, but I should decline. It's rather cold today, isn't it?"

Fox clenched his jaw. Not too cold to plan a drive with that jackanapes Stratham. "Just so."

"Time to take our leave," Carmody announced from behind the settee.

"I believe I'd like another cake." Miranda reached for the tray on the table before her.

"Never mind that." There was no mistaking the glower Carmody delivered to the top of Miranda's gilded head.

"Actually, Lady Miranda just agreed to take a turn about the room with me, if you don't mind, sir." Fox held his hand out. She looked up at him, one brow arched high. He held his breath while he waited to see if she would go along with him.

"Indeed, I have. Would you mind sparing us a few

minutes?" She took Fox's hand, and he had a desperate desire to continue what she'd started when he'd robbed her carriage. She threw a look over her shoulder at Carmody, who continued to eye her with irritation.

"All right, then." The older man waved them off.

Fox tucked Miranda's hand under his arm and escorted her in the opposite direction. The solar was a large room and if they walked along the windows on the south side, they would be relatively removed.

"That was bold of you." She kept her gaze forward as they walked.

"You didn't appear to want to leave." He kept glancing at her perfect profile as they strolled toward the windows. "As long as I'm being bold, might I suggest you and Mr. Carmody seem at odds?"

Her laugh brought a smile to Fox's face. She turned to look at him, her lips parted in a most provocative manner. He feared his lungs might seize. Bloody hell, but he'd never seen a more beautiful woman.

"Very bold, but I like bold." Her eyes twinkled with the first genuine merriment he'd seen in her.

He'd been about to say, "Yes, I remember," but then he'd have to explain *how* he remembered and that wouldn't do. He settled for, "Might I ask what brought you to our charming hamlet?"

"The Carmodys are cousins to my mother. My parents thought I might enjoy an invigorating visit to the country."

"And how do you find it?"

"It's very quiet. Indeed, it's so quiet I have trouble sleeping."

He strove not to think of her tossing sleeplessly in her bed lest he become fully aroused. "Mrs. Gates could recommend a sleeping tonic."

She threw him a quick, appreciative glance. "Thank you. I usually go for a short walk in the Carmodys' garden, though I'd enjoy that more if the weather were more temperate." She paused in front of the windows. "Overall, I have to say your village is quite lovely."

"Yes, it is." Only he wasn't looking outside, nor was he thinking of Wootton Bassett. The physical side of marriage to Lady Miranda Sinclair would not be a hardship. And he was fairly certain she was not already betrothed. He just had to get there before Stratham did.

She turned and her eyes widened slightly. He half-expected her to snatch her arm away. Pleasure warmed him from the inside out when she did not.

Beatrice approached them. Shamefully, Fox hadn't noticed her presence before now. "Good afternoon, Miss Carmody."

She inclined her head. "Good afternoon, Fox." Her attention moved to Miranda. "Father says it's time to leave."

He regretfully pulled Miranda's hand from his arm. Before he let go, he pressed an impulsive kiss to the flesh just above the glove.

She parted her lips. God, what he wouldn't give to taste them again.

"Good afternoon, Mr. Foxcroft. I'm sure I will see you at the orphanage."

He offered a bow and the women left. Fox then bade goodbye to the vicar and his wife. The afternoon hadn't been a complete failure. True, he had no more money than when he'd arrived, but he had perhaps made progress with his heiress. It had been worth being in the same room with Stratham for the better part of an hour.

Almost.

～

THE following afternoon, Miranda viewed her reflection in the too-small glass positioned above the chest in her too-small bedroom. The dark green bonnet made her eyes shine. The ivory ribbon set off her skin perfectly. She'd nearly fifteen minutes to spare before Mr. Stratham was due to call, but she refused to loiter in the inadequate entrance hall awaiting his arrival, despite her excitement to depart Birch House.

Beatrice pushed open the door. "I'm ready."

Was knocking not required in the country? Miranda turned to greet her, but stopped short upon seeing Beatrice's driving costume. "You can't think you're coming with us?" She flinched at how that sounded and smiled apologetically. "I don't mean to be uninviting, but I believe Mr. Stratham's invitation was for me alone."

Beatrice clasped her hands in a vee at her waist, her face completely placid. "I know. Father has bidden me to act as chaperone."

This wouldn't do. In London, one could ride in an open vehicle with a man without a chaperone. Was it too much to want to pretend she was back in London, if only for the afternoon? She brushed past Beatrice into the hallway. "Where is your father?"

"In his study, I imagine." Beatrice's footfalls sounded behind Miranda as they descended the stairs.

Miranda burst into Mr. Carmody's office without knocking, since that was apparently the norm. "I don't need Beatrice to chaperone. In London, I am allowed to drive with a gentleman provided we are in an open carriage. Mr. Stratham is driving an open carriage."

Mr. Carmody raised his thin face and arched a brow. "I'm fairly certain you aren't *allowed* to do anything in London at present. And since you are here, you will abide by my rules. You'll drive with Beatrice or you'll not drive at all."

Miranda clenched her hands at her sides. "Beatrice is young and unmarried. What kind of chaperone is she supposed to be?"

"As you so aptly pointed out, a chaperone isn't necessary. However, in your case, an additional person is warranted to ensure your good behavior." His eyes narrowed. "I don't trust you. Further argument will result in your staying here for the remainder of the afternoon and perhaps until next week."

Miranda opened her mouth, ready to deliver a scathing retort, when Fitchley stepped across the threshold. "Mr. Foxcroft is here for Lady Miranda."

She swung around. "Mr. Foxcroft, you say?"

"Indeed, my lady." Fitchley stared straight ahead. She had to admit he was a fairly accomplished servant for such a modest house.

Without giving Mr. Carmody the courtesy of a departing word, she swept from the room. Beatrice had remained in the hall, and Mr. Foxcroft stood just inside the door, hat in hand.

Before she could ask about his visit, he stepped forward. "I ran into Mr. Stratham in town, and unfortunately he has been detained. I should be delighted if you would allow me to escort you this afternoon."

Miranda would have gone for a drive with Satan if it got her out of Birch House. "Thank you." She gestured toward Beatrice without looking at her. "She has to come with us."

Mr. Foxcroft smiled. "Certainly, provided she doesn't mind riding on one of the back seats. I'm afraid I'm driving my cart."

At one time—say a fortnight ago—Miranda might have been deterred by his inferior vehicle, but her desire to get away from her jail exceeded her need for a landau, a carriage, or even a phaeton. "It sounds lovely." She turned to regard Beatrice. "Are you ready?"

Her eyes narrowed to tiny slits of displeasure. "Of course."

Miranda studied Mr. Foxcroft as they made their way outside. Though not as traditionally handsome as

Mr. Stratham or the gentlemen back in London, something about his features made him more real. Especially
the lines bracketing his mouth, which, like the tiny
crinkles near his eyes, indicated he smiled often. He
wore the buff breeches and dark brown coat he'd worn
at the vicarage yesterday—a much better costume than
he'd sported when she'd first met him at Stipple's End.

Mr. Foxcroft helped Beatrice into the rear of the
cart. "I apologize for the seating. I need to drive, and
there is only room for one other person next to me."

Beatrice nodded. "It's quite all right, Fox. I'm merely
here to play chaperone."

He raised an eyebrow, but said nothing as he
handed Miranda into the front seat. A cushion sat on
the wooden bench making it somewhat comfortable
despite the wooden back. At least it had a back. Miranda had never ridden in a cart before.

Mr. Foxcroft glanced at both of them. "If you are
ready, we should be on our way."

Miranda nodded, and it only took a moment to realize Mr. Foxcroft was quite adept at handling the
reins. She'd like to see him in a phaeton in Hyde Park.

He executed a flawless turn—Miranda never would
have guessed a cart could move so smoothly—with
minimal effort. "I thought we'd take a tour of Wootton
Bassett and some of the surrounding area. I presume
you haven't seen much of our town, beyond the church
and the orphanage. We very much appreciate your assistance there, Lady Miranda."

He seemed so genuine. Miranda felt a moment of
awkwardness because her motives for working at the
orphanage were not entirely altruistic. In fact, they
were rather selfish.

"I look forward to helping in a regular fashion." It
wasn't precisely a lie. She looked forward to anything
that evaded her house arrest.

"We are coming upon Cosgrove, Lord Norris's estate. It's up the drive to the left there." Mr. Foxcroft's tone held just a bit of scorn.

A large house peeked above the trees dotting the vast park land. "I don't believe I've met Lord Norris. Does he come to London?"

Mr. Foxcroft gestured toward Cosgrove. "He journeys to Town for the purpose of adding to his antiquities collection. I don't believe he attends Society events, however."

"And it's unlikely Lady Miranda encounters him at the Antiquity Society," Beatrice put in from the back of the cart. Miranda had almost forgotten her presence.

Miranda laced her tone with honey. "Actually, I do believe it's called the London Natural Society of Antiquities and Oddities. My godfather is a member."

Mr. Foxcroft laughed. "Touché, Lady Miranda! Lord Norris hosts an annual party in September in order to show off his most recent acquisitions. Perhaps you will meet him then."

"Like as not, since I plan to be back in London by then." God help her if she was still stuck in the middle of nowhere come the Little Season.

They left Cosgrove behind. Mr. Foxcroft kept his attention on her as much as on the road. If he were a lesser driver, Miranda might have been annoyed, but she found herself enjoying his pointed regard.

The fields lining the road were sodden and dark brown from last night's rain. Very few plants sprouted amidst the dirt. "Shouldn't the crops be visible by now?"

From Sunday's church sermon and from yesterday's tea at the vicarage, Miranda knew there was concern about the planting and the weather, but hadn't comprehended the severity. At her father's country seat, the fields were green this time of year.

"Indeed." Mr. Foxcroft sounded grave. "The unseasonably cool temperatures are playing havoc with our schedule. I am hopeful the plants will catch up, however."

The village came into view, the church spire rising high above the other buildings. They passed the church on the right before entering the town proper. Buildings that housed shops, a tavern, and an inn, The Swan, marched up both sides of High Street.

Beatrice sat forward in her seat. "I don't suppose I could trouble you to stop at Mrs. Abernathy's? I've a parcel to retrieve."

Mr. Foxcroft brought the cart to a halt before a small shop, which seemed to sell a variety of things. There was no telling what Beatrice's parcel might contain, not that Miranda much cared.

Beatrice's hooded gaze shouted, "Behave," as Mr. Foxcroft helped her from the cart. Miranda sighed and settled against the back of her seat.

Mr. Foxcroft resumed his position beside her and glanced over his shoulder down High Street. He fingered the reins lying across his lap. He wore dark brown leather driving gloves, the palms faded and worn.

She tore her gaze from his capable hands. "Did Mr. Stratham say what kept him from our appointment?"

His pupils dilated. "Ah, no, he wasn't specific."

Before she could censor herself, she asked, "It seems as though you and Mr. Stratham are perhaps not very friendly?"

Mr. Foxcroft glanced down at the reins in his hands, ran his thumb along the flat leather. "You could say that."

Miranda sensed a subtle change in him. He held a dark emotion just beyond her reach. She hadn't meant to cause him discomfort. "Forget I mentioned anything."

Before Miranda could ponder why she hadn't persisted in her inquiry, a landau turned onto High Street

and headed straight for them. Mr. Foxcroft mumbled
something under his breath that sounded suspiciously
like, "Son of a bitch." The vehicle halted in front of
them and Mr. Stratham exited. Yes, Mr. Foxcroft had
definitely muttered, "Son of a bitch."

Mr. Stratham approached the cart with a frown.
"Just what do you think you're about, Foxcroft?"

Mr. Foxcroft looked down at Mr. Stratham and
leaned back against his seat. "Lady Miranda and I are
enjoying a ride."

Miranda regarded both men. Mr. Stratham appeared torn between wanting to hit Mr. Foxcroft and
wanting to maintain his composure, whether for her
benefit or some other reason, she couldn't know.

After a moment, Mr. Stratham seemed to relax. He
circled the cart to Miranda's side and rested a hand on
the step. "Lady Miranda, I would be happy to see you
home. My landau is much more...comfortable." His
gaze roved the length of the cart.

"I do appreciate your offer, Mr. Stratham, but we
are waiting for Beatrice. I'm afraid she must return
with us." She wistfully eyed his luxurious vehicle.

"No matter." He stepped back and raised his hand
with a flourish. "I'm happy to escort you both."

Mr. Foxcroft laid his arm along the back of the seat.
A possessive gesture, the contact of his arm against the
back of her shoulders was not unpleasant. Awareness
prickled along her neck. First she'd been attracted to a
highwayman, and now she was apparently less than put
off by the attention of a farmer who operated an orphanage. What next? A blacksmith?

"Good afternoon."

Three heads turned to face Mrs. Abernathy's shop.

Beatrice held a wrapped package. "We were told you
were otherwise engaged, Mr. Stratham."

Mr. Stratham rested his hand on the step once
more. "Mr. Foxcroft was mistaken."

"But I was right about you being late." Though Mr. Foxcroft muttered this under his breath, Miranda caught every syllable. She was tempted to laugh but thought better of it given the palpable tension between the two men.

A carriage rattled up High Street and stopped behind Mr. Stratham's landau. Mr. Carmody departed the carriage and strode to the cart. This was turning into a social event.

Beatrice clutched her package to her side, almost as if she didn't want her father to see it. "Father, whatever are you doing here?"

"I've come to fetch you both home. The post arrived and with it, important news."

Miranda's heart leapt. This was what she'd been waiting for! Mother and Father had gotten her missive and decided her punishment too severe. They were rescuing her from this infernal backwater. She stood, and Mr. Stratham offered his hand to help her down. Mr. Foxcroft jumped to his feet and frowned as he watched her exit with Mr. Stratham's assistance.

Mr. Stratham held onto her hand a trifle longer than necessary. "Might I call for you tomorrow afternoon, then?"

Mr. Carmody's nasal voice cut off any response she might have given. "No."

Miranda pulled her head back as if she'd been slapped. Though she would be returning to Town, it was up to her to decline Mr. Stratham's kind offer, not his! "No?"

"No. Your parents have forbidden you from socializing. Except for church. You may attend church."

Miranda gasped, unable to keep her emotion in check. Humiliation stabbed through her chest. Was it necessary for Mr. Carmody to reveal this information in such a public venue? Of all the pompous, obnoxious—

"Come, gels." Mr. Carmody turned and walked toward the carriage, expecting Beatrice and Miranda to follow. Beatrice, of course, did just as she was told. Miranda's feet, however, were like lead. Though she stood in the middle of the street on a brisk summer afternoon, her chest constricted and her head pounded as if she were once more standing in her father's office while he interrogated her about what she'd done on the Dark Walk at Vauxhall.

After a moment, Mr. Carmody stopped and spun around. "Hurry it up, gel, or I'll suggest your parents ban you from helping at the orphanage, too."

She'd never felt so utterly alone in all of her life. But she refused to crumple. She raised her chin and walked to the carriage. Fitchley held the door and she climbed inside without saying good day to either Mr. Foxcroft or Mr. Stratham. Pity, for she'd have liked to have seen what happened next with them.

Once inside the carriage, she couldn't keep herself from glowering at Mr. Carmody.

He waved a hand at her. "Now, now, don't work yourself up. After all, you have church and the orphanage."

Miranda's face enflamed with her fury. "Church? You don't even socialize afterward. I can assure you, listening to the vicar drone on about the crops and the harvest and how we all must pray for warmer weather is no treat."

Mr. Carmody's lips thinned. "Such a spoiled brat you are. It's not as if you've been confined to your room. Yet."

Outrage fired her blood. "Why did you even bother to house me this summer? I'm clearly a burden."

"Mrs. Carmody is doing a favor for your mother." Ha, more like Carmody was trying to gain the support of one of England's most powerful dukes. "And believe you me, I'd no idea you would be so disagreeable. So far you've done nothing to assist Beatrice with her matrimonial goal."

Miranda folded her arms across her chest. Her body stiffened with anger, making the jostling ride more uncomfortable. "And I likely won't, given I can't *do* anything."

"If you can teach orphans how to comport themselves, I'm sure you can impart similar information to Beatrice. Your parents were very pleased Mrs. Carmody and I encouraged you to help at Stipple's End, by the by."

Encouraged her? They'd bloody ordered her to work there! Miranda glanced at the other occupant of the carriage. Beatrice peered out the window, her cheeks slightly flushed. Could she be angry on Miranda's behalf? Irritated because Miranda wouldn't be personally ensuring she was the toast of Wootton Bassett? Beatrice slid a mutinous glare at her father and for the first time Miranda wondered at the relationship between the Carmodys. Beatrice appeared to be the dutiful daughter, but perhaps everything was not as it seemed.

Miranda relaxed and settled back against the squab. She would find out. After all, she had nothing better to do.

CHAPTER 4

*A*FTER Carmody's coach pulled away, Fox plucked up his reins.

Stratham put his hand on the horse's flank. "Just what the hell do you think you're doing?" He reviewed Fox from head to foot in an insulting appraisal. "You believe she's going to be any more interested in your pathetic attempts at courtship than Jane?"

Fox jumped to the ground and knocked Stratham's hand away from his horse. Fox glared down at the vermin and sneered. "Jane was perfectly happy with me until you stole her away."

Stratham rose up on his toes and Fox briefly considered pushing him off balance. "You can't steal someone who doesn't wish to be stolen. And Lady Miranda isn't half as interested in you as Jane was. You had to lie to entice her to drive with you."

Oh, how Fox wanted to brag he'd kissed Miranda. She may not be falling all over Montgomery Foxcroft, but she'd thrown herself at the dangerous highwayman, found him dashing. Fox let out a breath and with it, some of the tension coiling his muscles. He wouldn't let himself be baited by Stratham. "We'll see what she really thinks. I'm sure we'll get to know each other quite well while she's working at the orphanage."

Stratham let out a dark laugh. "She said at the vicarage she's only here for the summer. She sees this
town and its inhabitants as beneath her."

Fox cocked a brow. "That doesn't bode well for you
then, does it?"

"You forget I spend a good deal of time in London. I
do believe Lady Miranda does not consider me in the
same *class* as the rest of Wootton Bassett."

"Because you're not. You're not fit to clean the
chamber pots of anyone I know."

Stratham's eyes narrowed. "Insolent ass—"

Fox jabbed his shoulder into Stratham's chest as he
turned. "Don't waste your time."

As he climbed back into the cart, Stratham backed
away. "She'll choose me in the end, you know. You're
the one who shouldn't bother."

Fox ignored the man's taunts and urged his horse
into a gentle trot. He was annoyed with himself for engaging Stratham, something he knew to be both futile
and frustrating. Perhaps they should have dueled over
the right to court her and saved everyone the plague of
prolonged competition.

A waft of spicy citrus hit him and he savored the
scent. His blood heated and the notion of marrying Miranda became more than about besting Stratham. More
than about money.

He wanted her.

Wanted her in a way he hadn't wanted a woman in a
very long time. It transcended mere physical require-
ment and the vanity that came with having such a
woman. No, she carried the promise of something
much more.

And for that, he'd fight to win.

～

*T*HE following Monday, Miranda found herself at the head of the long dining room table at Stipple's End. More than two dozen children stared at her—some with interest, others with disdain, all of them with hunger.

When she'd offered daily assistance to Mrs. Gates, the kindly headmistress had quickly—and gleefully—assigned Miranda to overseeing lunch. Fear overtook the appetite pulling on her belly. How could she possibly manage twenty seven children? Twenty seven party-goers, certainly. But this gathering was not a party. Even so, it had to be a far sight better than de-lousing. And if she was lucky, she would prove good enough at this to avoid delousing permanently.

A maid from the kitchen brought in the food, placing covered dishes throughout the table. As soon as one landed, a hand snatched off the lid and dove for the contents. Miranda's eyes widened at the lack of deco-rum. But that didn't actually begin to describe the...the *mayhem* erupting about her. Carrots spilled from the serving spoon onto the table more often than onto a child's plate. An unknown stewed vegetable—at least she assumed it was a vegetable—splattered a child's arm as he ladled a portion for himself. And did that small girl just devour a bite of turnips directly from the serving dish?

"Children." Miranda cleared her throat when no one responded. Why weren't they listening? She tried again, "Children, please stop." A few of the smaller girls looked up at her, their forks arrested in midair. When no one else halted their activity, they went back to their lunches. Presumably they gave Mrs. Gates their atten-tion. Why not her, the daughter of a duke? Didn't they realize her considerable position?

The kitchen maid shrugged at Miranda and took her leave. "Wait," Miranda called after the young woman, but her request was either not heard or ignored. Given the chaos in the dining room, Miranda rather thought it was the former, but couldn't dismiss the latter.

Squaring her shoulders, Miranda faced the raucous horde of children. Her knees trembled and nervous heat snaked down her neck.

"Hey, that's my roll!"

"No, it's mine. Get yer own!"

"Ouch, watch yer elbow!"

"I wanna glass of water!"

The cacophony was approaching a deafening roar. "Stop, please!" More children gave her their attention, but the majority continued to ignore her. Her anxiety gave way to ire. "I said, STOP!" Goodness, she sounded a bit like her father.

A few more children fell silent, but the skirmish over a roll continued at the other end of the table. Miranda stalked to the field of battle and seized the roll from the warring parties. Both lads stared up at her. One of them, she realized, was a shorn Bernard. Her scalp and neck twitched.

"There are plenty of rolls left. Why are you fighting over this particular one?" She hefted the bread in her hand, wondering if it would bounce off the boy's head if she threw it. No, she was civilized, unlike these heathens, and civilized people didn't throw food. Her job—and never did she more clearly understand it—was to civilize them.

The boys glared at each other a moment longer. "I guess I can get another one." And then she witnessed firsthand that the rolls did indeed bounce as Bernard nicked a roll from the tray and chucked it at his opponent's skull.

Instantly, other boys leaned over the table encouraging either Bernard or his foe. For his part, Bernard earned a spoonful of pudding aimed at his chest. A glop hit Miranda's arm and slid onto the floor. Unable to move, she gaped at the uncontrollable pandemonium around her. Children were yelling, tossing food, and crying. Crying? Miranda looked around for someone to help before recalling she was the only adult present.

Her brother had misbehaved. What had their governess done? Ah yes, *that*. Miranda reached forward, but pulled her hand back at the last second. Grabbing Bernard by the ear meant touching an area that was, and perhaps still could be, infested with lice. Risk the lice or allow the boys to completely devolve?

The crying made her decision for her. Miranda grasped both troublemaking boys by their ears and dragged them out of their chairs. They shrieked in unison. The rest of the table's occupants hushed almost immediately. Even the crying became a soft hiccupping.

"Both of you are finished eating. And you will clean up the table when our meal is over. Now go sit in the corner." She thrust them away, and they goggled at her, each with a reddened ear. Miranda felt a little bad about that, but not enough to summon regret. "Well, go on then." Reluctantly, they turned and shuffled toward the corner. "No, separately. One of you in that corner and the other in that corner." She pointed, and they split up as ordered. Her chest puffed up a bit as she watched them heed her directions. Her triumph was short-lived, however, when Bernard shot her a sharp glare.

Miranda turned on her heel and started back toward her seat at the head. A small girl halfway up the table resumed her crying. Miranda crouched beside her and tried not to gag at the sight of so much…gunk coming out of the urchin's nose. "What is it, dear?"

"I didn't get a roll. I wanna roll." Tears fell in earnest, dotting her stained dress. A roll she could manage, but what to do about the nose? Miranda picked up the urchin's hem and wiped her nose and mouth. One of the older girls looked at her curiously. What difference did it make? The dress was impossibly stained anyway!

Miranda turned to the boy seated to the girl's right. "Would you please ask for the rolls?" The boy stared at her for a moment as if he didn't comprehend. She gritted her teeth. "*The rolls*. This girl would like a *roll*."

He leapt onto his feet *on his chair* and reached across the table, his shirtsleeves dragging through a dish of turnips. When he shrank back to a seated position, he held a squashed roll in his grasp. He presented it to the girl with a toothless grin.

Horrified, Miranda waved her hand at nothing in particular. "You can't just lean over the table like that! You ask for the rolls to be passed. Goodness, have you no manners at all?" She directed the last to the table at large, but received no response.

Dazedly, she returned to her chair while the meal carried on in a symphonic discord of screeching children, audible chewing, and, good Lord, burping. Were those boys at the end having a contest as to who could burp loudest and longest?

Suddenly, she recalled a similar occurrence from her own childhood. Though her brother was several years older, they often ate together. On one occasion, Jasper had burped. They'd laughed because they could never have done such a thing in front of their parents, and to continue the hilarity, Miranda had copied the sound. Extremely effectively, too.

But should she—could she? She was out of ideas and the only thing resonating in her brain was her mother's admonishment, "If you can't think how to behave, simply mimic those around you. That way you shall always fit in." Perhaps her mother had never been more right. Miranda swallowed a great mouthful of air and burped it out as loudly as possible.

Everyone at the table froze. She couldn't help but smile at finally getting their attention. After a blissful moment of utter silence, Bernard clapped his hands from the corner. Soon everyone was whooping, laughing, or clapping wildly. And burping. She'd encouraged an epic tournament.

Ah well, she'd have plenty of days to fix their manners. For now, she was tired, hungry, and not at all interested in spoiling their fun. Surprisingly, she found she envied their carefree ignorance—stained dresses and all.

~

OX crouched low over the ground, scanning for the slightest sign of life. There! A tiny bit of green poked up from the soft brown earth.

"It's late." Rob frowned down at the meager sprout fighting to the surface of the orphanage's vegetable garden.

Fox stood. "Better late than nonexistent." He raised his gaze to the gray sky and was rewarded with a fat snowflake in his eye. Blinking, he said, "I was just going to say I brought a cartful of hay from Bassett Manor to cover the plants in case it froze tonight."

Rob squinted upward as a scattering of flakes fluttered toward the ground. "I'll get the wheelbarrow."

"And I'll get the pitchforks."

A few moments later, they were pulling hay from the cart amidst a flurry of cold, damp snow. The yard filled with the gleeful shrieks of the children as they played.

By the time Fox and Rob got back to the garden, a thin layer of white covered their tiny seedlings. Fox dumped the wheelbarrow. "Damn. It's really coming down. I'll spread this. You go and get another load."

A wet thwack against Fox's back made him turn. Philip stood maybe twenty feet away with a mouth-splitting grin. While Fox was anxious to get their precious plants covered, Philip was starting a snowball fight.

"Philip!"

Fox spun toward the voice calling out from the back of the house. Miranda stood at the door garbed in a dark blue gown, her blond hair pulled back from her face in a simple chignon. Even from this distance her beauty made his breath catch. She was a vision of domestic perfection. He imagined her standing on the back terrace at Bassett Manor calling him into luncheon.

His trance was broken when she stalked toward Philip, her brows drawn together. He strained to hear her admonishment over the sounds around him. "Mr. Foxcroft is working there. You mustn't throw snowballs."

Too late, Fox noticed Bernard launching a snowball at Miranda's back. With a gasp, she twirled around.

Fox ran to Bernard and yanked him toward the vegetable patch. "You will spread the hay over the plants. Quickly now." Fox pointed at Philip. "And you will go help Mr. Knott."

Philip nodded and took himself off.

Miranda gaped at him. "My goodness, they actually listen to you."

"It takes a stern tone. And several days supervising them working in the fields."

She hugged her arms around herself. "I can't believe it's snowing."

He repressed the urge to draw her to his body and warm her. "You should get back inside. You're not even wearing a cloak."

Snowflakes clung to her eyelashes, accentuating their lush length. "But you look as if you need help."

Fox watched as Rob and Philip hurried back to the garden with another load of hay. "It wouldn't come amiss. Do you think you can round up some children to help?"

She grinned at him and he thought his knees might give out. "I can try."

He stared after her, unable to tear his gaze away.

Rob cleared his throat as he sidled up next to Fox. "You going to gawk at her backside or take care of our beans and turnips?"

"If only I actually had a choice." Fox tore his gaze from Miranda's, yes, backside.

Rob waved at the boys in the vegetable patch. "Careful there! Cover the plants, but don't step on them!" Three more boys joined Bernard and Philip. They appeared eager to toss hay around in the middle of a snowstorm. Rob addressed Fox again. "You make any further progress with her, then?"

"Not since I usurped Stratham's place the other day when I took her for a drive." Fox steered the wheelbarrow back to the cart.

Rob walked alongside. "Brilliant move, that. You don't want him stealing her away." Color crept up his neck, and he looked away, either suddenly interested in the swirling snow or belatedly realizing he was a complete ass for saying such an imbecilic thing.

Fox glared at his friend. "You know full well Jane didn't choose him of her own accord, and neither will Miranda. I may not look as fancy as Stratham, but she'll recognize I'm the better man."

Rob glanced down at Fox's clothes: ancient gloves pocked with holes, work clothes, which were as patched and worn as the quilt his great-great grandmother had made, but nodded anyway. "I'm sure you're right. Besides, there's nothing wrong with a man who works."

They believed that, but did Miranda? The boys were throwing snowballs again. "Lads! If you're finished spreading that hay, move the snow away from the seedlings. We don't want them catching cold." Fox shook his head.

Rob pointed toward the vegetable patch, indicating the wheelbarrow was full and they should return. "You know, you could, ah, there is one way to ensure a trip to the altar."

Fox pinned him with an incredulous stare. "You aren't suggesting I abduct her to Gretna Green?"

"God, no! Just a situation that might infer you *needed* to marry her."

Fox stood rooted to the ground, not sure he'd heard his steward correctly. "Compromise her, you mean?"

Rob lifted a shoulder. "You know she's a bit brazen. Seems like it could work with little effort."

Yes, she'd proven herself more than a *bit* brazen. Still, the idea of trapping her was distasteful. "I'll take it under consideration. But for now, I prefer to court her as I am." He pushed the hay toward another part of the garden.

Miranda had come to supervise the nearly ten boys now tending to the plants. Aside from the occasional miniature snowball making its way down some lad's neck, they did a good job separating plant from snow.

She rubbed her hands up and down her arms. "These were all I could manage. The other children are too intent on making the most of snow in June."

"I'm impressed you got this many." And he was. She might look like a delicate flower, but she was proving to be as hardy as any wild rose.

Mrs. Gates joined them. "Lady Miranda, Mr. Stratham is here to see you. I brought your cloak." She wrapped the wool around Miranda's shoulders.

Miranda's cheeks were pink from the cold, but Fox detected a further blush. "How thoughtful. Thank you, Mrs. Gates."

Mrs. Gates couldn't help but mother everyone in her path—a fact that had probably saved Fox from following his father's example and leading a life of ruin. "It's no problem, dear. Go on in and see your Mr. Stratham."

Fox gripped the pitchfork. "Her" Mr. Stratham?

Philip took the implement from his hand. "I'll get the next load, Mr. Foxcroft."

"Thank you, Philip."

Miranda pulled her cloak more securely around her. "I think I'm needed out here. Would you mind telling Mr. Stratham I'm otherwise engaged?"

Mrs. Gates blinked. "I should round up the other children."

And now Miranda's face flushed even more. "Of course. I'll just run inside and send him on his way."

Fox shrugged. "You could make him wait. If he wants to see you, he'll come outside." *Or maybe he'll just leave.*

"Now, Fox, that isn't polite." Mrs. Gates clucked her tongue, but as she walked away, Fox could have sworn he heard her chuckle.

Miranda's tongue darted out and caught a snowflake. Fox couldn't move. The sight of that luscious pink tip was enough to cause his groin to heat despite the freezing temperature.

One side of her mouth turned up. "Sorry. A childhood habit I can't relinquish, apparently."

And Fox hoped she never did. The moment stretched toward two before Fox remembered there was a vegetable patch to protect from the snow. He opened his mouth to excuse himself just as he saw Stratham picking his way over the frozen ground.

"Lady Miranda!"

Miranda turned and smiled prettily. "Mr. Stratham. As you can see, we've been a bit surprised by the weather."

Stratham perused Fox and then the boys spreading hay. "Indeed. But, fortune has smiled upon you because

I've come to rescue you from your drudgery. My carriage awaits your beautiful presence." He grinned, his eyes crinkling as if he laughed often, as if he hadn't a care in the world—except perhaps whether his constituents could afford the tribute he demanded.

"I'm afraid I couldn't leave just now. We need to cover the fledgling vegetables." The sound of her saying, "we" made Fox's chest swell. Then she touched Stratham's sleeve briefly and he deflated. "Have you brought your donation today?"

Stratham allowed his gaze to rest a trifle too long on Miranda's bosom, and now he snapped his head up. "Indeed, I brought a donation. I will give it to Fox."

Fox's fingers itched to break the man's head clean off. Was his irritation due to a true depth of feeling for Miranda or the fear of losing to Stratham once again?

"It doesn't look as if you are contributing, "Stratham observed. "Why not enjoy the warming brick I have in my carriage?"

Did the idiot not realize he'd insulted her? Fox waited to see her reaction and wasn't disappointed.

Frowning slightly, she said, "Perhaps another time."

"Be assured of it." Stratham's lips parted in a grin. He hadn't recognized his faux pas at all. His straight, white, perfect teeth begged for Fox's fist to shatter them. And didn't he recall that Miranda wasn't allowed to drive with anyone? He was either incredibly obtuse or overwhelmingly self-involved. Both, Fox reasoned.

"Lady Miranda, would you mind helping me with Molly?" Mrs. Gates called from the other side of the yard. She held a coughing child whose dress looked to be sopping wet. Fox hoped she wasn't catching something.

"Here's the donation." Stratham tossed Fox a small purse.

The bag felt light. The biscuits and hairpins Miranda had stowed in his cloak the night on the road had weighed more. "Thank you for your *generosity*." Fox's gaze slid to Miranda who watched the exchange with a pleasant smile. No doubt she found Stratham a hero.

"Think nothing of it. See you next time." Stratham spun about and tiptoed back across the snow.

Fox wanted so badly to launch a giant snowball at Stratham's head.

"I'd do it if I were you." Rob came up beside him, reading Fox's mind.

"And I would if I wasn't trying to set an example for the boys." Responsibility was a terrible nuisance sometimes.

"What's that?" Rob inclined his head toward the bag in Fox's hand.

Fox opened the purse and surveyed the two shillings inside. "Stratham brought this."

Rob curled his lip. "Bloody plague, that one."

"Plague?" Yes, it was as accurate a description as any. Fox would add son of a bitch, corrupt, slimy, insincere, jackanapes—

Rob shook snow off his shoulders. "The assembly's coming up, and Miranda will surely be going. Stratham, too. You need to go. Do you have anything to wear?"

Fox pulled the pouch closed. He hadn't been to a quarterly assembly in years. Not since he'd courted Jane. "Of course, I have nothing to wear. Doesn't matter anyway, she won't be there. She's been forbidden from socializing. All of my courting will have to be done here, I'm afraid."

Rob frowned at Fox's clothes. "Unfortunately, I think you're right. You can't court her looking like that all the time, especially after seeing you next to Stratham." At Fox's sharp glare, he added, "Sorry, but 'tis true."

Fox's hand closed over the purse in his palm. He could scarcely believe he was discussing fashion—of all things—with his best friend in a vegetable garden in the middle of a snowstorm in June. "While I appreciate your statement of the obvious, is there a chance at all you'll leave this matter to me?"

"You said yourself you don't have any nice clothes. I'll ask Mrs. Knott to make you something."

"Your wife has supplies for such an undertaking?"

Rob grasped the wheelbarrow for another trip. "Eh, leave it to her. Mrs. Knott can make anything out of nothing."

If only she could turn snow into money, all of their problems would be solved.

CHAPTER 5

*L*ATER that night, Miranda sat at the small desk in her bedchamber and plucked up a quill to write a letter to her parents, only to drop it as a violent sneeze wracked her frame. Another threatened, but she quickly dabbed at her nose with a handkerchief. Wonderful—helping at the orphanage earlier had made her ill. So much for her nightly walk in the garden.

She picked up the quill, but then dropped it in resignation as another sneeze claimed her. Writing to her parents was a pointless exercise anyway, since they would likely respond that three weeks in the country hardly qualified as appropriate punishment.

Miranda begged to differ. Every evening stretched monotonously without the benefit of a book to read or people to talk with. Mr. Carmody shut himself in his study. Mrs. Carmody did needlepoint, *quiet needlepoint* as she seemed bent on reminding Miranda. And, after a bit of time spent with her mother in some inane after-dinner activity, Beatrice went to her room. Miranda didn't know what Beatrice did there, but she never invited Miranda to share her company.

A soft knock on her door interrupted her reverie. With a sniffle, she turned toward the door. "Enter."

Beatrice stepped inside. "I saw your light. I hope I'm

not disturbing you." Her appearance at this hour was a singular event.

Miranda gestured for her to come further into the room. "Not at all. Would you care to sit?"

She shook her head. "No, thank you. I merely wanted to ask if you might…would you show Tilly how to arrange my hair in a more fashionable style?"

Miranda wondered at this sudden interest. "I should be delighted. Tomorrow morning, after breakfast?"

Beatrice nodded. "Thank you. Good night."

"Is there someone whose attention you're trying to win?" Miranda couldn't resist asking.

The older girl blushed. "Perhaps, but that's none of your affair."

Actually, Miranda thought it might be, given the Carmodys' expectation she help Beatrice in her search for a husband, but decided not to argue. Instead she stood. "Beatrice, why don't Mr. Foxcroft and Mr. Stratham like each other?"

Beatrice folded her arms over her chest. Did she realize how closed and uninviting she appeared? "It really isn't polite to gossip."

Miranda fought the urge to roll her eyes. "I'm not asking for gossip. I just wondered why they are at such odds."

A sigh escaped Beatrice's mouth. "I guess it doesn't matter if I tell you. You'll hear about it eventually." She paused, and for a moment Miranda couldn't be certain if Beatrice would continue. "Fox, Mr. Foxcroft that is, courted a local girl, Jane Pennymore. Just when everyone expected them to announce their betrothal, she became engaged to Mr. Stratham."

"She chose Stratham over Foxcroft?" What a horrible girl to lead Mr. Foxcroft on and then throw him over for someone else.

"Without regret, I'm sure." Beatrice said this with absolute finality, but without rancor, as if he were the obvious choice. And wasn't he? "Stratham is very hand-some, he's the MP, and he's worth a lot more than Fox."

Miranda shook her head, fighting off another sneeze. "Which doesn't excuse Miss Pennymore's scandalous behavior. In London, her position in Society would have been drastically reduced, perhaps even ruined."

"Mr. Stratham carries quite a bit of importance in northern Wiltshire. Generally, people go along with whatever he does."

Interesting. "What happened to Jane?"

"She died of fever within a year of their marriage."

"How awful." And it was. Miranda sneezed, hoping she too wouldn't catch an ague and die.

"And please don't think I'm trying to excuse her behavior—what she did to Fox was perhaps cruel—but I understood why she chose Stratham. Whoever marries Fox will always come after the orphanage."

"What's wrong with that?" Miranda could well imagine what was wrong with that for *her*, but for these provincial folk? "I thought you liked working at the orphanage?" She dabbed at her nose once more.

Beatrice leaned against the doorframe. "Certainly I do, but it's not the focus of my life. It is, however, Fox's priority. Along with Bassett Manor. His ancient estate requires nearly as much work as Stipple's End."

Miranda couldn't help but pity the Mr. Foxcroft who'd been jilted by the woman he'd hoped to marry. No wonder the two men hated each other. Or at least, no wonder Mr. Foxcroft hated Mr. Stratham.

"You're not actually interested in either of them, are you?" Beatrice asked.

Miranda paused a moment before responding. She'd never consider either of them, would she? "No, certainly not. I was merely curious."

Beatrice arched one brow as if she didn't believe her. "Well, good night, then. I'll send up some hot tea.

You sound wretched." She closed the door behind her as she departed.

Miranda sat back down in the chair before her desk. Yes, and she was beginning to *feel* wretched.

It was no surprise Jane Pennymore had chosen Mr. Stratham. He demonstrated greater charm than Mr. Foxcroft, who had poked fun at Miranda for wanting to teach embroidery to the orphans. Perhaps he'd done something to offend Miss Pennymore. But to be fair, he'd also rescued her from Mr. Carmody that day at the vicarage, proving Mr. Foxcroft possessed at least a smidgen of social cunning.

Nevertheless, Mr. Stratham cut the much finer figure with stylish, well-tailored clothes and perfectly shorn hair, while Mr. Foxcroft's attire appeared second-rate and his too-long hair perpetually windswept. Even so, he was quite tall and seemed more impressive than the shorter Mr. Stratham. She had to give Mr. Foxcroft the advantage there. And the eyes. Mr. Foxcroft definitely won on that count.

Miranda shook her head. As she'd told Beatrice, she wasn't interested in either man. No, if she wanted to give in to impossible fancy, she'd much rather think about the highwayman. Such an exciting figure. She flattened her suddenly tingling palms against the top of the desk. Then she frowned. She shouldn't be thinking about him either. To lust after a criminal would only get her in trouble, and, sneezing again, she didn't need any more of that.

~

OX always spent a great deal of time at Stipple's End, but if anyone noticed his increased attendance over the past fortnight, they didn't say so. And if they had, he could've given them a dozen answers and still avoid the truth: he was on the hunt for an heiress.

Christ, that sounded positively mercenary.

Today he would investigate the orchard to see how the apples were coming along—*if* they were coming along, thanks to the persistently cool temperatures. It was July, and still summer lurked somewhere behind gray skies and damp earth. He strolled down the hill and immediately quickened his pace at the sight of Miranda standing beneath a particularly large tree.

Little Jemmy sat high on a branch, his tongue extended at Miranda. Frowning, she tapped her foot in a rhythm of peeved impatience.

Fox came up beside her. "May I be of assistance?"

She glanced at him before redirecting her disapproval toward Jemmy. "It's time to go inside, and Jemmy is refusing to come down."

Her lips twisted into a moue of annoyance, which Fox found completely distracting. Marshaling his self-discipline, he looked up at the young boy whose little face was scrunched into an expression of mutinous resolve. "And why is that, lad?"

Jemmy glared at Miranda. "She's gonna cut off my hair."

She crossed her arms over her chest. "No, I'm not. Mrs. Gates is. Or someone else. I'm not sure."

"I don't wanna cut my hair." He shook his head, his rather short, straight locks whipping about his head with the motion.

"He doesn't need a haircut."

Miranda exhaled loudly. "He has lice."

Right. And a nasty case if Mrs. Gates wanted to shear his hair.

"I'm not coming down!" Jemmy shook his head violently and nearly came tumbling out of the tree.

Fox leapt forward. "Careful there, Jemmy."

Jemmy leaned over and wrapped both arms around the branch, his eyes wide.

Miranda moved to Fox's right, joining him directly beneath the boy. "Are you all right?"

The boy nodded. Cautiously.

Fox understood Jemmy's recalcitrance, but some things in life were unavoidable. The loss of one's hair to obliterate a lingering case of head lice happened to be one of them. "Jemmy if you have lice, it's best to get rid of them once and for all. Cutting your hair is the best method." How to get the boy down? "If you come down I might be able to get you a spot of treacle."

The boys eyes lit and his grasp on the branch loosened. "You promise?"

Fox nodded, sensing victory. "I do."

"How do you accomplish these things so easily?" Miranda muttered before adding to Jemmy, "I'll even promise, too, if it will get you to come down."

"All right." Jemmy looked at the ground and then at Fox. "I can't get down."

"Yes, you can." Miranda waved her hand at the thick trunk with its many footholds and branches. "You climbed up there, and you can climb down."

Tears gathered in the boy's eyes. "No, I'm too scared."

Fox laid his palm against the trunk of the tree. "It's all right, Jemmy. I'll help you down." He spryly climbed up to the branch on which Jemmy perched. "I can't come out there because I'll break the limb. Jemmy, you'll need to scoot toward me and give me your hand." Fear creased the boy's dirty face, and Fox added, "I won't let you fall."

Jemmy looked down at Miranda, who studied the activity in the tree with a furrowed brow. Her obvious concern wouldn't help the situation. Sure enough Jemmy shook his head again. "No. I'll just stay here."

Fox took a deep breath. "Lady Miranda, perhaps

you could reassure Jemmy? Explain he'll be quite all right?"

Miranda's eyebrows arched. "Yes, certainly." She smiled at Jemmy and, jealously, Fox wished she'd given it to him instead. "When I was small like you, I climbed a very large tree at our estate. My brother, Jasper, dared me to climb as high as him. I couldn't make it, but then I got scared and couldn't get down, either." She paused with a thoughtful expression and darted a brief look at Fox before returning her attention to the child. "Jasper simply laughed and started to climb down without helping me, the rotter. I began to cry, and then Jasper fell and hurt his arm. And then I laughed. Served him right."

Jemmy's mouth gaped. "Your brother fell?"

"Only a little fall." She held her hands up to illustrate a very small amount. "And it wasn't a bad hurt. I shouldn't have laughed if that were the case."

Jemmy's expression turned to one of interest instead of trepidation. "How did you get down?"

"I believe Sherman, the gardener, aided me. He climbed up, and much like Mr. Foxcroft is doing, helped me to the trunk. Then he carried me down. I wasn't scared afterward and climbed that tree until just last year."

Fox joined Jemmy in a chorus of, "Really?"

Miranda laughed. "Well, maybe not last year, but I did climb it an awful lot."

Fox imagined a blond girl running around her family's estate, climbing trees with abandon and likely driving her brother to the brink of madness. How he would've liked siblings.

He pulled his admiring gaze from Miranda. "Jemmy, are you ready now?"

Apprehension flashed in the boy's eyes for a brief second, and then he nodded.

"All right, just come toward me a little and then give me your hand."

Unfortunately, Jemmy overreached and consequently lost his balance. With a shriek he fell through the air and landed...on top of Miranda. Both of them lay in a heap on the ground.

Fox jumped out of the tree and knelt beside them, his stomach withering into a tiny ball at the thought of either of them injured.

Jemmy giggled. The giggles became laughs and the laughs became guffaws. "That was fun!"

Fox's relief was replaced by mild irritation as Jemmy seemed unaware of the seriousness of falling on Miranda. She struggled to get up—an impossibility given Jemmy still sprawled on top of her. Fox plucked the boy from her midriff and set him on his feet. Assured Jemmy was as fit as ever, Fox held a hand out for Miranda and helped her to stand. "Are you hurt?"

She glanced down at the mud stains coating her dress. "Not that I can tell, though this dress is ruined."

Fox couldn't help but smile at her concern for her attire. She was definitely all right. He returned his focus to the boy. "Lady Miranda is very brave and strong to have caught you, Jemmy. Aren't you going to thank her?"

"Thank you, Lady Miranda."

Fox put a hand on the boy's shoulder. "Now, apologize for causing Lady Miranda to coax you from the tree."

Jemmy kicked at the dirt, all of his earlier glee disappearing. "Yes, sir. Sorry, Lady Miranda."

She took Jemmy's hand and squeezed it. "Thank you, Jemmy. I'll tell you a secret. I rather like boys with very short hair. Terribly handsome." Fox resisted the urge to run his hand through his overlong locks.

The boy blushed to the tips of his ears before turning abruptly and dashing to the house.

It was not lost on Fox that Miranda seemed different from when he'd first met her. She'd gone from being frightened nearly to death by Bernard's lice to coaxing a lice-ridden Jemmy from a tree. Rather cleverly, too. Respect joined the emotions he was beginning to feel toward her—he didn't want to think about what those other emotions were just now.

Miranda put a hand to her head. "You don't suppose any of those lice jumped from him to me, do you?"

Fox tried not to laugh, but couldn't help himself. She rewarded him with another smile, which surprised him a little. "If I were a louse, I'd abandon his head for yours in a blink."

"Well, I'm glad you're not a louse, then."

What an inane conversation. Fox grinned like a cat who'd just lapped up a giant bowl of cream.

She studied her formerly white gloves, the palms now brown with dirt. "What a mess." She looked back at him. "Thank you for helping."

He'd done nothing compared to her. "You were the hero."

She waved her hand. "Hah! Kind of you to say, but it was an accidental thing."

"Not you catching him, the story you told to ease his fears. I admit I'm surprised to learn you climbed trees."

She leaned toward him as if imparting a secret. "Well, only the one time." He caught her unique scent of cloves and orange. How he loved that smell.

"But you said—"

She straightened and he lamented the increased distance between them. "I know what I said, but as you pointed out, I was trying to ease his fears. I was the one who fell out of the tree when Jasper tried to help me. I couldn't use my left hand for a week."

She was full of surprises. Wonderful, exciting surprises. "So you were the one in trouble."

"Mmm, yes, I usually am." She arched a brow at him

and then shook the dirt from her hem. "My brother has rescued me from more than one scrape, I suppose."

"How nice that you have him." And how he wanted to spend the rest of the afternoon asking her about those scrapes.

She bent and flicked a large, clinging piece of mud from her skirt. "Have you no siblings?"

It had been a long time since he'd discussed his family. "No. I'm the firstborn, and my mother died in childbirth."

"Oh, I'm sorry. My eldest brother died when I was very small. I barely remember him. Were you and your father close then?"

Thoughts of his father intruded on the pleasant exchange like a dark storm cloud. "Not particularly." Her eyes flared briefly, and he regretted his terse reply. But he didn't offer more. He despised thinking about his father, let alone talking about him.

"I should go inside. And finish checking the children for lice." With a wrinkle of her nose, she took off toward the house.

A surprising desire for a future with this woman—and not just because of her financial benefits—skipped through his chest. "You really were wonderful with Jemmy. Working here seems to suit you."

She turned with a laugh. "You think so?" She cocked her head as if pondering his assertion. "I'll own it's not what I expected."

He watched until her muddied form disappeared into the manor. No, she wasn't what he expected, either.

~

*A*FTER dinner that night, Miranda followed Mrs. Carmody and Beatrice into the small parlor they retreated to every evening. What would tonight's torture be? Straining to embroider in the meager light provided by the too-few candles? Listening to Beatrice commit atrocities on the pianoforte? Or reading scripture, the only "literature" she was permitted?

When Mr. Carmody unexpectedly trailed them, Miranda despaired at having a new horror inflicted upon her person. Perhaps he planned to read the scripture aloud? Or, heaven forbid, try his hand at the pianoforte?

Mrs. Carmody claimed the seat she always took, an overstuffed floral wingback near the fireplace. Beatrice sat on the settee and Mr. Carmody stood near the pianoforte. Miranda held her breath waiting to see if he moved behind it.

Instead, he directed his gaze at her. "Sit, gel."

Miranda complied with alacrity, positioning herself beside Beatrice on the settee. Following his autocratic directives could only improve his disposition toward her, especially when he wrote to her parents every few days. She needed him to make positive reports.

Mr. Carmody clasped his hands behind his back. "Next week is the assembly and although you won't be attending, Lady Miranda, I expect you to assist Beatrice with her preparations. Teach her the latest dances, ensure her costume is de rigeur."

Disappointment stabbed Miranda's chest. "What assembly? I wasn't aware of an assembly."

Mrs. Carmody positioned the embroidery hoop stand before her and picked up her needle. "The quarterly assembly. You cannot accompany Beatrice given your parents' edict."

Of course. Rather than giving in to irritation and glaring at her jailers or saying something that would likely get her into trouble, Miranda tried to focus on doing what she must to escape Wootton Bassett. She composed her face into a serene expression. "I understand. I will do my utmost to ensure Beatrice is a smashing success."

If she didn't absolutely believe Mr. Carmody would ensure she was confined to her room for the duration of the summer, Miranda would already be plotting a way to sneak into the assembly. But there was no way she could enjoy herself at the event *and* keep her presence from them. Pity.

"Beatrice, perhaps we should spend our evening reviewing dances. And tell me, what do you plan to wear?"

The new curls framing Beatrice's face were an improvement over her formerly severe hairstyle, and a flattering dress could transform her into a very pretty girl. "My new gown will be ready day after tomorrow."

Miranda dearly hoped it wasn't pink or yellow. Beatrice's wardrobe seemed to be made up of only those two colors and neither did much for her complexion. She needed earthier tones, a rich red or a deep plum. "What color is it?"

"Daffodil." Mrs. Carmody answered for her, piercing her needle into the linen. "My favorite flower. Beatrice looks lovely in yellow."

Miranda weighed whether to speak or not. Good Lord, when had she ever thought twice about speaking? They had asked her to provide input and it didn't seem right for her to say nothing. "Daffodils are splendid flowers. However, I wonder if Beatrice might look more vibrant in persimmon."

"Oh!" Beatrice lit up. "I love red!" She glanced at her mother whose entire face had puckered. "But the dress is nearly finished."

Miranda nodded. "Perhaps next time, then." She paused a moment and then risked plunging forward. "You have beautiful skin, Beatrice, but pink tends to make you look pale and yellow tinges you, well, yellow."

She smiled apologetically. "I don't mean to offend, merely capitalize on your strengths."

Mr. Carmody tapped a finger against his chin. "Does her gown have so much effect, then?"

Miranda studied the older man, a bit surprised at his interest, but then he did want to marry Beatrice off. "It can. In London, one's wardrobe can greatly influence a person's acceptance. I'm sure the right gown will transform Beatrice. You would undoubtedly be pleased with the results."

His lips flattened, and he remained silent for a moment. At length, he said, "Tomorrow, Lady Miranda, you will accompany Beatrice to town and select a new gown for the assembly. You will also commission three other new gowns."

"Ouch." Mrs. Carmody shook her finger out after apparently poking it with her needle. "Four gowns? We can't afford such extravagance."

Mr. Carmody narrowed his eyes at her. "Don't question my authority. The chit made Bea's hair look better, so I'm inclined to listen to her opinion—at least in this. And no, I am not changing my mind about a new chair for your sitting room."

Mrs. Carmody glared, first mutinously at her husband and then malevolently at Miranda. Oh dear, she might've helped Beatrice, but at what cost? Miranda chanced a look at Mr. Carmody who didn't appear the least bit ruffled by his wife's irritation. Just as well, since Miranda was more concerned with his opinion of her than his wife's.

Beatrice fairly beamed. "Thank you, Father."

Miranda silently triumphed. Beatrice's excitement had been worth Mrs. Carmody's vexation.

Mr. Carmody stepped away from the pianoforte. "You may thank me by landing a husband."

"I will, Father." Beatrice looked back down at her hands.

Such a cold, unhappy family, not that Miranda's was any better. She loved her brother, but he didn't live at Holborn House and was quite content to stay as far away from their father as he could. Miranda had no such luxury. Except for when she misbehaved.

Now, to turn the disappointment of missing the assembly into something positive. "Since I will not be going to the assembly, perhaps I may spend the evening at the orphanage so Mrs. Gates and the others might attend. I suspect they don't enjoy many social occasions." And an evening alone in a library full of novels would be a treat indeed.

Beatrice's head snapped back up. She regarded Miranda with astonishment that quickly softened into admiring approval. "That's very thoughtful of you, Miranda."

A twinge of regret prickled Miranda's neck. Did it matter her offer was not entirely altruistic? Certainly she didn't mind helping and allowing Mrs. Gates to attend the assembly, but more importantly this endeavor might improve Mr. Carmody's opinion of her. And he'd share his new opinion with her parents, which just might get her out of here before fall. In addition, there was the library...

"Indeed." Mr. Carmody paused on his way out of the room. "I'm surprised at your offer, but perhaps you are learning from being here after all. Your parents will be pleased."

Miranda pushed her guilt away. A reprieve from the Carmodys' house was worth anything.

～

*O*N the night of the assembly, Miranda paced the girls' dormitory at Stipple's End while her charges readied themselves for bed. She tried not to think of the party taking place in town. Tried not to think of how charming Beatrice looked in her new persimmon gown. Tried not to think of how long it might be before Miranda enjoyed a similar event. Instead, she thought of Mrs. Gates dressed in her finery and smiled. The woman had been ecstatic at Miranda's offer to watch the girls tonight.

"Lady Miranda, will you tell us about London?" Flora sat cross-legged at the end of her bed, her eyes huge in the light cast by the fire and a scattering of candles positioned about the large room. The youngest girls were already drifting into slumber on the other side of the dormitory. The eldest girls had collected on Flora's and Delia's bed and the one next to it.

Delia pulled a blanket around her shoulders. "Yes, please. Have you met the Prince Regent?"

Miranda sank onto a small wooden stool at the foot of Flora's bed. "Yes. And his daughter, Princess Charlotte."

Flora's eyes twinkled. "You've met a real princess?"

"Indeed. I even went to her wedding in May."

A few of the girls gasped. All of them appeared awed. Comments and questions flew from their mouths.

"A royal wedding!"

"Was it in a grand cathedral?"

Miranda couldn't help but smile at the girls' excitement. Once upon a time she'd been equally enthralled with the trappings of Society. Now it was simply the way things were. Or had been. "No, it was at Carlton House."

"The Prince Regent's residence," Flora put in.

Miranda nodded. "Yes, but how did you know that?"

Flora plucked at the blanket across her lap. "My friend Rose sends letters. She lives in London now."

Delia pursed her lips. "Rose works in a bawdy house."

"Delia!" Lisette glared at the dark-haired girl.

"Well, she does!"

Miranda held up a hand. "Who is Rose?"

"She used to live here," Lisette explained from Delia's bed. "She went to work at the local brothel after she left the orphanage. Recently she moved to London to better her prospects."

"The local brothel." Miranda supposed that made sense. Such things would be as necessary in the country as they were in London. What did Mr. Foxcroft think of Rose and the choice she'd made when she left? All of that work and care given to her and now she sold her body. "And Rose went to work for an, er, establishment in London?"

"Yes, the White Palace." Flora rejoined the conversation, but lacked her earlier excitement. "She says it's very popular. She entertains fine, regular customers." A blush colored her cheeks as her gaze dropped to the coverlet.

Miranda knew next to nothing about this subject. Certainly she'd seen a few courtesans. Some of them blended so well into the upper echelon of Society it was sometimes difficult to discern them from actual Quality unless someone pointed them out, which someone always did.

But Miranda didn't want Delia making Flora feel bad because Rose was clearly Flora's friend. Miranda sought to put a smile back on Flora's face. "Perhaps she will find a wealthy protector and move even higher, become a courtesan."

"A courtesan?" Flora spoke the word reverently. "Could she really become a courtesan? Why, then she'd have her own house, maybe even a carriage."

Miranda wished to avoid a lengthy discussion of the benefits of selling one's body. "Probably. But there are plenty of things you can—should—do instead." She studied each girl. A couple of them seemed to barely hear her, their eyes drooping with exhaustion. Delia and Lisette nodded furiously. Flora merely smiled and hugged her blanket around her shoulders. Miranda stood. "Come girls, it's getting late. Time for bed."

The girls bid her good night, and she exited the dormitory. Shaking the conversation about courtesans away, she made her way downstairs to the library. She could hardly wait to find something to read.

She stepped over the threshold, poised to breathe in aged leather and paper.

"Good evening, Lady Miranda."

Mr. Foxcroft stood from a cozy, dark green chair situated before the fire. He held a book in his hand, his forefinger inserted between the pages.

"Mr. Foxcroft. I wasn't expecting anyone to be here." There went her carefully constructed plan, unless they could read in quiet company. Somehow she doubted that. She was far too...aware of his presence to simply ignore it.

He wore a slight smile. "Surely you realized someone would be supervising the boys?"

Miranda walked toward the bookcase to her right. She ran her hand along the soft, worn spines. Some were more tattered than others, but all appeared to have been loved. She'd missed such simple pleasures. "Yes, I just didn't expect to find that person in the library. Why aren't you at the assembly?"

Mr. Foxcroft ambled toward her. "I'd rather be here."

She turned her head and raised her brow at him. "I might have guessed as much."

He came to a halt next to the bookshelf. "What other assumptions have you made about me?"

She tapped her finger against her lip. "You don't dance, do you?"

He laughed softly. "Yes, I dance."

She wasn't sure why she baited him, but he seemed to be going along and so she continued. "Mrs. Gates has consented to allow me to instruct the children in dance soon. Perhaps you can assist me?"

He bowed, sweeping the book before him. "I should be delighted." Standing upright again—he really was quite tall—his lips quirked. "What do you have in mind?"

"The waltz." Miranda folded her arms across her chest and leaned against the bookshelf. Surely he'd never waltzed. Not when he didn't attend assemblies and hadn't been to London. She didn't think he'd been to London anyway. "Have you been to London?"

"Not in a long time." He tapped the book against his thigh. "That doesn't recommend me, does it?"

She lifted a shoulder. "I'm merely doubtful of your waltzing abilities."

"I could demonstrate. Now, perhaps." He cocked his head. "If you're willing." And now he was baiting her.

"I am. But there is no music."

"I will hum."

Miranda grinned. "All right, Mr. Foxcroft."

He set his book on the shelf behind her, his arm brushing her shoulder. He held his hand out and she placed her fingers in his. She stepped forward and he wrapped his other arm around her back, pulling her into his embrace. He leaned into her and said close to her ear, "You must call me Fox, as everyone does."

An inexplicable shiver traced down her spine. He straightened, arranged their positions in perfect form. Then he did exactly as he'd said. He hummed Haydn's Clock Symphony and swept her into the dance, one hand deftly cradling her back while the other clasped her fingers with seemingly effortless technique.

"Where on earth did you learn to dance?" She shook her head. "No, don't answer, for then the music will stop." Miranda closed her eyes briefly, imagined his voice was the sound of actual musicians, that they glided amidst a thousand candles, that they weren't trapped in an orphanage in rural Wiltshire.

The feel of his hand splayed against her gown was surprisingly pleasant. No, pleasant wasn't the right word for the flesh beneath her gown tingled with awareness and...something more. His touch grew firmer, bringing her a hair's breadth closer. She opened her eyes to find him gazing at her intently, his eyes seeming to glow from their amber center out past the jade and into the deep sapphire blue.

She was cognizant of his bare hand warming hers. Dancing skin to skin with him sent flickers of secret sensation—intimacy, she realized—through her body. She'd never removed her gloves with a gentleman before. In London, it would be inappropriate for them to share company without gloves. Just as their unchaperoned dance would be. Strange, but this hadn't occurred to her until now. Apparently country ways were leaving their impression on her. Her lips curved up.

"You look inordinately pleased."

She snapped her gaze to his. "You stopped the music."

"And yet you're still dancing." He continued to move her in time, as if the music played on. "Why were you smiling?"

"Our dancing alone together like this is a bit scandalous, isn't it? Or at least it would be in Town."

His eyes widened slightly, and his step faltered, but he didn't halt. His gaze was intense. "You said you *liked* bold."

"And that's why I'm here instead of in London." Miranda returned his regard. He looked handsome tonight. As clean and well-turned out as he'd been at the vicarage. Here was a man who worked hard, yet seemed as comfortable on an imaginary dance floor as in the field. Remarkable.

They swirled about the floor as if they danced every

night. "I'm surprised you didn't attend the assembly. You dance divinely."

He seemed to stand even taller. "Mrs. Gates insisted I learn to dance. And I, ah, I rather enjoy it."

She adjusted her hand on his shoulder, smoothed it over the blue wool. "Then I'm doubly surprised you didn't go to the assembly."

He flicked her an intense glance. "I'm too busy to bother with social endeavors."

She felt the burden in the knotted muscles beneath her hand. "The orphanage?"

His fingers splayed across her spine, and the divine closeness of their dance rushed over her once more. If he'd been any other man... "And other responsibilities, yes."

She tilted her head, working to ignore the shocking thrill of his touch. *Focus on his words, Miranda.* "Bassett Manor?"

He raised a brow, seeming to have regained his earlier sense of happy amusement. "Yes."

"Tell me about it."

He inclined his head. "It's been in my family for centuries. It was built in the late 1100s, destroyed by fire a few centuries later and rebuilt. When the house was ruined, our neighbors at Stipple's End invited my ancestors to stay with them. The prolonged visit culminated in the marriage of my several times great-grandfather from Bassett Manor to my several times great-grandmother from Stipple's End, thus joining the properties. Together they make up just over two thousand acres."

She'd no idea his holdings were so vast or the history so rich. "It's no wonder you're so busy, especially since the leak in the hall started up again." She studied him. He seemed so capable, and yet..."How can you let it go unchecked?"

He stopped. Abruptly. Miranda tottered on her feet, but he steadied her before dropping his hands. "It's not unchecked. I am well aware of the threat it poses." He turned and strode to the fireplace, keeping his back to her.

"I'm no expert, but surely you can at least throw a piece of canvas over the hole."

He turned and the stark lines of his face were cast into relief as firelight flickered behind him. "Do you have a spare piece of canvas, Lady Miranda?" His tone chilled her mood. The camaraderie they'd shared during the waltz gone as if it had never been.

Too late, Miranda wondered if he couldn't afford canvas. She'd no idea how much it cost. "There's no call to be boorish."

He took a step forward. His eyes sparked. "I can see you have no conception of how the real world works."

Why was he so angry? She hadn't insulted him. At least, she hadn't *meant* to. "Perhaps not. But what is the real world, Mr. Foxcroft? What is real to you may not be what is real to me."

The flesh around his mouth tightened. "Just because you don't see it, don't understand it, doesn't mean it isn't real. This orphanage, these lives," he swept his arm in a wide arc, "are more real than anything you'll ever encounter."

Now he was insulting her. "I'll just go back upstairs until Mrs. Gates returns. Good night, Mr. Foxcroft."

Miranda turned on her heel and quit the room. Only as she climbed the stairs did she realize she hadn't gotten a book.

CHAPTER 6

*F*OX slammed his fist on the mantel. Things had been going perfectly, and he'd allowed his pride to get the better of him.

She'd danced with *him*. Fox. Not the highwayman. Not Stratham. *Montgomery Foxcroft*.

Hell's teeth, he was an idiot. She hadn't meant to insult him. At least he didn't think so.

He pushed away from the mantel and stared into the fire. The repair they'd completed last month hadn't held, and the leak had begun dripping again yesterday. A review of the roof that afternoon had revealed further damage, courtesy of the cold, wet weather. They *could* cover it with canvas, and he was damned irritated he hadn't thought to do that. He'd been too focused on the repair. Or perhaps distracted by a tempting heiress.

The seemingly silly London chit had come up with a solution, at least temporarily. The canvas would probably be sufficient for the summer, provided the weather improved, allowing him time to come up with additional funds. And he'd obtain those funds...from marrying her?

Not bloody likely. Fox swiped his hand through his hair, not caring how tousled he appeared. She wouldn't be coming back. He clenched his fist. He'd held her in his arms and allowed her to slip away.

Would she have done so if she knew he and the highwayman were the same person? Had she even an inkling? She hadn't seemed to. With the highwayman, she'd flirted, she'd teased, she'd invited. What about him brought those things out in her? How could he, as Fox, elicit those same responses?

He'd been so close with the waltz. She'd been impressed, laughing, beautiful. Carefree. Unlike any woman he'd ever known. Ah, but to be as unfettered as she for even a short while. But he had been. In her arms.

Heels tapped in the doorway. His head snapped up.

Miranda paused just inside the library. She was lovely with her golden hair swept up from her neck, a few gentle curls wisping about her face. She wore an emerald gown, probably far grander than most at the assembly tonight. The color made her aqua eyes appear deeper, richer than any precious gem. Chin held high, swathes of color bloomed in her cheeks "Mr. Foxcroft. I came for a book. I forgot to take one with me."

"Is there a particular book you're looking for?" Fox cleared his throat for he sounded as if he'd eaten sand.

"Uh, no." Her gaze moved over the room. She hesitated for a moment and then stepped before the bookshelf.

He walked toward her, intent on making the most of this second chance. "I apologize for my behavior. I didn't mean to insult you." He stopped a few feet from her and rested his hand on the bookcase.

She turned her head, her lashes sweeping over her eyes quickly before she looked forward once more. "You're right. We're from different worlds. I shouldn't have presumed to know you or your work."

He ran his finger over a copy of *Lyrical Ballads*. "Actually, your tent idea is a good one. And you really must call me Fox. We might be from different worlds, but you're in my world now, and in my world everyone calls me Fox."

She pivoted and fixed her aqua gaze on him. His body, already in heightened awareness, heated beneath her regard. She plucked his book from the shelf. "What were you reading?"

"*Tristram Shandy*. It's a particular favorite of mine."

She handed the book to him. "It was my brother's favorite also. My eldest brother. The one who died."

He accepted the tome, wrapped his palm around the spine. "I'm sorry about that."

She glanced back at the bookshelf. "Don't be sorry for me, be sorry for Jasper. He went from careless spare to scrutinized heir in the blink of an eye."

He loved hearing these details, wanted to know everything about her. And not just because it might make his seduction easier. "That was hard for Jasper?"

The ghost of a smile played upon her face. Something kept her emotion for her family at bay. "Yes. He's very active and though our father encouraged athletic pursuits, he expected Jasper to be good at all things— including academia. Not that Jasper isn't terribly intelligent, but he's much happier riding than reading. These are all poetry here?" She inclined her head toward the row of books.

"Yes. Novels are down there." He turned to lead her down the wall, but paused. "I shouldn't assume you want a novel. Perhaps you'd prefer a treatise on crop rotation?"

She let out a soft, gentle laugh. It was short, but a sweeter sound he couldn't imagine. "A novel, I think."

They strolled a few feet down the shelf and he stopped before the novels. "There are quite a few."

"You're very knowledgeable about the orphanage library. Do you spend a lot of time here, then?"

"Yes, you could say this is my library in that I don't

keep many books at Bassett Manor. It makes more sense to keep them here where the children may use and benefit from them."

"Your dedication to the orphans is remarkable." She looked up at the shelves, strolled back and forth twice.

"Do you want to look up there? I'll get the stairs." Fox deposited his book on the shelf and went to the mobile stairs in the corner. He pushed the large oak contraption toward Miranda, its wheels squeaking along the wood floor. He brought it to a stop in front of the novels.

She turned to him, her pink lips parted. He imagined her tongue darting out and committing unspeakable acts. His temperature rose even higher, and suddenly his infernal cravat threatened to squeeze off his air supply. He held his hand out to assist her onto the stairs.

She took it, her soft flesh connecting with his. The jolt of pleasure he'd enjoyed during their waltz spread through his frame. She seemed unaware of her effect on him. "Thank you."

Fox merely nodded. He assumed a position at the base of the stairs and watched her ascend, trying not to ogle her swaying backside. She perused the shelf another minute or two and then removed a volume before turning. As she stepped out to descend, her foot caught something—truthfully he wasn't watching her feet—and the book flew out of her hands.

And into his nose.

"Oh!" She hurried down the stairs, stopping near the bottom so she stood at eye level with him.

Fox managed to catch the unintended weapon with one hand. The other he used to massage his stinging face. She brushed his hand away. "Let me see." She leaned forward and studied his nose while Fox tried not to think about how close her lips were, how alluring her spicy citrus scent was, how badly he wanted to kiss her again.

And then she made matters worse by *touching* him.

She reached out and ran her fingers along his nose. "It's not broken, is it? It doesn't look swollen, just very, very red." Her eyes met his. "I'm so sorry. Are you all right?"

"Fine." And then her words about boldness came back to him, and he gave in to impulse. "You could kiss it."

She pulled her head back the tiniest fraction, but seemed to consider, her golden brows drawing together.

Had he gone too far? "I thought you liked bold." He said this with less confidence, but infinite hope.

"Hmmm. Perhaps I should." She leaned forward again. If he took the first step, just below her, his mouth would replace his nose—

"Here you are!" Mrs. Gates bustled into the library, thoroughly shattering the moment.

Fox stepped back instead of onto the stairs, put his head down instead of up, urged his body to relax instead of enflame. He handed the novel to Miranda.

She took it without looking at him. "Good evening, Mrs. Gates. How did you enjoy the assembly?"

His surrogate mother clapped her hands together and beamed. "Delightful. Simply delightful. I can't thank you enough. And the children, they were no trouble?"

Miranda shook her head. "None at all."

Mrs. Gates looked at Fox. "The boys were no trouble, either?"

He stared at her while trying to form a coherent answer. His mind was still kissing Miranda, disrobing her, savoring the feel of her body...Christ, he couldn't fantasize about that right now. "Perfect angels."

Mrs. Gates chuckled. "Now I know that can't be

true. Lady Miranda, the Carmodys are waiting outside in the carriage to see you home."

Miranda clutched the book to her chest.

Fox inclined his head. "You can take the book with you."

She ran her palm over the cover, longing etched in her features. "Thank you, but no. Mr. Carmody doesn't allow me books." She sighed and then held it out to him. "I'll read it next time."

Surprising. Bold, risky Miranda following someone's ridiculous dictates? "I'll save it for you." He accepted the book, his fingers grazing hers. He suppressed the need to breach the space between them.

"Thank you." She lifted one brow and gave him a small, saucy smile. "For everything."

With the loss of her presence, the room tinged to gray. Fox stared at the doorway until Mrs. Gates coughed, a small smile playing about her mouth. "It's good to see you like this. It's past time you started looking forward instead of back. Time you left Jane behind."

They rarely spoke of Jane. "I moved on long ago."

She straightened a table sitting askew. "By 'moved on' I hope to heaven you aren't talking about that awful Mrs. Danforth." She frowned and shook her head. "I forgot to tell you she came by last week with some clothing for the children."

He set Miranda's book on the shelf, his hand lingering on the cover as if he could draw every bit of her essence from where she'd caressed it. "We can't afford to deny Polly's charity, regardless of how you feel about her."

Mrs. Gates bustled about the room tidying things unnecessarily. "Can't she send her donations over instead of coming personally? Better still, you could have Rob fetch them. It galls me to have to see her after she lured Rose away to work for her."

They'd had this argument before. Fox tugged at his cravat. "Rose was a troubled girl. She came to us older than most children and was already well down the path she chose. I regret her decision as much as you, but we did our best to convince her to stay—the best she let us anyway. And you oughtn't blame Polly. Contrary to what you believe, she comes here to offer what help she can, not entice our girls into prostitution."

Mrs. Gates sniffed in disdain. "Your mother wouldn't approve of you spending time with her, either." His mother and Mrs. Gates had been close friends until Fox's mother's death. Mrs. Gates sometimes invoked her name when she wished to inspire guilt.

And Fox refused to feel guilty about needing the company of a woman after Jane had married Stratham. "I'm not spending time with her." Mrs. Gates raised a brow at his declaration. "Anymore." And he wasn't. Not since Miranda arrived.

She went to fuss with a pile of books on a table near the windows. "Do you mean to pursue Lady Miranda, then?"

He'd never been able to hide his motives from her. "I do."

After aligning the books in a neat stack, she turned to him. "Is she amenable? I can't tell if she's happy here."

"I think she finds the country quite pleasant, and I have reason to believe she might be open to my suit." At least he assumed so given she'd been about to kiss him.

Mrs. Gates grinned at him. "That's wonderful news, Fox! You need a wife, and I've been surprisingly impressed with her work here. You should see her at lunch with the children. The improvement she's managed is astonishing. And they truly adore her. But how can they not? She's..." Mrs. Gates shook her head as she passed her hand over the top of the book pile, "one of a kind."

Yes, she was. Fox couldn't quite believe his luck, but reasoned he was well overdue. "I may not compare to the gentlemen she's used to in London, but I'll take that as a mark in my favor."

"As well you should," Mrs. Gates agreed with a firm nod.

"And you might be a wee bit prejudiced." Fox pinched his fingers together and smiled.

Mrs. Gates's chuckled as she walked towards him. "Perhaps, but with good reason. You're an extraordinary man. Who else would've forgone university to stay here and care for a struggling orphanage? You could have easily sent the charges to the workhouse and carried on with your life. No one would have blamed you."

"You give me far too much credit. After Harrow, I was tired of lectures and rules. It was far easier—and more exhilarating—to come home and manage two estates." Was that true? Fox realized he'd never know, but didn't regret the path he'd chosen.

"Lady Miranda will have no trouble seeing what a fine gentleman you are." She stood on her toes and bussed his cheek.

Tonight had gone much better than he imagined. He was more than encouraged and his resolve had never been more strong.

He was going to do it. Ask Miranda to be his wife.

Right after he purchased some canvas.

~

THE following afternoon, Miranda walked into the orphanage, sorry to be going indoors when they had a true summer day at last. For once she hadn't minded traveling to Stipple's End on foot, especially given Beatrice's excellent mood.

Last night on the drive to Birch House, Beatrice had

talked incessantly about the assembly and how her dance card had never been so full. Instead of hanging on her every word—as Miranda would normally have done for any other girl extolling the thrills of a social event—Miranda kept thinking of Fox and how she was certain he'd been about to kiss her in the library. And how she hadn't minded. No, that wasn't precisely true. *How she'd wanted him to.*

She was still thinking about that shocking revelation today.

Maybe her parents were right after all. Men showed a slight interest in her—or not, in the case of her initial encounter with the highwayman—and she crumbled at their feet.

Beatrice turned toward the stairs. "I'll be in the schoolroom." She paused. "Miranda, thank you for your help. Last night was the first time I had...fun."

Miranda smiled. "I wish I could have seen it."

Beatrice looked away, as if she were uncomfortable with Miranda's kindness, before hurrying up the stairs. Could this possibly be the only joy the poor girl had ever known? Now Miranda felt doubly glad to have helped her.

Miranda glanced at a clock adorning the mantel over the enormous medieval fireplace. The children were still outside enjoying their post-lunch exercise. Mrs. Gates had insisted Miranda skip luncheon at the orphanage today in exchange for being here last night. Miranda had been disappointed and not just because it meant she'd had to take luncheon at Birch House. She'd missed being here. Goodness, but the country was full of surprises.

A heavy rap sounded on the front door, like the head of a walking stick striking the wood. Miranda turned, but no one came to respond to the caller. With a shrug, she went to open it.

Mr. Stratham stood on the threshold, his beaver in

hand. Moisture dampened his forehead, likely a result of the warmer temperature. His eyes widened slightly and then crinkled at the edges as he smiled broadly. "We missed you at the assembly last night, Lady Miranda." He stepped inside without invitation.

Miranda closed the door behind him. "I was here tending the children."

"Lucky children." He threw her a flirtatious glance. "I hoped today might be the day I convince you to take a drive with me. I'll be tied up with district business for the next few weeks and will be heartbroken if you don't come away with me immediately." He leaned on his walking stick in a most elegant manner, presenting a stylishly attired leg. Buff breeches clung to his compact frame and disappeared into magnificently shined Hessians.

While she'd love a drive on such a fine day, she daren't risk the consequences. Besides, she wanted to conduct her duties. She *liked* working with the children. She laced her fingers together in front of her waist. "I'm afraid I must decline. I have only just arrived."

"Oh come now, surely Mrs. Gates will excuse you from your duties for one afternoon. Particularly since you spent your evening here instead of at the assembly last night."

Had he forgotten she was forbidden from attending social events or partaking in social excursions such as driving? Or had he simply not been paying attention that day in Wootton Bassett? Fox had been paying attention.

Mr. Stratham took advantage of her silence. "Excellent, I'll wait here while you inform her of our plans."

Miranda unclasped her hands. "I'm afraid I can't. I'm not allowed to drive with you."

"With me?"

"With anyone, actually. Please don't take offense."

She smiled, truly not wanting to upset him. He seemed like a jovial fellow, even if he had stolen Fox's fiancée. Had she cast Mr. Stratham into the role of villain? Her mind chased that thought and missed whatever he said next. "I beg your pardon?" she said.

"I merely suggested we could take a turn about the grounds then, if you aren't allowed to drive. It's such a lovely day." He plucked up his walking stick, tossed it into the air, and caught the slender piece of wood and ivory in his fist.

She ought to have declined but suspected his persistence would continue. Mrs. Gates would likely not object to delaying the children's afternoon schedule on their first real summer day. "I'll need to check with Mrs. Gates. She's probably out back."

Miranda led him down the back hall and into the yard. Bright sunlight met her eyes, and she held her hand against her brow as she sought the floral muslin skirts of Mrs. Gates. She stood past the vegetable garden talking down the well. Down the well?

Panic drove Miranda through the yard. "Mrs. Gates?"

The headmistress turned and waved, heralding a rush of relief. "Good afternoon, Lady Miranda."

Mr. Stratham followed as Miranda made her way to the well. She stopped next to Mrs. Gates and peered into the blackness. "Is something down there?"

"Just me," came a voice. Miranda's neck tingled despite the day's heat. She'd heard that voice before...on a dark road perhaps?

Mr. Stratham sidled up to the well and placed his gloved palms on the stones. "Fall down, did you, Fox?"

Fox? He was the voice in the well? She'd imagined, for a moment, she'd heard the highwayman. Stupid fancy. She'd been thinking of Fox nearly kissing her last night and had dreamed of the highwayman who had *actually* kissed her.

A rope tied to a nearby tree and dangling over the side of the well into the abyss went suddenly taut. Another moment later Fox pulled himself hand over hand to the top, a bucket looped over his right elbow. His shirtsleeves were rolled up and his muscles flexed with his effort. Society dictated she be offended by his state of undress, but such outrage was for other, more virtuous women. Instead, she studied his exposed flesh and found him to be quite well-formed. Her dress clung heavily to her breasts, but she blamed it on the temperature.

Fox grasped the side of the well and hoisted himself up and over, swinging to the ground with ease. He set the bucket on the ground and then pushed his hair back from his forehead. He looked dewy and hot, his forearms wet, presumably from the well. The opening at the collar of his cream-colored linen shirt exposed his neck. Miranda stared for a moment before realizing the scandal of her behavior and steered her gaze to Mrs. Gates, who frowned at the bucket.

With a shake of her head, the headmistress gave Fox a cloth. "I'm sorry you had to climb down there. So terrible of the boys to cause you such bother."

Fox wiped his face and hands. He chuckled. "It's all right. I remember being a lad with mischief to spend."

"What happened?" Miranda asked.

Fox looked at her, his gaze burning into her as warmly as the sun on her back. "A couple of the boys put the bucket down the well without the rope."

"Insolent pups." Mr. Stratham had stepped back from the well and now swung his walking stick through the grass, breaking the blades as it arced.

Fox glared at him, but said nothing. Mrs. Gates took the cloth from Fox and shoved it into the pocket of her apron. "I should round the children up."

Mr. Stratham raised a hand toward Mrs. Gates. "Before you go, I must beg you allow Lady Miranda to stroll with me and enjoy this fine day for a small while."

Mrs. Gates looked at Miranda, who answered the headmistress's silent question with a slight nod. For some inexplicable reason, she looked at Fox. He bent his head and a lock of hair fell over his forehead. A proper miss would find his disarray appalling, but Miranda liked the way he looked. Rugged. Strong. Overwhelmingly male.

"It would be a shame not to enjoy this pleasant afternoon after all the dreary weather we've had," Mrs. Gates said. "I'll give the children extra time outside. Let me know when you're ready, dearie." She took herself off toward the back of the house.

Mr. Stratham held out his arm. "Shall we, then?"

Miranda took his arm but snuck a glance over her shoulder at Fox. To her surprise, his smoldering gaze fixed on her in return. She hurriedly turned back, lest she trip over her foolishness.

~

OX watched Miranda walk away on Stratham's arm and wondered how easy it would be to persuade Philip and Bernard to throw Stratham into the well. Too easy. Fox pulled up the rope he'd used to climb down the well and tied it to the bucket.

With a muttered curse, he turned and strode from the well. Damn Stratham. Fox refused to lose Miranda to him. His extortion and corrupt election processes were bad enough.

But maybe she wouldn't want Stratham. Last night, she'd danced and laughed with him. Not Stratham, not some London fancy-pants. *Fox*.

He walked to the edge of the yard. Farmland rolled away beyond the fence. His farmland. Summer was well upon them, but the crops were behind. Too behind. He pushed the worry away. He couldn't control the weather. He could, however, control his own actions. And he needed action.

He glanced back at Stratham and Miranda strolling through the yard, now heading toward the orchard. Then he looked down at himself. They weren't his worst clothes, but he looked like a serf next to Stratham with his tailored coat and intricately wound cravat. Hell, Fox wasn't even *wearing* a cravat. He touched his throat and felt the moisture there. He was also dirty and sweaty.

Not the finest picture to present to one's lady, but he couldn't afford to wait until properly attired. Furthermore, if he wasn't mistaken, Miranda had looked at him at the well with anything but contempt.

Fox walked toward the orchard. He crested the slight slope that blocked the view of most of the apple trees from the yard and paused. Stratham was leaving. He'd just bent over her hand—and probably slobbered all over it, the lecherous sod—and she waved him off with a smile.

Did Fox need to rush down there now? Looking like he did? The threat was gone. For now.

And then he heard it. A high-pitched cry down the hill to his right. The water hole!

Miranda had heard it to, too. She looked around for a source. But then she didn't know the property very well and was likely unaware of the small pond.

Another screech spurred Fox into action. He ran down the hill and called out, "Miranda, this way!"

She hitched up her skirt and followed him as he sprinted toward the sound of the child's cries. Flora nearly doubled him over as she came through the shrubbery and slammed into his chest. "Oh, Fox! It's Clara. She's drowning!"

Fox grabbed the girl by the upper arms to steady

her. "Go fetch Mrs. Gates. Go!" He let Flora loose and she tore up the hill.

Miranda had caught up to him and they ran the last few yards to the water together. Several children were standing on the bank. Philip swam out to a flailing Clara.

"He's too slow." Fox pulled off his boots. He dived into the water, knowing from experience it was deeper here than on the opposite side. Stretching his arms and legs, he swam out to Clara, quickly passing Philip who had paused to catch his breath.

In another moment he grabbed the girl under her arms. "Are you all right?"

She nodded furiously, water flying in every direction from her sodden hair.

Fox glanced at the bank where the children were collected and then to the opposite shore. It would be easier to carry her from the water on the shallow side. "I'm going to take you to the other bank. Just hold on to my arm." He positioned her on her back and secured his right arm across her chest and under her arms. She clung to his arm with the strength of five children. As he swam, he saw Miranda circuiting the pond to meet them on the other bank.

His feet met the ground. He swept Clara into his arms and walked the last several feet.

"Mrs. Gates!" Miranda waved her arms wildly. Fox turned to see the older woman hurrying along the side of the pond with a bundle of toweling.

Nearly to shore, Fox struck something solid. Pain sliced into his left ankle and he slipped. Clara shrieked, Miranda dove forward to catch her, and he fell to his knees.

Miranda, now calf-deep in water, clutched Clara before directing her concerned gaze at Fox. "Are you all right?"

Fox nodded despite the excruciating pain in his leg.

Mrs. Gates rushed to the edge of the water. Miranda waded out with Clara and delivered her to the fussing headmistress who wrapped the small child in a blanket. "Good heavens, Fox. Thank the Lord you heard them."

Miranda held out her hand to him. Fox accepted her solicitation and got to his feet. They made their way to dry land, her fingers never leaving his.

She pointed to the ground and, much to his disappointment, dropped his hand. "Sit." Then she turned to Mrs. Gates. "Go ahead and take Clara back to the manor. I'll help Fox."

Fox sat down next to where Mrs. Gates had dropped the toweling. The headmistress's face was drawn, her expression somewhere between fury and extreme relief. She glanced at Fox's ankle. "I'll see about a poultice for the cut on your leg." Still clutching Clara to her chest, Mrs. Gates hurried away, pausing only to herd the rest of the children toward the house.

Miranda knelt beside him. "Let me see."

He stretched out his left leg, his ankle throbbing. She gently pulled his stocking off, her fingers grazing his flesh. He watched her closely, almost forgetting the pain in his ankle amidst her devoted attention.

She gingerly dabbed at his wound with a square of toweling. "Philip told me what happened. He and Bernard tied a rope—I'm guessing the rope from the well—to a tree branch over there and were taking turns swinging into the water."

Fox turned back to look at the other bank. He saw the telltale rope. Yes, it was from the well. He leaned back, putting his hands palm down behind him. "And they let Clara have a turn."

"Not exactly. Lisette explained that the other children were wading on this side of the pond. No one noticed Clara going to the rope until she fell into the water." Miranda sat flat on the ground, still holding the toweling to his leg. "She got out quite far, as you saw."

Fox remembered the hot summer days of his own childhood. "The little ones always do."

Miranda raised her brow in that half inquisitive, half challenging way of hers. "You speak from experience?"

He looked at her intently, enjoying this intimate moment. "Yes. Did you have a place to swim? Next to the big oak tree you fell out of perhaps?"

She nodded. "Benfield—my father's estate outside London—has a large lake. My brother loves to fish." A shadow flickered in her eyes, just as it had done last night when she'd spoken of her family. She peeked under the toweling at his leg. "We should get this properly cleaned. Can you walk?"

He smiled, enjoying her ministrations. "It's not so bad."

Her gaze met his. Sunlight filtered through the still branches of the apple trees and turned her hair to golden silk. Her chignon had come loose, probably as she'd run to the pond, and long waves caressed her shoulders.

"I'm sorry you were hurt. You were wonderful saving Clara." Her eyes were soft, her mouth set into a sweet smile just for him. "Let me help you up."

She stood then offered him her hand. He considered pulling her down to sprawl on top of him and kissing her senseless. Damn, he couldn't think about that, not with wet clothing that would surely advertise his state of arousal. Willing himself to think of something else—which was bloody impossible—he took her hand and used his other palm to push himself up.

She tugged him up until he was standing. In fact, she continued to pull so that he almost crashed into her. He grabbed her waist lest she go tumbling backward.

She blushed a bit. Utterly charming. Then her gaze met his, and he saw a curiosity in her blue-green eyes that matched his own. Her lips parted. He inched forward and lowered his head.

Her breath gusted over his lips as she stepped back. "You can't kiss me."

He couldn't keep the frown from his mouth. "Why not?"

"It isn't appropriate."

God, how he wanted to argue that kissing him was far more appropriate than kissing a highwayman! "Why not?"

She pressed her lips together and tilted her head. "You know why not."

"Then marry me and make it appropriate."

She laughed unsteadily and gave his upper arm a light tap. "Fox!"

He reached for her, clasping her waist between his hands. "I'm serious. Marry me."

She stared at him a moment. "I can't."

"You absolutely can. I'll have the banns read on Sunday."

She shook her head. "My parents would never allow it." He opened his mouth to interrupt, but she spoke over him. "Nor do I want to. You're a...friend. That's all."

Anger sparked in his belly. He'd wager Stipple's End and Bassett Manor she'd been about to kiss him. "Tell me you didn't want me to kiss you." He leaned forward and brought his cheek a hair's breadth from hers. "Tell me to leave you alone, and I will. Or, ask me to kiss you, and I'll make all your dreams come true."

She was still a moment, and then he felt something stir inside of her, the echo of a sigh, perhaps. Her cheek grazed his. He turned his head to claim her mouth. Her hands closed over his... And pushed them away.

She stepped back once more. Her eyes took on a frigidity quite at odds with the steamy afternoon, and she donned an air of arrogant detachment he hadn't seen since her first day at Stipple's End. Alone, her icy stare would have been as effective as another dunk in the pond, but then she spoke and drove the knife in deeper. "What dreams of mine could you possibly bring to pass?"

And there it was. She didn't remotely consider him as a potential mate. Hell, she didn't even consider him as a potential lover. The highwayman had one up on him there.

Her refusal cut to the quick, but was it because he needed her money so desperately or because she'd sliced some buried emotion?

He ached to kiss her anyway, show her how good they'd be together, but pride kept him rooted to the ground. Instead, he gave her a lazy, sardonic smile and said, "Looks like you'll never know."

CHAPTER 7

*R*AIN battered the windows facing the drive to Stipple's End. In mute boredom, Miranda focused on the water running down the glass as she awaited the Carmodys' carriage to fetch her to Birch House.

Her gaze traveled to the clock on the mantel. The Carmodys were at the vicarage today for tea, which is why they even bothered to stop and retrieve her. She could only guess how long she would have to wait.

Ah well, at least she could bide her time in the library.

Miranda took herself to the book-lined room in the back corner of the manor. Tall, diamond-paned windows provided an expansive view of the yard and orchard beyond. One could just make out the watering hole amidst the apple trees.

She tried not to think of the disastrous day over three weeks ago when Fox had nearly kissed her and then proposed marriage. And since Fox now rarely spoke to her—seemed to avoid her company altogether actually—it appeared he had chosen to ignore the occasion as well.

Except if they were truly ignoring it, they would be going on as they had before—as friends. Now awkwardness passed between them, and little else save banalities such as, "Good day" or "Dismal weather we're having."

Miranda was sorry for it. She'd come to like Fox. He possessed something that drew her—and almost everyone else—to him. He was attentive, kind, and from what she could tell at the orphanage, fiercely loyal and dedicated to those who depended upon him.

Plus, she constantly wondered what it would have been like to kiss him. And whether he might try again. And if he didn't, if she might conjure the nerve she never seemed to have trouble summoning with other gentlemen and kiss him.

Where had that daring gone? She'd suffered no qualm about kissing a common highwayman, for goodness sake. But there'd been nothing common about that kiss. A thrill shot up from her toes and spread through her abdomen. Surprisingly, she was almost certain kissing Fox would've provoked the same response. Whereas Darleigh had scarcely aroused more than curiosity, both a thief and then a farmer—he was more than that, but she wasn't feeling particularly charitable at the moment—had actually induced…lust.

"Ah, here you are, Lady Miranda!" Stratham entered, carrying his ivory-tipped walking stick in the air like a staff.

She dragged her focus from Fox to Stratham and was surprised to feel a crest of disappointment in her chest. Because she was raised to be polite, she offered him a smile and said, "Good afternoon, Mr. Stratham. Did you enjoy a successful trip to London?"

He took her hand and floated a kiss above her glove. "Indeed. Though I'll be traveling again soon, I'm afraid. Which is why I've come today so I may spend a bit of time with you while I am in Wootton Bassett." He looked from side to side and raised a brow, giving the appearance he was about to impart some dire secret.

"In truth, I came straightaway from the vicarage after determining the Carmodys would visit for another half hour at least. I knew we would not be interrupted." He finished with a grin and a tap of his stick on the polished oak floor.

Miranda wondered who had let Mr. Stratham into the manor. Another notion crept up her spine. One that went quite along with his furtive manner. Perhaps he'd snuck in. It reminded her of London, and how she and her friends threw caution over a cliff at nearly every opportunity. Such behavior seemed a bit hazardous now. Perhaps her banishment was altering her behavior after all. *Oh, perish that thought.*

"Come, sit with me." Mr. Stratham took her hand and led her to a settee facing the fireplace. "I understand it has rained almost incessantly since I left."

"Indeed." She sat down and retracted her hand from his to smooth her skirts. "Everyone is quite worried about the harvest. Apparently it is several weeks behind schedule."

Mr. Stratham set his walking stick against the end of the settee. "I'm sure it will catch up."

Miranda turned toward him. "You don't seem concerned."

"Not really." He stretched his arm along the back of the settee. "Things have a way of working out." He winked at her, and she couldn't decide if he was incredibly optimistic or purposely obtuse.

Her eye caught the door over his shoulder, and she noted it stood half closed. Since she'd left it wide open, she had to conclude Mr. Stratham planned some kind of impropriety. She should put a stop to his scheme. Unlike with the highwayman and, to her astonishment, Fox, her body didn't quiver with anticipation in Stratham's presence.

Although perhaps she hadn't given him the opportunity. Now was the time to prove she was above

common   thieves   and   impoverished   country
bumpkins.

Mr. Stratham moved his fingers from the back of
the settee to lightly graze her shoulder. "Lady Miranda,
your beauty steals my breath."

So he wasn't a poet. She wasn't interested in poetry.
She leaned a bit closer, willing a spark to tingle along
her shoulder blade, up her neck, *anything*.

He responded in kind, his head angling toward her,
his lips parted. His pupils were dilated. At least
someone was affected.

He touched his lips to hers, and Miranda strove to
find the thrill that ought to accompany his kiss. The
thrill that had accompanied the highwayman's kiss. Instead, nothing.

A loud crash jolted them apart as surely as if Mr.
Carmody had put his skinny arms between them. Miranda looked over Mr. Stratham's shoulder, saw the
door shuddering as it bounced back from the wall
where Fox had thrown it.

Fox.

He looked as if he might tear Mr. Stratham's head
from his shoulders and then mount it on the wall.

Miranda leapt to her feet. She swallowed the large
ball of guilt lodged in her throat. "Ahem. Ah, well. Good
afternoon, Fox."

Fox glared at her, his eyes dark and slitted. "The
Carmodys are here. I suggest you be on your way."

"Yes, thank you." Miranda wanted to say something
else, but words would not come. What could she say to
mitigate this disaster?

Mr. Stratham rose, walking stick in hand. "I'll see
you to your carriage."

There were so many reasons he could *not* walk her
to the Carmodys' carriage, not the least of which was
that Mr. Carmody would likely become apoplectic at
the knowledge Mr. Stratham had paid her a social call.

And really, why else would he be at the orphanage he'd steadfastly avoided until she'd begun working there? And what if Mr. Carmody assumed the worst? Given what her parents had told him, he only waited for her ruination. Oh no, she could not be seen with Mr. Stratham…never mind Fox had witnessed their ill-conceived kiss.

Fox continued to glower in their direction. "I will escort her."

The way in which he delivered his pronouncement brooked no argument. With her head high, Miranda walked from the room, her pulse racing even faster as she passed Fox in the doorway.

He turned and fell into step beside her. Anger resonated in the heat from his body. His hair and clothing were damp as if he'd been working in the rain without a hat. That errant lock had fallen over his forehead making him appear dashing, careless. He looked as if he couldn't be contained. Primal.

She hated what she'd seen in his eyes when he'd barged into the library. "I'm sorry." The words sounded pathetic.

"What for? I'm not your guardian." He slid her an acidic glance. "Or your husband."

If he'd slapped her, she would have felt better. Instead, her stomach threatened to shrivel up and disappear.

"I would counsel you to beware of your choices. You've made it clear Wootton Bassett is not to your liking. With him, you might spend a decent portion of the year in London, but he'll always come home."

Another person who sought to know what was best for her! "I'd thank you to keep your counsel to yourself." They were passing through the main hall. Fox walked ahead to open the door.

"As you wish." He swept his hand in a grand gesture, ushering her outside.

She plucked her bonnet from a table and shoved it on her head, not bothering to tie the ribbons. With a final glare of her own, she stalked out into the rain.

And flinched as the door slammed behind her.

~

*F*OX turned from the trembling door and balled his fists at the sight of Stratham twirling his walking stick and grinning like an imbecile. Fox wanted to shove the stick up his—

"Fox, you look peevish. Something else around here fall apart?"

With supreme effort, Fox flattened his palms against the sides of his thighs and willed himself to relax. There was no point pounding Stratham, much as he'd like to. "We still need to fix the roof. Thanks to generosity like yours, we haven't been able to afford the proper repairs." Fox sneered, unable to keep his emotions in check.

Stratham pressed his lips together. "You're always so disagreeable. I don't understand why you blame me for Jane. At least I assume that's the reason for your behavior. She made her choice and risked condemnation by the entire district for it."

She'd risked nothing. "Who would dare slur the MP's wife? Especially one who wields such power." Fox stepped toward the smaller man. "Shouldn't you be out collecting 'tributes' or whatever you call the money you extort from northern Wiltshire?"

Stratham clenched his walking stick in both hands before his chest as if it were a shield. "Watch what you say, Foxcroft."

"Are you threatening me?" Fox took another step forward. "After everything my father did for you? After everything he gave?"

Stratham looked to the side and threw his shoulders back. "Your father was a good man."

"My father was as morally deficient as you. I'm sure that's why you got on so well." The anger Fox had conquered moments before reared its head once more. "You'll have to excuse me, I need to get on the roof." They'd installed the canvas a few weeks ago, but a drip had started again that morning, meaning the covering must've come loose.

"In this weather? Even you aren't that daft." Stratham paused. "Are you?"

Fox pushed past the little rat. "Get the hell out of my orphanage, and don't come back unless you're invited."

A few moments later, Fox walked out into the gray day and approached Rob stationed at the base of a ladder. "Are you ready?"

"Aye." Rob inclined his head toward the front of the house. "Was that Stratham's carriage in the drive?"

Fox nodded. The idiot certainly wasn't surreptitious about his unauthorized visit. Fox assumed Stratham was still prohibited from calling on Miranda. Else, why would he have come here?

Because he stood a better chance of finding her unchaperoned.

Fox's mood darkened to the color of the storm moving from the west. "Caught him kissing Miranda in the library." He started up the ladder.

"Son of a bitch. Suppose he's proposed yet?" Rob called the last.

Fox couldn't answer Rob's question and be heard. He climbed onto the roof so Rob could follow. Carefully, he made his way to the corner. As expected, the canvas had blown back, exposing part of the hole.

When Rob stopped beside him, Fox responded, "If he has, she's given him the same answer she gave me." This thought gave him a modicum of relief. And if she'd turned Stratham down as well, what was he doing kissing her? Trying to compromise her? Christ, he basically just had. If anyone other than Fox had walked in... Fury built again. Dammit, if anyone was going to compromise her, it should be *him*, not that slimy Stratham.

Fox looked down at the battered roof tiles. They desperately needed a large influx of money to replace the tiles and the timber frame beneath.

Rob let out a low whistle. "Can you imagine if this was still covered in thatch?"

The medieval hall had been built with a thatched roof, which had been replaced by Fox's forebears when they'd converted the building to an orphanage. Fox usually took comfort in thinking about his ancestors who had sacrificed so much and worked so hard to give those less fortunate a better life. But then he thought of his father's transgressions and became angry. Why had his father failed them all and left them in this disastrous mess?

Fox kneeled to pull the canvas back into place. Rot had destroyed most of the wood frame. The tent was keeping things dry for the most part, but he couldn't tell how long the structure would be secure. Fox only hoped it didn't buckle and hurt one of the children. He'd tell Mrs. Gates to avoid holding activities in the hall. Perhaps he needed to start thinking about moving them to Bassett Manor. His home wasn't quite as large as Stipple's End, and it hadn't been renovated as an orphanage, but it was at least free of potentially catastrophic leaks.

They went about securing the canvas back into place. As they nailed the canvas to the wood, Fox wracked his brain for a solution to their financial problems.

"What if I steal Stratham's tribute money?"

Rob, kneeling near the corner, looked up, his hammer poised over a nail. "How do you propose to do that?"

Fox sat back on his heels. The rain fell a bit harder now and he wished he'd grabbed his hat and a coat. "He starts collecting soon. Then he delivers the money to Norris. Why let the money line their pockets when there are people who need it far more?"

Water dripped from the rim of Rob's hat. "You'd be risking a great deal if they caught you. No telling what kinds of lawlessness those two are tangled up in."

Fox futilely wiped the rain from his face. "Even so, it's the only way I can think to obtain a lot of money quickly."

Rob glanced away, weighed the hammer in his palm. "I'm sorry things didn't work out with Lady Miranda." He turned back. "You sure that way's closed?"

"Quite."

She'd been more than clear. Oh, he still wanted her, but he'd be damned if he'd propose to her again. At least not until she realized he wasn't a second-class match.

Rob swung the hammer. "You don't mind being the highwayman again? I'll go along, if you want."

"No, I'll do it alone. I'm not risking you or anyone else this time." The idea of donning his mask again made him think of the first time he'd done so. When he'd kissed Miranda.

He *could* compromise her, couldn't he? Better him than Stratham, who'd nearly done it today. Actually had done it today if Fox wanted to advertise what he'd seen. Which he most certainly didn't. Fox closed his eyes against the rain. He'd been reduced to thieving, but God help him, he wasn't a cad.

Not yet.

≈

*T*EN days later the rain continued, drumming against the roof of the carriage as Miranda and Beatrice returned home from Stipple's End. They were nearly to Birch House when Beatrice finally spoke. "What's happened between you and Fox? He goes out of his way to avoid you."

Miranda recalled the furious look on Fox's face when he'd walked in on her kissing Stratham. "Nothing's happened. He's incredibly busy, isn't he? What with Stipple's End and Bassett Manor."

Beatrice gave her a gimlet eye, but said nothing. After a moment, she turned back to staring out the window. "Mrs. Gates told me you invented a new fragrance of soap today. You thought you'd be teaching the children. How surprising that you've learned from them." Was Beatrice needling her? "Mrs. Gates believes it will sell well at Mrs. Abernathy's." She contemplated Miranda with a pensive look. "I'm impressed."

Miranda shifted in her seat. She'd been complimented on her hair, her clothing, her laughter, and a hundred other things, but never for something as mundane as creating soap. Why then did pride bubble in her chest?

"It's fun making soap with the girls." Shockingly so.

"Then being here isn't as tedious as you imagined?"

"I suppose it's no use trying to convince you I wasn't expecting tedious." And anyway, that wasn't really true. "I enjoy many things about Wootton Bassett." Miranda eyed the dirty hem of her favorite day dress. The constant mud was not one of those things. With resignation, she raised her gaze once more.

Beatrice focused her attention out the window in what was probably supposed to be a careless manner, but Miranda could see the tension bunching her shoulders. "Mr. Stratham is one of those things."

Comprehension dawned. Miranda would set Beatrice straight right now. "No. That is to say, my interest in Mr. Stratham is of a purely pragmatic and likely temporary nature."

Beatrice looked at Miranda, blushing profusely. "Not romantic?"

At the word romantic, an image of sapphire, jade, and amber eyes jumped into Miranda's mind. Good Lord, that was an alarming—and completely unacceptable thought. "Beatrice, you must realize that while I don't hate it here, I will return to London. I've no desire to remain in Wiltshire—for romantic reasons or otherwise."

"But Stratham's carriage was at Stipple's End after the last vicarage tea. He left hurriedly, apparently to see you." Beatrice's color faded. Her level gaze dared Miranda to prevaricate.

Miranda had already been interrogated by Beatrice's father. She narrowed her eyes and gave Beatrice the same answer she'd given Carmody. "Yes, he came to see me. But I was busy."

Self-preservation demanded she didn't admit they'd been alone together. A thought struck Miranda—clearly Beatrice had been ruminating on this for days. "I didn't realize you hoped for his attention."

Beatrice's cheeks reddened again as the carriage rambled to a full stop. She opened her mouth to speak, but merely said, "Oh, never mind," and jumped out.

Miranda followed, eager to pursue a discussion of Beatrice's feelings toward Stratham. The match began to take shape in Miranda's mind, and she smiled. Putting them together would be like being back in London with her friends.

Fitchley opened the door to the house, and Beatrice disappeared inside. "I've a letter for you, Lady Miranda." He handed her the missive, effectively halting her progress.

She turned the parchment over in her palm. Her father's seal. Her heart quickened and her plan regarding Beatrice fled. "Thank you." She dashed up the stairs, tempted to take them two at a time. Once in her room, she closed the door firmly and shook off her pelisse. She pulled her bonnet off and laid it over the end of the bed with her gloves.

She stared down at the missive. Would it be good news or bad? Happy tidings or blistering admonishments? She plucked it up and tore it open, her eyes scanning its length. It was short. Maddeningly, disappointingly short.

> *Miranda,*
>
> *Please stop pleading to come home. You ruin not only yourself with your behavior—you infect the entire family.*
>
> *Do everyone a courtesy and stop writing.*
>
> *Holborn*

The paper fell from her fingers and drifted to the desk. The gray-white walls of her room blurred before her eyes. It was a miracle Father hadn't sent her to a convent instead of rural Wiltshire.

She grabbed the poker and went to stoke the fire. Anguish clogged her throat, made it ache as she stirred through the embers. If only her parents hadn't been so controlling. They were certain she would ruin herself, gave her no credit for making her own sound judgments. The memory of Stratham kissing her at Stipple's End made her insides cringe. Perhaps she'd never given them reason to.

Her efforts with the fire were as pointless as thinking about how she might earn her parents' trust. Replacing the poker in its stand, she sat on the side of the bed and pulled a blanket around her shoulders. She flopped back and gazed up at the ceiling. A crack marred a crooked path from one corner to the center of the room. How long had it taken to get that far? How long before it met the other corner and split the room in two?

How long would she be consigned to this abyss? She was alone and separated from everything she knew. Everyone she loved.

And for the first time, she wondered if she didn't deserve it.

~

*M*IDNIGHT had come and gone, and still Fox leaned against a tree, surveying the quiet drive leading to Stratham Hall. He'd wait ten more minutes. How did true highwaymen not die of boredom waiting for their next quarry?

Though just past mid-August, the crisp scent of autumn already hung in the air. Fox usually loved this time of year, but the disaster of the harvest weighed heavy, smothering his anticipation of the coming season.

He'd stationed himself outside Stratham's estate every night over the past fortnight. When the rat left his nest, Fox followed him, hoping he was headed to Cosgrove. It made sense that Stratham would take the tribute money to Norris as he was the driving force behind the scheme. Fox knew this because his own father had collected money for the earl until Norris discovered the elder Foxcroft had pocketed a share to make up for his losses at the gaming tables. Norris had ended the relationship. Though he couldn't prove it, Fox believed the earl had then done whatever possible to foster Fox's father's gambling addiction. If an attack of the heart hadn't killed him, he likely would have bled both Stipple's End and Bassett Manor completely dry.

Could the people afford the money Norris demanded this year? Not that they had a choice. They either paid Norris, or he'd do whatever necessary to ruin their livelihood, just as he'd done with Fox's father.

The lights of Stratham's pretentiously extravagant house were visible through the trees. Built a mere fifty years ago, Fox admitted the estate was far grander than Bassett Manor, but in his opinion its lack of character and history made it the lesser home.

Stratham's carriage rattled around the drive from the back. Fox pulled himself astride Icarus while he waited for Stratham to get in the vehicle. Within a few minutes, the carriage rumbled toward Fox. He stepped his horse behind the tree.

A coachman rode on the box and a footman stood on the back. Stratham didn't normally take the extra man. Could this mean he carried the tribute money tonight and needed the additional security?

Fox checked his pistols and ran his palm over the hilt of his saber. Despite his armament, he was still out-numbered—not that he counted Stratham in the equation.

A twig snapped behind Fox. He pulled a pistol from his waistband and turned in the saddle.

"Hold there." Rob, wearing his mask, walked his horse closer. "It's just me. I thought you could use some help."

Fox exhaled, the air hissing through his clenched teeth. "I told you I didn't want to risk you."

"But there're two of them on the coach."

Fox nodded. "All right, but stay hidden unless I need you." He led Icarus into a trot, and they followed Stratham in silence.

After a few minutes, Rob asked, "Where do you plan to do this?"

"Assuming he's on his way to Cosgrove, just before the bridge. I'm going to cut across Wickersham's field to beat them there."

Rob grunted in response, and they made their way

across the field. They stopped just shy of the bridge and heard the distant sound of Stratham's carriage. He was headed for Cosgrove then.

Fox and Rob moved into a copse of trees. Fox climbed down from Icarus and ran to the middle of the road just as the coach rounded a bend and came into view.

The coach slowed. The coachman half-stood in his box. "You there! Get out o' the road!"

Fox took his pistols from his waistband and pointed them at the coachman. Careful to disguise his voice, he shouted, "Stand and deliver!"

The coachman brought the horses to a shuddering halt.

Fox kept the pistols steady, his arms wide. "I know there's a footman on back. Come 'round slowly. I've got a bullet fer the coachman and one fer you if need be."

The footman appeared from the right side of the coach. The moon was but a sliver in the sparsely clouded sky, but the lanterns on the coach provided ample illumination.

Stratham opened the carriage door and jumped to the ground behind the footman, who made his way forward. "What is the meaning of this?"

Fox pointed a pistol at the coachman. "You, get down. Slowly." He fixed his other weapon on the footman. "Keep yer hands up where I can see 'em."

Stratham stepped around his servant. "You're that damned blackguard! Thought you'd run off or, better yet, died."

"Not at all. I've been waiting fer you." Fox smiled malevolently beneath his mask. A satisfying idea struck him. "Coachman. Loose the horses."

"Are you mad? Those beasts cost a fortune!" Stratham shrieked.

Fox chuckled low in his throat. "You'll find 'em again, no doubt." The coachman hesitated. "Coachman, I've still got a pistol on you or have you forgotten?"

The servant freed the horses. They wandered to the side of the road and grazed.

Fox gestured toward them with his pistol. "Coachman, give 'em a good pat to send 'em on their way." The coachman complied, and Stratham yowled like a wounded animal.

The small man stepped forward, throwing his face in shadow as he moved away from the light. "You'll pay for this. I won't rest until you're strung up."

"Fer what, turning yer horses loose?" Fox waved at him with a pistol. "Step back into the light, please."

Stratham moved backward, his eyes narrowed. "I presume you've another reason for stopping my coach."

Fox kept one pistol trained on the footman and the other on the coachman. "Aye."

Stratham inclined his head toward Fox. "You've only two bullets there. And there are three of us."

Fox looked Stratham up and down in an exaggerated fashion so the weasel would know he was being appraised even though the appraiser wore a face-covering mask. "That's a bit generous, don't you think? I'd count two and a half at best."

Stratham balled his fists and surged forward, but his feet didn't leave the ground. "We can overtake you."

"No, I've other men in the trees." Fox called out, "Give a whistle, will you?" Rob responded in kind. "Assuming yer satisfied with our ability to quash any rebellion you might mount, let us move on to our transaction. I'll take all the money you're carrying tonight." He moved the pistol slightly, training it on Stratham's chest. "All of it."

"Christ." Stratham ran a hand through his hair, tousling the always-immaculate tresses.

Fox grinned. Adrenaline poured through his veins. Luck was finally his. "You," he gestured to the footman standing just behind Stratham, "fetch the money. Take off yer coat and leave it on the ground. My men have their guns trained on you. If you come out of the carriage with a weapon, they'll shoot you. Do you understand?"

The footman nodded and backed up slowly before bending into the open door of the carriage. Fox couldn't see the servant, and hoped Rob had a good view of the man's movements.

"How do you know I'm carrying money? Do you work for Norris? He better not be stealing his own money only to make me collect it again."

Not a bad ruse. Fox wouldn't put it past the old codger to come up with something so vile. And he saw no harm at all in allowing Stratham to think the worst about the man who pulled his strings. "Believe what you will."

The footman emerged from the carriage with a tapestry bag. Fox could hardly wait to see how much it contained. From Stratham's reaction, it seemed a lot. Perhaps more than Fox dared hope. It couldn't be more than he needed, however. He doubted there was a number high enough. He inclined his head toward the line of trees in which Rob hid. "Put it down over there and then step back here. Slowly."

Once the footman deposited the bag near the trees, Rob stepped out and picked it up with one hand, his other clutching a pistol trained on the servant.

Stratham's hand twitched, as if he was missing his third arm—that damned walking stick of his. "I hope for your sake you work for Norris. If you don't, he will exhaust every resource hunting you down."

"Why, when as you pointed out, he can simply make you collect more?" Even as he said this, Fox inwardly cringed. Having to come up with another payment could wreak disaster for some people.

Before he regretted his actions, Fox backed toward

the trees. The footman had returned to Stratham's side and the coachman lingered on the other side of the now-empty traces.

Fox heard the breathing of their horses, knew Rob was mounted and had Icarus ready to fly. "Good evening then, gentlemen." He dashed into the cover of the trees and tucked one pistol away. With his free hand, he pulled himself onto Icarus's back and they sped from the roadside copse as fast as the horses could manage. They kept clear of the road and made their way toward Bassett Manor, not daring to stop and count the money now tied to the back of his saddle.

How would he explain the influx of wealth to Mrs. Gates or anyone else who might ask? The sudden repairs would not go unnoticed, especially when he'd been asking everyone over the age of fifteen for a donation. If he told them he sold something valuable, they'd simply wonder why he hadn't done so before. No, he'd have to spend it judiciously and not draw too much attention. If asked, he would say they had an anonymous donor. He would have to be careful, lest Stratham or Norris grow suspicious. He'd sit on the majority of the money for at least a fortnight.

Breathing a sigh of relief now he'd formed a plan, Fox allowed himself to relax. They passed the road leading to Birch House and he slowed. Did Miranda still walk the Carmodys' garden at night? More importantly, did she still lust for the highwayman?

"Rob," he called ahead to his friend.

Rob stopped and waited for Fox to come up beside him.

Fox reached back and untied the bag of money. "Here, take this back to Bassett Manor."

Rob took the bag. "We're awfully close to Birch House. What are you about, man?"

"I'm taking your advice." He gripped his reins in apprehension. How did one go about compromising a woman? Simply climb into her room and declare himself? Wait for her to come out for her nightly stroll and then raise the hue and cry?

Rob chuckled. "Good luck to you, then." Raising his hand in farewell, he took himself off.

Fox led Icarus around the back, dismounted, and tethered him to a tree. Stealing across the disappointingly empty yard, he studied the building. Which room was hers? He'd only been to Birch House a couple of times and had never been on the upper floors.

He paused, sheltering himself next to a tree. What the hell was he about? A compromise required something scandalous. But didn't it also require someone witnessing the scandal? Who would witness anything at this hour? The house was completely dark. He'd have to make a commotion.

But I'm dressed as the bloody highwayman. He glanced down at his clothes. The highwayman couldn't compromise her. Montgomery Foxcroft had to do it.

His body stopped in mid-motion—one hand palm down against the tree, his torso turned toward the house, his feet ready to flee at a moment's notice.

Indecision battled opportunity. He was here. Dressed as the bandit. She liked the bandit. She'd kissed the bandit. He could steal into her room, perhaps steal another kiss or two, and depart before anyone was the wiser. Or, he could remove his mask, kiss her as Montgomery Foxcroft and bind her to him forever.

Put like that, he had nothing to lose.

Fox raised his hand to his mask and froze as the back door of the house swung open.

CHAPTER 8

*M*IRANDA stopped short on the small landing outside the back door. Though dark enough for her eyes to deceive her, she felt certain someone stood not twenty feet away.

Reason told her to turn around, but reason was vastly overrated. Besides, the nape of her neck tingled with anticipation. Somehow she knew who lingered in the yard. She stepped into the soft grass. "Who's there?"

"You promised we would meet again. I got tired of waiting."

The highwayman.

He sauntered toward her, pausing a few feet away.

The cool night breeze stirred her hair. Miranda brushed a stray lock from her face. "Have you been skulking about the back entrances of every house in the district, or did you somehow know to find me here?"

"I have ways of finding what I need." He leaned against a small pear tree not far from the stairs she'd just descended into the yard.

Miranda heard the smile in his voice. *Go inside,* her mind screamed. But other, less sensible parts of her body drove her forward until she stood before him. He wore the same dark clothes he'd worn the night of the robbery. A mask covered his entire head, save his mouth and chin. Pity, for she dearly wanted to see his face.

"Did you say need?"

"Mmm. I did." His deep voice sounded husky, alluring. He stepped closer and she could feel the warmth of his body. "You seem in a precarious position. I couldn't help but overhear that man berating you after we first met. What is your relationship to him?"

Her throat went dry. "He's my jailer." The words came out croaky. The highwayman laughed. A deep, cleansing sound of mirth that made Miranda smile, but she quickly sobered. "You risk a great deal coming here."

"Perhaps some things are worth any risk." He tucked her hair behind her ear, his finger tracing along her sensitive flesh. Shivers of anticipation raced down her arms, through her belly, along her thighs.

She pulled her dressing gown tighter against the chill night air. So many nights she'd walked in the garden, and she'd never considered she might encounter someone. Let alone her highwayman.

"It's cold." The highwayman pulled his cloak from his shoulders and wrapped it around her. Immediately, she was ensconced in delicious heat. A fresh, earthy scent, something infinitely masculine enveloped her. Recognition tickled the back of her mind. She had to be recalling their first meeting.

"But now you're cold."

He reached out and pulled her against him, his arms encircling her back. His legs were parted and he positioned her between them. "Now, I am not."

She swallowed with difficulty. She should rip his cloak off and run back into the house, but she couldn't move. Couldn't do anything but gaze up into his masked face. Her flirtation with the highwayman was reckless, dangerous, forbidden. A thrill shot up her spine.

Miranda tipped her head back. Her highwayman was rather tall. "Have you come to ransom me? If you knew where to find me, perhaps you know about my family, too."

His hands held her close. "I know you've been deprived your usual comforts. And, forgive me for saying, but your usual comforts are more luxury than people like me will ever see. It didn't occur to me to ransom you, but that is an excellent notion."

She ignored the last, for it seemed to have been said in humor. "And what 'people' are you like, then?"

He chuckled, low and soft in the darkness. She pressed closer.

He dipped his head and said against her ear, "I prefer not to classify myself."

Her heart beat a staccato rhythm in her chest. "If you aren't here to take me away, why have you come?"

"For another kiss, perhaps." His warm breath caressed her temple.

Miranda shivered. "I should go back."

His lips brushed her cheek. The rough cotton of his mask grazed the side of her face, her ear. "I won't stop you."

She placed her hands on his shoulders, opening the cloak, leaving less between them. He removed his hands from her back and put them against her neck, caressing her, drawing her closer. And then his mouth touched hers, and her knees went weak. She gripped him tighter, moving her hands behind his neck, holding onto him lest she tumble to the earth.

Her frustration and loneliness—yes, loneliness she now realized—faded in his kiss. Where she'd been bold during their previous encounter, she let him lead her, content to do his will. One of his hands cupped the back of her head as his lips parted over hers. His tongue swept against her, and she opened for him, welcomed him inside.

His kiss deepened, his hands holding her firm, steady, captive. Her head dropped back under his on-slaught. *Yes, command me.* Desire pulsed through her body, throbbed between her thighs. *Make me yours.*

He trailed kisses along her jaw. Finding her earlobe, he nipped it, eliciting a shudder of longing that seemed to make her body curl in upon itself. His right hand tangled in her hair while his left coasted over her shoulder and settled just above her breast, the warmth of his bare palm heating her flesh through the thin cotton of her nightrail.

She did falter then, slumping against him with a faint moan. He turned with her, pushing her back against the pear tree. His hand moved down her body, cradled her hip, pulled her against his hardness.

She tugged at the fabric covering most of his face. "Won't you take off your mask?"

He shook his head against her neck, as he kissed and licked a path back to her mouth.

She pleaded, "I won't give you away."

"Shhh." He kissed her, his mouth open, slanting across hers, devouring any response she might have given.

She arched against him, and his hand moved be-tween them once more. He found her breast, her nipple hardening against his palm. His fingers closed around her, and she gasped into his mouth.

A thump from the house froze their movements. He stood straight, breathed against her forehead.

She pushed his cloak from her shoulders and thrust it at him. "You have to go."

He looked at the house as if he were waiting for someone.

"I can't be caught out here with you. Not again! Please go!" She shoved at him, and finally he stepped back.

She pivoted and hurried to the house. At the door she turned to see if he remained.

His silhouette was recognizable next to the tree. "Until next time, then."

She stepped inside and pulled the door shut. There couldn't be a next time.

~

*N*EARLY a week had passed since the highwayman's visit to Birch House, but Miranda could still feel his hands on her body, still longed for his kiss. For the hundredth time, she bade herself focus on teaching the dance to the children. Between Miranda's flights of fancy and the boys' lack of interest and grace, today's lesson was a mess.

"Ow!" Beatrice hobbled off the makeshift dance floor, precisely where Miranda had waltzed with Fox several weeks ago. They danced in the library since Fox had deemed the hall too hazardous.

"Sorry, Miss Carmody." David, the oldest boy at Stipple's End, studied the floor sheepishly.

Now one of her dancers was wounded. First, there had been strife over who partnered whom, a process that had taken far too long. Then the girls had pouted over not learning the waltz before *The Touchstone*. Who could have foreseen dancing would be Miranda's toughest challenge?

Beatrice sat in the green chair by the fireplace and reached down to massage her foot. "Continue on without me."

Miranda nodded and turned back to the children who were still assembled in their positions. David and Beatrice had been leading, but now David merely stood there looking perplexed.

"Take a seat, David." Miranda waved at the settee. This left six couples on the floor.

"Why don't you dance with him, Lady Miranda?" Lisette asked.

"It's too difficult to direct all of you if I have to do the steps myself." It was too difficult to direct them even when she *wasn't* dancing.

"Aw, I'm tired of dancing. Can't we be done?" Bernard threw himself onto the settee next to David, and the rest of the boys broke their formation.

"No, wait!" Miranda held her hands up and tried to beckon them back. Coaxing some of the boys to participate had been difficult, but Mrs. Gates had promised lightened chores if they were agreeable. "We are almost through *The Touchstone*, and then we will be done for the day."

Several of the boys pulled faces while others simply stared blankly, as if they were too tired to continue. She let her hands drop. Though she hated not finishing, it was probably for the best.

Flora's face fell. "But you said we could waltz!"

Miranda hated disappointing the girls, but more than one dance was really too much to expect from the boys. Actually, just *one* dance had proven too much. "I never promised." She'd been noncommittal, adopting one of her mother's favorite methods. *We'll see*, was an excellent tactic, she had to grudgingly admit.

Bernard shuddered. "I don't want to waltz anyway. Don't you have to touch their *waists*?"

David and another boy looked at the floor, their ears turning red. As they were the eldest, Miranda wasn't surprised they wanted to touch a girl's waist— and probably more if given the chance.

"We'll have to waltz another day, then." Truthfully, Miranda hoped she'd leave before trying to teach dancing again. But they'd be so disappointed…regret twisted in her chest.

Delia approached Miranda. "Can't you at least demonstrate the waltz for us?"

Though tired and frustrated, Miranda bent beneath the girl's pleading gaze. "With whom? Beatrice? She's hurt her foot. No, I'm sorry, but we'll have to wait for another day."

"You could dance with Mr. Foxcroft," Delia suggested.

Every head in the room swiveled toward the door. She spun around. Fox leaned against the doorframe. He arched a brow, and she couldn't determine his reaction at being called out like that.

She crossed her arms over her chest. "How long have you been standing there?"

"Long enough to see that the instruction of dance may not be your forte."

She arched a brow at him in challenge. "And you think you could do better? The children have asked for a waltz demonstration, if you are so inclined."

"I'm willing to give it a go. Though I'm not wearing the right shoes." He glanced down at himself. True, his scuffed brown boots were not at all conducive to an elegant waltz, but he looked rather nice today in tan breeches, dark blue jacket, and simply knotted cravat.

"Are you begging off, then?" Had she sounded hopeful? While he danced superbly, she didn't want to get that close to him. Not after they'd done such a good job avoiding each other.

"Certainly not." He joined her in the center of the room and looked around. "Is there music?"

Miranda gestured to the eight-year-old boy sitting near the windows. "Young Martin has been playing his flute."

Fox smiled at him. "Can you play something to which we can move like this?" He stepped his feet in three-quarter time.

Martin nodded and began to play.

Fox faced her and bowed. Cornered, she took his hand, not at all sure she wanted to touch him. Since turning down his marriage proposal, she'd barely spent any time with him, let alone in close proximity. She held her breath, sure their awkwardness with each other would translate into a disastrous demonstration.

He swept her into the waltz, transporting her back to the perfection of their first dance. Today, with the accompaniment, they moved as one, and it was the closest she'd been to her old life since she'd been forced to leave it.

She closed her eyes briefly and let him lead her, let the music relax her tension, let herself enjoy the moment. When she opened them again, his gaze burned strong, intent, reminding her exactly of their first waltz. She couldn't look away, nor did she want to.

And so they danced.

Until Martin finished his song. In fact, she didn't realize until after he finished that the music had stopped. As with their previous waltz, they'd continued to dance without music.

"So beautiful," one of the girls murmured.

"Yes," Fox agreed, but Miranda knew he and the girl were not commenting on the same thing. A spike of heat burned her neck, and Miranda stepped back. The jade of Fox's eyes seemed to drown out the gold, as if the flame within him had been doused, before he looked away from her.

"When can we learn it, Lady Miranda?" Lisette clasped her hands before her in an urgent plea.

Miranda smoothed her suddenly dewy palms against her skirt. "Soon, I'm sure. But we've had enough today."

As if she'd overheard, Mrs. Gates appeared at the doorway. "It's time for afternoon chores. Past time actually." She smiled. "But I hated to break up such a beneficial lesson. Did you all enjoy your dancing?"

"Oh yes!" The girls twittered all at once, both to Mrs. Gates and to each other. They began to file out of the library. As the last pair passed, Miranda overheard a conversation.

"Maybe Lady Miranda will marry Mr. Foxcroft, and then she'll be with us forever!"

"Nonsense. Why would she stay here when she could go back to London?"

"But they dance so divinely together!"

Miranda looked away from them, and her gaze connected with Fox's. From the way he stared at her, she guessed he'd overheard them too.

Beatrice got up from her chair. "Miranda, I'll be ready to leave in a trice. I just need to run up and fetch, er, something." She ducked out of the library before Miranda could ask what. Besides, Fox was still staring at her.

And now they were alone. Again. Good Lord, but the country was unconcerned with propriety. When she thought of it that way, Wootton Bassett seemed the perfect place for her to be. Ironic that her parents believed her safe from herself out here—or at least safer than she'd been in London.

Her brain urged her to pick up her feet and flee Fox's presence.

He stood maybe twenty four inches from her. "Do they know you're leaving?"

Miranda's gut clenched and her feet remained rooted to the floor. "No. But *I* don't even know that I'm leaving."

His body shifted, opened up somehow. "You mean there's a chance you'll stay?"

She caught the hope quickening his voice and remorse twitched her shoulders. "No. I was speaking sarcastically. Of course I'm leaving. I just don't know when."

He exhaled, as if he'd been holding his breath during her response. "They love you, you know. And you seem to have grown fond of them. Why wouldn't you consider staying? Or perhaps visiting?"

"Oh, I may visit." But Miranda couldn't think of when or how. Once she returned to her life, there would be an endless succession of social engagements and obligations, as there had always been. At one time, she'd been sure she could never endure a summer without such activities. Except she had. And, in truth, didn't miss them as she anticipated she would.

The gold in his eyes reignited. "Is that why you turned down my proposal? Because you can't see yourself living here?"

Miranda's insides heated. "Partly, yes."

"And the other partly?"

"There are many other 'partlies.'"

"And you're not going to offer any of them, are you?" The tone of his voice deepened. It rustled over her like a silk chemise.

"Why did you propose?" As soon as she asked the question, she wished she hadn't. She didn't like any of the probable answers: he wanted her money, he needed to beat Stratham in some primeval masculine competition, or he lusted after her. The last possibility renewed the heat that had tripped along her spine a few moments ago.

He stared at her a long moment. "I hold you in high esteem."

That was not what she'd expected to hear. "Esteem? You want to build a marriage on esteem?" It was good enough for most people she knew, but Miranda wanted more. "No, thank you."

His eyes darkened and he moved toward her. "Among other things." He took her hand and a shiver raced up her arm. "Esteem is an excellent basis for a successful marriage. As is mutual respect. Similar interests. Dancing compatibility." His lips curved into a dangerous smile. "Attraction."

A flame sparked to life in Miranda's belly, warming her body from the inside out. She'd felt like this when the bandit had kissed her... Damn if she wasn't attracted to both a highwayman and Montgomery Foxcroft, of all people! Why couldn't she conjure even a modicum of desire for someone like Stratham, or better yet one of those milksops in London her father would approve of?

She snatched her hand away just as Beatrice reentered the library. Miranda took a step back lest Beatrice draw a disastrous conclusion about their proximity.

Fox's mouth hardened. As engaging as he'd looked a moment before, he appeared the complete opposite now—his features cold, unyielding.

Beatrice clutched a package. "Are you ready, Miranda?"

Fox's mouth turned up once more, but there was bitterness in his expression. "We were just enjoying a nice, *private* discussion."

Miranda caught his inflection on the word "private." What was he about? She narrowed her eyes at him. "Thank you for your assistance this afternoon. Good day, Fox."

Beatrice said goodbye and exited with Miranda. In the hall, Beatrice picked up her bonnet from a table and tied it under her chin. "The children really do adore you. Today was chaotic, but everyone had such a good time. You bring that to them. A sense of...joy." She blinked at Miranda as if she couldn't quite believe it.

Miranda should have felt happy, but while she'd given the children an afternoon to cherish, she'd given Fox another memory he'd probably like to forget.

And what would her lasting impression be? Would she recall her time here fondly or be glad to leave it behind her? She hoped it would be a combination of the two because she didn't want to miss them.

But she suspected she already did.

~

*F*OX looked down at the ledger, staring at the columns of numbers until they blurred together. The money he'd stolen from Stratham hadn't been as much as he'd hoped, but would've been sufficient to fix the roof. If half the food store hadn't gone rotten because the kitchen now leaked. If a half dozen of the children hadn't fallen ill and required medical attention. If three of the boys hadn't needed new clothes and shoes.

Money was always short at this time, but the upcoming harvest usually promised an influx of funds that would see them through another year. Usually. But what crops hadn't died over the cool, wet summer wouldn't provide enough product. It was going to be a lean winter. And spring. And summer.

Fox rested his temple against his hand and looked out the window into the backyard. The children were playing ball. Miranda came into view, her golden hair swept onto her head, her peach dress, like everything else she wore—like her—still too fancy for their humble orphanage.

With fall nearly upon them, he supposed she would be leaving soon. And she'd confirmed she'd be going. He chastised himself anew for not taking her into his arms and kissing her senseless when Beatrice had entered the library after the dance lesson last week. A perfect opportunity to compromise Miranda wasted.

And he'd made the decision to compromise her. He'd done it on the road after stealing Stratham's tribute money and kissing her had only stoked his need.

That day he'd stood in the doorway at least a quarter hour watching her lead the children in the complicated steps of some dance. The task had been difficult, but she'd shown patience, compassion, and some other emotion…could it be love?

Love.

The word drove a knife clean through his heart. Did he love her? He didn't know, but he wanted her for more than money. More than desire. He wanted her here. With him. With all of them. He'd never seen the children so happy. So light. *He'd* never felt so happy or light—and that said a lot given his cursed financial woes.

And they were as bad as ever. He slammed the ledger shut. He was running out of time and she was clearly avoiding him, ensuring they were never alone together. Making a compromise all but impossible. Dammit, but he wished he could turn back the clock to the night of the assembly. He got to his feet and strode into the corridor. As he entered the main hall, Mrs. Gates was just letting Mr. Carmody inside. He'd be an excellent witness to a compromise.

The older man nodded. "Good afternoon, Fox. Where might I find Lady Miranda?"

Mrs. Gates answered before Fox could. "I'll just run and get her." She bustled from the hall, leaving the two men alone.

Carmody's gaze traveled the length of the hall and settled on the barrel in the corner. The roof wasn't dripping, but they'd left the barrel just in case. "You've got a leak there?"

Fox swallowed a sarcastic retort. "Yes."

Carmody continued his perusal. "Must be a lot of work, a building this old." He looked directly at Fox. "But then, your own estate is just as ancient, is it not?"

Fox said nothing, gritting his teeth instead.

After a few moments of awkward silence, Miranda entered the hall and suddenly the tattered furniture and threadbare rugs seemed even more decrepit. She glanced over at Fox before fixing her attention on Carmody.

Beatrice followed on Miranda's heels. "Good afternoon, Father. If you've come to fetch us home, we're not ready to leave."

Carmody glanced at his fob watch. "You may stay. I've come to collect Lady Miranda. Her parents have arrived."

Fox's stomach collapsed on itself.

Miranda's eyes widened. "My parents are here?"

Carmody nodded. "At Birch House. I bade them rest after their journey while I came to fetch you."

Fox noted Miranda's heightened color and the flexing of her hands against her skirt. After a moment she said, "Am I to return to London?"

Carmody slid a bored look at Miranda beneath hooded lids. "I'm sure I don't know Their Graces' plans. But you'd best not keep them waiting."

Beatrice touched Miranda's arm. "Would you like me to accompany you?"

Carmody straightened. "That won't be necessary, Beatrice. I'll send the carriage back at the appointed time. Your presence is not required."

Beatrice pursed her lips and gave a slight nod before retreating from the hall.

Miranda shook her head as if she'd drifted off for a moment. "I should say goodbye to Mrs. Gates and the children." She looked at Fox, and the sadness in her eyes twisted his gut.

Carmody cleared his throat. "There isn't time."

She turned toward the back of the house. "It won't take but a moment."

"Once again you demonstrate why your parents sent you here in the first place," Carmody snapped. "We should have been on our way already if not for your argument."

Fox plastered his hands against his legs lest he do

something foolish like hit Carmody or embrace Miranda. He wanted to do both.

Miranda spun about. "I wasn't—" She pressed her lips together, and Fox imagined her teeth were clenched behind them. "Never mind. Let us depart at once."

Fox stepped toward her and reached out as if to touch her arm, but then dropped his hand. "I'll talk to them. They'll understand."

"Thank you." Her eyes shone with unshed tears. "I—tell them I'll be back."

Fox wasn't sure he believed her. Not when she'd been yearning for this day. "It's all right. It's nearly fall anyway." He didn't say the words: *you won't be back*.

Miranda gathered her bonnet and gloves from a table near the door. She looked at Fox as if she would say something, but then glanced at Carmody. "I'm ready."

Carmody touched the brim of his hat. "Good day, Fox."

The door closed behind them. The winter would be dark and mean indeed.

CHAPTER 9

*T*HE carriage ride to Birch House was both interminable and over far too soon. Thankfully, Mr. Carmody said nothing. Although even his annoying conversation might have been better than the anxiety threatening to eat Miranda's stomach away.

Her parents' coach stood in the drive, the perfectly matched bays tended by one of the footmen. As Miranda alighted from Mr. Carmody's carriage, she raised a hand to the coachman. He smiled and waved in return. The friendly gesture gave her just the fortitude she needed to go into the house and face uncertainty.

Carmody stepped inside behind her and handed his hat to Fitchley. He turned to Miranda. "His Grace and Her Grace are in the drawing room."

Miranda nodded and slowly opened the door of the largest room at Birch House—though it would fit inside Miranda's bedchamber—situated off the foyer.

"There you are, gel," the duke stalked toward her from the other side of the room. "Sit." He gestured to a chair positioned near the settee, where her mother perched with a distasteful expression creasing her classical features.

Wishing to appear dutiful and respectful, Miranda did as she was told and sat in the chair her father indicated. "Good afternoon, Father, Mother." She inclined her head at both of them and dared to smile. "Did you have a pleasant journey?"

The duke clasped his hands behind his back. *Let the pacing commence.* Miranda gripped her hands together even as she maintained what she hoped to be a placid expression.

He strode behind the settee where her mother perched. His brows drew together in his most stern countenance. "Carmody tells me you've been quite popular despite your social prohibition."

What on earth did he mean? She wasn't exactly certain what he knew of her activities this summer, other than Carmody had informed him of her ill-conceived kiss with the highwayman on their trip to Wiltshire. Thank God no one knew she'd repeated the offense. She shoved the memory away. She could *not* think about that right now! Likely, Carmody had told him about Stratham attempting to court her, damn the man.

"Mr. Carmody is mistaken."

"Don't lie to me." Her father continued his circuit of the room, pausing by Miranda's chair. "The local MP has been courting you. I hear he's been spending time at the orphanage where you're supposed to be *working*."

Miranda tamped down her anger. Her father despised emotional displays. "Mr. Stratham has visited the orphanage, but I have not encouraged him. What has Mr. Carmody told you?"

Father wagged his finger at her. "Don't deflect this on Carmody. I've no doubt he's shared the complete truth of the matter. I'll call on this Stratham myself and instruct him to leave you alone."

Apprehension gnawed at Miranda's belly. "Why would you need to do that if I am to be leaving?"

"You're not leaving." Her mother's voice might have soothed Miranda's frayed temper, but the words she uttered had the opposite effect.

Forgetting—as she usually did—that she meant to retain a calm demeanor, Miranda shot to her feet. "But it's September! My friends will be expecting me in town!"

"Sit." The duke loomed over the settee.

Miranda exhaled loudly and dropped back onto the chair. "Why did you bother coming if you planned to leave me here? I've done nothing to warrant this."

"Nothing?" Her father's blue eyes widened. "Attending pugilistic bouts in Covent Garden is nothing? Nearly compromising yourself on the Dark Walk at Vauxhall is nothing? Embracing highwaymen is nothing?" His voice rose with each subsequent question until it reached a near-deafening crescendo.

Miranda winced. "I meant I've done nothing recently. I've been a model, er, prisoner."

"You think this a prison?" Her father spread his arms to indicate the meager drawing room. "This is nothing," he spat.

His words flayed her better than any physical punishment. Could she do nothing to please them? She'd redouble her efforts at the orphanage. "I'm sorry. I know you've been...lenient." She prayed this is what they wanted to hear. "I like working at the orphanage, and I believe it's had a positive effect on me. Perhaps you will come see what I do there?"

Her mother's face registered a flash of emotion—distaste, maybe—her eyes and nose flaring quickly before she regained her composure. "A pretty speech, but I'm not sure I believe you've learned a thing since arriving here. We'd hoped you'd have at least ascertained a shred of humility." She completely ignored Miranda's invitation to visit the orphanage. Had she really expected them to take interest in any endeavor that didn't directly affect them, either positive or negative?

"We received your letters." Her father drilled her with a probing stare. The kind that made her feel as if she was eight years old and had just made her governess cry. "The one thing they lack is contrition for your scandalous behavior. Now, your seemingly regretful attitude in our presence weakens your credibility. You must change the way you act, not speak empty promises."

"I am. I mean, I will." The words sounded hollow, even to her ears. Even so, it was what they wanted to hear, and she couldn't stop herself from trying to please them. She had their attention, but that was easy to obtain. She needed their approval.

Her father's lips whitened. After a moment, he turned from her and resumed pacing.

Her mother sat as stoic as ever. "Your father and I believe your reputation is improving with your absence from Society. But you must behave appropriately, even in this place."

Her reputation couldn't be in tatters. None of her friends' reputations were in danger. They'd engaged in harmless amusements. "Francesca, Lord Dunbar, Darleigh—they haven't been adversely affected."

Lines accentuated her mother's mouth and eyes, likely from her wearing an expression of perpetual disappointment. "Francesca was compromised by Lord Dunbar at a house party in July."

Miranda nearly raised her hand to her mouth, but kept it firmly in her lap lest her parents see how this news shocked her. She refused to give them the satisfaction. Poor Frannie. Dunbar was a jolly fellow, but not at all husband material. Miranda wondered if she hadn't been too extreme in her behavior. If she'd kissed anyone but a highwayman in front of Beatrice and Mr. Carmody, she'd be married by now. She swallowed against her tightening throat.

Her father halted before her chair. "And what have you to say about that?"

Would she always feel the recalcitrant child in his

presence? She looked up at him. "I'm sorry for Francesca. And I understand how my past actions could have negative effects." And she truly did, but she was smarter than featherheaded Frannie.

"Harrumph." Her father continued pacing. "Because you've proven time and again you can't be trusted, we've decided you must marry as soon as possible. We will find a suitable husband and send for you as soon as we do. In the meantime, you will go on as you have here. Without this Stratham's attention, of course."

Miranda's stomach caved in as if she'd been punched. They didn't want her anymore. They were anxious for her to be someone else's problem. Yes, they saw her as a problem. But, marry? Wasn't she far enough out of the way in Wootton Bassett? Gathering her courage, she dared to ask, "Have you anyone in mind?"

He didn't pause, but continued on his path around the room. "We are on our way to a house party at Wokingham. The duke is interested in a wife of appropriate breeding and money for his second son."

"I'm not good enough for his heir?" She muttered the words, but her mother had the hearing of a hound.

"His heir is already betrothed." The duchess's blue-gray eyes held no warmth. How Miranda wished for even the slightest sign of affection.

"But Lord Walter is paunchy and sallow. And he smells of cheese." Miranda wrinkled her nose. "If my prospects are so awful, why not encourage the attention of Stratham? He's wealthy. Though not titled, he's an MP. Surely I could do worse." Such as a highwayman.

Father smacked his hand down on the back of the settee. "Dammit, girl! You'll marry well. Not some common oaf from the country. I don't care if he is an MP..." He went on, but Miranda's attention turned inward.

For some reason her father's disdain for Stratham made her curl her fingernails into her palm. It wasn't that he maligned Stratham specifically, because in truth she wouldn't want to marry him in any case. No, it was his overall derision for the *country*. Her thoughts arrested for a moment. She'd practically made a pastime of deriding her banishment, particularly her locale! And now she found herself wanting to defend Wootton Bassett and its inhabitants. She shook her head and tried to focus on whatever her father droned on about.

"Your duty is to marry as we see fit." Ah, he'd continued on about the marriage. Nothing new there. She'd been listening to the same diatribe her entire life.

Miranda looked at her mother, hoping to appeal to her feminine sensibilities. "Am I to have no say then? You were allowed to choose each other." Even if her parents didn't love each other—and Miranda was fairly certain they didn't—they'd entered into their marriage willingly. Certainly Miranda wasn't selfish to want at least that much for herself. But was that all she wanted?

Her father opened his mouth, but her mother held up a staying hand. "You would have had a choice, but you squandered that with your appalling behavior. We will endeavor to find a gentleman who is both worthy of your heritage and your admiration. Lord Walter fits both of those requirements."

Miranda swallowed her protestations that she could never *admire* Lord Walter. She stared at her parents, trying to quell the mutiny building inside of her.

Her mother finally stood. "We will take our leave now. I know you're still angry, Miranda, but I hope you will see in time that we want only what is best for you." She walked to Miranda and patted her hand. At last, a small morsel of care.

Yes, she was still upset, but Miranda took her mother's touch as eagerly as the children grasped for dessert at the orphanage. "Will you at least write to me?"

Mother withdrew her hand and stood straight. "Yes."

"Come then, dear." Father went to the door and held it open. "We need to pay a visit to this Stratham fellow on our way to Wokingham."

Miranda cringed thinking about them calling on Stratham. Mortified, she considered retiring to her room for the rest of her banishment.

Her mother paused at the door. "Do remember what your father said. Don't encourage Mr. Stratham or any other socially inferior gentlemen you may encounter." And they were gone.

~

SEPTEMBER was supposed to be a cheerful month. Warm, late summer days, the orchard brimming with apples, happy tenants celebrating the harvest. Fox turned his horse into the drive at Stipple's End. The road was as wet and rutted as late October.

His dismal mood matched the weather. He usually looked forward to being at the orphanage, even after Miranda had refused his marriage proposal. Just being in her orbit made the day a little brighter. And this summer he'd needed all the light he could get.

He led Icarus to the small barn and situated the horse before turning toward the manor. Wind buffeted the canvas covering the hole on the roof. As if the leaky roof wasn't bad enough, three children had arrived last week, all of whom needed new clothes and shoes, and one of them, medicine. He'd tried to turn them away— he was simply at the breaking point already—but they had nowhere to go. Every time he got close enough to see a light ahead, blackness closed in once more. He needed to consider resurrecting the highwayman.

Warm laughter rushed over him as the children rushed into the yard, their bundled-up bodies eager to be outdoors despite the overcast sky and cool temperatures. At least it had stopped raining.

Fox trudged to the back steps and stood at the threshold before he saw her standing at the door.

Miranda.

He stared for a moment before finding words. "You didn't leave?"

She quirked a smile and held the door for him to walk inside. "No. My parents didn't come to fetch me. They came to tell me I'm to be married."

Fox froze in the middle of knocking dirt from his boots. His heart thundered and a loud rushing noise cascaded in his ears. "When?"

Miranda waved a hand and shrugged her shoulders. "Oh, I've no idea. They haven't selected a bridegroom as far as I know." She appeared utterly unconcerned. Fox, conversely, wanted to put his fist through the nearest wall.

He finished cleaning his boots off and met her gaze. They stood in the dim light of the back hallway, on either edge of the tattered carpet running the length of the corridor. To Fox, it seemed as if heat collected between them, forming an almost solid mass that would inevitably draw them together. He pushed everything else from his mind and allowed himself to sink completely into this moment with her.

"I think we should have an orphanage meeting." Her business-like tone doused his mood.

He blinked. "A meeting?"

She turned then and led him toward the small office. "Yes. We need to come up with a plan for raising the money to fix the roof."

"We?" Fox shook his head as he followed her into the office. "But aren't you leaving to get married?" The words cut into his chest.

"I didn't say so. Anyway, never mind that now." She went to stand by the window and gazed outside at the children playing. Such a lovely domestic portrait she presented…"Tell me, Fox, why is there never any money?" She pivoted and the milky light from the window made her eyes an arresting gray-green.

Fox shifted his weight and pondered her question for a moment. He picked up a quill from the desk and rolled it between his fingers. "My father gambled it away. The reserves, that is. I inherited a mortgaged estate and a nearly destitute orphanage."

She sat in a small wooden chair. "Why didn't you close it?"

He'd considered it. Instead, they supported fewer children than in the past, but he could never bring himself to close permanently. "Surely you've been here long enough to answer that yourself."

Her eyes widened briefly and then she nodded. "Yes. You need a lot of money then. Don't people make donations like Mr. Stratham did?"

This would be the perfect opportunity to tell her Stratham's donation had been an insult, but he couldn't draw attention to the fact since he *had* come up with money after robbing Stratham.

"Few people have made donations this year because of the harvest." He glanced outside at the meager fields.

"We need to target wealthier people. I've yet to meet Lord Norris. Does he give money?"

Fox looked back to her, seated in the chair with her ungloved hands resting on her lap. Her nails were not quite as pristine as when she'd arrived. Oh, they were still well-tended, but not as long and not all the same length. They were the hands of a genteel country lady and the sight of them drove a stake of wanting directly into his heart.

"Lord Norris is more interested in his antiquities than with local affairs." With the exception of ensuring he had everyone's money via the tributes Stratham collected for him.

"But there must be other people who could give money?"

"Could, but don't. What are you scheming in that pretty head of yours?"

She looked up at him and raised her right brow in the quintessential Miranda look that nearly always made him smile. "I'm trying to figure a way to raise money for this place. I'm thinking we need to do something to encourage people to part with their purses. I know it's a lean year, but presumably there are people with reserves—unlike you—who can help the orphanage." She tapped her finger against her lip.

Fox went back to looking outside because he *couldn't* stare at her mouth.

"What have you done to raise money in the past? Aside from donations?"

Committed highway robbery. Fox stifled a laugh. "The orphanage has always lived on the kindness of my family and others. Unfortunately, my father wasn't as kind as our forebears."

"Yes, so it would seem." The chair creaked, but Fox didn't turn.

From the corner of his eye, he saw her slide up beside him at the window. "This year more than ever, people won't want to part with their money unless they can get something in exchange." If he reached his hand out, he could touch her, draw her to him, bind her to him…

"I see." Miranda paced behind his desk and around the other side of the small room. "We ought to have an event then, something diverting like an assembly. People will pay to attend."

"And how will we afford to put it on?" He turned to watch her move about the room. She looked so comfortable here, as if they often spent time in the office discussing the orphanage's business. He pushed the warmth away from his heart, lest it become too comfortable. He mustn't forget this was a temporary thing —she would be married soon. God, he was going to lose her, not that he ever had her. He looked at her hair, her face, the column of her throat. He was willing to compromise his morals to have her, but what kind of marriage would that be? Oh, but he would have a lifetime to make it up to her…

"I may have a solution."

Fox dragged his mind back to their conversation. She had an idea about how to raise money? He shouldn't have been surprised. She'd reminded him of covering the roof with canvas when he and Rob had been too preoccupied with an outright repair.

He opened his mouth to ask, but she shook her head. "No, don't ask just yet. Leave this to me." She resumed pacing. "I wonder if we might have some sort of fair as well. We could sell the girls' soap. And a group of them have taken to embroidering." She arched a brow as if daring him to say something to disparage their needlepoint. "They can make handkerchiefs."

Fox allowed himself to smile. "You seem to have everything in hand."

"Not yet." She glanced up at him and grinned in return. "But I shall."

In that moment, he resolved to find a way to make her marry him. Whatever the cost.

CHAPTER 10

*T*HE next afternoon, Miranda's boot sunk into the mud to her ankle. With one hand she held her skirt up in an attempt to keep it clean, but a ring of dirt clung to the hem despite her efforts. With the other she gripped an umbrella she now wished she hadn't brought. With two hands, perhaps she could have saved her dress.

She could scarcely believe she dared show up at Stratham Hall or any other place looking like this, but what choice did she have? The walk from Birch House to Stratham Hall stretched two miles, and she and Beatrice had undertaken it on foot. The alternative was to ask for the carriage, which meant revealing their destination to Mr. and Mrs. Carmody, and since Miranda wasn't allowed to pay social calls...well, there *was* no alternative.

"Is it much farther?" Miranda squinted against the sky. Clouds covered any trace of blue, but it was a light cover at the moment and the sun glared brightly behind the gray.

Beatrice walked a few steps ahead, swinging her umbrella at her side. "No, we're on the Stratham estate now."

"I appreciate you coming with me today."

"What could I do, let you visit him alone?" Beatrice looked back, criticism lining the flesh around her mouth. "I agreed to accompany you because you have an excellent reason for paying this call. Even so, the fact you are forbidden from socializing with Mr. Stratham and are ignoring that directive does not sit well with me."

"I'm not socializing with Mr. Stratham. I'm conducting orphanage business. Whatever you may think of me, Beatrice, I've no desire to place myself in a compromising position." Miranda recalled Frannie and her marriage to Lord Dunbar. It could have been her in the parson's trap.

Beatrice slowed her gait. "Truthfully, I am constantly revising my opinion of you. Three months ago I never would have believed you would be planning a benefit for the orphanage. I still don't believe Mr. Stratham will agree to your scheme." She stepped through a stand of trees. "There it is."

Miranda came abreast of Beatrice and paused. The drive leading up to the manor was to the right. Constructed of stone with tall windows along the front, Stratham Hall presented an imposing façade. This looked much more like the houses Miranda typically visited.

"Why don't you think Mr. Stratham will help us?" Miranda gestured at the looming manor as they walked onto the drive. "He has a large estate and from what I can tell, the means with which to host a decent rout, even by London standards."

Beatrice shook her head.

"What?" Miranda stopped, aware of the fine gravel of the drive adhering to the soles of her boots, or rather to the thick cake of mud coating the soles of her boots.

Beatrice turned to face Miranda, pursing her lips. "There you go again. Just when I think you're not nearly as arrogant as I originally perceived, you say something like that and verify my first impressions."

A fat drop of rain hit Miranda's cheek. "What did I say?"

Beatrice opened her umbrella against the coming shower. "You insinuated no one in Wiltshire could have a 'decent rout' even at one of the nicest houses in the district."

Miranda put up her umbrella as well. "That's not so. I said Mr. Stratham likely *could* host a decent rout."

"But you give the impression such a thing is an unexpected boon."

Miranda twirled her umbrella over her head. "And isn't it? We're in rural Wiltshire. There are people in London who can't even host a decent rout by London standards. I'm still not at all certain what was wrong with my statement."

Beatrice shook her head again and began walking toward the house. "Never mind. Forget I said anything. I'm sure you're right."

Frowning, Miranda continued up the drive. She knew Beatrice had passed judgment on her as soon as she had kissed the highwayman, if not before. They'd never discussed the specific reasons behind her banishment, but Miranda could only assume the Carmodys had told their daughter everything they knew, which was probably a complete catalogue of her transgressions.

"I'm a good person, you know." Miranda spoke before she realized she'd planned to.

"Because you're helping the orphanage? I was given to believe you had no choice in the matter."

Miranda stopped and reached out to stay Beatrice. "I could just as easily go to Stipple's End and do my work with nary a word about anything. Instead, I am trudging through muddy fields and multiple rain showers to organize an event that may save the orphanage. Really, Beatrice, you've been working there for years, and it doesn't bother you to see the trouble they are having?" Irritation corroded Miranda's good humor.

Beatrice froze. After a brief moment she turned to look at Miranda. "Yes, it bothers me. I just never...ah, I never considered how I might contribute something other than what I already do." Her cheeks were red, but Miranda suspected the color resulted as much from emotion as from their exercise.

"I never meant to suggest you were somehow lacking." Miranda patted the other girl's arm and then withdrew her hand. "Together we will put on a grand event, and money will flow into the orphanage."

Beatrice shrugged. "You say together, but I scarcely know what to do."

Miranda turned toward the house and started back up the drive. They couldn't stand outside and talk all day. "There will be plenty for you to do. In fact, this will be an excellent opportunity for you to plan a grand event, a very useful skill for a wife." She winked at Beatrice. Unfortunately Miranda would need to flirt with Stratham today to achieve their goal for the benefit, but she would do what she could to further Beatrice's interests in that direction.

Beatrice stopped. "Are you making fun of me?"

Miranda paused long enough to link her arm through Beatrice's, then dragged her toward the manor. "Goodness no! I'm quite serious. When you're married, you'll need to plan parties, balls, routs."

"Nonsense. If I do marry—and that is debatable—I doubt I'll need to do any of those things." Beatrice started up the stone steps leading to the house.

Miranda squeezed Beatrice's arm, not liking the way she disparaged herself. "Don't speak that way."

Beatrice slid her a skeptical glance. "Do you really believe people will come to the benefit?"

Miranda couldn't see why not. It wasn't as if Wootton Bassett and its surrounding area boasted a plentiful social calendar. Still, she needed to ensure an appropriately attractive event so that people not only wanted to attend, but felt as if they simply *had to*. All the best parties in London were *have to* events.

"Trust me, Beatrice. Everyone will be clamoring to be at the social event of the Season." She dropped Beatrice's arm and curved her mouth into a smile. "And, you'll marry."

The front door opened. Pristine marble gleamed beneath a large Aubusson carpet whose oranges, reds, and browns warmed the entry. A gorgeous Rococo painting adorned one wall. The comfort of being in such a grand home drove away the discomfort of her discussion with Beatrice in the drive.

Beatrice collapsed her umbrella and handed it to the footman. She turned to address the butler in the center of the oval room. "We're here to see Mr. Stratham."

The butler nodded. "Allow me to show you to the Gold Room."

After delivering their umbrellas and pelisses to the footman, they followed the butler through a sitting room into a large drawing room where the upholstery, carpet, window hangings, even a tapestry over the fireplace were all predominantly gold.

Miranda found the display garish. The butler departed and she took a wingbacked chair near the crackling fire.

Beatrice positioned herself on the settee facing the hearth. Her gaze traveled over every wall and piece of furniture as if she were memorizing each detail. "I've never been here before. It's very, er, gold."

Mr. Stratham entered through another door. He was smiling, as usual. "Good afternoon, Lady Miranda, Miss Carmody. It's been too long since I visited the orphanage, but I've been away on business. I'm glad you've missed me as much as I've missed you." He went first to Miranda and took her hand, giving it a perfunctory kiss.

Given his behavior, Miranda had to assume her parents had not found him in residence when they'd called at Stratham Manor. Thank goodness she didn't have to explain that nuisance. "Your presence has been missed by all."

Mr. Stratham bowed over Beatrice's hand. Then, with a flick of his coattail, he sat in a chair adjacent to the settee. "Brooks is bringing some tea. He said you walked here. Very industrious of you."

Miranda clasped her hands in her lap, intertwining her fingers. "We have an urgent matter to discuss, Mr. Stratham. We are in dire need of your assistance."

Mr. Stratham looked from Miranda to Beatrice and back again. "Your visit sounds critical indeed. How may I help?" He leaned back in his chair and draped one hand over the arm.

Miranda glanced at Beatrice. She gazed at Mr. Stratham and didn't turn her attention. Miranda plunged onward. "I know you are aware of the leaky roof at Stipple's End. There are other needs as well, and we are planning a benefit for the orphanage."

Mr. Stratham's brows drew together. He seemed very concerned. In fact, she'd never seen his face so pinched before. "I'm sure I don't know how I can be of assistance."

Smiling brightly, Miranda put her attributes to best use. She blinked, knowing her lashes fluttered in a becoming manner and drew attention to her blue-green eyes. Mr. Stratham's attention was riveted, as it ought to be.

"Mr. Stratham, I need a place in which to host this benefit. Stratham Hall is the perfect location. You have ample space and, judging from your excellent appointments, you are no stranger to entertaining. Tell me, do you have a ballroom?" She leaned forward and settled her lips into what she knew to be an arresting moue. Predictably, Mr. Stratham stared at her mouth. Miranda didn't dare look at Beatrice, lest she see the other woman's certain jealous anger.

"Yes, there is a ballroom. It's not overly large—"

Miranda jumped to her feet. The thick cake of mud and gravel pasted to the soles of her boots made her stance uneven. Embarrassing, but what did one do about it in the country? "Please, will you show us? I'm sure it's more than adequate. I should like to see how many musicians might be accommodated."

Beatrice also stood, her features schooled into impassivity, but Miranda knew better. Oh, she'd make it up to her!

Mr. Stratham had no choice but to join them. He wore a befuddled expression, his mouth partly open and his brow furrowed. If he wanted to decline the use of his property, he didn't say so.

Miranda stepped toward him to deliver the coup de grace. She took his arm, linking hers through it and then rested her other hand on top. She cocked her head so she displayed the column of her neck to its best advantage and gave him a flirtatious smile. His eyes crinkled at the edges as they narrowed almost imperceptibly.

"I will be eternally grateful for your pledge of assistance, Mr. Stratham." She peered up at him using the same hooded gaze she'd employed with Charles Darleigh when she'd convinced him to take her to a fight in Covent Garden.

Stratham's mouth relaxed into the familiar grin, and she knew victory was hers. He patted her hand. "I should be delighted to share my home."

The trio exited the Gold Room and entered another sitting room decorated in mostly yellow, and yes, some gold. From there, they stepped into a large room, which was clearly the dedicated ballroom. A semi-circular dais sat at the far left end, while on the opposite wall four sets of glass paned double doors led to a patio. Wide windows filled the spaces between the doors and gave an expansive view of a well organized garden and the park land beyond.

Miranda noted the very new parquet floor. Lady Hess had had a similar floor installed in her London townhouse several months ago. "What an elegant space, Mr. Stratham. When did you last entertain?"

Mr. Stratham didn't look at her as he answered. "Over two years ago, before my wife passed."

"Oh yes, I had heard of your tragedy. That must have been very difficult." Miranda gave his arm a gentle squeeze.

"Indeed, but life moves ever onward and so must we." He smiled, but it wasn't his usual effusive grin and a shadow haunted his eyes.

Miranda wondered if his marriage had been a love match. If so, then Fox had merely been the recipient of poor luck. Miranda didn't like this scenario, and not because she felt particularly sad that Mr. Stratham had lost his wife. No, it meant Fox had known a series of misfortunes from his father's financial betrayal to the loss of the woman he hoped to marry to his current state of ceaseless worry over the orphanage. Why did she want to fix things for him? She didn't want to answer that question and promptly pushed it to the back of her mind.

Miranda stepped away from Mr. Stratham and looked down at the gleaming wood, ignoring her inner thoughts. "This floor looks brand new. Parquet is quite the rage."

Mr. Stratham clasped his hands behind his back and surveyed the room as if he, too, were assessing the floor. "I just had it put in over the summer."

Miranda gestured for Beatrice to come further into

the room. "Beatrice, have you ever seen such a beautiful pattern of wood?"

Beatrice came to stand by Miranda. Dirt flaked from her boots and Miranda noted they'd both left a bit of a trail. She would have apologized if she hadn't been so annoyed. He'd been redecorating his already splendid estate while the orphanage leaked? And to what end if he didn't even entertain?

She'd only thought to have him cover the cost of the decorations for the fundraiser, but now she'd include the food and musicians as well. "It's lovely. And it will provide the perfect backdrop for our party. This will be *the* event of the season, Mr. Stratham. Everyone who is anyone in northern Wiltshire will come." Miranda turned as she said the last, putting her back to the windows.

Mr. Stratham paused in the middle of the room. "Lord Norris hosts a party in September. I'm not certain he'll attend." A muscle in his neck twitched, giving Miranda the impression he was somehow disquieted. She couldn't imagine why, but neither did she particularly care.

"I recall you telling me about Lord Norris's annual party." Miranda turned in a circle, contemplating how to attract the district's most esteemed resident to attend their benefit. She stopped upon seeing Beatrice. "Beatrice, have you any thoughts as to how we might encourage Lord Norris's attendance?"

Beatrice's tone was ice cold. "He is particular to antiquities."

Miranda recalled their conversation in early summer in Fox's cart. It seemed forever ago. "Ah yes, he's a member of the London Natural Society of Antiquities and Oddities along with my godfather." Miranda clapped her hands. "I will write to Lord Septon at once! He will know precisely what will draw Lord Norris's attention. Perhaps we could display antiquities, like in a museum?" As soon as she said this, she realized they'd likely never find enough to rival an actual museum. "Or maybe we could *sell* something he'd like to buy. Of course, we'll have to procure the item at little or no cost." Her voice trailed off as her mind churned.

"You seem to think of everything." It was impossible to overlook the sarcasm lacing Beatrice's statement.

Turning to Mr. Stratham, Miranda ignored Beatrice's discomfort. "Now, let us discuss the date of our event, as well as the refreshments. Mrs. Gates assures me we will be able to procure the musicians who play for the assemblies." If Mr. Stratham had an opinion regarding their using the same people who provided music for the local assemblies, he didn't show it. "Should we return to the Gold Room? I find I'm in desperate need of tea."

Instead of taking Mr. Stratham's arm, Miranda took Beatrice's and preceded their host from the room without waiting for his response. After all, Miranda didn't really need it.

~

*F*OX shifted in his chair and wondered, not for the first time, how he'd ended up in a meeting with four women discussing decorations and music and food. Miranda stood at the head of the dining room table at Stipple's End. Mrs. Gates and Beatrice sat on one side, while Felicity Knott, Rob's wife, sat on the other. At least Fox was safely ensconced at the opposite end.

"What do you think, Fox?" Mrs. Gates sat forward and peered down the length of the table. Not safe enough, apparently.

"Er, about what?"

Miranda answered. "About selling antiquities to garner Lord Norris's attention. My godfather, Lord

Septon, will be coming from London with a few of his antiquity society friends. I'm counting on their presence to attract Lord Norris, but we'll need things to sell. Mrs. Gates thought you might have something at Bassett Manor."

Fox drummed his fingertips on the tabletop. Bassett Manor was filled with ancient things, most of them utterly worthless. Anything of import had been sold over the past eighteen months to pay the accumulating debts and to keep the children fed and clothed. Even so, there were a few tapestries some female relative had woven back in the fourteenth century that still had a measure of color to them. "I have some tapestries. You're welcome to them."

"Tapestries, you say?" Mrs. Gates sat straight in her chair. "We have some tapestries on the third floor in the dormitory wing. I'd forgotten all about them. They used to hang in the great hall. Perhaps they are worth something?"

Miranda clapped her hands together. "Excellent!"

Fox ignored whatever she said next. He preferred to focus on the alluring way her eyes flashed when she spoke in the animated fashion she currently employed. She was so engaging, he'd no doubt they'd all donate their firstborn to aid her cause. He was only glad her cause was his cause.

For now.

Then she said "Stratham," and he snapped to attention. "What does Stratham have to do with any of this?"

A pale flush of pink tinted Miranda's cheeks. "I've been meaning to tell you. We're holding the event at Stratham Hall."

Fox leapt out of his chair before checking his temper. "No. Absolutely not. We'll have it here."

"Now, Fox, we can't have it here. With respect to you and Mrs. Gates, Stipple's End is not the appropriate place to have an elegant party, even if it were in the best of condition." She used a sweet, soft tone likely meant to placate, but it grated against his nerves.

"Bassett Manor, then."

Mrs. Gates stood. "Fox, Stratham Hall will encourage people to attend. Mr. Stratham hasn't opened his house since"—her gaze flicked down—"well, he hasn't opened it in years."

Fox knew very well the last time Stratham had entertained, not that he'd attended. It was before Jane died. Fox had been invited to the occasion, their first ball, but he'd preferred grooming his horse or perhaps counting the blades of grass in Bassett Manor's park— whatever he'd done—to spending an evening at Stratham's garish house.

"I don't care if he wants to host the bloody Prince Regent, I'm not having the event there." He strode from the room without giving them a chance to respond. Before he made it halfway down the back hall, Miranda stopped him by grabbing his arm.

"Wait. You must listen to reason." She raised her brow in a thoroughly supercilious manner, daring him to continue his flight.

"Fine." He leaned against the wall and crossed his arms. "Persuade me."

She straightened her spine and raised her chin. "As Mrs. Gates said, Stratham Hall itself will draw people to attend. Further, I've convinced Mr. Stratham to donate considerably more than his home."

Fox pushed away from the wall. "What's he doing?"

Shadows fell across her face. "He's paying for the decorations, the food, the music."

At once, Fox was pleased Stratham would finally put his money to good use, and disgusted he had to rely on the man who'd extorted that money from so many in the district.

She stepped forward and tipped her head up. Light

splayed across the upper half of her face. "We can't do it without him."

She might as well have driven a knife into his gut.

Fox put his hands on his waist. "So he's hosting this party then. With you."

Her eyes widened briefly and her lips parted. "No, he's not the host. Well, yes, I suppose he is. But it's not as if we're giving a party *together*."

He felt his lip curl. "And this activity is within the confines of your punishment?"

She closed her mouth tight. Tiny lines formed on her forehead belying her irritation. "My punishment is none of your concern, but yes, I'm allowed to oversee this event because it is part of my work at Stipple's End."

"How convenient for you. I presume your parents must approve of Stratham, then. Perhaps he will even be your mysterious bridegroom."

She arched her brow. "Actually, my parents believe he's quite beneath me. They are currently husband hunting elsewhere." She moved a hair's breadth closer. "I'm not marrying Stratham."

While her words mollified him, they didn't change the fact she wasn't marrying him, either. And if Stratham was "quite beneath" her, then Fox had to be positively inconsequential—not even worth discussing, he'd bet. In that moment, his pride dearly wished he could tell Miranda and her infernal father to go to the devil.

"Oh, Fox." Mrs. Gates entered the back hallway and Miranda immediately stepped back. Another opportunity for compromise squandered. "Would you mind showing Miranda the room we use for storage up on the third floor? I've a baking lesson this afternoon." She continued to the end of the hall and then outside.

Fox leaned forward, still angry at having to accept anything from a man he despised—and probably more than a bit irritated at his missed opportunity. Perhaps he should pull Miranda into an embrace and call Mrs. Gates back? Instead, he said, "I'm sure you don't need my help. Should I send for Stratham?"

She put a fist on her hip. "You're being obnoxious. We're saving *your* orphanage. I know you can't abide Stratham, but can't you put your anger aside for the sake of the children?"

Put like that, Fox was a selfish ass. He started down the hallway toward the great hall and the main staircase. "Follow me."

They went up to the second floor. When they reached the landing, he took her past the dormitories to the end of the hall where another staircase led to the third floor. The stairs were covered with a threadbare carpet that might have once been red. They creaked as he took the first step.

"I haven't been up here in awhile." Was he trying to excuse whatever disrepair or dishevelment they might find on the third floor?

Servant rooms lined the corridor, but none were currently used. An odor of aged wood and mildew assailed his nose. Christ, a leak probably trickled around this corner of the building as well. He swiped a hand over his face and crossed the hall.

He opened a door and stepped into a cluttered chamber. Trunks were lined against one wall and a sturdy wardrobe stood in the corner. A large window facing the front drive illuminated a film of dust covering everything.

Miranda came in behind him and immediately went to an old table, upon which were draped a pile of tapestries. Skimming her fingers over the muted threads, she said, "Help me turn this over."

Fox went to help her and together they flipped the heavy piece. She gasped at the vibrant beauty on the reverse—a bucolic scene with rich green and gold fields and dancing children with rosy cheeks. "This is stunning." She glanced up at him. "They seem very dear, don't they?"

Fox knew next to nothing about tapestries. "I can't say. They're in far better condition than the ones at Bassett Manor. I'd wager Norris will at least be interested enough to come to your event."

"It's *our* event, Fox." Miranda flashed him an exasperated look and then lifted the edge of the tapestry. "There are at least five of them here." She grinned at him.

He felt her excitement as well as saw it in the sparkle of her eyes and the wide set of her mouth. Clinging to his foul mood was proving difficult.

"Let's see what else we can find up here," she said, moving to the armoire in the corner. She tried to open it, but the door wouldn't budge.

"There's a latch at the top." Before Fox could get there and open it for her, she stood on her toes and pulled at the latch. Still, it didn't move, and neither did she.

"My dress is caught."

Fox went to stand beside her—*right* beside her since he had to get close enough to work the fabric free—and plucked at her sleeve. The ribbon trim at her wrist had unraveled and caught on the latch. Inadvertently, he loosed the latch and the door immediately swung open, taking her along with it. She skipped to the side, but lost her balance anyway.

Fox grabbed her around the waist. "Put your other hand around my neck." While he held her with his left arm, he tried again to free her wrist with his right hand. Her spicy orange scent conquered his senses. Her golden hair tickled his chin. Her arm curled around his neck, her fingers splaying over his right shoulder. Heat spread from that shoulder to every part of his body. He needed to get her arm free, but at the same time couldn't bear to let her go.

Her breathing came steady while his seemed shallow and uneven. He hoped to God she didn't notice. After what seemed forever, he untangled the ribbon from the latch and set her on her feet.

He expected her to inspect her tattered dress. Instead, she cradled her wrist in her right hand and looked up at him. "Thank you."

Fox stared at her, studied every nuance of her reaction. Her pulse beat in her throat, strong and maybe a tad fast. Perhaps she wasn't as immune as he'd originally perceived. "I've wanted to apologize for the day at the pond. I meant to ask you in a different setting."

She massaged her wrist and her fingers played with the torn velvet ribbon, avoiding his gaze. "I hope you understand my choices are not really my own."

Was she saying she might have chosen him if she could? Maybe he should drag her off to Gretna Green...

She dropped her hands. "My marriage will be for my parents, not for me. Fox, you'll make someone an excellent husband." She reached out and touched his hand, igniting a fire of need that would not—could not —be doused. "I truly hope that for you."

And she did. He could see it in her eyes. Even so, it did nothing to assuage his disappointment. He'd fallen in love with her. Not that it mattered. She'd be leaving soon to marry someone else, unless he did something drastic. Perhaps something that would ensure she never loved him in return. Could he do that?

"Shall we look through the armoire, then? We did go to an awful lot of trouble." She smiled impishly, but Fox wasn't in the mood to return the sentiment.

"I'll let you continue the search. I've other matters that require my attention." He glanced down at her hand, still resting on his. He clasped it between his and used every bit of his willpower not to press a kiss to her palm. "Thank you for all you're doing. Stipple's End will sorely miss your presence when you leave."

Something flickered in her eyes, but he couldn't discern her emotion. "And I shall miss it, too." She retracted her hand, and he felt the loss all the way to his toes. "I'm not gone yet, and before I go, I mean to raise so much money that you won't need to worry at all."

God, but he had never wanted to touch another person more than he wanted to touch her in that moment. "If anyone can, it's you, Miranda. I've no doubt it's you." He wracked his mind for another tortured moment, but in the end, he couldn't bring himself to do anything but let her go.

CHAPTER 11

*T*HE following week, a carriage rattling up the drive to Birch House drew Miranda's attention from the list of food she was making for the benefit. Though the day was dim and gray, and the view from the drawing room window was distorted from sheets of rain sluicing down the panes, she could just make out her father's crest on the coach.

Had they come to fetch her? How ironic of them to appear at the moment she actually wanted to stay.

Beatrice leapt to her feet, exhibiting the excitement for Miranda's parents' arrival that Miranda couldn't muster. "It looks as though your parents are here to take you to your betrothed."

The coachman jumped down and approached the house—alone. If Miranda's parents were here, they wouldn't wait for her outside. "I don't think my parents are in the coach."

Fitchley entered and held out his hand. "A letter for you, Lady Miranda."

"Just a letter?" Beatrice sounded a tad disappointed.

Fitchley gave a perfunctory nod and departed.

Miranda tore open the paper and scanned the missive. Her heart dropped into her stomach. Beatrice had been right, although her parents hadn't come to escort her. "They've found a potential husband and wish me to come to Wokingham at once."

"Are you betrothed, then?"

"Not yet." But she would be soon. Probably to Lord Walter. "Oh, I can't leave now!"

"Well, you can't disobey your parents." Beatrice blinked. "Can you?"

Miranda ignored the question and began to pace. "I've four days until the benefit. Wokingham is a day's journey. I can leave in the morning, arrive tomorrow night, spend a day doing whatever it is they require, and return in plenty of time."

Beatrice made an inelegant snort. "You think you can swoop in, become engaged, and be allowed to rush back here?"

Did Beatrice not want her to come back? She didn't seem disappointed Miranda had to leave. And did Miranda hope for Beatrice to miss her? She shrugged the idea away, unwilling to admit she might want Beatrice's friendship. "I'll be back in time for the benefit. I can't expect you to oversee things."

Beatrice visibly bristled. "It's not as if I couldn't manage it. In fact, perhaps it would be best if you didn't return. I'll be the one who's here in the future, not you."

Hadn't Beatrice bemoaned the fact she wouldn't ever get married, wouldn't ever have to plan an event like this? And now she acted as if it was as natural to her as reading a hymnal. "My guidance is necessary, Beatrice. You're learning quite nicely, but surely you realize this event requires experience and polish. I'm certain I will return in time. Count on it, in fact." Throughout Miranda's speech, Beatrice's eyes had narrowed, but Miranda didn't have time to smooth the girl's ruffled feathers.

Miranda picked up her letter and her list. "I'm going upstairs to pack. Would you please inform your parents of my departure?" She didn't wait for Beatrice's response.

~

OX timed his arrival at Stratham Hall the following day perfectly. The Carmodys' carriage pulled up the drive as he climbed out of his landau.

He glanced down at his new coat, glad he'd let Rob talk him into having it made along with the ensemble he would wear to the benefit. How could he refuse his friend when Rob had offered to pay for it?

Fox shook his head. Pathetic he had to rely on the kindness of others. But then, he worked hard to ensure people like Rob lived with a small measure of comfort. Even if it meant he didn't.

The Carmodys' carriage came to a stop behind Fox's landau. Fox stepped toward it and waved up at the coachman, indicating he'd open the door. A little bubble of anticipation worked its way up his chest. He wondered if Miranda would notice his new coat.

Pulling the door open, Fox lifted his hand to help the ladies out. He tamped down his disappointment when Beatrice appeared first. After delivering her to the ground, he turned back to the carriage and saw her maid. He searched the shadowed interior for another person.

Beatrice stood in the drive. "There's just me, I'm afraid. And Tilly."

Alarm constricted Fox's lungs as he helped the maid out. "Where's Lady Miranda? She's supposed to be with you."

Beatrice took in his new coat. She'd noticed, then, but it wasn't the same. "Indeed. However, she's gone." Beatrice turned and walked toward the house.

Fox gaped at her back for a moment before hurrying to her side. "Where has she gone? When will she return?"

Beatrice paused part way up the steps, but the door opened before she could speak. Stratham stood framed in the entryway wearing his usual ridiculous grin. Fox took a bit of pleasure from watching the man's face fall upon noticing Miranda's absence.

"But where is Lady Miranda?" He looked past Beatrice, Tilly, and Fox—Fox wasn't even sure Stratham had seen him yet—in utter puzzlement.

Beatrice stepped inside the house, her maid close on her heels, brushing past the stupefied Stratham. "She's gone to meet her betrothed. We'll need to continue on without her."

Fox stumbled on the last step. Stratham noticed him now—his gaze dropped to Fox's feet. Then he smirked. Jackass.

As he walked by Stratham into the foyer, Fox threw his elbow out, catching Stratham in the upper arm. "Surely Lady Miranda plans to return for the benefit," Fox said, "after all she's done." He seemed as though he tried to convince himself of this fact as much as anyone else.

"I'm afraid not." Beatrice handed her pelisse to a footman and loosened the ribbons of her bonnet. She perused them with a confident gaze Fox had never seen her wear before. "I will have no trouble ensuring the event is a success."

Fox took a deep breath. He couldn't believe Miranda had gone and wasn't coming back. He had tried to prepare himself for her inevitable departure—and marriage—but now faced with the reality, he ached, and probably would ache no matter what.

Stratham frowned at Beatrice. "I say, I'm a bit worried Lady Miranda isn't here."

Beatrice's eyes flashed. "There is no cause for concern, Mr. Stratham. I have everything well in hand. Besides, it's not as if we can cancel. Some of our guests are traveling to attend and have likely already begun their journey."

Stratham shrugged. "That's no matter. You refer to Lord Norris's friends from the antiquity society. They're also coming to attend his party, which is very soon after the benefit. Canceling the benefit won't put them out."

Fox wrenched himself from self-pity and glared at Stratham. "It would put the children out, you self-centered cad."

Stratham turned on Fox. "There's no need to be vulgar."

Fox stepped forward with menace. "I haven't begun to show you vulgar."

Beatrice cleared her throat. "While this display of male virility is, er, enlightening, I suggest we complete our tasks for the day. Fox, did you bring the items to be auctioned from the orphanage?"

Fox itched to plant the man a facer, but he forced himself to look at Beatrice and respond to her inquiry. "Yes."

"And we're displaying the items in the sitting room off the ballroom, is that correct, Mr. Stratham?"

"Indeed. The room is all prepared. Lady Miranda saw to it the other day."

Beatrice rolled her eyes.

What was that about?

"I'll have my men bring in the items." Stratham turned to go, contemplating leaving on foot while his retainers—two of the ten he managed to keep on staff— unloaded the landau.

"Mr. Stratham, why don't you go to the sitting room and I'll join you shortly? I've a few things to discuss with Fox." Beatrice smiled prettily, exuding a self-possession Fox had never seen in her.

Stratham gave her a bow, but before he left, his gaze

lingered on her. It looked as if he'd noticed Beatrice's newfound sense of whatever-it-was as well.

Beatrice gestured for Fox to follow her outside and then called to her maid who'd stood silent in the corner during the entire exchange with Stratham. "Tilly, you can stay inside."

Once the door closed behind them, Beatrice turned to face him on the portico, her more usual stern expression firmly in place. "Do you think you could manage to be civil to Mr. Stratham? I realize you dislike him because of Jane, but really, isn't it time to leave the past behind? She loved him, you know."

The familiar anger tasted bitter in his mouth. "I'm not certain she did."

Beatrice jerked her head back, perhaps as a reaction to the emotion Fox probably couldn't keep from his eyes. "That's absurd. I knew Jane. She was ecstatic over Stratham's proposal. It was a boon for her to land such a gentleman."

"By 'such a gentleman,' do you mean a corrupt MP?" Fox could scarcely believe he'd uttered the words aloud. He'd made a point of not accusing Stratham because he couldn't actually prove anything. Even so, he *knew* and the knowledge burned a hole in his mind, especially when everyone sang the rotter's praises.

She stiffened. "Now, see here. You can't go about denigrating Mr. Stratham's good name."

He should stop, retreat, leave Beatrice to think whatever she would. But the words rushed from his mouth before he could halt them. "Would it surprise you to learn Jane was forced into the marriage? Things happen in this district that would dearly offend your maidenly sensibilities, Miss Carmody."

Beatrice's hand flew to her chest. Her mouth gaped. "But...but Jane was happy."

"Jane was whatever her father told her to be. I'm sure you can appreciate such an attitude." At her widening eyes, Fox instantly regretted his loose tongue. He hadn't meant to offend her.

Her mouth snapped shut and she nodded. "Yes, I know precisely how that can be. Poor Jane." She stared at him a moment. "And poor you. I didn't realize."

Christ, he didn't want her pity. Nor did he want to turn her against Stratham. Long ago, he'd tried to convince himself it wasn't worth despising Stratham, but perhaps he should try again. "Don't you go hating Stratham, too. He's doing a service for Stipple's End." Saying those words made his stomach curdle.

Beatrice's features softened and again Fox saw a hint of the beauty hidden in her stoic manner. "You said there are things I would be surprised to know. Is it possible you could be just as surprised? Perhaps Mr. Stratham is not all he seems."

Fox could tell by the way she said it that she hoped it was true.

He recalled the night of the robbery and Stratham's suspicion that Norris had hired someone to steal the tribute money. Apparently, Stratham thought Norris was even more underhanded than Fox believed him to be. Could it be possible Stratham was under Norris's thumb, a reluctant participant in the corruption that beleaguered the district?

With a jerk of his shoulder, Fox threw off the notion. He didn't give a damn. The man was an extortionist and nothing else mattered. It was past time he and Norris and whoever else was involved in the scheme paid for their crimes. And if Fox could settle his financial problems, perhaps he could be the man to see justice wrought.

But, for now, the need for money loomed as surely as the dark days of winter ahead. "Did Miranda give any indication as to how much she estimated the items would garner?" Fox knew how much money he needed and how much money he wanted—they were two different numbers—and ought to be sure he wasn't completely off the mark.

Beatrice's brows rose. "*Miranda*? Oh, Fox, never say you've fallen for her too?"

Fox shifted his weight between his feet. The only people who'd any notion he'd desired Miranda were Rob and Mrs. Gates, but even they didn't know the depths of Fox's longing. "I haven't." The lie burned his tongue. "You first-name her, why can't I?"

"Because you're an eligible gentleman." Beatrice waved a hand. "Never mind. I don't want to discuss her. She's gone, and she won't be back. Now, let's bring in the items for the auction and get them arranged. I've an appointment with Mr. Stratham's kitchen staff this afternoon, and I don't wish to be late."

Fox descended the steps to the drive and signaled the retainers who were still seated on the box. They jumped to the ground and went about transporting the goods inside. Fox stood on the gravel and looked up at the gray sky. Then he looked down at his now-useless coat. There was no point staying. He might as well head to Stipple's End and start on the apple harvest. They were due to begin tomorrow morning anyway.

Sadly, it wouldn't take long at all.

～

*M*IRANDA stood before a mirror in the dressing room of her chamber at Wokingham. She hadn't been so finely dressed since last spring. The evening gown felt odd on her frame, as if she'd have to walk slowly and softly to avoid creasing it. A maid clasped a strand of pearls around Miranda's throat. She tilted her face away, her gaze settling on the trunk that transported her gowns, her jewels, and yes, even some of her books to Wokingham. The books had been a surprisingly thoughtful touch by her grim-faced parents.

Anne stepped back to admire her handiwork. "Why are you frowning, my lady? You look lovely."

"Mmm, yes, thank you." Why was she frowning? She ought to be happy to have her things and be back in the bosom of the Society that had nurtured and loved her. Why then was she obsessed with thoughts of the children at Stipple's End and the benefit?

Because she worried she wouldn't be able to get back in time. The journey to Wokingham had taken an extra day because of the weather. They'd had to take shelter overnight at a posting inn and had finally arrived that afternoon.

Anne hurried to answer a knock on the door. Miranda's mother swept into the room, a vision in dark blue watered silk and sparkling sapphires. The sight reminded Miranda of the countless evenings she'd watched her mother dress for Society events. Miranda had been so eager to have her own gowns and jewels. Desperate to be a part of the routs, parties, and balls intrinsic to their position in the *ton*. She'd spent most of her exile filled with the same craving. Hadn't she? But now as she was about to reenter the world she adored, she couldn't stop thinking about what her girls would think of it.

Her girls? When had they become that?

The duchess gave Miranda an assessing look. Her mother nodded, her features settling into a pleasant mien of approval. It was always thus.

Until Miranda spoke. "Who is the victim? Lord Walter?"

As expected, her mother's mouth turned down. "No. And he is not a victim. He is a potential bridegroom."

Her parents hadn't bothered to share the name of their intended husband. Knowing it wasn't Lord Walter, Miranda found she didn't particularly care.

Her mother glanced at her own reflection, avoiding Miranda's gaze. "Lord Kersey."

Suddenly, Miranda cared. "You jest."

"Absolutely not. Unlike you, I do not make light of such things." The duchess turned from the mirror, her hand pressed against the jewels at her throat.

"If you are so concerned about my reputation, why align me with him?" Lord Kersey was generally regarded as a worthless dissolute cut in the image of his father, the Earl of Stratton. Miranda had been forbidden from speaking the elder's name in polite company.

"He's been distancing himself from his father. Many believe he is trying to improve the family name."

Miranda pulled an ivory glove over her left hand and tugged it up her arm. "I am baffled by this turn of events."

Despite Lord Kersey's lack of social standing, Miranda found him more personally desirable than Lord Walter. Lord Kersey wasn't paunchy or sallow, nor did he smell of cheese. Truth be told, she'd never gotten close enough to determine if he smelled like anything.

The scent of crisp grass, earth, and rosemary came to her. Who smelled like that?

Fox.

She missed that smell.

"Miranda, finish with your other glove. We need to get downstairs." Her mother turned and glided toward the door.

With a shake of her head, Miranda pulled on the second glove. She glanced at her reflection once more and stared as if she didn't recognize the person she saw. She wasn't used to seeing herself dressed in this fashion, with her hair artfully styled and jewels sparkling at her ears, throat, and wrist.

"Miranda!" Her mother perched at the threshold, impatience etched into her attractive features.

Miranda followed her mother from the room and couldn't help but feel she was walking backward.

~

THE people at the entrance to the ballroom clustered as thick as Bond Street on any sunny afternoon. Friendly faces greeted Miranda as she pushed through the throng.

"We've missed you this summer!"

"Brighton wasn't the same without you!"

"I wish you could have been at Lord Leavitt's house party!"

Miranda could scarcely answer all of the people clamoring for her attention. From the corner of her eye, she saw her mother's half-smug, half-amused smile as she too was surrounded by a gaggle of her friends. After several minutes, the crowd thinned, leaving Miranda amidst a handful of girls her own age. In turn, they were surrounded by a circle of lesser-known friends.

Rebecca Jones-DeWitt leaned close. "Did you hear about Frannie?"

Miranda fanned her face, employing the device as a shield. "Yes. Is she here?"

"Goodness, no. She and Dunbar were married a few weeks ago. They're rusticating."

Unfortunately, Miranda feared Frannie would be rusticating forever. She scanned the ballroom for Lord Kersey, but could barely see past the circle of people who still loitered in her orbit.

Lady Georgiana Farraday sidled up next to Miranda. "We're so glad you're here at last. The country wasn't too dreadful, I trust." Georgiana's eyes focused on the ballroom, ever seeking the latest thing.

"Actually, it wasn't dreadful at all. In fact, I'm hoping to return."

Rebecca gasped. "Never say so, Miranda!"

"Not *permanently*. It's just that I'm—"

Georgie put up her fan and whispered to Miranda and Rebecca, "I've just seen Lord Kersey. No, don't stare at once. He's over by the terrace doors."

Miranda swallowed her frustration at being cut off and craned her neck. Lord Kersey was easy to spot for he stood quite tall, nearly as tall as Fox. But Lord Kersey's shoulders were very broad, and he wore the most current fashion from his magnificently tied cravat to his impossibly shiny dancing slippers. Even from this distance, Miranda could appreciate his good looks.

"He came to Lord Leavitt's house party, too." Rebecca fluttered her eyelashes in his direction. "If he successfully reconquers Society, he'll be quite a catch."

Georgie sniffed. "Oh come now, Becca, your parents would never entertain an offer from him, despite his title."

"You're probably right. Still, I can look my fill, can't I?" Rebecca's deep chuckle was answered by Georgie's.

Miranda saw no need to inform them of her parents' ill-conceived plan regarding the viscount. Was Lord Kersey even interested in wedding her? If he wished to elevate his social position, Miranda supposed she was an appropriate target for a wife. Irritation blossomed, and she fanned her face again. Did no one want her for her?

And now he was cutting through the ballroom directly toward them. "Block me."

Georgiana swung her gaze to Miranda. "Why? Maybe he's headed for me. Or Rebecca."

"Excellent, you two stay here and wait for him. I'm for...something else." Miranda hurried away from her friends and fortunately saw her brother lounging against the wall. Dressed in immaculate black and wearing the special smile he reserved just for her, he was a welcome sight. She made her way to his side.

"Little sister." Jasper took her hand. He studied her for a moment. "You look different."

Miranda glanced down at herself, smoothed her hand over her waist. "I do?"

"The country seems to agree with you." He lifted his gaze over her head to the ballroom beyond.

Miranda stood beside him, putting her back to the wall. Jasper had the same blond hair and penetrating glacial blue eyes of their father, but thankfully less of his uptight demeanor. Still, he had to be described as arrogant, which he had fair reason to be. Attractive and possessed of a fine wit, he sat a horse better than almost anyone and was at the top of everyone's list of potential husbands.

Beatrice had called Miranda arrogant. Was that true? She turned to her brother. "Am I arrogant?"

Jasper laughed, a low, throaty sound. "Probably. But you say it as if it's a bad thing. Confidence is often misconstrued as arrogance. You're a strong young woman, and most people prefer the fairer sex to be malleable and meek."

Miranda raised a brow. "Is that what you prefer?"

His eyes widened in mock horror. "I'm not discussing women with my sister."

"Fine." Miranda watched Lord Kersey who talked with Georgiana and Rebecca. "Why are Mother and Father keen to marry me off to Lord Kersey?"

"Because you're a bloody pain in their arses." Jasper never censored his speech around Miranda, a trait she adored him for. She turned her head as he shifted to face her.

Miranda darted a glance at Lord Kersey, still entangled with her friends. "I don't have time for this right now. I need to get back to Wootton Bassett."

"You can't be serious. You've written all of us letters begging to come home."

That much was true, but she hadn't written such a

missive in at least a month. "I did. I do. Just not right now. Lord Septon is coming, and I'd hoped to visit with him."

"What's your godfather doing in Wiltshire?"

Miranda opened and closed her fan in rapid succession. "We're having a benefit for the local orphanage. We're auctioning antiquities."

"'*We're*'? Who on earth is '*we*'?" Jasper crossed his arms over his chest with a bemused expression.

Miranda dropped her fan, recognizing she looked as agitated as she felt. That simply wouldn't do. "Beatrice Carmody, the gentleman who owns the orphanage…"

Jasper held up a hand. "Wait a minute. What gentleman? Is this the fellow who is courting you? Mother mentioned an MP whom they tried to warn away. Apparently, he wasn't around to suffer the duke's lecture about social stratification and how it's important each level maintain its own relationships."

"No, Fox isn't the MP."

"*Fox*?" Jasper's eyes widened. "Regardless, it sounds as if this fellow's the real threat."

"Why, because I call him what everyone calls him? A bunch of nonsense." Fox was his surname for heaven's sake, not an endearment. "I need your help to get back. I simply must be there for the benefit. It's a huge undertaking—Lord Septon is bringing several friends from the antiquity society and none of those people in Wootton Bassett have ever hosted a London event."

Jasper's eyes crinkled as if he wanted to laugh. "But this isn't a London event, Miranda. It's a benefit for a backwater orphanage."

Miranda swatted his arm. "Do not besmirch Stipple's End. Those poor children have nothing. No one."

He arched a brow and his mouth quirked into a half-smile. "Apparently they have you. Lucky brats."

"Will you help me, or do I have to sneak back on my own?"

Jasper gave an exaggerated sigh. "You do know how to appeal to my darker nature. The duke and duchess will not approve."

"But you'll help me anyway?"

"Yes. However, Holborn's lost to the gaming room for the night, so it will have to wait until tomorrow." They both knew better than to interrupt their father whilst he was at the gaming tables.

Miranda wanted to leave tomorrow. "Fine, but I want to be on the road by afternoon."

Jasper's eyes narrowed. "Just because you're in a desperate rush doesn't mean things will happen quickly. I need to talk to Kersey, and then I'll need to convince Holborn to let you leave. It's going to take more than a five minute conversation." He shook his head. "You're always so impulsive. Planning and execution should not be underestimated." And with that, he pushed away from the wall.

"Wait, you're not leaving me here alone, are you?"

Jasper chuckled softly. "Miranda, you're the least helpless female I know. You'll manage."

Miranda scowled at his departing back. If he hadn't agreed to help her, she'd have chucked the fan at his head.

CHAPTER 12

*M*IRANDA darted out onto the terrace from the overheated card room. She'd spent the day rejoining the life she'd left three months ago, and her face hurt from smiling so much. Cool autumn air rushed over her face, soothing her aching cheeks and restoring her ability to think clearly.

Where on earth was Jasper? She'd wanted to leave that morning, but hadn't seen him since the previous night. She had to assume he'd spent the day doing as he'd said—talking to Kersey and their father. At least, she hoped he had.

"Good evening, Lady Miranda." A low masculine voice rumbled in the darkness.

She started, hoping it might be Jasper, but knowing as soon as the figure stepped from the shadows it was not.

Light from the room behind her splashed across Lord Kersey's upper body, illuminating his handsome features and superbly tailored black coat.

"Good evening to you, Lord Kersey." Miranda glanced back over her shoulder. They were in clear view of the card room so she wasn't likely to be endangering her reputation. But if her parents were to be believed, she was incapable of knowing when she *did* threaten her reputation, so really, who knew?

Lord Kersey moved further into the light, but not closer to her. "I went riding with your brother today."

Miranda turned so the doors were on her left. "Indeed? Were you able to keep up? Jasper is nearly unbeatable on horseback."

Lord Kersey's warm chuckle filled the air around her. "Yes, I managed to hold my own. Thank you for your concern."

Where most would have used the last comment as a means to flirt, she had the impression he teased her. In fact, he hadn't yet tried to sidle too close or to find an excuse to touch her.

Miranda eyed him warily. "Well, I suppose I should return indoors. A pleasure seeing you, my lord."

"If you would pause but a moment, Lady Miranda."

Again, she waited for a staying hand, but he didn't move. Miranda didn't either.

He gestured toward her, but still didn't come too close. "I'm not exactly sure how to say this."

Miranda's stomach seized. The urge to run screaming from the balcony nearly overpowered her. Her father had convinced him of the match and he was going to propose! "Lord Kersey, I really don't think—"

"Please, allow me to finish." The viscount lifted one side of his mouth, but his eyes darkened slightly and she rather thought he didn't like being interrupted. "Your brother discussed your father's, er, his plan with me, and I must admit I am not interested in pursuing a courtship. I am given to understand from Jasper this is acceptable to you."

Miranda exhaled audibly. "Oh, yes. Quite acceptable. Thank you, Lord Kersey." She cocked her head to the side. "Forgive me for saying, but it's odd you didn't jump at the chance."

He pulled his head back and his lips quirked into a bemused expression.

Miranda laughed softly. "I don't mean to overestimate my own appeal. It's just that I haven't yet met a man who didn't want something from me."

"You just did."

His meaning took a moment to truly sink in. He didn't want to link himself to her because doing so wouldn't help to elevate his position. He needed someone with a perfect social record. Someone sedate. Someone well-mannered. *Someone else.*

She really was the pariah her parents alleged. Good Lord, she wanted to get as far away from this house party as possible.

"I appreciate your candor, Lord Kersey." Miranda tossed her head, looking for her suddenly misplaced self-respect. "And I especially appreciate your disinterest." A laugh that might have come out as a sob bubbled in her chest. She stifled it, so she'd never know for certain. "Good evening."

She spun on her toes and reentered the card room before Lord Kersey could say anything else to further destroy her equilibrium.

"Oh, Miranda, there you are!" Georgie rushed toward her, cheeks flushed and eyes sparkling.

Rebecca followed close behind. "You'll never guess who's just arrived!" She looked at Georgie who could barely contain herself and indeed let out a little squeal.

They turned to Miranda with identical expressions of glee. "Darleigh!" they cried in unison.

Miranda resisted the almost painful urge to roll her eyes. *Where in the bloody hell was Jasper?* "Have you seen my brother?"

Georgie stared at Miranda for a moment and then glanced at Rebecca who mirrored the exact same movement. Georgie looked back to Miranda. "Didn't you hear what we said?"

Miranda grasped her fan in her palm as if it could be used as a blunt instrument. "Yes, I heard you. I'm looking for Jasper."

Rebecca rattled her head as if she were trying to shake moths from her ears. "But *Darleigh* is here."

Georgie reached out and touched Rebecca's arm. "She wants to know where Lord Saxton is so she can meet Darleigh without being suspected." Georgie turned a beatific smile on Miranda. "Never fear, for we are your dearest friends. We've arranged for you to meet Darleigh in the garden."

"You've what?" Miranda gripped the fan until she felt the delicate wood bend. "I don't want to meet with Darleigh. I need to find Saxton so I can return to Wootton Bassett. As I've tried to tell you, I—"

Rebecca thrust her lower lip out in a most unattractive frown. "You aren't as fun as you were before. What did they do to you in that horrible little village?"

"You weren't pilloried, were you?" Georgie's caramel-colored eyes were wide, and for the first time Miranda realized her two closest friends in the world were a wheel short of a barouche.

"Oh, for heaven's sake. Wootton Bassett isn't a 'horrible little village.' There are nice people there doing nice things."

She recalled her charges and how different their lives were from Georgie's and Rebecca's. Miranda had shared with the girls the trappings of being ladies, but beyond their accomplishments with needlepoint and dancing they were, quite simply, good girls. Girls who didn't waste their time arranging clandestine meetings that would likely get Miranda compromised.

Just when she feared she might knock her friends over in an effort to leave, Miranda spotted Jasper's tall frame near the corner of the card room. With a muttered, "Never mind," she took herself off, not caring to look back at Georgie and Rebecca, who were now whispering madly.

Jasper's eyes lit on Miranda as she closed the distance between them. "Good evening, Miranda."

Miranda took in his casual stance, the way he watched the faro game at a nearby table. "Where have you been?"

"What, no jovial welcome? No sisterly affection? No appreciation for a brother's good deeds?" He said the last with an exaggeratedly elevated eyebrow.

"Yes, yes, thank you for talking to Kersey." Miranda had no desire to revisit that conversation, even in her own mind. "But you will get no sisterly affection from me until we are on the road. When are we leaving?"

He went back to watching the card game. "About that...I've encountered a snag. With the departure of Kersey from the field of potential suitors, Holborn has simply moved on to the next target."

"And that would be?" Miranda was afraid of the answer, but had to know just the same.

Jasper didn't look at her. "Lord Walter."

"Can't you talk them out of it?"

Now he turned. "You think I hold some sort of influence?" He snorted. "The country air has weakened your mind."

Miranda wanted to brain him with her fan. "But the benefit is tomorrow night! I need to leave immediately. If the roads are at all bad, I'll risk missing the entire thing!"

Two of the gentlemen seated at the faro table threw angry glances in their direction. Jasper grabbed Miranda by the elbow and escorted her from the card room.

"I can see you've still not learned the art of moderation." Jasper let her go as soon as they'd walked several feet down the corridor. "You're going to have to get over this obsession with a silly benefit."

Miranda gasped. "It's not silly." She gritted her teeth. "And I'll get back there with or without your help."

Jasper shook his head. "You are the most stubborn, difficult girl." He fell silent for a moment. "I've no doubt you'll sneak off by yourself and cause even greater havoc. I'm beginning to wonder if the duke and duchess aren't correct in their treatment of you. You really have no notion of how your behavior appears."

Miranda's shoulders drooped. "What happened to you? I used to be able to count on you being as mischievous as me."

Jasper chuckled. "There you are dead wrong. No one is as mischievous as you." He sobered. "And it nearly got you into serious trouble. Still might if you aren't careful." He raised his hand to his chest. "Because I am a kind and helpful brother, I will escort you *in the morning.* I promise we'll get you to your precious benefit in plenty of time."

"What about Mother and Father?"

"I'll explain that Lord Septon has journeyed to Wootton Bassett for this benefit in the hopes of seeing you, his goddaughter. They won't want to disappoint him. Of course, I'll have to promise to bring you back the very next day, you realize." He cocked his head to the side in brief contemplation. "The only problem is where I shall stay when we get there. Is this Stratham's house adequate?"

"Yes, more than. You'll be quite comfortable. Are you sure you're *allowed* to stay there?"

"Ah, sweet sister, when will you realize the rules are not the same for you and me?"

But Miranda knew all too well. Perhaps that was why she always broke them.

~

*F*OX sat in his landau in the drive of Stratham Hall. Daylight was fading along with his interest in this benefit. Oh, he was pleased the orphanage would reap the rewards, but did he really need to be there?

"Are we getting out?" Rob asked from the opposite seat. He'd ridden over with Fox from Bassett Manor. "I need to get inside. I told Mrs. Knott I'd arrive a little early."

Fox leaned his head back against the seat. "Go ahead. I'm still thinking about it."

Rob kicked him in the shin. "This is a bloody benefit for *your* orphanage!"

Fox looked down at his leg. "Are you trying to ruin my new clothes?"

"No, but if you aren't going to make use of them, what difference does it make?" Rob's brows drew together over his flashing eyes. "I never knew you to be a coward, Fox. Besides, we discussed the potential for other opportunities, if you'll recall."

Of course he recalled. Rob had suggested several days ago that perhaps one of the out-of-town guests might be a marriageable *moneyed* female. Since things hadn't worked out with Miranda, why not move on to someone else? "Hadn't worked out" was a disingenuous way to describe the hollowness in Fox's chest. But he hadn't shared the true nature of his feelings for Miranda with Rob. Hell, he'd barely admitted it to himself.

Rob jumped down. "Come on. Surely drinking a goodly amount of Stratham's liquor will improve your mood."

This argument was the best he'd made yet. Fox climbed out of the landau. "Fine. I'll go to the damned party."

They walked into the house together. Servants bustled to and fro doing whatever it was they did to prepare for such an event. A footman directed them to the Gold Room where Mrs. Knott and Mrs. Gates were reviewing the display of antiquities.

Laid out in one room, it presented an impressive collection. There were tapestries, both from Stipple's End and Bassett Manor, silver pieces, a few portraits and a handful of landscapes, some jewelry, though nothing terribly dear as far as he could tell, and some ancient looking earthenware from Stipple's End supposedly dug up in the yard. For the first time Fox allowed himself to believe this might actually raise enough money to get them through the winter.

Rob had stopped to speak with his wife and now came to stand beside Fox. "Mrs. Knott is going to see about getting us some brandy."

Fox nodded and tried not to pluck at his stiff cravat. Stupid waste of money. He was supposedly dressed in the height of fashion, not that it mattered. He'd wanted to impress Miranda, and now she was gone. Hell, where was that brandy?

Footfalls carried from the doorway. Fox turned, expecting to see the footman bearing a tray. Instead, Stratham sauntered in wearing the same smug grin he always wore. And a green waistcoat.

Dammit. Fox looked down at his chest. Stratham's garment was incredibly similar to his own emerald waistcoat. He looked up and Stratham's gaze registered the same likeness.

The footman stepped into the room behind Stratham, and Fox went directly for the brandy.

Stratham tried to look down his nose at Fox, but it was nearly comical given his vertical shortcomings. "Dipping into my cellar so soon?"

Fox grabbed a glass from the tray. "Yes." After taking a fortifying sip, he turned to leave and stopped short as two gentlemen walked in. He nearly spewed his brandy at the ridiculous sight of Lord Norris stuffed into a puce-colored waistcoat like a sausage into its casing. The man stood even shorter than Stratham, but twice as wide. The gentleman at his side provided an amusing counterpoint as he was unearthly tall and thin.

"Lord Norris!" Stratham swept by Fox to pay his sycophantic respects to the man who likely controlled his every move.

Norris blinked, his lids stretching over eyes as fat as the rest of him. "Stratham, capital evening. Hope you don't mind we came a bit early. Wanted to sneak a peek." He wagged a corpulent finger at the items spread throughout the room. "This here's Septon. Down from London."

Miranda's godfather. It bothered Fox that someone close to her was so friendly with the likes of Norris.

Septon bowed. "Good evening, gentlemen. Thank you so much for the kind invitation. Is my goddaughter about?"

Fox opened his mouth, but Stratham beat him out. "My apologies, Lord Septon. Lady Miranda has been called away by His Grace. She was sorry to disappoint you."

The older man nodded, but Fox detected a bit of sadness around his eyes. He'd been looking forward to seeing her, then. And who wouldn't?

The footman delivered Rob's brandy and then departed. Fox wanted to follow him so he could procure the bottle.

Norris wandered over to study the tapestries hanging from the ceiling. All five from the orphanage had been cleaned. The colors were vibrant and the designs breathtaking. The four from Bassett Manor were larger, but dull in comparison. He'd be lucky if someone bought them as scraps.

The squat earl stood with his hands clasped behind his back. He turned to face Fox and the others. The buttons of his coat looked as if they might pop off. "Where did you find these tapestries? They're a far sight better than yours there, Fox." Norris had been interested in buying Fox's tapestries last year. He'd viewed them, negotiated a price, and then never returned to actually purchase them. Fox had been counting on that money.

Fox downed the rest of his brandy. "They're from Stipple's End. And, yes, they're exquisite." He pinned the earl with a hardened stare meant to skewer him like a juicy piece of game. "And very, very expensive."

Norris ran his fingers over one of the embroidered edges. "I should think so. What do you say, Septon, thirteenth century?"

Septon stepped toward the tapestries and removed a quizzing glass from his coat. "Hmmm. Yes. Excellent depiction of the lists, this one." He studied a scene in which two knights charged toward each other on horseback, lances drawn at the ready. The crowd cheering the event was incredibly detailed. One could almost hear the shouting.

Norris chuckled. "I can see we'll be driving the price up in our competition. Looks like your little orphanage is going to get lucky."

Fox clenched his hand around the glass. They should be "lucky" anyway. Norris could easily feed all of them for the next year. A tap on Fox's arm made him turn his head. Rob whispered, "Ignore him."

Fox relaxed his muscles. "I'm for more brandy." He strode from the room before something else could halt his progress. He left via the door the footman had taken and after traversing several rooms, ended up in the foyer. Bloody maze of a house.

He turned to go back the way he'd come and his eye caught Beatrice coming down the staircase. She wore a purple gown that sparkled in the candlelight. Her dark hair was swept up and decorated with what looked to be tiny jewels. He'd never seen her look so...beautiful.

Cool air rushed over his back as the footman

opened the door. Beatrice froze near the bottom of the stairs. Her gaze arrested on something behind Fox. Her lips turned down.

Fox spun about, nearly dropping his brandy glass in the process.

Framed in the doorway was heaven herself.

CHAPTER 13

*M*IRANDA stopped short. At first she didn't recognize the man in the entrance hall, but then she looked at his face—really looked at it —and realized it was Fox.

Only a Fox she'd never seen. Dressed in a crisp black evening coat and pantaloons, a rich emerald waistcoat, and pristine white shirt and cravat, he was terribly handsome. He even wore dancing slippers. *Dancing slippers.*

His brown hair had been neatly trimmed and was combed back from his rugged face. Still a touch too long for London, it curled at the top of his collar giving him an aura of raw masculinity that combined the Fox she knew with the Fox standing before her.

"Are you going to move out of the doorway?" Jasper pushed her over the threshold.

Miranda stumbled as she took a larger than normal step. A swish of skirts drew her attention, but she had a hard time dragging her eyes from Fox.

Beatrice came toward her and stopped near the center of the room. Near Fox. Too near Fox. "Miranda, we weren't expecting you."

Miranda groped about for her voice. "I don't know why not. I told you I'd return."

"You did?" Fox took a step forward. Away from Beatrice.

Miranda suppressed a smile. "Absolutely. I wouldn't miss this for anything." Jasper cleared his throat and moved to stand beside her. "Oh, pardon me. Jasper, you remember Miss Carmody, and this is Mr. Montgomery Foxcroft. Beatrice and Fox, this is my brother, Lord Saxton."

Jasper took Beatrice's hand. "A pleasure, Miss Carmody." He swept Fox with an assessing look from head to slipper. "Mr. Foxcroft."

Fox returned Jasper's perusal. "Good evening, Lord Saxton. So kind of you to escort Lady Miranda."

Jasper's lips quirked. "She's been prattling on about this benefit since she arrived at the house party, so I had no choice. I'm sure you've realized my sister is a force of nature when it comes to something she wants."

Fox looked at her, the golden center of his eyes fired by the hundreds of candles overhead. Or maybe something else.

Beatrice pursed her lips and clamped her hands together. "How nice of you to find time to return, Miranda. I'm sure you understand, however, you needn't have bothered. I have things well in hand."

Fox still stared at Miranda. "That may be, but Miranda's presence is very welcome." His voice softened. "Lord Septon was asking after you."

"Thank you, I'm looking forward to seeing him." Miranda glanced down at her traveling costume. "But I need to dress." She turned to a footman. "I wonder if Jasper and I might be shown to rooms upstairs. In fact, my brother will be staying so he'll need a bedchamber." The retainer nodded and took himself off. He returned immediately with the butler in tow.

"Do follow me, my lord. My lady." He led them toward the stairs at the back of the entry hall.

Miranda walked by Fox. He smelled less like fresh

grass and more like rosemary, but it was a lovely scent either way. "I'll be right back. Don't let Beatrice manage *everything.*"

He chuckled. "Never fear. I'll watch out for you."

How curious they could banter given what had gone between them. Something was different. Perhaps it was simply that she'd never seen him at a social engagement —that long-ago day at the vicarage didn't signify.

Running her hand along the smooth, polished wood of the balustrade, she looked down. Fox watched her ascend as if he couldn't take his eyes from her. Little thrills of sensation raced up her arms and along her spine. Yes, something was very different.

Jasper whispered next to her ear. "I knew Foxcroft was the bigger worry."

Miranda flinched. She peeled her gaze from Fox and focused on the butler's back. Normally she'd snipe back at her brother, but she couldn't seem to find the words. Probably because she feared he was right.

But she didn't want to be attracted to Fox! It was bad enough she still dreamed of the infernal highwayman! Her parents would faint dead away if she were to become entangled with someone like Montgomery Foxcroft.

The butler showed her to a well-appointed chamber decorated in hues of rose and burgundy. "Do you have an attendant, my lady?"

"No, but I'm sure Mr. Stratham has a maid he can spare." Miranda looked out into the hallway at her brother. "I'll see you shortly. Unless you'd rather not come downstairs."

Jasper shook his head. "I worked hard to get you here in time, and you want me to miss the fun? I don't think so. Besides, I haven't seen Septon in awhile. Nice of him to come to your little benefit."

"Septon, unlike some people in my family, is more than eager to provide his assistance and concern. When

I first wrote to him about the event, he responded with a lovely and *lengthy* letter." Miranda playfully glared at him.

Jasper held up his hands. "Sorry, not much of a writer."

A footman appeared with her dress and a small bag filled with her other necessities. She'd insisted Jasper allow her to hang her gown in the interior of the coach so it wouldn't be creased. She knew their time would be precious once they arrived.

The butler gestured down the hall. "If you'll just continue with me, my lord." Jasper gave Miranda a pointed glance—Lord only knew why—and followed the retainer.

Miranda went to close the door behind the footman when Mrs. Gates appeared in the hall.

The older woman's face lit up. "Miranda! Fox said you'd arrived. But then, I always knew you would." She beamed as she walked into the room without invitation and gave Miranda a hug.

Miranda froze for a moment. No one hugged. At least no one *she* knew hugged. She patted Mrs. Gates's back, unsure of what to do. After a moment, Miranda pulled away, and Mrs. Gates turned her around to help her out of her gown. "You'll be pleased with how we've pulled everything together."

Miranda untied the ribbons of her bonnet and sent it sailing to the bed. "It certainly appears as if Beatrice has everything in hand." And was quite territorial about it.

"Oh yes, I've never seen her work so hard. She seems very motivated. And, I daresay, she might be catching the eye of Mr. Stratham."

Miranda stepped out of her dress. She'd purposely worn the undergarments she'd need under her ball gown, despite the awkward fit the lighter chemise had provided for her traveling clothes. "How fortuitous for

Beatrice."

Mrs. Gates took Miranda's gown from the armoire. The dark green gauze overlay whispered against the pale green silk underneath as she swept it toward Miranda. "Such a lovely gown." She helped Miranda into the garment and went about fastening her up.

Miranda surveyed herself in the mirror. Strands of hair had escaped her chignon. Her coiffure didn't at all go with the elegance of her dress. She touched the back of her head.

Mrs. Gates clucked her tongue. "We'll get your hair fixed up in no time. Where are your baubles and pretty things?"

Miranda went to the bag near the armoire and retrieved her jewelry box. "In here." She handed the case to Mrs. Gates.

"My goodness, this is a bit heavy." Mrs. Gates put the box on a small table and peered inside. She gasped as she reverently extracted various pieces and set them on the tabletop. "You've never worn any of this before."

The jewelry hadn't been in Miranda's possession of course, but would she have worn such things to the orphanage? Actually, she might've worn the pearl-encrusted brooch. Or the cameo. And most assuredly the garnet cross. Miranda plucked up an emerald pendant and clasped it around her neck. "Can you use the emerald combs in my hair?"

Mrs. Gates held up two large gold combs studded with emeralds and diamonds. "Certainly. Sit on the edge of the chair here." As Miranda complied, the older woman continued, "We weren't expecting your return. I expect Fox is thrilled to see you."

Thrilled? Had he discussed her with Mrs. Gates? She thought of Fox's reaction when she'd arrived. Yes, thrilled seemed an appropriate description. The notion trickled heat through her limbs.

The headmistress pulled Miranda's hair down and

went about braiding two lengths of it. "I do hope you'll be fair with him. He is as dear to me as a son. I should like to see him happy. He's had enough heartache."

"Are you speaking of Jane Pennymore?"

"You know about Jane, then." Mrs. Gates's fingers moved quickly and deftly. "More than that is how deeply his father betrayed and disappointed him."

Miranda recalled Fox telling her about his father. He hadn't elaborated, but she knew enough. "By endangering everyone's livelihood with his gambling."

Mrs. Gates clucked her tongue. "Fox told you about that? He rarely speaks of his father. He must care for you a great deal."

Mrs. Gates's observation gave her a rush of pleasure. At the same time, Miranda didn't want to think too closely about Fox's underlying feelings—that was a dangerous path.

Finished with the braids, Mrs. Gates swept up the loose portion into a bun and wrapped the braids around it. She stuck one comb into the right side and was poised to put the other on the left.

Miranda held up her hand. "If you please, Mrs. Gates."

The older woman relinquished the comb, and Miranda pushed it into the left side, but more toward the top. Now the combs were not exactly opposing each other. "It's better to have them offset a bit, don't you think?" She needn't explain asymmetry was in style. This gave her pause. She never used to censor what she said. Another curious development.

Mrs. Gates clapped her hands together. "I do! A lovely effect. You've quite an eye, Miranda."

"Thank you, Mrs. Gates. I can find my other accoutrements if you'd like to go on to the party. I'll be down shortly."

Mrs. Gates glanced at the small gilded clock on the bedside table. "The auction is due to start in thirty minutes. It's lovely to have you back with us, dear." She smiled before hurrying from the room.

Miranda dashed a bit of fragrance behind her ears and along her neck. Locating her ivory gloves and dancing slippers, she completed her toilette—my, but she'd become adept at readying herself in a trice—and followed in Mrs. Gates's footsteps. Laughter and conversation rushed up the stairs as she made her way toward the party. People filled the entry hall, including Delia, Lisette, and Flora. Miranda went to greet them.

"How splendid you girls look. Let me see!" Miranda bade them all turn around and show their gowns. "Lisette, did you make all of these?"

Lisette blushed prettily. "We got them used from Mrs. Abernathy. I trimmed them a bit with some lace and whatnot. Flora's even has a few sparkles."

"Why, yes it does. You've done beautifully, Lisette. You all look lovely."

Flora moved toward her with outstretched arms. "I'm so glad you've come back!" Goodness, she was going to hug Miranda, too.

Miranda reached out and clasped the girl's hands before she got too close. Hugging in the privacy of a bedchamber was one thing, but in the middle of a bustling entry hall it was completely unacceptable. Flora's brow furrowed, and Miranda rushed to say, "We don't want to crush your dress, sweeting."

Flora nodded vigorously. "When does the dancing begin?"

Miranda had no idea if they'd kept to the schedule she'd laid out. Given the timing of the auction, it seemed they might. "I believe the musicians will start after the auction. In the meantime, would you girls like to have something to eat?"

They nodded, and Miranda led them to the dining room where an elaborate buffet supper spread across five tables. The girls went directly to the sweets table.

Beatrice stood inside the doorway. She had just finished speaking to a servant who scurried off to presumably do her bidding.

Miranda paused beside her. "Beatrice, you've done very well. Everything appears to be exactly as I arranged. I'm so glad my lists were helpful."

Beatrice quirked her mouth into a nasty smile. "I knew you'd assume responsibility for this."

Miranda startled at the venom in the other girl's tone. "In fact, this was my—"

Beatrice rounded on her, jabbing a finger in Miranda's face. "See, there you go! This isn't about you. Yes, this was your idea. Yes, you organized much of it. But *I* brought it to pass. I made sure it all came together. Me, me, *me*."

Miranda stood rooted to the floor. She'd never seen so much emotion from Beatrice. Miranda was silent for a moment, trying to think of something that might soothe the other woman.

Mrs. Gates's hug stole into Miranda's brain. She wondered if Beatrice had ever been hugged either. Despite Beatrice's dither, Miranda couldn't bring herself to physically demonstrate the fact she cared—and she did. Instead, she used the method that had always served her well: gifts. "I brought you something. A novel. I know your father doesn't allow them, but I fancied you might like to read one."

Beatrice flushed, and her eyes widened, but she quickly reined her expression into subtle—or rather she tried for subtle—curiosity. But there was no mistaking her interest. "That was, er, thoughtful of you."

Miranda wasn't fooled. Beatrice's initial reaction had been too…happy. And blast it all if Miranda didn't like seeing that expression on Beatrice's face. Miranda recalled the mysterious wrapped packages Beatrice toted about. "Is there a chance you already read novels?"

With crimson-tinted cheeks, Beatrice nodded.

Miranda suppressed a giggle. So they shared a love for novels and perhaps memories of parents who never hugged them. Suddenly she found it imperative to ally herself with the too-dour Beatrice. To that end, Miranda would do everything possible to ensure she snared Mr. Stratham.

Miranda gestured toward the door. "Come, show me the auction. I shall give you the book when we get back to Birch House."

Beatrice walked beside her. "You're coming back?"

"I told you I would. I'm certain my things have already been delivered." Miranda smiled at people as they moved through a growing throng.

"But aren't you going to be married?" Beatrice spoke in low tones.

Miranda waved a hand. "Heavens no. At least, not yet."

"But I thought your parents had found a husband for you."

"We didn't suit." Lord Kersey's gentle rejection still stung. And she simply refused to think she might be allied with Lord Walter.

They stepped into the Gold Room. Rows of chairs had been set up along with a podium. An auctioneer from London stood at the front of the room—or what had been designated as the front.

"Miranda, my dear! I was told you wouldn't be here. What a splendid surprise." Lord Septon came forward and took her hand between his, giving it a hearty squeeze. The angular planes of his face crinkled as he grinned down at her. "Such a display you've arranged for us. 'Tis very well done of you."

Miranda withdrew her hand after clasping his in return and gestured to Beatrice. "Dear Septon, this is my friend Miss Beatrice Carmody. She is the one you should be lauding. I have only just returned from Wokingham." Miranda was pleased to see Beatrice's mouth curve up.

Beatrice glanced at Miranda before giving Lord Septon her attention. "We are honored to have you and the other members of the antiquity society with us."

"It is you who honor us. This is an impressive collection. I daresay we might come to fisticuffs over a few of the items." He laughed heartily.

Miranda scanned the room, taking in the various people, nodding at those she knew, and then arresting when her gaze fell on Fox leaning against one of the doorways. He stared straight at her, his eyes blazing. A shiver crept across her shoulders.

Beatrice clasped her hands together. "We should take our seats."

Lord Septon offered his arm to Miranda. "May I see you to your chair?"

Miranda pulled her gaze from Fox. "No, thank you. I'm just going to stand in the back."

"Very well then. I require a position very near the front." He offered them a bow and moved to the first row of chairs.

Beatrice turned to Miranda. "Aren't you going to say something to everyone before the auction?"

Miranda shook her head. "No, I can see you have everything well in hand." At Beatrice's momentary look of panic, Miranda rushed to add, "Unless you want me to say something?"

Taking a deep breath, Beatrice squared her shoulders. "No, you were right. I've been doing my part out of a sense of obligation my parents have instilled in me since childhood. I realized over the past few days I'm doing this because I want to. And I want to because you've shown me how much it matters."

"Me?" Miranda had inspired Beatrice? This evening was full of surprises. Around them people were sitting or moving to the sides of the room and conversation began to die. Miranda gave Beatrice a nudge. "Go on."

Beatrice answered with a small smile and went to the podium. Miranda retreated to the back of the room. Her brother entered with a stunning, raven-haired beauty on his arm. He guided her to a seat in the back row and sat beside her, whispering in her ear. She looked at him with the same expression Miranda used with the opposite sex when she wanted something. Except she was fairly certain what the unknown woman wanted was *not* anything Miranda had tried to obtain.

After Beatrice's introduction, the auctioneer began describing the first item, a landscape painting. Septon bid first. He'd brought at least a half dozen people from the antiquity society, maybe closer to ten even. She'd write him a special note of thanks.

"You look beautiful."

Miranda hadn't seen Fox walk up beside her. His low-spoken compliment fluttered across her bare collarbone. She turned and was once again astonished at the change in his appearance.

"Thank you. You look nice, too." What a terribly inadequate remark. But neither could she wax poetic without looking a complete fool. They lapsed into silence for a moment, their gazes locked in some sort of quiet struggle in which they thought of something to say, or perhaps something not to say. Finally, Miranda opted for safety. "Who is the woman sitting with my brother?"

Fox looked at the back row. Though she now studied him in profile, Miranda noted his nostrils flared.

"Mrs. Danforth."

Miranda glanced back at Mrs. Danforth leaning close to Jasper. "I've never met her. Does she live in Wootton Bassett?"

Fox didn't take his gaze from the voluptuous woman. "Not far, yes."

"She's very flirtatious for a married woman." In truth, she was no worse than any of the married women in London. "Unless she's a widow."

At last, he turned back toward Miranda. His eyes were impossibly vivid this evening. Every time he looked at her, it felt as if he were touching her. "Yes, in fact, she is widowed. Has been for quite some time."

Miranda had lost all interest in Mrs. Danforth. "I'm going to check on the musicians. The dancing is due to begin after the auction." She expected him to accompany her, had practically invited him to do so. Her breath halted in her lungs as she awaited his response.

The gold in his eyes burned against the green and blue. Before he could say anything, Beatrice came up beside them. "Did I hear you mention the musicians? I was just on my way to make sure they were all set. Why don't you join me?"

Caught, Miranda could only nod and leave with Beatrice. Over her shoulder she gave Fox a lingering look. He continued to watch her. A warm flush suffused her limbs as she glided out of the Gold Room.

Miranda busied herself over the next hour, floating between rooms. The auction was going smashingly well. The orphanage would have a comfortable winter. The last items up for bidding were the tapestries from Stipple's End. Lord Septon, the rotund man pointed out to her as Lord Norris, and a third gentleman from the antiquity society battled over the precious items. In the end, Lord Norris emerged the victor.

Glad the auction had finally concluded, Miranda went to the ballroom where the music had begun and people were already dancing. She'd made a point of ensuring there would be a waltz in the first set.

Positioned opposite the dais, Miranda could see all of the doors leading into the ballroom. She scanned the faces pouring in for Fox. As the reel drew to a close, she finally saw him enter. He perused the crowd until he found her and then his lips lifted into a smile. He came toward her.

Patience had never been one of Miranda's skills. She met him halfway just as the strains of the waltz started up. He took her hand. "Would you care to dance?"

She smiled up at him. "I would."

He led her to the middle of the ballroom and swept her into his arms. The memory of their prior dances washed over her like a warm, welcome, rosemary-scented bath.

He guided her toward the terrace doors and then toward the dais. "This music is better than our first waltz."

She laughed. "I liked it fine."

He arched a brow. "Well, then surely I look more the part."

"You look every bit the part." She smoothed her hand over the black wool covering his shoulder. The jacket wasn't made from the finest cloth, but it fit him perfectly. But then, he had a frame made for display.

His eyes darkened except for the gold at the center, which seemed to spark. "Stop looking at me like that, Miranda."

"Like what?"

"Like I'm a sweetmeat on the buffet table." His low voice rumbled over her bare flesh.

Miranda's eyes widened. Was she so obvious? "Sorry." Even after she'd rejected his proposal, he'd made it clear he still wanted her. Had he changed his mind while she was gone? His behavior didn't seem to indicate such. "I didn't mean to make you uncomfortable."

His lips tightened into something like a grimace. He stared over her shoulder. "I'm not uncomfortable, exactly." He glanced down at her face and quickly averted his gaze once more. "Yes, I'm uncomfortable, but likely not for the reasons you suspect."

Miranda wanted to smile for she knew *exactly* what he meant.

"I have to ask." He took a deep breath. "Are you betrothed?"

Miranda nearly tripped over his foot at the anguish she detected in his tone. "No." She leaned a fraction closer.

"You're torturing me. Do you know that?" He looked down at her again, but this time kept his incredible eyes fixated on her face. "I still, that is—"

"Don't say it." Now Miranda looked away. What could she say? Even if she wanted to—and she wasn't absolutely sure she did—she shouldn't encourage him. Her parents had cautioned her against associating with "socially inappropriate" country gentlemen. But tonight she felt so... A rebellious idea came to her, as usual. If she really wanted him, they could simply elope to Gretna Green. Someone Georgie had known since girlhood had done that very thing last fall.

She returned her attention to Fox, but he'd gone back to staring over her shoulder, his face an impassive mask. Despair rooted in Miranda's chest. Was she doomed to be attracted to unsuitable men like the highwayman and Montgomery Foxcroft? She *could* run away with him, but too much of her couldn't bear the disappointment her parents would surely bestow upon her.

The dance drew to a close and before she could savor the touch of his hand at the small of her back, he stepped away from her. They stood facing each other for a moment.

Lisette rushed to Miranda's side and grasped her hand. "Lady Miranda, you must help. Flora has left."

Miranda reluctantly turned from Fox. "What's wrong? Is she ill?"

"No. She's gone." Lisette's lower lip quivered and tears shone in her hazel eyes. "She left with Mrs. Danforth." She ended her declaration on a gasp.

Miranda shook her head. "I don't understand. Why did she leave with Mrs. Danforth?"

Fox stepped toward them. "Come, let's move to the side." His face had darkened and his brows were drawn together.

Lisette dabbed at her eyes with a handkerchief. "Mrs. Danforth is the one who took Rose away."

Miranda froze as they neared the corner. "Isn't Rose the prostitute?"

"Yes." Lisette began to cry.

Miranda patted the girl's shoulder. "There, there. We'll take care of this. I'll deliver you to Mrs. Gates, and then we'll figure this out. I'm sure someone knows where Mrs. Danforth has taken her."

Lisette looked at Fox and then at Miranda. "Fox knows. She's his friend."

Miranda turned on Fox. He'd reacted to the woman when she'd come into the auction with Jasper. "She's your *friend*?"

Fox pressed his lips together. "Let's find Mrs. Gates. Then I'll go to Mrs. Danforth's and fetch Flora."

Before Miranda could question him further, he guided Lisette toward the door, leaving Miranda to trail in their wake. Rather than waste time looking for Mrs. Gates, Miranda reasoned it would be better to go directly after Flora. Which meant she had to go to Mrs. Danforth's. Hopefully it wouldn't be difficult to find. Perhaps she could yet overtake them if she left right away.

Instead of following Fox, Miranda exited through a different door and made her way to the entrance hall. A footman let her out onto the front portico. She shivered as the cool autumn night air greeted her bare neck and shoulders, but there was no time to fetch a pelisse or a shawl. Hurrying down the stairs, she focused on the carriages parked in the drive, willing her eyes to adjust to the semi-darkness. Carriage lanterns splayed light onto the sides of the vehicles and onto the gravel below, but she had no idea what to look for. Which carriage belonged to Fox?

She could take the carriage she and Jasper had brought, provided it had returned from delivering her things to Birch House, but she presumed Fox's driver would know how to get to Mrs. Danforth's. Anger flared up her spine again, but she pushed the emotion away. She'd have plenty of time to query Fox about his *friendship* with Mrs. Danforth.

There! A dark, somewhat shabby landau that looked to be nearly as old as Miranda. She strode to the man leaning against the side. He tipped a flask back and wiped a hand over his mouth.

She came to a halt before him. "Excuse me, is this Mr. Foxcroft's landau?"

The coachman stashed his flask inside his coat. "Indeed, ma'am."

She smiled her coquette's smile and the man's features softened. "He requested you drive me to Mrs. Danforth's."

The coachman's eyes widened and his mouth gaped. "Surely there's a mistake."

Miranda fluttered her lashes at him and sidled closer. "No. I need to fetch something. It won't take but a trice. Fox demanded we hurry."

The coachman glanced at the house, indecision marked in his features. He looked back at Miranda, and she curved her lips into a provocative moue. He blinked. And then he opened the door.

With a satisfied intake of breath, Miranda climbed inside. Settling against the squab, she folded her arms across her chest. She'd just run in, grab Flora, and hurry back to the benefit before anyone noticed her absence. What could go wrong?

～

OX found Mrs. Gates in the Gold Room overseeing the auctioned goods. Some were being paid for and taken this evening, while others would be delivered or collected the following day. Fox should have been helping with this endeavor, but he'd been too distracted by Miranda.

Mrs. Gates rushed forward, her forehead crinkling with concern. She smoothed a hand over Lisette's brow. "Goodness, what's happened child?"

"It's Flora!" Tears coursed down Lisette's cheeks. "She's left with Mrs. Danforth."

Mrs. Gates snapped her gaze to Fox. It had been years since she'd directed such an angry look at him. "I thought you told that woman to stay away."

Fox was transported back to when he'd ruined a bucket of good apples by throwing them at a target he and another boy had set up in the orchard. Mrs. Gates had made him clean the library every day for a fortnight. Defensively, he said, "I did." In a note. That Polly hadn't responded to.

Lisette hiccupped. "Where's Lady Miranda?"

She wasn't behind him? Fox spun around to empty space, but saw Lord Saxton enter. Unease settled into Fox's bones like an unpaid debt.

Saxton took that inopportune moment to overhear Lisette's question. He strode further into the room. "I'm looking for her myself. Have you seen her?"

Lisette gulped air as she gawked up at Miranda's brother. "Yes, she was just here."

Fox shot Mrs. Gates a speaking glance. With a subtle nod, Mrs. Gates turned Lisette from the gentlemen and whispered something in her ear.

He turned to address Saxton. "She was with us in the ballroom. However, she's gone to Stipple's End with one of the girls who's taken ill." That would explain both Miranda's and Flora's absences for the rest of the night. He had no intention of letting either of them return.

The headmistress threw a look over her shoulder at Saxton. "My apologies, my lord. She's very upset about her friend."

Saxton's pale blue eyes briefly widened. "You say Miranda left the party to care for a sick child? My sister, Miranda?" He studied Fox, the quirk of his mouth belying his skepticism.

Mrs. Gates allowed Lisette to turn back around, but held the girl close. "Yes, my lord. Miranda, that is, Lady Miranda has become very close to the girls. Indeed, we quite rely on her at Stipple's End."

Saxton cocked his head to the side. "I might not have believed this if I hadn't heard you say it, ma'am. It appears people do change."

Fox was growing irritated with this conversation. Not because it somehow demeaned Miranda—and he supposed it did—but because she was Lord-knew-where. Actually, Fox had a suspicion as to her location, and if he was right, he needed to get her out of there immediately.

Donning his most benign expression, Fox bowed to Mrs. Gates and Lisette. "I've some things to see to, if you'll excuse me." He was halfway to the door before he realized Saxton trailed him. *Dammit.*

"Foxcroft. I understand there's a certain, ah establishment in the area where a gentleman might go…"

Fox then recalled Miranda's brother had been sitting with Polly Danforth during the auction. If Miranda had gone to Polly's, as Fox surmised, it was the absolute *last* place Saxton needed to be.

Fox paused outside the Gold Room, his mind

churning for ways to dissuade the other man. "That would be Polly Danforth's. It's a bit early yet. Best time to go is around midnight."

Saxton nodded. "Excellent. And how might I find this oasis of pleasure?"

"I presume your carriage is in the drive?"

"It should be if it isn't at present," Saxton said. "My coachman had to deliver Miranda's things to Birch House."

"I'll give your coachman the direction." Fox planned to conveniently forget.

"Brilliant. I suppose I'm for more of Stratham's brandy then. He's got a damn fine cellar."

Because a displaced Frenchman in the next town over offered the brandy as a tribute, but let Saxton believe what he would. Fox had more pressing matters than calling out Stratham's illegal behavior.

Fox bowed stiffly and took himself off. Thank God Miranda's brother didn't follow. Fox raced through the entry hall and out into the drive to...where his carriage was no longer parked.

"Hell's teeth!"

A couple of coachmen who were standing nearby looked over at him. "What?"

"I need a horse." Fox muttered the words and then repeated them much louder. "I need a horse!"

"Stable's over there." One of the coachmen gestured around the side of the manor where the gravel drive disappeared from view.

Fox sprinted in the designated direction and immediately swore. There was a reason these shoes were called dancing slippers. They were woefully inadequate for running or even walking fast. The rocks of the drive dug into the soft soles. He felt every edge of the ground as he sped toward the light of the stables.

Once he reached his destination, he paused a moment to take stock. A young groom brushed a horse while several animals were stabled.

Fox looked in the direction of the tack room, but there wasn't time to saddle the beast. "Which is your fastest?"

"I beg your pardon, sir?" The carrot-topped lad stopped his work and gaped.

Fox tapped his hand against his thigh. "I have urgent need of a horse."

The groom turned slightly, his brush-shod hand poised over the horse's flank. "I suppose Gawain here's as fast as any." And as luck would have it, Gawain still had a bit in his mouth.

"Get the reins on, lad." Fox swung himself up before the groom even moved. "Quickly, then!"

The boy dropped the brush in a bucket and ran to the tack room. Rushing back with the reins, he fastened them just as Fox reached down and plucked the supple leather from his hands.

"Thank you!" Fox called as he took the horse into the night, urging him into a canter. Within moments, his face blistered with the cold air. Stratham Hall's grounds vanished beneath him as he drove the horse faster.

A scant quarter hour later, he turned up Polly's drive. Situated in a wooded parkland, the house sat completely isolated from any surrounding property and from the main road. He galloped to the front of the house and jumped from Gawain's back before the horse had come to a full stop. He tossed the reins to Barton, Polly's head groom.

Light leaked from the windows and shone against the man's bald pate. "'Evening there, Fox. Been quite awhile since we seen ye here."

Fox had no time for pleasantries. It was after eleven. If he didn't get Miranda out of there before her brother showed up, assuming he found directions...

Christ, it didn't bear thinking about. "I'm looking for a young blond woman who would have just arrived. Or for Polly and a girl she brought here. All of them, actually."

Barton let out a low whistle. "The blonde got here maybe ten minutes ago. Just took her landau—say, I thought it looked familiar, but you only brought it here the one time…" He rubbed his smooth head.

"And Polly?"

"Blonde was looking for her, too. She got here a bit ago, but I don't know if she had anyone with her. She took her coach to the rear door. Sorry, Fox. Try her office, maybe?"

"Thanks." Fox leapt up the steps and paused at the threshold, taking a moment to compose himself.

A footman in scarlet livery swept the door open. His expression seemed carved in stone, completely disinterested.

Fox moved into the empty foyer, expecting to see Miranda immediately, but instead saw no one save the doorman. Where could she be? Polly's office? Taking Barton's advice, he made his way upstairs to Polly's sitting room office.

Flickering candles illuminated the floral wallpaper of the corridor. Polly's office was to the left.

Suddenly a flash of green appeared at the end of the hallway. Fox took off at a dead run and grabbed Miranda by the elbow.

"You little fool! What the hell are you doing?"

Miranda tried to shake his grasp away. "Looking for Flora, of course. It's a good thing, too, since it took you so long to get here." Her aqua eyes flashed up at him.

Fox gripped her more firmly. "I might've come sooner if someone hadn't taken my transportation. Nonetheless, your earlier arrival seems to have benefited…nothing." He spat the last, anger overtaking every other emotion. "You need to get out of here. I'm putting you back in my landau, and you're going directly to Birch House."

"I'm not leaving without Flora." She planted her feet in the carpet. Fox pulled her arm, and she went sprawling against him.

He ignored the delicious sensation of her pressed against his chest and set her away. "I'll take care of Flora." Realizing the volume of his voice did nothing to disguise their presence, Fox took a deep breath to calm himself. "Can't you see this is no place for you?"

She glared at him, crossing her arms over her chest.

"I begin to understand why your family shipped you to the country, *and* why they are so desperate to marry you off. You're the most reckless, headstrong—"

Fox froze as he heard a click, like a door opening or closing. Moving quickly, he opened the nearest door and shoved Miranda inside. He stepped in after her and shut them in a room the size of a closet.

Candlelight shone from a small window cut into one wall. On the other side was another, much larger room. With a bed in the middle. On the bed...*holy shit*.

A woman sucking a man's cock.

Fox dared to look at Miranda. She stared straight ahead. At the couple on the bed. Pressed against her side, Fox realized they'd have more room if he stood behind her. He heard the distinct sound of footfalls outside the door, but after that he heard nothing save the sounds of sex and the deafening roar of his blood pounding from his head directly down to his hardening cock.

Sanity told him to flee, but desire kept him rooted to the floor. Miranda swayed back against him, and his mind completely shut down in favor of his body.

CHAPTER 14

*M*IRANDA couldn't believe what she was seeing. One of the scullery maids at Benfield had given her a verbal education about what occurred between men and women in the bedroom but hearing about the act didn't compare to seeing it.

The man knelt on the bed, in profile. Candles flickered around the room, throwing light on his bare, muscled chest. One of his hands tangled in the woman's dark blond hair. She kneeled also, but bent at the waist. Her mouth moved up and down over his shaft, her tongue darting out at intervals. At one point she laved the tip of his penis, and the man groaned. The woman's hips undulated, and he stroked his hand down her neck, splaying his fingers over her shoulder blade. He moved against her mouth, urging her to take his entire length.

Miranda heard their erratic breathing. Or was that hers?

The room was tiny, probably only intended for one person. As a result, Fox pressed against her back, his heat burning through her gown to scorch her flesh. She couldn't see his face, which only served to heighten her senses.

A hunger started in the pit of her belly, moved

lower. Desire dampened her thighs until she wanted to press her hand between her legs to appease the desperate need growing there.

The man on the bed guided the woman up until she faced him on her knees. He brushed her hair away from her breasts and ran his thumbs over her nipples. Miranda's hardened in response.

The woman cast her head back, her long, pale hair floating down her back, grazing her behind. He cupped her breasts, lifted them, blew on the rosy circles at their tips. Miranda felt as if she were sinking into a state of semi-consciousness. Her breasts swelled. She leaned back against Fox, seeking whatever surcease he might give her.

Fox slid his hands under her arms and skimmed them up her ribcage, settling them beneath her breasts.

Miranda took a slow, deep breath. Would he give her what she craved? What if they were caught?

The man on the bed licked the woman's breast. She moaned, her hands moving between her thighs.

Fox cupped Miranda, then moved his palms up over her aching nipples. She rested her head back against his chest, arching the column of her throat, but maintaining her view of the couple on the bed. Fox's breath rushed against her ear, the side of her face. The sound was deeply erotic.

The woman's breathing quickened as the man suckled first one breast and then the other. She thrust one hand into his crop of dark hair and held him close. He squeezed one of her nipples and she gasped, thrusting her chest forward in blatant offering.

Miranda pushed herself back against Fox more firmly. The steel of his arousal pressed against her lower back. Wicked thoughts came to her. How she could do to him what the woman on the bed had done to the man. Miranda need only turn and kneel…

The man on the bed spun the woman around, her

back to his chest. Now their position nearly mimicked Fox and Miranda's. But then the man pushed the woman down on all fours. Miranda's eyes widened.

Fox teased her nipples through her gown, then dipped one hand into her bodice and dove beneath her chemise. His bare hand caressed her flesh and she moaned softly as his fingers closed over her breast. Miranda swiveled her hips, pressing back against his shaft. He sucked in his breath and tugged at her nipple.

On the bed, the man caressed the flesh of the woman's behind, kneading her soft flesh. She whimpered softly as she pushed backward, seeking his touch. He ran his fingers along her inner thigh, and they disappeared inside her. She arched her neck and moaned loudly. She moved against his hand, slowly at first and then more quickly. Her breathing increased, as did her cries.

Fox continued to fondle Miranda's breast while his other hand slid down over her belly. His fingers came to rest over the apex of her thighs, and Miranda jerked against him. She had learned to bring herself to release, but she'd never ached with such desperation. Instead of a tentative act born from curiosity and rebellion, this was a visceral need, a primal craving only he could satisfy.

The woman on the bed cried out, her fingers twined in the bedclothes as she pulled the sheets loose from the mattress. Then the man drove into her from behind.

Miranda pushed herself into Fox's hand as he pressed his fingers between her thighs. His lips touched her neck and a small, simple word escaped her mouth, "Yes."

Soft crying burst the cocoon of their lovemaking. "I want to go home." Flora was in the corridor outside the door.

Fox's hands froze, and Miranda turned, pressing her back to the window. Muted light filtered in from behind her and she could just make out Fox's strained features. His breathing came fast, but deep. Her gaze dropped to the bulge in his pants and without thinking she reached out to touch it.

"Don't." He turned to the side, pushing himself against the wall so as not to touch her. He took several long breaths and after a moment, he opened the door.

Cool air rushed into the dark, overheated cabinet. Miranda's cheeks were as enflamed as every other part of her. She fanned herself with her hand before stepping out. Fox was already halfway down the hall. She closed the door behind her, shutting out the passionate sounds of lovemaking from the couple on the bed.

Flora and Mrs. Danforth were turning to go downstairs as Fox ran to catch up with them. Miranda hurried to hear the conversation, embarrassed that in her lust she'd all but forgotten about Flora. She hoped the girl was all right.

"Miranda!" Flora launched herself forward and threw her arms around Miranda's waist. She'd hugged more people tonight than in her entire adult life.

This did not include the embrace in the dark closet with Fox. God, she could *not* think about that right now.

Fox turned to look at Miranda. His eyes were flat, his features barren of emotion. "Take Flora back to Stipple's End."

Miranda nodded. "Yes, let's go." She took a step toward the stairs, keeping one arm around Flora.

Fox grabbed her arm and the contact nearly sent her to her knees. They might have walked away from the closet, but her body still reeled from the effects.

He dropped his hand and looked at Mrs. Danforth. "They need to leave by the back door."

"Yes, of course." Mrs. Danforth had the grace to look a bit ashen. Her lips were drawn. "Follow me." She led them to the servant stairs and then descended into a small room seemingly used for storing linens. Mrs. Danforth opened the door and checked the corridor before gesturing for them to continue.

They followed the hallway to an exterior door, which Mrs. Danforth opened and guided Miranda and Flora through before stepping out after them. "Jenks! Fetch Fox's—" She looked at Fox without completing the sentence.

"Landau." The single word came clipped and hard.

"Landau, and have the coachman take these girls to the orphanage, please."

Miranda spun on her heel in the damp earth. "Fox, aren't you coming with us?" Even as she asked the question, she knew he wasn't. He was going to stay here. With Polly Danforth. He and his lust were staying here.

His gaze threatened to freeze her to the very bone. He didn't move from the doorway. "Go, Miranda."

She clenched her teeth. At the sound of the wheels churning the ground behind her, she gave him a final glare and turned away. The coachman helped Flora and then her into the landau. Mrs. Danforth disappeared inside and the door closed before the vehicle pulled away.

Whereas on the journey from Stratham Hall, she'd been chilled, Miranda's flesh burned, especially where Fox had touched her. She wiped a hand over her brow.

Flora fidgeted beside her. "I'm so sorry, Lady Miranda. Mrs. Danforth has always been so kind to us. And when you said a courtesan had a nice life, I just imagined—"

"What?" Miranda stared at the girl.

Flora blinked. "You said courtesans lived comfortable lives. I'm going to have to leave Stipple's End next year. I've been thinking I could come to work here, like my friend Rose did."

Miranda took the girl's hands. "No! I didn't mean it

was a decent life, Flora. Not for you. Never for you."
Her heart raced. "Not for any of you girls."

"But I'll never be rich like you," Flora said softly, her
tears glistening in the meager light weaving through
the windows from the swaying lanterns. "You live such
a fairy tale."

Miranda dropped her hands and sat back, at a complete loss for speech. This girl knew nothing about Miranda's life. She'd told them about the things she did in
London, but if her life were such a fairy tale, why was
she nearly betrothed to a man she didn't love while
lusting after an impoverished gentleman who was even
now making love to somebody else?

Her hands shook. She laid them palm down on her
lap in an effort to keep them still. "Flora, a courtesan's
life is no fairy tale. Having nice things and attending
parties and balls and such nonsense does not make one
happy." She said these things because she believed they
were the right things to say to the girl, but there was a
truth she couldn't deny. Miranda had expected to be
miserable in Wootton Bassett. Had counted on it, in
fact. But when she'd tried to make the best of it, well,
she'd made the best of it.

Until she'd rather liked it.

In fact, she'd gone back to her old life and couldn't
wait to return here. She'd come to finish the task she'd
started with the benefit, to ensure her godfather and his
friends had a good time. But she'd missed these people.
And their silly little village.

Miranda closed her eyes. This was a disaster. Soon
her parents would find a suitable lord, and she'd be
forced to marry him. Even Jasper wouldn't be able to
help her.

Jasper!

Lord, where did he think she'd gone? Fox's anger
came back to her. She had been reckless. And stupid.
And perhaps compromised herself.

With him.

But no. No one had seen them together. Well, Flora and Mrs. Danforth had, but they didn't signify.

It was just as well. Compromise meant she would have to marry him, and she simply couldn't. She wouldn't put it past her parents to try to cover it up in order to prevent her from making such a ghastly mistake as marrying so far beneath her station.

Flora began to cry again.

Miranda patted the girl's hand. "Are you all right? Nothing happened to you there, did it?" She waited a breathless moment for the girl's response, irritated with herself for not ensuring the girl's welfare before wallowing in her own selfish thoughts.

She sniffled. "Nothing happened except that Mrs. Danforth didn't want me to leave her house."

"I'm certain she didn't." Miranda wished she'd pushed the woman down the stairs. Images of her making love to Fox like the couple on the bed scalded her brain. "How long has she known Fox?"

Flora shrugged. "She comes to the orphanage sometimes and gives us clothes or shoes. She was always so nice." Her tears fell in earnest.

Miranda put her arm around Flora and drew her close. How could Fox befriend such a woman? Well, chances are he more than befriended her. The idea of him paying that woman to have sex with him made Miranda's stomach pitch.

The landau stopped in the drive of Stipple's End and Miranda helped Flora from the coach. Mrs. Gates met them at the door. "I've just arrived, dearie." She wrapped her arms around Flora who now sobbed against Mrs. Gates's chest. "There, there, my girl. It's all right now." Mrs. Gates raised her gaze to Miranda. "I've some tea started in the kitchen, but I'm going to take Flora upstairs to my bedchamber. She doesn't need to sleep in the dormitory tonight."

The headmistress and Flora left as one, leaving Miranda alone in the great hall. The air seemed nearly as frigid as outside owing to the lack of a fire and the draft caused by the poorly patched hole in the corner.

She could have Fox's landau take her to Birch House. Or, she could go to the library where a fire usually burned. Her feet carried her toward the latter, despite the fact her mind continued to mull her options. Why stay? Fox likely wouldn't return. He'd be spending the night with that harlot.

Reason told her to go back to Birch House. But since reason had never been her forte, Miranda curled up in a chair by the fire and waited.

~

*F*OX leaned against the wall in Polly Danforth's corridor while he waited for his landau to leave and Polly to come back inside. Cold rage such as he'd never felt before threatened to consume him.

Finally, Polly's ebony head appeared in the doorway and she closed the door behind her, shutting them into the flickering half-light.

He cleared his throat. "Tell me you did not cultivate a relationship with me to recruit the girls at Stipple's End."

Her hand fluttered to her ruby-clad neck. Despite the dimness of the hallway, he could see the apprehension in her eyes. "*Relationship* is a rather strong word."

Fox slammed his fist against the wall. "Dammit, Polly! We were friends!" He couldn't bring himself to catalogue the history because he was afraid to look too closely. "Or was your kindness after Jane married Stratham a lie too?"

She stepped toward him, but he backed away. Anguish lined her tired face. A face he'd found pretty until tonight. "I'd like to think we're *still* friends."

His skin felt dirty. "And Rose coming to work for you was a coincidence?"

She flinched and then looked away, unable apparently to withstand his glare any longer. "When I visited you one day at Stipple's End, she talked to me. She knew who I was and—"

"And *what* you are." He let the insult hang between them.

Her eyes flashed. "Yes. I have no shame about that, Fox. I've done what I had to in order to survive. You do the same for your precious orphans."

Fury crested in his chest, made his lungs ache. "I don't prostitute myself."

Polly moved toward him, her hand set provocatively on her hip. "Can you honestly say you never slept with me hoping I might leave a donation?"

Her question stabbed straight into his gut. She'd befriended him after Jane had married Stratham, and a physical relationship had naturally bloomed. He'd never paid her for her favors. She'd given money and goods to the orphanage. He'd judged her a kind and caring woman. But at some level, had he expected her to repay his physical attention with charity for Stipple's End? As if *he* was the whore?

Refusing to answer that question, even in the darkness of his own mind, Fox pushed past her toward the door, intent on leaving. Mrs. Gates had been right about Polly all along. "I can see now our objectives were completely different." He put his hand on the knob, then spun on his heel to face her. "Your money— or anything else—is no longer needed at Stipple's End. You will cease all interaction with me or any of my charges."

Her lips quirked up. "You can't stop them from coming here."

He squeezed the doorknob as though he might tear it from the wood. "I just did."

"If she wants to badly enough, she'll come back."

Fox shook his head. "She won't. Want to, that is. Miranda will see to it."

Polly tapped a painted fingernail against her chin. "'Miranda'? What makes you so certain?" Her voice dipped. "Or is she your lover now?"

Fox released the door. "Certainly not, she's a lady." His body quickened. Miranda might not be his lover, but God, how he wanted her to be. "She cares for those girls. Genuinely cares."

Polly arched a shoulder. "The way Flora told it, your precious Miranda encouraged her to seek my way of life. Said the girl could do quite well for herself as a courtesan in London. You claim to have been wrong about me, what makes you think you aren't wrong about her?"

He couldn't believe Miranda would do such a thing. She wasn't that careless.

Doubt laced through his mind, but he shook his head. He couldn't be wrong about Miranda. She'd rushed back to Wootton Bassett tonight when she didn't have to. And it certainly hadn't been for him. She had to have come back for the children.

Emotion darkened his voice. "I'm not wrong about her." Fox pivoted and opened the door. The cool night air provided a welcome balm to his heated flesh, but he detected dampness. Rain threatened.

He went to the post where he'd tied Gawain. Stratham would have to do without his horse for the remainder of the night.

Once astride, Fox pointed the animal toward Stipple's End. He started out fast, but slowed his pace. Why hurry? After depositing Flora at the orphanage, Miranda would have continued to Birch House. At least she would if she had any sense.

Which meant she'd be at Stipple's End waiting for him.

It was just as well for he'd several things he wanted to say to her. First and most importantly: *go away*. She'd all but turned him down *again* during the waltz—after staring at him with barely concealed lust—and then she'd driven him to complete sexual frustration. She was going to kill him.

Which meant she had to go.

Fox's landau stood in the drive at Stipple's End when he arrived. He asked the coachman to take care of Gawain and then turned to the manor. Entering the great hall, he noted the chill, but continued toward the library, certain she waited there.

Light spilled from the open doorway into the corridor. Fox paused at the threshold, scanning the room. She sat tucked into the green wingback chair by the fire —the one he'd been sitting in when she'd happened upon him here the night of the assembly. Her head rested against the side and her chest rose and fell with the gentle breath of sleep.

He wanted to move closer, but didn't dare. She was a vision. Her golden hair framed her face, so perfect in sleep. Too perfect. It lacked the animation and passion that made Miranda, well, Miranda.

But he couldn't let her sleep there. He stepped into the room. A floorboard creaked and her eyes opened. Blinking, she rolled her shoulders back and brought her feet out from under her. She looked up at him and froze. The beauty of her face twisted as she jumped out of the chair.

"How could you befriend a woman like that?"

Fox nearly staggered backward at the ferocity of her anger. In response, his own fury rose anew after cooling almost completely during his ride and upon finding her sleeping so peacefully. So innocently. Hah.

"How could you go charging off to a brothel? Good

God, Miranda, did you know your brother is planning to go there tonight? What if he'd seen you there?" Fox knew he shouldn't discuss such things with her, but he wanted her to understand the foolishness of her actions.

She blanched. "I was merely trying to rescue Flora."

"Which I would have done." In retrospect, he should have sent Miranda and Lisette to find Mrs. Gates while he raced off to Polly's, but he couldn't change what had happened. "Do you ever think of the consequences of your actions?"

She didn't answer for a moment. Fox wanted to roll his eyes. *Now*, she took the time to think. "Fine, I shouldn't have gone."

Fox momentarily deflated. He had been so sure she would argue with him.

It was a brief respite. The virago reared her head once more with hands on her hips and aqua eyes flashing. "But those girls see *that woman* as your friend. Or more than your friend. They feel comfortable with her, and Flora was ready to entrust her entire future to her. A future as a…a *harlot*."

Fox ground his teeth. His words came out like a growl. "Polly said you'd encouraged her, that Flora acted on your suggestion." He could still scarcely believe this was true.

Miranda took a deep breath. She fidgeted with the sides of her dress. Her nostrils flared. "I may not have appropriately discounted the potential of life as a London courtesan."

Fox lunged forward. "What?"

She took a step back, her eyes wide. "Flora told me about her friend Rose and how she'd made a nice place for herself in London at a brothel. I only told the girls they needn't consider such a life. I never imagined Flora was serious about it. Things are so different here. Any young girl in London would have known better."

Did she not realize these girls idolized her? "You aren't in London!"

"I'm quite aware of that fact, thank you!"

They stood there glaring at each other for a moment. She didn't flinch, and neither did he.

"You never answered my question about Mrs. Danforth. How can you befriend someone like her, allow her access to the girls?"

He lowered his voice, but his fury did not diminish. "I don't have to explain myself to you."

At length, she huffed. "I suppose you don't. I believed we were friends and knowing you share a relationship with her...well, it bothers me." She crossed her arms over her chest.

Fox sputtered. "You're jealous? You've no right to be, not when you could easily have had me."

She dropped her arms. "I did want you. At the brothel."

He laughed, but it was as hollow as his storeroom in January. "For a tup." He watched her face register his coarse language, her eyes widening, the subtle parting of her delicious lips. "I want more than that. If you do too, I'm right here."

With her fists clenched at her sides and her eyes blazing in the firelight, she was more stunning than he'd ever seen her. He could feel her anger, her doubt, her confusion, her desire. He willed his body to stay cold, not warm to her passion, to her very presence.

"My father will never let me choose you. Your station is unacceptable enough, but knowing you keep time with the local bawdy house owner further demeans your credibility."

"*My credibility*? Every nobleman I've ever known has a mistress—and often a wife at home. Even now your brother is enjoying the very bawdy house *you* just came from. Next to you and your kind, I'm positively sedate. With your reputation and penchant for reckless behavior, any man who marries you will likely regret doing so."

She flung an arm out as her features deepened with anger once more. "So you don't deny she's your mistress?"

Fox could scarcely credit her question. "After everything I just said, this is what you fixate on?"

She recrossed her arms over her chest. Her cheeks were flushed, and he could practically see steam rising from the top of her head. "I'm leaving after Lord Norris's party."

"Good." He said the word, but every emotion behind it was the complete opposite. He reached for her, intending to finish what they'd started. He couldn't let her go like this—

"Did I hear yelling?" Beatrice walked into the library and Fox swung around.

Fox wanted to push Beatrice back out of the room so he could put Miranda in a position from which she couldn't deny him. A position like the one they'd shared at the brothel. "No."

"Oh." Beatrice looked at Miranda. "Are you ready to leave?"

Miranda dropped her arms to her sides. Gone was any hint of their emotional exchange. "What are you doing here, Beatrice? The party hasn't concluded, has it?" She looked stricken, as if it would be a horrible crime for the party to be over when the clock hadn't yet chimed one.

"No, my parents made me leave." She rolled her eyes. "It wasn't well done of them because we hadn't completed the auction accounting. Since Mrs. Gates and Fox had already left, there is no one there to finish save Mrs. Knott, and I do believe she and Mr. Knott are having far too much fun at the party to conclude the business. Your brother said you'd come here with a sick child and asked if we'd fetch you to Birch House. Very conscionable of him."

Miranda glanced at Fox. He quirked a brow at her. She seemed a bit surprised, or maybe she was thankful, that Fox had covered for her with Jasper. "Mrs. Gates is here to care for Flora, so I suppose I can leave. Still, perhaps we'd better return to Stratham Hall to finish up."

Fox cleared his throat. "I'll see to it." He needed to return Stratham's horse anyway. Furthermore, he was suddenly nervous about no one overseeing the accounting besides Rob and his wife.

Miranda's shoulders slumped. "Thank you, Fox. Let's go then, Beatrice."

Beatrice nodded. "Good night, Fox." She turned to Miranda as they fell into step beside each other walking out of the library. "It was a splendid evening even if I did have to leave early."

Miranda glanced back over her shoulder. She looked at him as she'd done during their waltz. As if she wanted to devour him. As if she simply wanted *him*. Regret pierced his heart, and he turned away.

He stared into the orange flames of the fire for longer than he knew. When he finally moved, his neck ached. He rolled his shoulders to relax his muscles.

He needed to get back to Stratham Hall. At least the night hadn't been a complete disaster. Now he could fix the roof and pay for a myriad of other necessary things. And he could finally use his own money for Bassett Manor. Clinging to the positive, he turned to go.

A loud crash sounded from the great hall and he sprinted into the corridor. Immediately he felt the cold air rushing toward him and smelled the moisture. The rain had come.

And it fell in bucketfuls, directly into the hall through a brand new gaping hole in the roof.

CHAPTER 15

*M*RS. Gates flew down the stairs and rushed into the great hall. "Good heavens, Fox! The roof!"

Fox stared, speechless, at the dark night sky bleeding rain all over the already ruined wood floor. The barrel sat useless, catching only a portion of the torrent.

Mrs. Gates halted beside him and shivered. "What are we to do?"

Fox pushed his shock away. "I'll have to hire architects and carpenters."

She glanced at the floor, shaking her head. "Oh, Fox, it never ends. I suppose we'll need to replace more than just the roof."

Yes, this would be far more expensive than the original repair. It was a damned good thing they'd had the benefit. His anxiety over the money returned. He should've been there to count it and take it away. Instead, he'd been chasing Miranda all over hell and yonder.

He frowned, worried the proceeds were still at Stratham Hall. He needed to get the money right away, not only to determine how much they'd made but also to ensure its safekeeping. "I'm going back to Stratham

Hall to get the money from the benefit. In the meantime, keep the children in their dormitories and close every room up to try and keep the cold out. Tomorrow we'll start moving everyone to Bassett Manor."

Mrs. Gates gaped at him. "You want us to live in your home? Fox, you need your privacy. You already do far too much."

No, he hadn't done enough. He should've moved them all to Bassett Manor back in June. "It's the only solution until Stipple's End is repaired. I can't leave you and the children to live like this. It will take time to move everything, but we'll manage."

Mrs. Gates nodded, and Fox took his leave. Outside, he instructed the coachman to fetch Gawain and tie him to the landau for the drive back to Stratham Hall.

Rain, steady and monotonous, drove against the vehicle as it clambered toward its destination. The ride jostled him mercilessly, but the ancient springs had no hope of replacement.

Dammit. He'd expected to finally get ahead after this benefit. Stow money in the coffers instead of trying to stretch each penny past its worth. But tonight he'd been very close to getting his money another way—if he'd stayed in the brothel a little longer with Miranda, perhaps her brother would have arrived and they'd be betrothed even now. Then he'd never have to worry about money again.

Why did he keep coming back to compromising her into marrying him? Rob had suggested it months ago, after she'd first arrived. There were any number of times he could've done it. In fact, he had done it—as the highwayman. Hell, even as Fox. Their private waltz the night of the assembly last summer might have been enough to send them to the vicar.

So why didn't he just do it? After all, he wanted to marry her. He allowed his mind a moment's luxury while he thought of her body pressed against his. And then her repeated refusals intruded, shattering the illusion. Even though she admitted to wanting him physically, she'd made it clear he wasn't worthy of her hand in marriage, and never would be. *That* was why he didn't compromise her. What kind of life would they have with that between them? His pride demanded that she choose him.

He didn't want to think about her anymore. He'd tried to let her go, and she kept falling back into his lap. But soon she'd be gone for good. He needed to focus on Stipple's End. He'd always focused on Stipple's End. Why was it so difficult now? No need to answer that. He'd already decided not to think about her anymore.

Finally, the landau pulled up Stratham's drive. Though thinned, a group of coaches still awaited their occupants. Light shone from the elegant manor, and as Fox stepped onto the gravel, the revelry coming from inside washed over him, making him feel more alone than he already did.

But he had no desire to join the party. He wanted the money and nothing else. In fact, he would've preferred to wait outside while someone brought it to him. With a weary sigh, he climbed the steps, rain dampening his hair and his new clothes. Too bad he couldn't have worn his highwayman's cloak. Made from thick wool it provided warmth, and more importantly, covered him from head to boot, er, slipper. Fox glanced down, realizing his shoes had been horribly abused tonight. They were likely ruined, but he couldn't do anything about it now. Dancing shoe replacement was just about dead last on his list of needs.

The door opened wide and Fox stepped around a couple who were taking their leave. He made his way to the Gold Room. Devoid of people, it contained several packaged auctioned items, though not all. Presumably, some had been taken already. A quick perusal did not reveal the money.

Stratham sauntered into the Gold Room. "I was informed you'd returned. Come to drink more of my brandy?"

Fox barely had patience for the man while in the best of moods, but now, he restrained himself from outright knocking him down. "I'm here to pick up the money. Where is it?"

Stratham clapped his hands together. "I've put it in my study. I'll just go and get it. He crossed the room, but turned back before continuing. "Aren't you coming?"

"I didn't realize I was invited." Fox didn't really want to go along, but the sooner he got the money, the sooner he could leave. He trailed Stratham to a corner of the house. A low fire burned in a massive fireplace decorated with gold-flecked Italian marble. A huge, gilded mirror hung over the mantel—probably so Stratham could see himself while he counted his ill-gotten fortune.

Likely because of his black mood, Fox couldn't control his anger. "So this is the heart of our district's corruption?"

Stratham turned on his heel. Candles and firelight brightened the room enough for Fox to see the diminutive man's nostrils flare. "You keep throwing accusations about, but have you any evidence?" When Fox said nothing—what could he say, *Yes, I stole your tribute money?*—Stratham went on. "I didn't think so. You'd do best to keep your mouth shut, lest someone close it for you."

Fox allowed his anger to win out and advanced on his foe. "Don't threaten me unless you can see it through."

Stratham blinked and stumbled backward. He unlocked a drawer in his desk and withdrew a wooden box. He thrust it at Fox. "Here. This is the last time I do you any favors."

Fox took the box. He wanted to clobber Stratham over the head with it. "You think tonight a favor to *me*? This was for a group of children who have no family. No money. No prospects. A group of children who, without Stipple's End, would be in workhouses, or worse. Have you no concern at all?" Fox had always seen people like Stratham as going about their lives without thinking of the world around them. But now he realized Stratham likely did contemplate such matters and that he simply didn't care.

Stratham rested a hand on his hip and said nothing. Really, what could he say? Fox opened the box. There appeared to be a lot of money inside, but he had no idea how much there ought to be. "Where is the accounting sheet?"

"That other woman has it." Stratham waved a hand. "Tall, sturdy—married to your steward."

Fox's fingers curled around the box, gripping it tightly. "Mrs. Knott is her name. Are the Knotts still here?"

"No idea. As the host, I can't be expected to monitor the comings and goings of your employees." Stratham gestured toward the door. "I think our business is concluded."

Fox hefted the box in his hands. "I want to count this. You go ahead."

Stratham shifted his weight and fidgeted with a button on his coat. "No, not in here. Take it back to the Gold Room."

Fox arched a brow. "What's this? Afraid I might search your desk and find something incriminating?"

Stratham inhaled audibly, and his color deepened. He opened his mouth, but nothing came out.

While it was satisfying to bait the man, Fox didn't have time for it just now. "Fine. I'm going."

He made his way back to the Gold Room and looked around for an accounting sheet. It was too much to hope they'd just left it lying around, but without it, counting the money would be somewhat pointless. Nevertheless, Fox sat down and counted the bills and coins. It amounted to an impressive sum, but not quite what he expected. Had Stratham lightened the purse? Fox couldn't know if they were missing funds without the ledger. He'd been far more drawn to Miranda's neckline than how much money the auction had been making.

Since he didn't want to go looking for Rob and his wife in the ballroom, Fox opted to quit the manor altogether. He'd see Rob in the morning, and then they could figure this out. In the meantime, he'd go home.

Alone. He always went home alone, but tonight it was lonelier than usual.

~

*M*IRANDA'S trunk waited in her cupboard-sized room when she arrived at Birch House. She'd almost forgotten how small and dingy everything appeared here after spending the last several days in her grand chamber at Wokingham.

She stood in the center of the room and...did nothing. Her mind could barely sort through everything that had happened. Remembering the book she'd promised Beatrice, she threw open the trunk and shuffled through her belongings until her fingers closed around the spine.

With quiet feet, she picked her way to Beatrice's room at the other end of the house, stepping particularly lightly as she passed Mr. and Mrs. Carmody's door. She rapped softly once she reached her destination.

"Who's there?" Beatrice called from the interior.

"It's Miranda."

Beatrice opened the door, already wearing her

nightclothes. Her gaze dropped to the book in Miranda's hand.

"I've brought you *Emma*." Miranda held it out to Beatrice.

"Come in." Beatrice tugged her by the wrist into the room. She grabbed the book and ran her palm reverently over the crisp new cover. Sitting on the edge of her bed, she opened the tome and began to read the first page.

Miranda glanced around the chamber, nearly twice as large as Miranda's room, but just as sparsely furnished. Even so, Miranda noted, rather enviously, Beatrice's bed was much bigger and appeared infinitely more comfortable.

Beatrice looked to be already engrossed in the novel, but Miranda didn't want to be alone just yet.

She sat on the bed next to Beatrice. "How long have you been sneaking novels?"

Beatrice glanced up from the page. "Since I started working at the orphanage. I read all of the ones in Stipple's End's library before I began ordering them with my pin money."

"The day we went to town with Fox, you were picking up a novel?"

She blushed. "Yes."

Miranda chuckled. "And here I fancied you were as proper as they came."

Beatrice arched a brow. "I wouldn't say I'm as scandalous as you. Sneaking novels under my father's nose is hardly gadding about with inappropriate people or kissing highwaymen."

Miranda exhaled loudly. "True." She rested her hands palm-down on the lacy coverlet. She almost told Beatrice about the situation with Flora. The words formed in her brain, but she couldn't bring herself to share her foolishness.

"I have to say something." Beatrice turned her head.

Her brow scrunched up and her lips twisted as if speaking took great effort. "Thank you for organizing the benefit. You've done a wonderful thing for the orphanage. Everything you've done has been...well, you've made a good impression with the children."

No one ever thanked Miranda. She wasn't comfortable with the praise, not now when she'd almost led poor Flora to unequivocal disaster. Emotion bubbled up and Miranda only hoped Beatrice couldn't see or hear her exaggerated swallow. "You've done a lot too, Beatrice. And the benefit wouldn't have happened without you."

Beatrice's face sparked with life as her lips curved into a smile. "I've never felt so needed. People never paid attention to me before. Did you know Mr. Stratham danced with me tonight? Twice."

Miranda rocked back on the bed and gave a delighted cry. Beatrice raised her finger to her lips, and Miranda straightened. "How wonderful, Beatrice. It means he's interested. At least it does in London. I daresay he'll be taking you for a drive soon."

"Do you think so?" Her dark eyes glistened with excitement.

"Indeed. But, Beatrice, are you sure? Is Stratham someone you want?" Miranda recalled what Fox had said about him, that he'd been a willing party to corruption.

"I believe so." She nodded. "Yes, he is. Do you know, my parents will be shocked if he courts me."

"Well, then for that reason alone, I hope he proposes!" Miranda laughed, but stopped when she saw Beatrice gaped at her. "I'm sorry. Sometimes I speak before realizing I've said something very likely inappropriate."

Beatrice sighed. "I wish I could do that."

Miranda sobered. "No, you don't." It can be hurtful —both to others and yourself, she added silently. "You're better off as you are."

Beatrice's brow furrowed. "Why, you sound regretful. Has something happened?"

Again the words explaining the disaster with Flora came together in her brain but got lost on the way to her mouth. "No, I imagine I'm just a little sad to be leaving soon."

"And I believe I'll actually miss you. I'm sorry I was so awful about the benefit. It's just I've never received such attention before. I...liked it."

Maybe it was all the hugging from earlier, but Miranda wanted to embrace Beatrice. Tentatively, she put her arm on Beatrice's shoulder, but when Beatrice gave her a quizzical look, she settled for a gentle pat.

Miranda stood. "Well, good night, then."

"Good night, Miranda. You truly did do a good thing. Everyone is going to miss you."

With a nod, Miranda left and made her way back to her room. Her good deed had been canceled out by the mistake she'd made with Flora, but maybe she could fix that too. She could help Flora be something other than a courtesan. Before Miranda left Wootton Bassett, she'd ensure Flora's talents were put to the best possible use.

As she climbed into bed a short time later, Miranda's stomach tossed with uneasiness. Was she still upset about Flora? No, she had a plan. Was it because she would be leaving soon? No, because she'd been trying to leave for months. But even as she thought it, her skin crawled. What did she have to look forward to, besides a husband her father would choose for her?

She pulled the bedclothes tight around her body, burrowing into their softness. Sleep, she needed sleep. But when she closed her eyes, the memory of Fox's hands on her body assailed her.

A long, long time later, slumber finally soothed her aching spirit.

～

OX tapped his fingers against the top of the desk in the office at Stipple's End. Rob was late, but then the rain affected everything—even a short jaunt from Rob's house to the orphanage. It had continued to fall in earnest all night and into the morning. The great hall was wet and cold. Despite keeping the rest of the manor closed off, the damp chill permeated everywhere he went in the building.

He paused and looked at Mrs. Gates, seated in a wooden chair near the window. They'd already decided to delay moving to Bassett Manor until a relatively dry day. Hell, he'd settle for something less than a torrential downpour. "Perhaps we should hang my old tapestries at the top of the stairs to better guard the second floor from the elements."

The water sluicing against the window above Mrs. Gates's head threw mottled shadows onto her white bonnet as she nodded. "An excellent notion, Fox. The upstairs hallway is quite cold."

"But you passed an acceptable night?" Fox had tossed and turned in his own bed, concerned about the inhabitants of Stipple's End.

Mrs. Gates twisted her hands in her lap. "Yes, though I'm worried about the money from last night. We hadn't completed the accounting when I left, but there ought to be more money. Lord Norris should have paid half what you have in that box for the tapestries alone."

Fox leaned back in his chair. Precisely as he'd suspected. Either Norris hadn't paid—the louse—or Stratham had taken some for himself. Of all the things Fox regretted about last night, not being there to oversee the accounting was at the top of his list.

Rob came in and handed a book to Fox. His brows gathered over his eyes, creating a rather dire expression. "Here's the accounting. You're not going to like it."

Fox flipped open the ledger and found the page he sought. He perused the entries and frowned. "Everything here is checked off except the tapestries. Does that mean everyone paid except Norris?" He handed the book to Mrs. Gates.

She studied the numbers and nodded. "He hadn't paid when I left, and it looks as if Mrs. Knott continued my technique of noting the payments."

Rob stood next to the desk. "Mrs. Knott said Norris didn't pay. She considered asking him to do so, but didn't know how to approach him." He shot Fox an anxious glance. "We thought you were going to be there."

Fox clenched his hands together and swallowed his frustration. Damn Miranda and her recklessness. "I meant to be there, but there was a…problem. I apologize for leaving Mrs. Knott in a terrible position." Of course someone like her couldn't address a pompous, self-absorbed criminal like the Earl of Norris. Fox ran a hand through his hair. "Thank you, Mrs. Gates. We'll handle it from here."

Mrs. Gates replaced the open ledger on the desk in front of Fox. "I'm so sorry, Fox. I shouldn't have left with Lisette."

"No, you wouldn't have been able to get the money out of Norris, either." Fox was the one who shouldn't have left.

Mrs. Gates exited, closing the door behind her. Rob leaned against the wall and crossed his arms over his chest. "What do you mean to do?"

Fox rested his forehead on his palm and stared down at the accounting book. Why did everything have to be so goddamned difficult? "Go to Cosgrove and get the money."

"You think he'll give it freely? After he didn't pay you last year?"

Fox dropped his hand and looked up at Rob. "I'm

hoping, perhaps foolishly, since he actually took possession of these tapestries, he'll pay for them."

Rob arched a brow. "And if he doesn't?"

"You've seen the damage to the hall, Rob. You and I can't fix this. We need to hire a carpenter. Plus, we need to repair the interior now as well." He slammed the ledger shut and shoved it to the edge of the desk. "We never seem to get anywhere!"

Rob stood straight. "I'll take care of contacting some folks about the repairs. You've got enough blunt to move forward on that at least, right?"

Fox glowered at the far wall, his hands fisted on the arms of his chair. "Move forward, yes. Complete it? Not bloody likely." Never mind the other thousand things he needed to do with the money Norris hadn't paid them.

"You're in a right dither over this, Fox. Something else eating at you?"

Fox stared up at his steward. "The potential ruin of this orphanage, not to mention my tenants, my servants —hell, *me*—that's not enough?"

Color rose up Rob's neck. "Aye, it's plenty. I've just never seen you quite so worked up."

Fox pushed out of his chair, crashing it into the wall behind him. "I'm for Cosgrove to bleed that prick of what he owes us."

Rob stepped aside as Fox strode to the door. "I'd wish you luck, but I don't think it'll matter."

Frustratingly, Rob was probably right.

A half hour later, Fox stood in a large sitting room at Cosgrove decorated in the Chinese style. Colorful vases from the Far East adorned every available tabletop. Two swords marked with Chinese characters crossed each other over the fireplace. Rich tapestries embroidered with black-haired, almond-eyed people decorated two walls.

Before he could further catalogue the richness of

the antiquities, Norris ambled into the room. His lavender waistcoat nearly screamed with the effort to encase the man's massive gut. He seemed more corpulent every time Fox saw him.

"Good afternoon, Fox. Twice in two days. I haven't seen you this much in the past half-year." Norris dropped himself into a gold chair, eliciting a creak from the aggrieved piece of furniture.

Fox sat on a sky blue settee opposite Norris. He'd do best not to put the bounder on the defensive from the beginning. "I wanted to thank you for your support at the benefit. You've no idea what your generosity means to the orphans. Or to me personally." The last words were uttered at great cost. Fox would rather have choked on them.

Norris waved at the maid who entered with a tea tray. She placed it on a low table in front of the earl. He gave her a brief glance. "You'll need to pour."

Fox didn't think the instruction necessary. Norris likely couldn't lean forward to put on his own shoes.

The maid poured out and handed Norris a cup. He winked up at her, and Fox felt a moment's revulsion on the poor woman's behalf.

Norris sipped his tea. "Very kind of you to pay a personal visit."

Fox took a drink of his own tea, mostly to school his emotions. He needed to tread carefully. "I also came to collect the payment for the tapestries you purchased. They're lovely specimens, and I'm certain you've already decided where to display them."

Norris tipped his head to the side. "Indeed I have. But I assure you I already paid for them. Cost me a pretty penny too."

Fox clenched the saucer in his hand and then put the delicate piece on the table lest he shatter it. "Perhaps there has been a mistake. Did you pay for it yourself? Neither Mrs. Gates nor Mrs. Knott recalls you paying for them. Yet you took them with you last night, did you not?"

"I certainly did. Couldn't wait to get them home. But do not forget yourself, Fox. They've been paid for." Norris's fish-shaped eyes hardened into coal. He chuckled then. "Surely you wouldn't rely on the word of a headmistress at an orphanage and the wife of a common steward over my own?"

He found the man's arrogance infuriating. But what could Fox do? If he said Norris hadn't paid for them, the earl would say he did. And unfortunately he was right: an earl trumped any woman, especially those as low-born as Mrs. Gates and Mrs. Knott.

Fox willed himself to smile. "Where do you plan to hang the tapestries?"

"They're being hung right now. I'll show you, if you like." He beamed as he lumbered to his feet, the jowls of his cheeks shimmying with his movement.

"Lead the way." Fox trailed the earl from the room, mentally noting everything he saw. Unlike Stratham Hall, Cosgrove was well organized and Fox easily committed its layout to memory.

Norris slowed, his breathing labored. "I get a bit winded now and again. They're just up here, past my office."

Fox nodded, a small smile playing about his lips. He didn't give a fig where he stuck the damned tapestries, only where the son-of-a-bitch kept his money and his records.

∽

*T*HE luncheon of mutton and boiled potatoes sat like lead in Miranda's belly. Her anxiety was less about the food and more the horror of finding the roof had fallen in. And seeing Fox after last night's argument—not to mention their tryst in the closet. She tried to focus on her embroidery, but even in the best of circumstances, her skills were lacking. Laughable, really, that she meant to "teach" the girls something at which she enjoyed so little facility.

The dreary weather only compounded her glum mood, but at least it had provided a reason for her to stay. With the heavy rain, she'd easily convinced Jasper they should postpone their return journey to Wokingham.

Rain streaked along the windows of the library at Stipple's End and the gray sky required them to work their needles by candlelight. She glanced over at Flora who methodically plunged her needle into the linen, creating a beautiful cross pattern. The girl seemed remarkably calm and comfortable after last night's near-disaster.

Jasper strolled into the library. Miranda promptly stuck her needle into her finger. Tossing the square of linen into the basket at her feet, she gave up the pretense of embroidery altogether. "Good afternoon, Jasper." To a one, the girls arrested and stared at her handsome brother. "Jasper, these are my girls. Girls, this is my brother, Lord Saxton."

He bowed to the room at large and offered a hearty grin. "So this is how my sister spends her days? How fortunate for all of you to have the wealth of her knowledge." He stepped toward the closest girl—Delia —and peered down at her needlework. "Although, I can already see your embroidery skills have surpassed Miranda's."

Miranda stood. "Yes, every single one of them is better than I."

"Have you taught them how to paint? Or did you decide not to even bother?" He glanced around at his captivated audience. "As bad as she is with a needle, she's even worse with a paintbrush."

Miranda rolled her eyes. "Do you see what I have to

put up with in London? Perhaps I'll just stay here in Wootton Bassett."

Lisette dropped her needle. "Really?" She turned to Delia. "I told you she'd stay!"

Delia frowned. "Don't be silly. People like Lady Miranda don't live in places like Wootton Bassett. Perhaps Lord Saxton has come to fetch her home."

Jasper arched a brow at his sister. "Actually, I have come to fetch her home—to Birch House, that is. We'll be leaving as soon as this rain lets up."

Miranda gave her brother a sharp glare. She hadn't told the girls when she would be going. Lisette still looked at her with wide, sad eyes. Unable to bear her scrutiny another moment, Miranda turned her back and whispered to Jasper, "What are you really doing here?"

He leaned in and adopted a hushed tone. "Why so suspicious? I wanted to see you at work. I admit I'm a bit shocked. This place is a shambles. How long has the roof been caved in?"

"It just happened last night, but it's been leaking intermittently all summer."

"And it hasn't been repaired before now?" Jasper shook his head.

Miranda bristled. "Fox and everyone else work very hard to keep Stipple's End in order. It's been a difficult year with the weather. And the harvest is devastatingly poor. We planned the benefit in order to raise money to fix the roof."

"Well, I hope you made a lot of money. That looks to be an expensive repair." He straightened. "Are you ready to leave now or do you need to botch some more of whatever you were working on?" He finished with a light-hearted wink, but his cavalier attitude irritated her.

She glanced at the clock. Their lesson had ended anyway. "Girls, this concludes our time today. I'll see you tomorrow." She had every intention of remaining in Wootton Bassett for Lord Norris's party, and if the rain didn't continue, she'd simply convince Jasper she needed to spend more time with Lord Septon. Surely their parents wouldn't fault her for that.

Taking Jasper by the arm, she dragged him toward the door. He bowed to the orphans before following her into the corridor. Frigid air greeted them and wrapped its icy tendrils around her bare fingers and neck.

She went to retrieve her bonnet and spencer from the hall, but remembered she'd left them in the dining room in order to keep them out of the cold of the great hall. "I'll just be a moment."

Leaving the dining room, she stopped short when Fox intersected her path. He looked completely different today, garbed once more in his work-aged clothing, his brown hair slightly tousled. Nevertheless, Miranda found him as attractive as he'd been the night before. Perhaps more so, which made no sense to her.

He studied her from head to boot, seeming to assess her appearance just as she'd done to him. "You're still here. I thought your lesson concluded."

"It is. I'm just leaving." Neither of them moved. "I'm sorry about the roof. It's fortunate we had the benefit last night. Will you be able to fix it soon?"

He flinched. Had she said something wrong? She probably shouldn't have asked about the repair. She knew he did his best to keep things together, but he couldn't mask his sensitivity about Stipple's End. Maybe he'd spent an awful night like she had. Had he recalled their interlude at the brothel, their argument afterward?

She smiled even though her mind and body threatened to split in two. "I'm sure you'll have everything back to normal very quickly. They're lucky to have you." She searched his half-turned face for any hint of emotion.

"You should go." His voice sounded deep, dark, as if he'd swallowed gravel.

Her heart clenched and she grabbed his hand though her brain screamed for her not to. "Fox, I'm so sorry about last night. If I could change things—"

He clasped her fingers in a fierce grip and pierced her with a furious glare. "You can't. Thanks to you and your recklessness, we didn't collect Norris's payment and now we're short."

Miranda gasped. "What happened?"

His lip curled, showing her a Fox she'd never seen before. "I wasn't there to oversee the accounting and now Norris claims he paid, though Mrs. Knott assures me he did not. It's his word against hers."

Her knees felt weak as dread curled through her body. "It's all my fault—"

At the sound of Jasper's throat clearing, Miranda dropped Fox's hand as if it had sprouted thorns. Fox pivoted toward Jasper and offered a slight nod.

Jasper came further into the hallway. "Good afternoon, Mr. Foxcroft. Looks like you've got your hands full here. Damned noble of you to look after these poor souls."

Fox's hand fisted against his thigh. "Yes, well, they're my responsibility, and I take it very seriously. Now, if you'll excuse me. As you said, I have my hands full." He walked away without looking at Miranda, without saying goodbye.

Jasper helped Miranda into her spencer. "Glad I'm not in his place. Can you imagine having to see to all of this? Plus he has his own estate—and it's no small thing from what I hear."

With shaky hands, Miranda tied her bonnet beneath her chin and took her brother's arm. She focused on speaking calmly instead of giving in to the chaos of her thoughts. "I've never been to Bassett Manor. I've no idea of its size."

Jasper led her outside and handed her into the carriage. "Well, let's pray it's an improvement over this. Better him than me to worry about such things as faulty buildings and dirty orphans." He gave a pitying glance at Stipple's End before climbing into the carriage. He settled back against the plush, royal blue velvet squab while the footman closed the door.

"Jasper, they're not dirty! They're well cared for! Indeed, I should hope other orphanages are run so well, but I'm confident they are not." No, even if they had far more resources than Stipple's End, Miranda felt certain no one ran an institution as successfully as Fox. The children were safe, learned, and happy. She frowned at her brother. "You should hear yourself."

Jasper pinned her with an icy stare, reminding her far too much of their father. "You should hear *yourself*. You are quite changed. Defending orphans, exhibiting great concern, planning a benefit." He laid his palms on the cushion on either side of him as the coach pulled forward. "I'd suggest you don't need to continue working there while we're stuck, but I daresay you wouldn't hear of it. And if I hadn't seen evidence of your obvious care for the girls, I might think you desired to stay here for Foxcroft."

Miranda's pulse quickened. "Don't be absurd. I've no interest in Mr. Foxcroft."

He cocked his head. "Indeed? It seemed you two were sharing some sort of intimacy when I walked into the hallway."

Intimacy? Surely nothing so personal. Nothing like they'd shared at the brothel. Her flesh began to heat and she took a deep breath. "Aren't you a Meddlesome Mary? I was merely demonstrating my concern about the roof. What would I see in a country bumpkin like him?"

His arresting eyes and the way they twinkled when he smiled. His work-roughened hands and the way they held her so gently when they danced and so erotically when—

"He cares about the same orphans you do." Jasper spoke and she tried to focus on his words. "Seems like you have a commonality."

"Perhaps. But that is all." She pressed her lips together. Couldn't he talk about something else?

His lips pressed into a firm line. "It's just as well. Can you imagine if you actually had a tendre for Foxcroft? You'd never be allowed to marry him."

There. He'd said what she'd been telling herself since last night. What she'd told Fox. A future with him was impossible. A tiny voice in the back of her mind chanted it wasn't, that she'd done as she'd pleased thus far. "And look where it's gotten me," she muttered under her breath.

"What's that?" Jasper moved his attention from the sodden countryside to her.

"Nothing." Miranda folded her hands in her lap as Jasper turned his head toward the window again.

Things were so much easier for him. Living at Saxton House, he was able to do what he pleased, when he pleased. He was able to avoid their parents almost entirely, though he usually put in an appearance at Mother's bi-weekly tea. Miranda recalled one such tea last spring. Jasper had been romancing an opera singer and Father had clapped him on the back, congratulating him on such an excellent conquest. The closest the duke ever came to looking at her like that was when she entered a ballroom and her dance card was immediately filled or notable people sought her acquaintance. At those moments, his chest puffed up, and he gave her a stiff nod.

What she wouldn't give for the duke to be truly proud of her. Not of her beauty or her attributes, but of *her.* If her parents came to Stipple's End as Jasper had, would they nod with approval and lavish her with praise? Not if she dawdled with the likes of Mont-gomery Foxcroft.

Experience told her she'd be better served if she could realize happiness without her parents' approba-tion. But her heart feared it wasn't possible.

CHAPTER 16

OX slammed the door of the office at Stipple's End. Rob, seated behind the desk entering numbers in the estate book, startled, dropping his quill. His brow furrowed as he looked up at Fox. "Things didn't go well at Cosgrove?"

Fox threw himself into the small, wooden chair by the window. "Son of a bitch says he paid Mrs. Gates and warned me against making an issue of it. After all, why would anyone believe her over him?" Fox saw no point in telling Rob the earl had cast aspersions upon Mrs. Knott's credibility.

"Jackass." Rob expelled the word on a pent-up breath, baring his teeth. They sat in silence a moment before he asked, "What do you plan to do?"

Fox stretched his legs out in front of him. "We need that money. We'll never have enough to fix this place otherwise." He gestured toward the book on the desk. "The ledger tells the truth of it."

Rob set his quill down. "Aye, it's worse than we expected. I reckon you're thinking what I am."

"I'm not certain what you're thinking, but I'm going to steal the money. What else can I do?" He threw his hands up. "Hell, it's not even stealing since it should be ours anyway."

Rob rested his hands on the arm of the chair. "You have a plan for this?"

Fox nodded. "I've been thinking about it since I left. As luck would have it, I walked around inside Cosgrove a bit. I found Norris's office. It has three windows. I can't be certain the money's in there, but I'm guessing I'll find something."

They needed the money, but he also wanted to find proof of the earl's corruption. Perhaps a list of people who paid tributes and the amount they paid. Anything he could provide to the House of Lords who would in turn mete out some form of punishment. Would transportation be too severe? No, it sounded just right.

Rob drew him from his thoughts. "You may recall Freddie works as a groom at Cosgrove."

Freddie had been an orphan at Stipple's End. He'd been hired on at Cosgrove a few years back. "What do you have in mind? I've no wish to endanger the lad's position."

Rob lifted a shoulder. "I'll talk to him, see if he knows anything about what's in the office or if he can at least make sure one of those windows remains unlocked."

"That would be most helpful. But I won't get the boy in trouble."

"Understood. What's your plan?"

Fox pondered for a moment. "I've never gone into a house wearing the mask, but I don't see another way."

Rob picked up the quill from the desk and rolled it between his fingers. "Isn't he having a party in a couple of days?"

"I wasn't invited." Fox wouldn't let that stop him. "No matter. If I'm caught, I'll pretend I'm a guest. Most of the people attending are his antiquity friends from London and won't know me."

Rob rubbed his chin. "I don't know. Seems risky. On the road, it's easier to get away. Furthermore, if you're caught inside Cosgrove with the mask, people will think you're the highwayman."

"Maybe, but that was a long time ago. No one knows about the other robbery with Stratham. I'll have to risk the connection to Carmody's highwayman." Fox stood, eager to move forward with this plan. He wanted to storm Norris's stronghold and take what the man owed right now.

Rob fixed him with a piercing, cautionary look. "I don't see how it signifies. You're committing this robbery, and that's enough to see you hang."

Fox opened the door to go. "Well then, I'd best not get caught."

~

*W*ITH the nearly full moon obscured by a thick covering of clouds, it was beyond dark on the night of Norris's party. Thankfully the rain remained at bay. Fox left Icarus tied a good distance from the drive at Cosgrove and crept toward the house as stealthily as his voluminous black cloak would allow.

There were coaches in the drive, which meant footmen and grooms loitering about. Careful to keep to the shadows, Fox prowled to the corner of the building in which Norris's office sat. Once he reached the building, he pressed himself up against the gray stone, the rough surface catching at the wool of his cloak.

He eased along the façade until he reached the first window of the office. Here is where he'd learn if Freddie had been successful. The groom hadn't been able to learn anything about what Norris kept inside, but he'd been fairly certain he could unlock a window. Freddie had been more than happy to help Fox, to whom he apparently held more loyalty than his employer. The boy had also left a crate under a nearby shrub to better access the window, for it was rather high off the ground. As soon as Fox could afford it—assuming he ever could—he'd hire Freddie away from the earl.

Standing on the crate, he reached up and pushed at the first window but it didn't budge. He moved the makeshift stool and tried the next one with the same result. At the third window, he met victory. He slid the window open, thankful for his superior height.

The muted symphony of music and laughter drifted through the open window. It sounded as if the office door was open. Climbing into the room would be difficult wearing the cloak. He wrapped the thick fabric into a ball and dropped it to the ground. He pulled himself up to the casement and swung his feet over, easing himself onto the floor as silently as possible.

Near-darkness shrouded the interior of the office. As anticipated, the door stood ajar, allowing faint light to slither inside. Once he closed it, the room would be black as coal. He scanned the room, moving about quietly until he spied a branch of candles on the desk. Taking a spill from the fireplace, he lit one of the wicks and hurried to close the door.

He turned back toward the desk, contemplating where to begin his search. The desktop contained small curiosities, probably expensive antiquities purchased with other people's money. He hadn't expected an open ledger filled with names and monetary amounts under a heading of "Tributes," but it would've made for an easy task.

He gently slid the first drawer out when the door suddenly creaked open. In one fluid motion, Fox pinched out the flame and crouched behind the desk.

The door latched shut. The rustle of skirts filled the room as the person—woman—moved toward the desk. His senses jolted to high alert and he immediately caught a spicy waft of clove and orange.

Miranda.

The devil's own luck. He held his breath, wondering what in the hell she was doing there. She came closer—too close. She stepped behind the desk, and he couldn't move fast enough before her foot connected with his.

She gasped.

He shot to his feet and pressed his hand over her mouth. "Shhh." When she nodded, he released her.

"Is that you?" she asked breathlessly.

Fox didn't dare ask for clarification. Besides, he already knew who she meant. Christ, this was a mess. Dropping his voice, he said, "You have to go."

"What are you doing here? Are you stealing from Lord Norris?"

Though she spoke softly, he feared their conversation would draw attention. He wrapped his hand around her arm and whispered, "You have to go. Now."

She shook her head, and her scent of citrus and spice overwhelmed him. It took every effort not to bury his face in her hair.

"I can help you."

"What?" He worried he'd given himself away when she stilled. He hastily added in what he hoped was a throaty, unrecognizable tone, "You can't help me."

"Yes, I can. I won't raise the hue and cry, if that's what you're worried about. I didn't when you came to Birch House, did I?"

No, she hadn't. Being with her here in the dark, smelling her essence, wearing the mask he'd worn when he'd kissed her...all of it played merry hell with his resolve. His goal of searching Norris's office faded beneath a driving need to enfold her in his arms.

"I have but one caveat," she said. "You'll need to give me a portion of what you find."

Fox's thoughts came to a sudden and thorough halt. "What?"

"Lord Norris owes money to the local orphanage, and I mean to ensure they get it." She came closer, stopped so near him her breath tickled his chin. "So, you see, I'll help you steal his money, but I want a portion. For the orphanage."

He'd never wanted to kiss her more.

Too late he noticed the bright splash of light spilling under the door. A hand on the knob.

Bloody hell. No time to run. No time to hide. Only time to take off his mask.

And, though it hadn't been his intent, to compromise her at last.

∼

*T*HE door behind her opened. Miranda froze, riveted on the highwayman. As he pulled the mask from his face, candlelight illuminated his features.

Fox.

She blinked.

Fox.

She sucked in a breath.

Fox?

Her eyes widened, and her jaw dropped. She simply couldn't keep the shock from escaping. And she'd been moments from kissing him again only to stop herself because she'd been thinking of Fox instead of the highwayman. Except Fox was the highwayman.

Wasn't he?

"What the devil is going on here?"

Miranda spun about, her heart colliding with her lungs at the sight of Lord Norris clutching an oil lamp in the doorway. Then her heart and every other piece of her insides plummeted to her feet as she saw who stood behind him, surprise and disappointment etched in his face. Jasper.

"I say again, what are you about in my office—Foxcroft? I don't recall inviting you this evening."

Jasper pushed past Lord Norris and strode into the

room. "If you aren't a guest, what the hell are you doing closeted in the dark with my sister?"

Fox looked from Jasper to Lord Norris to Miranda and then back to Jasper again. What could he say? He'd come to steal from the earl?

Miranda stepped toward Jasper. "He came here to see me." She spoke without thinking of anything but preventing Fox getting caught.

Jasper turned on her, his eyes hard. "You made some sort of assignation with him here, of all places?"

Lord Norris hadn't stopped staring at Fox. "No. I think Fox had another objective in coming here. Didn't you, my boy?" The earl's round, bobbling eyes narrowed, though it seemed impossible for them to do so.

Fox looked at Miranda, raised one brow the tiniest fraction as if asking her what he should do. Quickly, she had to choose: save him and in the course ruin herself, or...let Norris continue. Time stretched with three pairs of eyes watching her, waiting for her to be savior or executioner. Jasper's brows gathered, reminding her too much of their father.

She was a coward.

Norris gestured toward the window. Barely open, it still provided adequate evidence as to how Fox had entered the office. "He came in through there. What kind of man sneaks into a party to steal a moment with a woman? No, he came here to steal from me because he thinks I owe him something." He shook his head while his thick upper lip curled. "I warned you, Fox." The earl glanced at Jasper. "I think if you search his person, you'll find at least a few thousand of my pounds."

Fox held up his hands. "I've got nothing of yours, Norris."

Lord Norris grinned maliciously. "Then you won't mind Lord Saxton taking a look." He gestured at Jasper to do as he bade.

Miranda's gut twisted. What would he find?

Jasper stood before Fox. He looked marginally less angry than when he arrived, but his face was still drawn with tension. "Empty your pockets."

Fox held Jasper's gaze, a tic pulsing in his jaw. A moment passed before he reached inside his coat and pulled out...nothing. "That's my only pocket."

"Mind if I check it?" Jasper put his hand forward.

Fox raised his arms perpendicular to his body.

"What's that?" Lord Norris pointed at a bulge in Fox's right sleeve.

Fear raced along Miranda's spine.

Jasper grabbed Fox's arm. He reached up his sleeve and pulled out...the mask.

"Aha!" Lord Norris crowed. "He's here to steal all right. With a mask!" He pursed his fat lips for a second. "Wonder if he's the highwayman who, ah, never mind."

Jasper turned to face her. "Wait, weren't you held up by a highwayman on your way to Wootton Bassett last June, Miranda?"

Miranda's heart sank. "Yes. But I don't think it was Fox."

The earl's eyes were round as her pearl earrings. "You don't think? Well, what would you know, gel? He wore a mask, didn't he?"

Miranda opened her mouth to say she'd know the highwayman's kiss anywhere, but she'd never kissed Fox. Even so, she knew in her bones they were the same person, that all this time she'd been attracted to not two different men, but one. Fox.

How could he be a thief? Tears pricked her eyes as Fox dropped his arms to his sides. He didn't look the least bit defeated. No, he looked defiant, the gold centers of his eyes flaming in the dim light.

Jasper held the mask out. "Have you nothing to say, Foxcroft?"

"Not to you." Fox glared at Lord Norris, sparing not so much as a glance for either Jasper or her.

"I'll notify the mayor." Lord Norris clucked his tongue. "Damned shame. What will happen to those poor orphans after you're transported, Fox?" He turned to address Jasper. "I'd rather not interrupt my party with this nonsense. Might as well lock him up in the stables overnight."

Miranda whirled to face the earl. "The stables? Surely that isn't necessary! He didn't steal anything!"

"Maybe not tonight, but I'm willing to bet he stole from Carmody and who knows what else he's done. And he entered my house unlawfully with the intent to thieve. Sorry, my dear, but the law doesn't allow for people like him."

"You hypocritical son of a bitch." It sounded as if Fox had growled the words. His hands were fisted at his sides, and a vein throbbed in his neck. Miranda wanted to wrap her arms around him. God, if only she'd said they *were* having an assignation!

She turned pleading eyes on her brother. "Jasper, do something!"

Jasper's eyes softened briefly. Nevertheless he took Fox's arm. "Where do you want me to take him, Norris?"

"No!" Miranda grabbed Fox's other arm as if she'd tug him away from her much stronger brother. "You can't take him. He hasn't done anything."

Jasper turned to Lord Norris. "It's true he didn't steal anything from you."

"Just because you didn't find it doesn't mean he didn't take anything. Maybe he threw it outside." The earl pushed open the window and looked below. "There, I see something on the ground."

"It's my cloak. I didn't take anything." Fox had never sounded so cold, so removed.

"If what you say is true, which I don't think it is, I'd wager the only reason you're empty-handed is because you were interrupted. I'll have someone go out and fetch whatever it is."

Panic bubbled in Miranda's throat. "If you don't find anything, you can't prove he took anything. Isn't that right, Jasper?"

Lord Norris shook his head emphatically. "It doesn't matter. He still stole from Carmody."

Miranda wanted to claw the earl's bulbous eyes out. "But you can't prove it!"

Jasper stared at her. "Can you prove he *wasn't* the highwayman?"

Wildly, Miranda cast about for a response. She couldn't say she just *knew*. That she'd been rather intimate with both men and knew them to be different—never mind this was an outright lie since they were the same bloody man! She'd just begun to make progress with her family and this would kill all of it.

Defeat slumped her shoulders. "No." She chanced a look at Fox and cringed at the stark disappointment in his eyes.

"Let's go, then." Jasper pulled Fox into the hallway. Miranda followed close behind. Her brother turned a weary gaze on her. "Go back to the party, Miranda."

She wanted to argue, but didn't dare. Fox stood half-turned from her and said nothing. What did she expect? For him to absolve her and simply march to his doom?

Lord Norris stepped in front of Jasper. "This way. We'll take him out through the back."

Miranda stood rooted to the floor as she watched her brother haul Fox away. Emotion clogged her throat until it ached. Transportation? Would they really send him to a penal colony? And what would happen to Stipple's End? Horror ate away at her insides until she felt hollow. She had to find a way to stop this.

But as far as she could tell, the best way, the easiest

way—perhaps the only way—would be to sacrifice what little reputation she had left.

~

*F*URY coursed through every vein in Fox's body until he feared he might burst. She could have saved him if only she'd claimed he'd come to see her, that they'd plotted the secret meeting. Norris likely wouldn't have believed it, but everyone else could have been convinced. And to think he'd felt guilty about having contemplated compromising her. Now he wished he'd just done it without a backward glance.

They entered a servants' hallway and immediately came upon a footman. Norris directed the man to get help and search the ground outside the windows of his office. He then asked him to send Stratham to the stables. Hell's teeth, but this night couldn't get any worse.

They exited the house. The stable lay a few hundred yards away. Norris addressed Miranda's brother. "I'll ask Carmody to come by in the morning and verify Fox is the highwayman who robbed him. Then we'll turn Foxcroft over to the mayor."

Saxton's grip remained strong. "What if Carmody can't identify him? Miranda bore witness and, ah, had reason to be quite close to the criminal. If she says Fox isn't the highwayman, you'll have conflicting testimony from two witnesses."

Norris's breath came in gasps as he waddled faster to keep up. "Bah. She's just a silly chit. No one will believe her."

Saxton looked down at the squat earl with an arrogance Fox recognized from Miranda. "I beg your pardon, Lord Norris, she's the daughter of a duke." His tone dripped cold enough to freeze the River Wylye.

"Yes, yes, of course." Norris nearly panted now. He slowed his lumbering gait while he spoke. "I only meant she couldn't possibly know. Not unless she saw him unmasked or got close enough to see something of his features despite the mask."

Fox wondered if Saxton would elaborate. It seemed he knew she'd kissed the highwayman, but he said nothing. Apparently preserving Miranda's precious reputation was worth any cost. To anyone.

They reached the stable, and with it the pungent odor of the earl's horses. Lanterns illuminated the interior where two grooms hurried to cast aside their tools and stand straight to receive Norris and his guests. Fox noted Freddie was one of the grooms. The boy had grown since Fox had seen him last, but he would be nearing twenty by now. He gave Fox a fleeting glance that likely no one else caught.

After catching his breath somewhat, Norris addressed the older groom. "Lock this man in the tack room." He gestured toward Fox.

The groom nodded and went to a door between two stalls. He held it open and waited for Saxton to lead Fox inside. Norris followed them. Once inside the tack room, Norris turned to Saxton. "Thank you, Lord Saxton. I'll take things from here."

Saxton looked as if he were going to object, but gave a slight nod and departed.

Norris closed the door and finally set down the lamp he'd been clutching since he'd walked into the office. "There's no point in pretense, Fox. I am well aware you came here tonight to take the money for the tapestries. Foolish notion, that, but I can credit your daring, to be sure." He chuckled and Fox wanted to wipe the smug smirk from the man's greasy, fat face. "Unfortunately, they'll find money in your cloak, and then it'll be hanging. Transportation if you're lucky."

"They'll find nothing in my cloak, Norris. Not unless you put it there." Genuine fear iced his neck.

"Now, now, there you go with your accusations

again. They'd be so much more valuable if you had anything to back them up. But I have to assume you do not, else you would have said as much in front of Lord Saxton. Careful what you say now, you're soon to be recognized as a criminal."

Norris would ensure Fox's formal arrest and the subsequent trial for his crimes, including the one he hadn't committed tonight. His mind raced, searching for a way to turn the tables somehow. "I'll prove you've been extorting money for years, how you bleed this district until people barely have enough to eat."

For the first time, alarm registered on the earl's face. He mopped a hand over his sweat-laden brow. "You stole the money from Stratham, didn't you? I was certain he lied, that he'd taken the money himself."

Victory, however small, burgeoned in Fox's chest. At last the man admitted his sins. So Stratham had reported the robbery to Norris. But how could Fox tie that money—all of which was gone—to their extortion scheme? He didn't know, but he'd figure out a way. In the meantime, he offered a cagey smile. "Yes, I took the money. My actions were no worse than what you're doing."

Norris's chest puffed out and Fox expected the earl's lemon yellow waistcoat to pop open. "I didn't steal from anyone. Those people gave me money in exchange for a service."

Fox wondered if Norris actually worked to satisfy the interests of his constituents in the district. "I have a hard time believing you would do anything that wouldn't serve you, regardless of the money involved. Would it be difficult, do you suppose, to find a person who's been forced to pay you? And might that person be convinced to testify against you?"

Norris's eyes bulged and he sputtered. "No one would be so foolish. Besides, what can you hope to accomplish from in here?" The earl's lip curled, but his eyes reflected a shade of fear.

Eager to further sow the seeds of doubt, Fox lifted a shoulder. "You'll just have to wait and see."

A knock on the door interrupted further conversation. Norris called, "Enter."

Stratham poked his head inside. Without looking at Fox, he addressed the earl. "You sent for me, Lord Norris?" What, no taunting remark directed at Fox? No obnoxious show of power or self-importance?

Norris picked up his lamp. "You'll be pleased to know I've caught the highwayman who stole from you."

Stratham's widening eyes moved to Fox. "You?" His mouth continued to move, but no sound escaped.

Fox refused to admit to anything. He did, however, enjoy a measure of satisfaction at Stratham's reaction.

The earl lumbered his corpulent frame toward Stratham. "Sleep tight, Fox. Come morning you'll be transferred to the mayor."

The door closed behind them, and the chill darkness of the tack room embraced Fox. He hadn't heard the lock—maybe they'd stupidly leave him in here without securing it. He crept to the door and listened. The voices outside faded, as if Norris and Stratham were retreating to the house. Perhaps Freddie would be able to help him.

After another moment of quietly pressing his ear to the door, Fox straightened. Just as he did so, the wood pushed against him, nearly knocking him off balance. Light cascaded into the room once more and illuminated the face of Miranda's brother. He carried a lantern with a tallow candle into the room and closed the door behind him.

Fox had a suspicion about this visit, but remained silent. Saxton set the lantern on an overturned bucket and faced Fox. The meager light of the single flame so low to the ground cast his face in eerie shadow. Nevertheless, the man's anger was evident in the set of his chin and narrowed eyes.

"Just what in the hell is going on between you and my sister? She claims you are nothing to her, but I keep finding you in close quarters."

Fox chose his words carefully. "Why don't you believe her?"

He gave Fox a look that seemed to ask, *are you simple?* "Because she's Miranda. Don't you understand why she was banished here in the first place? She'd been cavorting around London with a group of miscreants—wealthy and even some of them titled miscreants, but fools the lot of them. I won't bore you with the specifics, but our parents expelled her from London after she was observed on the Dark Walk at Vauxhall with a certain gentleman. I'm sure you're well aware of what occurs on the Dark Walk so I needn't explain."

"Actually, I've never been to Vauxhall." But Fox suspected upon hearing the tale he'd want to kill that Certain Gentleman.

"Well, then let me enlighten you. Well-respected young daughters of dukes do not take the Dark Walk with lascivious bounders interested in a bit of fluff and perhaps a large dowry. But Miranda, in all of her foolishness, not only went with this man, but engaged in a rather lurid embrace. Thankfully the witness was a close family friend, and we were able to prevent the story from leaking to London at large. It would have been an absolute calamity."

That explained her experienced kisses. Yes, he definitely wanted to kill the Certain Gentleman. And he wanted to throttle Miranda as well. Had she no sense at all?

Saxton continued, "So you can see why I am suspicious of your relationship with my sister. It's seems obvious to me you want her—whether for her beauty or her money, I don't know. Not that it matters since she isn't eligible to someone like you."

Of all the arrogant jackasses. Fox sneered, unable to keep his anger in check. "Someone like me? What does that mean, exactly? I'm poor? Or I run an orphanage? I'm not titled? Or is it that I live here instead of your beloved London?"

Saxton's stony stare yielded nothing. "All of those things, if you must know. If Miranda has shown you any interest, it's because she likes a challenge, and more than that she enjoys tweaking convention. You are the worst possible gentleman for her, and so she finds some perverse pleasure in engaging your attention."

His words sunk into Fox's furious brain. They held a note of truth. Why else would she have kissed a stranger—a highwayman to boot? She'd been shipped to the country and at the first chance she rebelled by flirting with a highwayman, something guaranteed to shock those around her. Was it possible she'd never felt anything for him at all? That every moment they'd shared, even the night at the brothel were mere episodes of a girl playing at being a woman?

Saxton interrupted his thoughts. "I'm surprised she defended you tonight. Usually when pushed to choose propriety over her lapses in judgment, she chooses the former, but then I suppose in the end she did. You didn't really come here to see her, as she suggested." Though not a question, uncertainty tinged the words. Fox's ire pounced on it.

"Would that be so hard to believe? As you pointed out, she's beautiful and wealthy. God knows I need the money. And she does have a penchant for this highwayman, so why not sneak in wearing a mask and seduce a fanciful young girl? You said yourself she seeks such adventure so it seems a perfect plan—"

Saxton's fist cut short Fox's speech. He staggered

backward but didn't fall. His face throbbed. Christ, the man had a vicious swing.

Saxton moved forward again, and Fox gave in to his anger, swiping at the other man's face. His knuckles slammed into Saxton's cheek, just below his eye. He fell back. Both men stood glaring at each other, fists raised.

Much as Fox would appreciate an exhilarating brawl to expel his emotion, he needed to think. "I haven't seduced her."

Flexing his hands, Saxton paused. Even in the semi-darkness, the man's eyes glimmered like the hard, impenetrable ice that covered the lake at Bassett Manor in January. "If I believe otherwise, we'll finish this. I'll call you out, and either run you through or shoot you dead. I'm equally proficient with either method." Saxton straightened his coat. "It's a shame, really. I rather liked you. I gather you lack funds, but to steal?" He shook his head.

Fox's fury renewed. He wanted to pummel Saxton into oblivion. "Someone like you would never understand."

Fox could tell him he hadn't stolen from Norris, could tell him Norris was even now setting him up for the crime. But he doubted Saxton would believe it. Especially not now when the man clearly wanted to thrash him.

Saxton turned Fox's words back on him. "By 'someone like me' you mean someone who has money?"

"And opportunity and security. Tell me, Lord Saxton, would you be able to provide for over a hundred tenants? Forty orphans? Two staffs? Do you have a legacy that requires you to work your hands to their very bones with little or no personal comfort? Do you have responsibilities that all but ensure you will never be able to pursue the things *you* might like to do? When was the last time you *didn't* put yourself before all others? Better still, when was the last time you deprived yourself in order to serve another—and not because you had to, but because you wanted to? Make no mistake I choose this life, as difficult and capricious as it might be. What life do you choose, Lord Saxton?" Fox's chest heaved. He took deep gulps of air to calm his thundering heart.

Saxton said nothing.

Suddenly weary, Fox sat in a rickety wooden chair set in the corner. "Just go. Please."

Saxton stood a moment longer and then exited, pulling the door shut behind him. This time, Fox heard the lock click.

Saxton had left the lantern. Shadows danced on walls covered with saddles, reins, and all manner of tack supplies. Fox gazed into the flame, his pulse finally slowing to a moderate pace for the first time since Miranda had opened the office door.

His mind worked, frantically searching for a way out of this disaster. He had to ensure Carmody didn't identify him as the highwayman. Not that it mattered. Norris would plant money—maybe already had—in Fox's cloak as proof he'd stolen from him tonight. That evidence along with the mask would be difficult to discount, especially when an earl would be giving testimony. If only he had something on Norris!

Fox nurtured a small hope Freddie would be able to help him. A hope that faltered when no one came to the door, and diminished with the dark silence of each passing hour. Still, he clung to it, because he had nothing else.

CHAPTER 17

*M*IRANDA suffered through the remainder of the evening knowing Fox was locked in the stable. So close, but absolutely untouchable.

When Jasper rejoined the party, he glowered at her across the room. She did her best to avoid him, but now as the festivities drew to a close, he caged her in a corner of the drawing room. "I'm not comfortable with you staying here tonight."

Lord Septon had asked for Miranda to stay at Cosgrove so they could have breakfast in the morning and perhaps go for a ride afterward. Jasper frowned at her. "You should come with me to Stratham Hall."

Miranda shook her head. "No, I have plans in the morning with Septon. We're to go riding. I haven't been riding all summer, Jasper."

"That better be the only thing you do in the stables." He gave her his most obnoxious brotherly glare. "I'm warning you, Miranda, stay away from Foxcroft."

"What am I going to do? Let him out and run away to Scotland with him?" The idea gave her a thrilling jolt.

His mouth pressed into a disapproving line. "This is not a situation to make light of. The man's future is at risk. And from what I can tell, you've done enough to falsely encourage him. Leave him be."

Falsely encourage him? Had Fox told him about the marriage proposal? She hadn't encouraged that! "I haven't done anything wrong. Fox and I are friends. Nothing more."

His lip curled in a half-smile lacking actual amusement. "Friends don't look at friends the way you two look at each other. You'll keep your distance, or I'll ship you back to Holborn in the morning."

His observation made her flesh tingle. How did they look at each other? Fox had told her not to look at him as if she wanted to eat him. Was it her fault he'd looked so devastatingly handsome at the benefit?

"I'm going to bed." She turned to leave but Jasper placed a staying hand on her arm.

"Maybe I should have a maid sleep on a pallet in your room."

She swung back to face him and pulled from his touch. "Stop! I'll stay in my room. Go away." She fled the drawing room before he could say another word. By the time she got to the staircase, she'd calculated the time she'd need to wait while everyone settled in their rooms for the night. As she ascended, she plotted her path to the stables. When she entered her room, she could scarcely wait to leave.

An interminable two hours later, Miranda crept into the hallway. She'd pulled her riding skirt over her nightdress—which she'd donned to avoid arousing the maid's curiosity—and topped it with the matching spencer. She didn't look terribly appropriate, but she didn't plan to meet anyone who would care.

Making her way down the faintly lit corridor, she wondered if Fox would be easy to find. There couldn't be many rooms in the stable in which to lock him. Was he comfortable? Maybe she should bring him some food or water. Her half boots tapped softly against the stairs as she descended. She couldn't risk meeting anyone in the kitchen. Sticking to her original plan, she looked around the foyer for the footman on duty. Hopefully he slept in a cupboard under the stairs.

Luckily, she saw no one. She eased open the front door and slipped outside into the cool night, pulling her spencer more tightly about her. The stables were to the left. Thankfully the drive appeared as vacant as the foyer had been. She made her way quickly along the side of the house to the end of the building. Turning, she saw the stable and doubled her pace.

By the time she reached her destination, her breath came in short gasps. Stopping outside, she pressed herself against the exterior wall and gulped air. After a moment, she peered into the doorway, careful to keep herself out of sight. Two grooms sat at a table drinking. Behind them marched a line of stalls. Had they stashed him in one of those for the night?

She craned her neck, trying to see the other side of the building. She glanced back at the table. One of the grooms stared straight at her! She flattened herself against the wall once more, panic shortening her breath again.

Reason told her to run back to the house, but she couldn't abandon Fox when she'd come this far. His imprisonment was her fault! But if the groom caught her, what would she say? Her mind worked for explanations of why she might be there—

A hand closed around her arm and dragged her away from the door. The groom held his finger to his lips. "I've only got a moment. You're here to see Fox?"

She blinked up at him. "You know him?"

He nodded and released his grip. "I'm Freddie. And if I'm right, you're Lady Miranda."

"How do you know that?"

A smile flitted across his lips. "My brother Philip told me all about you."

Could she be this fortunate? "Philip? From the or-phanage?"

"Yes. I used to live there, too." He looked back over his shoulder. "Are you here to help Fox?"

Hope swirled through her chest. "If I can. Where is he?"

"In the tack room." He jerked a thumb in the direc-tion of the building. "I've been trying to get rid of Tom all night, but he thinks we both need to stand guard. So I started giving him whisky, and I'd say he's about ready to knock over. Just be patient, and I'll come get you when he's out."

Miranda shivered. "Thank you."

He twisted his mouth, appearing regretful. "Sorry I can't let you inside where it's warmer. Will you be all right?"

She hadn't come this far to give up to the cold. "I'll be fine."

Miranda huddled in the shadows next to the building and waited. She wrinkled her nose at the prevalent scent of horse manure. While she loved to ride, she never spent much time in the actual stable.

When her fingers tingled with the onset of numb-ness, Freddie finally came back out. "Follow me."

The groom led her into the barn. The figure slumped over the table had to be Tom. Freddie un-locked a door partway down the left row of stalls. Mi-randa hurried into the tack room. A tallow candle burned low, barely illuminating Fox stretched out along the far wall on a makeshift pallet of horse blankets.

"Fox!"

He jumped to his feet and her heart tightened at the sight of him in his rumpled clothes and mussed hair. "What the hell are you doing here?"

She stopped abruptly at his angry tone. Had she expected him to welcome her with enthusiasm? Foolishly, she'd hoped he might.

Fox turned his glare on the groom just inside the door. "Freddie, why did you let her in?"

"Keep your voices down. The other groom is sleeping out there. She said she came to help you."

Fox nodded but then returned his attention to Miranda. "Do you have a plan?"

Seeing him here, consigned to sleeping on the floor in the rank darkness, made her heart ache. Accommodations on a ship to a penal colony would be far worse. She swallowed her emotion as best as she could. "Can we talk about this privately?"

Fox clenched and unclenched his fists. "Fine. Freddie, you'll let us know if anyone comes?"

The lad nodded. "I hope you'll let me know how I can help." He frowned sadly. "I wish I could just let you go, but I don't dare."

"Certainly not, Freddie. I understand. Do not concern yourself." Fox quirked a brow at her. "Miranda apparently has a plan."

"I'll be out here if you need me." Freddie closed the door, but didn't lock it.

Now alone with Fox, Miranda's nerves spiked, and she couldn't think of what to say.

He sauntered toward her, stopping an arm's length away. "So what's your plan, Miranda? Or like everything else, have you not quite thought this through?"

Now that pricked her anger. "Would you rather I leave?"

They stared at each other, the tension palpable in the small, dark room. Though shadow cloaked his face, the hard glimmer of his eyes pierced straight to her soul. "No."

And with that simple word, relief pulsed through her veins and her knees wobbled. "I've considered this, Fox, and I'm sure Carmody won't identify you. I'm going to tell him I know you can't be the highwayman. He knows I kissed the highwayman and will have to believe me."

"How do you figure? Unless you plan to kiss me too?" He leaned forward and she shivered.

She glanced at his mouth. "I have kissed you."

"As the highwayman, but you can't tell them that." The ice in his voice made her cold. "Obviously."

"Obviously." Fear he wouldn't let her help him stole a bit of her resolve. "I've never seen you like this."

"I've never faced hanging before." The words were clipped, raw.

"You aren't going to hang!" Fear he might made her voice shrill. "Without Mr. Carmody's testimony, there's nothing to convict you of this crime."

"Nothing except the money Norris planted in my cloak."

Miranda gasped. The room tilted a bit. She shook, as much from emotion as from the cold.

Fox took her hand and stroked her fingers. For the first time since she arrived he seemed like himself. Like the Fox she knew.

"Are you all right? You're freezing."

He guided her to the blankets and sat down with her on the soft pile of wool. Grasping both of her hands, he warmed them between his own.

Her teeth started to chatter. Fox sat back against a saddle and pulled her between his legs. He grabbed a blanket and threw it over them, wrapping his arms around her. The heat of his chest warmed her back, and she tucked her head under his chin.

She held the blanket up. "It's cold. Put your arms under here."

He hesitated but ultimately complied. He crossed his arms over her chest, settling his hands on her elbows. They sat quietly for a moment, while her body absorbed warmth and her shaking subsided. Slowly she became aware of his breath tickling her hairline, of the hardness of his frame around the softness of hers.

Sitting against him like this reminded her of the brothel. Her heart beat faster again, but not with fright. It pounded steadily, mounting in its speed along with her yearning. Her yearning for him.

She turned in his arms. He gazed down at her, the gold of his eyes glowing in the sputtering candlelight. She ran her fingers along his jaw, prickly with the growth of his faint beard, but tantalizing. His pulse beat in his throat and she traced along the vein to the edge of his opened shirt, staring at the flesh bared to her gaze.

He smelled of rosemary and hay and man. He never smelled like the men she knew in London with their carefully crafted perfumes. No, his scent was real and impossible to duplicate. She rested her fingers in the hollow at the base of his throat and raised her gaze to his. He didn't move and she took his lack of response as acquiescence.

Coming up on her knees, she pushed his coat from his shoulders, running her hands over the muscles of his upper arms and then back up again as he shrugged out of the garment. He didn't touch her, but rested his hands at his sides on the blanket.

She massaged the backs of his shoulders, his neck. His muscles relaxed as she worked, and his eyes lost a bit of their ferocity. She skimmed her palms over his collarbones and down the front of his shirt. His chest shuddered as he took a particularly deep breath. Without pause, she continued her journey downward and tugged the linen out of his waistband. Keeping her gaze locked with his, she ran her hands up, bunching the fabric as she traversed his heated flesh. His eyes widened slightly, but not with surprise. With pleasure.

When he didn't move to take off the garment, she

clutched the hem. He grabbed her hands. "I won't let you start something you don't intend to finish."

Raw desire raced along her flesh. She offered him what she hoped to be her most seductive smile. "I intend to finish."

He gripped her hands more firmly. "I'm quite serious. I will not be trifled with, Miranda. I've offered myself to you before and you turned me down."

The smile fell from her face at the intensity in his gaze. "I won't turn you down." She squeezed his hands in return. "I want you."

"Your brother told me there were others." The muscles around his mouth tensed, his gaze hooded. "In London."

What had Jasper revealed? Any games she'd played with Darleigh were mere shadows of what she felt for this man. "No. Never. At least, not like this. You're... you're different."

His features relaxed slightly. "I would still marry you." His voice dipped low, until he sounded hoarse.

"I know." She pulled her hands free and he let them go. Grasping the hem of his shirt, she whisked it up over his head, and he helped toss it away.

Bare-chested, he was magnificent. His muscles were clearly defined, with a light covering of pale brown hair trailing downward until it disappeared into his waistband. Intrigued, she wanted to follow where it led, but first she must explore that which lay exposed to her hungry gaze.

"You're staring at me like I'm food again." His words heightened her arousal and further emboldened her.

She feasted on his male beauty. "I've never seen anything as delicious as you."

"Christ, Miranda. Ladies don't talk like that."

She traced her fingers around his nipples and watched them tighten. Her own hardened in response. "You don't like it?"

He swallowed audibly. "I like it fine." The pulse in his throat quickened, and Miranda felt a surge of pleasure.

She flattened her palms against him and glided them down to the alluring path of hair leading into his pantaloons. He sucked in a breath as her fingers found the buttons of his fall. The fabric fell away with her ministrations and her knuckles brushed against the swell of his penis, hidden from her gaze by his drawers. He flinched, but still didn't move to touch or assist her in any way. She looked back to his face as she stroked her fingertips along the length of his erection. His tongue darted out and wetted his lips.

Her breasts grew heavy, and her entire body thrummed with pent-up desire. Still, he simply sat there. "Aren't you going to touch me?"

He raised a brow and she couldn't be sure if she'd interrupted a lust-filled reverie in which touching her hadn't occurred to him or he'd simply been waiting for her invitation. His lips spread into a slow, wicked smile. "Yes."

With great speed, he leaned forward and took her in his arms. He pressed her back onto the blankets and covered her body with his. Poised above her face, he touched a finger to her mouth, traced first the lower lip and then the upper. Her body screamed with need.

And then he splayed his palm against her cheek and lowered his mouth to hers, capturing her with a kiss so full of passion, so overwhelming, it crowded all thought from her mind. She quivered beneath the onslaught of his tongue as it stroked her lips and then the recesses of her mouth. Her response encompassed everything she could give, desperate for it to be enough to ease the hunger building between them. She'd never been kissed like this, not even when he'd been the highwayman. He seemed to be drawing something from her, coaxing something to the surface of her conscious-

ness. A wild craving exploded in her breast and between her thighs.

He cradled the back of her neck while he angled his
head to better plunder her mouth. She tangled her hands
in his hair, holding him to her, never wanting to let go.

Working the buttons of her spencer free, he delved
his fingers inside and paused for the briefest moment.
Then he pulled back and looked down at her chest.
"What are you wearing?"

She moved her hands to his shoulders. "A
nightdress."

"You came out here dressed in your nightclothes?"

She shrugged. "It seemed unnecessary to dress for a
social occasion."

He laughed then. A deep, throaty, wonderful sound
that slammed heat into every corner of her body. "Miranda, I adore you."

Heady sensation careened through her until she
feared it would leak out in the form of a giggle. Swallowing the emotion, she arched up off the blanket and
kissed him, running her tongue over his lower lip. With
a groan, he opened his mouth and hastily stripped the
spencer from her. His hand moved to her waistband
and found the hooks of her skirt. Deftly, he loosened
the garment and pushed it down over her thighs. She
wiggled her hips in assistance.

Fox whispered against her lips, "Be still. I'll do it."
He sat back and pulled the skirt from her legs, exposing
her nightdress, which came to her knees. His fingertips
caressed her calves in turn as he removed her half-
boots and set them to the side. He glanced up at her
with a half-smile and skimmed his palms up her right
leg until he found the garter above her knee. "Will your
feet be cold if I take these off?"

"I don't think I'm capable of being cold around you."

"Mmm. Exactly as I'd hoped." He bent over her and

unfastened the garter. His warm fingers massaged her flesh, and then his lips were against the back of her knee. His touch tickled, too captivating to resist, and she shivered. His breath heated her skin. "Divine." No, there was no chance of being chilled now.

Slowly, he rolled off her stocking and flung it away. With infinite patience he repeated the ritual with her other leg, flicking his tongue into the dimple at the side of her knee.

Having bared her legs, he crouched over her ankles and brushed his palms up to the heat of her inner thighs. She opened herself instinctively and cast her head back against the blanket. Her nightdress bunched around her waist, but he pushed at it, exposing her belly.

Anticipation sparked her nerve endings, made her arch up and seek more of him. She wanted to feel his body over her as he'd been before.

Then his thumb pressed against her sex, and she cried out. Sensation spiraled through her, immediately driving her to the brink of desperation. She thrust her hips into his hand, but he stroked her with maddening softness. She gasped, taking air into her lungs until she nearly panted with longing.

He moved up her body, pulling the nightdress from her in a fluid movement. All the while, his fingers played a slow, methodical rhythm against the burning flesh between her legs. His tongue flicked against her nipple, further battering her patience. She clasped his head and he closed his hot mouth over her breast. Furious whimpers tumbled from her as he used his tongue to tease the tip into a throbbing bud of sensitivity. She pushed her breast further into his mouth, begging him for more.

And then he kissed her, his tongue driving into her mouth just as his finger pierced her moist sheath. She jerked upward and pulled at his hair, returning his kiss with a lust that surely lacked sanity.

She rocked her hips against his hand. He stroked in, out, his finger working her toward the frenzy that promised to claim her, give her peace.

He sat back abruptly, and she at last felt a blast of cold. Propping herself up on her elbows, she watched him remove his boots with quick movements.

Barefooted, he shed his trousers and paused beside her, staring over the length of her body. "I've never seen anything as beautiful as you." He caressed her breasts, her belly, her thighs. "So perfect." He gazed into her eyes. "That you would give yourself to me is incredibly humbling."

A twinge of embarrassment heated her face. "Why?"

He smiled. "Because you're Miranda. A goddess to my mere mortality. I am a beast beside you."

She shook her head, not at all comfortable with his comparison. "I'm just a woman. Your woman."

He fell on top of her with a primal growl, and she recalled the hard labor he performed daily. His work-calloused hands cradled her face while he ravaged her mouth with stark need. He settled himself between her legs, his smooth hardness caressing her sex.

Pressing against her, he put his hand between their bodies and stroked her softness.

"Wait."

He froze at her command, closing his eyes as if he were pained. "Please don't tell me you've changed your mind."

"No, I just…want to touch you." She reached between them and found his hand. "Show me what to do."

He opened his eyes and the gold centers burned as hot as her core. "Here." He wrapped her fingers around his shaft. "He was soft but hard, like wood sheathed in silk. "You can move your hand if you like."

He groaned, and she smiled in appreciation. Experimentally, she closed her hand around him more firmly and slid her palm down to the base and then up again to the velvety tip. Amazing this would fit inside her, but she supposed it must.

His breathing increased with her movements. "Miranda, I need to come inside of you. Now."

She withdrew her hand and kissed his mouth. "Then come."

CHAPTER 18

OX'S hand shook as he probed her wet satin. Her sheath contracted around his middle finger until he reluctantly withdrew it. With great care, he replaced his finger with his cock, closing his eyes as paradise engulfed him. He breathed deeply, willing his hips to remain steady instead of driving forward and causing her undue discomfort. She stretched around him, rocking her pelvis back to accept his invasion.

She drew in a sharp breath. Fox stilled. "Are you all right? I didn't hurt you, did I?" He had absolutely no experience with virgins.

"It's fine." Her voice strained and he didn't believe her. "Truly. I just need to accommodate this…" Her muscles contracted, and Fox worried he'd spill himself too soon. "There, better." She smiled against his neck and kissed the flesh there.

Her grip on his cock nearly undid him, but he drew back and plunged again with a bit more force. He clasped her legs around him, angling her hips for the optimal position. She complied with abandon, opening herself to him completely, her hands keeping him close. As if he'd ever leave.

He basked in the thrill of her passion, stroking in

and out of the shelter her body so eagerly gave. Their breath came fast and hard against each other. Her eyes were closed, her head cast back with the graceful column of her neck exposed. Fox licked her heated flesh and nipped at the velvety softness just beneath her ear. She shivered and clutched him even tighter between her legs.

Ecstasy built and threatened to devastate his carefully held control. He forced himself to hold back, to prolong the pleasure as long as possible. The first moment he'd seen her on the highway he'd deemed her perfect. The first time he kissed her, he'd lost his footing in the only reality he'd ever known. Now, emotion pulled him over the edge, pitched him into the sparkling beyond. Quickly, he reached between them and stroked her until she cried out. He covered her mouth with his, suffocating the sounds of her undeniable rapture, taking them deep inside of himself where he would cherish them forever.

She clenched around him, her arms clutching his back, her tongue dancing with his while her throat elicited erotic sounds of joy and sheer satisfaction. He welcomed the crushing orgasm shuddering through his frame and poured into her. He held her close, broke their kiss and gasped against her neck. With a final thrust, he spent himself. When his breathing slowed, he pressed his lips to her neck, pushed stray strands of her golden hair away from her face.

Shimmering aqua eyes met his gaze and crinkled at the corners as she smiled. "Is there more?"

Fox leaned up on an elbow. "You're not satisfied?"

"Yes, quite. But, are you?" She glanced down, and he knew she referred to the fact he hadn't left her.

His lips curved up. "More than I've ever been in my entire life." He eased away from her and settled against her side. He pressed a kiss to her blond head, still thunderstruck she'd chosen him, come to help him.

She turned in his arms. "Why does Lord Norris want so badly for you to be convicted? I don't understand."

Fox pulled a blanket over them. "He knows I know about his extortion. I stole a good number of his annual tributes, which Stratham had collected."

Her eyes widened. "You robbed Stratham?"

He smiled. "You don't believe I'm capable of such an act?"

"Well, I saw you steal from Carmody with my own eyes, so I suppose you're capable. I just hadn't heard about it."

He stroked his fingers along her shoulder and upper arm. "Because Stratham and Norris didn't tell anyone. What were they to say? A highwayman stole a great deal of money they were transporting for the purpose of corruption?"

She sat up, clutching the blanket to her chest. It didn't leave much fabric for him. Her hair tumbled around her shoulders in gorgeous disarray. "Why couldn't Stratham have just said the money belonged to him?"

Fox pulled another blanket over his lap and sat back against the saddle. "I suppose he could have, but it seems Norris didn't believe Stratham's story anyway. He reckoned Stratham probably took the money himself."

Miranda shook her head. "What are you going to do?"

"I'm not sure. I don't have any evidence against Stratham or Norris."

Her eyes lit. "Maybe Stratham will help you!"

He scoffed. "He wouldn't give me a drink of water if I were dying of thirst."

She raised a creamy-white, bare shoulder. "He's not so bad. He did give the benefit for the orphanage."

Fox knew he should focus on this conversation because he needed a plan, but he'd be damned if her disheveled state and the scent of their lovemaking wasn't making it nearly impossible. "Because you forced him into it."

She seemed oblivious to his rising lust, tapping a finger against her kiss-swollen lips. "But you said Norris thought Stratham stole the money, that Norris didn't believe he'd been robbed. Surely Stratham wasn't very happy about that. Perhaps he'd be willing to help bring down Norris?"

Unable to stop himself, Fox leaned forward and kissed her. Though brief, the connection affected her enough to leave her looking slightly dazed. He grinned. "Miranda, you've a brilliant mind. He's likely to have evidence of some kind. Now how do we persuade him to help me, of all people?"

Miranda dropped the blanket. Her breasts arched like perfect ivory globes, their tips proudly pink and so luscious. He started to lean forward again but she'd jumped to her feet and collected her clothes. "I'll do it. I'll go now."

Fox stood. "You can't go now. It's the middle of the night."

She tossed her nightdress over her head and then sat again in order to fasten her garters. "Actually, it's closer to morning. We need to get you out of here as soon as possible. Oh!" She froze in her movements and looked up at him. Her gaze paused at the juncture of his thighs, and God help him, his body responded. Beautiful roses bloomed in her cheeks as she jerked her attention to his face.

For the sake of her modesty, Fox pulled on his drawers and then his pantaloons before dropping to his knees before her on the blanket. "I appreciate you wanting to help me, but I need to be the one to see Stratham."

He finished dressing and she followed suit. "How

are you going to do that when you're locked in here?" she asked as she tried to tame her hair with her fingers. It was no use; she looked absolutely ravished. Ridiculous male pride surged in his chest.

"I've a plan." Fox went to the door and pulled it open a sliver. Still draped over the table, Tom snored loudly. Fox pushed the door wide and gestured at Freddie sitting in a chair near the exterior entrance, likely keeping watch on the manor house. The good lad hurried to the tack room.

Fox took Miranda's hand and led her over the threshold. He turned to Freddie. "Can you make sure Lady Miranda gets back to the house?"

Freddie nodded. "Aye."

"If you run into someone, you'll need to explain why you aren't here guarding me." Fox knew they weren't going to like what he said next, but he refused to allow Miranda to go to Stratham Hall. She couldn't continue to behave in a reckless fashion, especially on his behalf. "You'll say I escaped."

"What?" Miranda dropped his hand and turned to face him.

"Miranda, this is the best way. I've got to be the one to see Stratham. And if things work out as we hope, my escape won't matter because there will be nothing to charge me with."

"But how will you have escaped? You're supposedly locked inside with two men guarding you. You don't want to get Freddie in trouble." Her gaze flicked to the helpful groom.

"No, of course not." He glanced at Freddie whose face had gone a bit pale. "Freddie will tell them I called to use the privy and when Tom opened the door, I hit him. He's already unconscious, and the whisky will likely prevent him from recalling what actually happened."

Freddie looked from the snoring Tom to Fox. "Are you going to hit him? In case someone looks him over?"

Fox shrugged. "I suppose I could if you think it's necessary."

"Nah, I'll do it. He's an imbecile anyway." Freddie picked up a bucket and whacked Tom on the head. Miranda flinched, but Tom didn't move. Freddie took Tom's arm and pulled him off the chair. Fox rushed to help him drag the man to the tack room.

Freddie stepped over the prone Tom. "I suppose you have to hit me then too."

Fox would sooner hit himself. "Why can't you have gone out to use the privy yourself? It makes sense for me to wait for one of you to leave before launching an escape attempt. You came running back when you saw me ride out of the stable."

Freddie nodded. "Just might work. Aye, I think it will."

Miranda looked between the two men. Fox could see the wheels of her mind turning as her expression changed from alarm to wariness and finally to acceptance.

Fox smiled to allay her fear. "Are you ready?"

Her gaze softened and she reached up to touch his jaw. "Please be careful."

He leaned down and pressed his lips to hers. She kissed him back, but it ended too soon. Later there would be time. "Now, go." He gestured for both of them to leave.

Freddie turned back. "Take the bay." He pointed to a horse in a stall near the door. "Stone's as fast as any of his lordship's mounts."

"Thank you, Freddie. For everything. And when this is over, I'll expect you to come work for me."

The boy grinned. "Happy to, sir."

Freddie and Miranda left. She turned and waved, reminding him of the first time they parted—after their kiss on the highway. Fox ducked into the stall and quickly readied Stone, not bothering with a saddle.

He rode out into the coming dawn but slowed the animal upon seeing three figures outside the manor house, instead of two. Alarm pricked his neck. He squinted in the near-darkness, trying to determine the third person's identity. Tall, broad-shouldered. Not Norris. Taking Stone closer, he swore as recognition hit him like a fist to the gut. Saxton. Why the hell wasn't he at Stratham Hall?

Fox wanted to stop and face Saxton with Miranda, but he had to go. If he didn't leave now, he might not have another chance. Kicking Stone into a gallop, he forced himself not to look back.

~

URKY gray clouds swirled against the deep purple of the predawn sky as Miranda and Freddie made their way from the barn. She knew the color well, since she often arrived home at precisely this hour when she resided in London. That seemed a lifetime ago.

During their progression to the house, she kept looking back to watch for Fox's departure. When Freddie gasped, she jerked her head forward and nearly stumbled into Jasper.

"I knew I couldn't trust you." Jasper's flat tone and tense features reflected his disappointment. "I instructed the maid to check in on you at intervals."

If she wasn't panicked about Fox's plan failing, she would've been outraged by her brother's actions. Instead, she only wanted to delay him so that Fox could get away.

She tugged at his arm. "Come inside, Jasper. I've something to tell you."

His gaze judged her from her tousled hair to her inappropriate attire. "From the look of you, I can well imagine what you're going to say. At least no one else has seen you. Yes, I agree we need to get inside."

A horse whinnied and hooves pounded over the earth. All three of them pivoted toward the commotion. Miranda cringed and felt Jasper's muscles tighten beneath the sleeve of his coat.

Her brother turned blazing green eyes on her. "You let Foxcroft go?"

"He escaped, my lord." Freddie's voice trembled, making it seem more like a question.

Miranda squeezed her brother's forearm. "Jasper, Fox didn't steal anything, and he's not the highwayman."

Jasper's lip curled. "Actually, Norris found a great deal of money in Fox's cloak, and the same amount went missing from his office. I'm afraid your lover lied to you."

Miranda stumbled backward at the derision in Jasper's expression and tone. He'd assumed the roles of judge and jury, and would no doubt like to be executioner. Anxiety curled in her stomach. Had she really expected to spend the night with Fox without anyone finding out? The truth brought a wash of shame to her face: *yes.*

Jasper targeted Miranda with a merciless stare. "Now, tell me where Foxcroft went."

She shivered and not because of the predawn chill. She had to make Jasper understand that Fox wasn't a criminal. At least not today. "He didn't steal anything from Norris. Norris planted that money in his cloak. And what's more, Norris never paid for the tapestries he bought at the auction. Fox came here tonight to take the money Norris owes the orphanage!"

"He told you this?" At her nod, he continued, "And you believe him? Of course, you believe your lover. Where did he go?"

She had to give Fox time to convince Stratham to help him. "I don't know."

"Horseshit!" Jasper grabbed her arm. "This is not some mindless dalliance, Miranda! The man is a criminal. You ruin all of us with this! Where is Foxcroft?"

Miranda recoiled. Could she ruin their entire family? Her mind churned, trying to sort out how she could preserve her family's reputation and still help Fox.

"Christ." Jasper thrust her away and she just managed to keep her balance. He rounded on Freddie then. "I assume you helped Foxcroft escape, though I've no idea why. If you want to avoid prosecution for aiding a criminal, you'll tell me right now where he's gone."

Freddie cast an apologetic glance at Miranda, but she knew he had no alternative. "Stratham Hall."

Jasper pulled his head back, a look of confusion quirking his mouth and narrowing his eyes. "Why would he go there? He's not trying to escape?"

"No." Miranda put her hands on her hips. "I told you he's innocent. He's gone to prove it."

Jasper spun about and walked toward the house. "I'm going to rouse Norris, and then we're off to Stratham Hall."

Miranda hurried after him. Fox's plan had better work. She started to say, "I'm going with you," but realized Jasper would never allow it. She'd follow at a reasonable distance, for she'd no intention of staying behind.

CHAPTER 19

*D*AWN had fully broken over the east when Fox drew Stone to a halt in the drive at Stratham Hall. He hoped Miranda hadn't gotten into too much trouble and wished he'd been able to help her. For now, escaping the hangman's noose had to be his first priority.

He ran up the steps and pounded on the front door. Almost immediately a footman greeted him. "Mr. Stratham is not accepting visitors at this hour."

Fox pushed past him into the foyer. "I'm not a visitor. Go wake your employer and tell him to meet Foxcroft in his office." Fox already stalked toward the corner of the house. Once Stratham learned he'd arrived and had already gone to his office, Fox wagered he'd be down in a hurry.

The footman followed Fox for a moment. "I'm afraid I can't allow this."

Fox swung and faced the shorter, slighter retainer. "I don't think you understand. I'm not asking for your permission. Now fetch Stratham." Fox spun back around and quickened his pace. Anxiety curled up his spine as he wondered if the footman would do as he bade or instead raise the alarm. Part way through the Gold Room, he heard the pursuit. He looked over his shoulder. Two liveried men rushed after him. Alarm then.

Fox broke into a dead run for the office. Heaving, he pushed inside and slammed the door behind him before the footmen caught up. He turned the lock and hoped they wouldn't try to break in.

Milky gray light spilled across the large mahogany desk from the windows. Fox opened drawers, aware of the footmen outside the door speaking in low tones. Then the hammering started.

"Sir, you need to come out!"

Fox ignored them as he rifled through the contents of first one drawer and then another. Frustration mounted as he tossed estate papers and other worthless —at least to him—documents to the floor.

Finally in the next to last drawer, he found a locked wooden box. He'd seen a key in the first drawer he'd searched. Was Stratham simple enough to keep the means to open the box so close? Fox located the key on the desktop where he'd cast it haphazardly and inserted it into the lock. Nothing. Apparently Stratham lacked that amount of stupidity, at least.

The pounding stopped, replaced with more talking he couldn't discern. Then a knock. "Fox? Open the door." Stratham.

Fox looked wildly through the piles of paper on the floor. No key. More knocking. "Fox! I'm going to send for the mayor if you don't open the door!"

In desperation, Fox threw the box against the expensive marble fireplace. The wood splintered and fell to the floor in a tangled mess.

"What was that?" Stratham pounded on the door.

Fox dropped to his knees and sorted through the ruined box. Quickly, he scanned the papers. *Yes.*

He stood and opened the door. Stratham and three footmen rushed inside.

Fox held up the papers. "There's no need to call the mayor unless it's for you."

Stratham's eyes widened. He turned to his retainers. "Go." The footmen left and Stratham closed the door.

On the way from Cosgrove, Fox had rehearsed what he might say to Stratham, but the words stuck to his tongue like mud to the bottom of his work boots. How it grated to have to align himself with this man. But what choice did he have if he wanted to save his neck? "I need you to help me." There, he'd said it.

Stratham cocked his head. "How can I possibly do that?" His gaze barely moved from the papers in Fox's hand.

"Norris is framing a story in which I stole several thousand pounds from his office last night. You know that story is false."

Stratham pulled his attention from the sheaf of papers. "He says you stole the tribute money from me on the road? Is that true?"

Fox took a perverse pleasure in revealing the truth. "Yes."

Stratham exhaled. "Then Norris will do whatever he must to ensure you're punished for the crime."

Fox's heart beat faster as his apprehension increased. "Except you know he can't report that crime, so he's fabricated another."

Stratham's eyes narrowed and he adopted his annoying, most supercilious tone. "Which doesn't change the fact you're a criminal."

Fury exploded in Fox's brain. He lunged forward, waving the papers at Stratham as if they were a weapon. "Stealing from criminals! For the sake of my charges!" His chest heaved with his anger. "I'm not proud of what I had to do, but I would do it again."

Emotions played across Stratham's face. Fox couldn't see the man's thoughts, but he seemed to be wavering.

Fox pressed his advantage. "It's only a matter of time before Norris has to use you to cover his own crimes. He told me he believed you'd stolen the extortion money. That can't have been pleasant for you. What did he do, make you come up with the money yourself?"

Stratham's eyes darkened with doubt. "Yes, how'd you know?"

"Because he's a greedy, selfish son of a bitch. All he cares about is stuffing his house with overpriced relics while everyone else in the district suffers from the worst harvest in over a decade." Fox tried to breathe out his anger.

Stratham's shoulders stiffened. "My harvest was poor, too. I'm not completely unaware of your struggles."

The man knew nothing. So the harvest would mean he went without a new waistcoat or pair of gloves. For Fox and the people who depended upon him, it meant so much more. "Then help me! If I go to prison, or worse, there will be no one to help the orphans or my tenants. You know this is wrong."

Stratham's gaze flicked to the papers. "Are you going to use that to coerce me?"

The itemization in Fox's hand included names and dates, but he hadn't seen any mention of Norris. "I could, but I need Norris to be the guilty party and only your testimony will ensure that happens. Only you can link him to this list of tributes and the fact you've been collecting them for him."

Stratham's chest seemed to compress. "How'd you know, anyway? Did one of them tell you?"

Fox clenched his teeth together. He didn't have time for the familiar anger of their shared past. "Pennymore. After Jane died, her father admitted Norris bargained her hand in marriage to you in exchange for his future support. Norris promised that he and the MPs—including you—would continue to represent Pennymore's interests in Parliament, and, more importantly, that he would receive preferential treatment in the district."

Stratham sank into a plush ivory velvet chair. "She didn't love me?"

Fox shrugged. "I've no idea. Perhaps by happy coincidence she did." Surprisingly, Fox no longer cared.

Stratham shook his head. "I don't think so. I believed she possessed a reserved nature, but perhaps she masked something instead. When she agreed to marry me after such a short courtship, I assumed her sentiments matched my own." Stratham had loved her then. He'd been a pawn in Norris's machinations, just as Fox was now. Stratham looked up at him. "Why would Norris want her to marry me though? I don't understand."

Unwanted pity invaded Fox's array of emotions. "Who knows how the man's mind works? Maybe he planned to use it against you some day—you wanted something, and he gave it to you. You have to admit it's a clever way to keep someone indebted."

Stratham wiped a hand over his face. The clock ticked Fox's freedom away. Norris would be here soon. Fox's throat constricted until he feared suffocation. He'd come so close. Too close to watch it all slip away. "Stratham, I need you to tell the truth about this extortion scheme, and I need you to tell the mayor Norris planted the money in my cloak. If you don't, I'll lose everything, and I just…can't."

In that moment, Fox knew he would fall to his knees and beg if he had to. But he didn't have to. "You either help me or I'll ruin you. I've got nothing to lose, Stratham. They might not hang you, but you'll lose your seat, probably go to prison, and perhaps even lose your land."

A commotion in the hallway drove Stratham to his feet. Both men turned toward the door and waited.

Saxton opened the door while Norris's wide girth shambled over the threshold. The earl grinned while mopping his brow with an orange handkerchief. "Not much of an escape, eh, Foxcroft?"

Saxton followed Norris into the office. While Norris looked as if he'd just eaten a vastly satisfying meal, Saxton looked as if he wanted to tear Fox's limbs from his body. He'd seen Miranda and must've made his own assumptions. Fox thrust the thought away—he'd deal with it later. Right now, he needed to focus on gaining his freedom. He glanced at Stratham, trying to discern whether the man would help him, but his features were inscrutable.

Norris tucked his handkerchief into his coat. "We've got you now, Fox. The mayor is on his way. Never understand why you came here instead of running for parts unknown."

Fox worked hard to keep his temper in check, a difficult endeavor as the world fell out from under him. His grip tightened around the evidence he'd use to prove Stratham's crimes, but without Stratham testifying that Norris had planted the money in Fox's cloak, he would still be prosecuted as a thief.

"I've no intention of running from a crime I didn't commit. Not when you're the one who's been extorting money from our district." Fox looked to Stratham, waiting for him to corroborate his story. The shorter man glanced at Fox and then back to Norris who sank into the chair Stratham had vacated.

Saxton assumed a stance near the garish fireplace. "That's a strong accusation, Foxcroft. Are you able to substantiate it?" The set of his mouth gave Fox to believe he didn't think so.

An uncomfortable moment stretched during which Fox wanted to throttle Stratham. Finally, his former foe stood as tall as his diminutive stature would allow. "I've collected this money for Lord Norris. Fox is holding a list of the people who have paid us the past four years in exchange for our promise not to adversely affect their properties."

Norris's face bloomed a vivid scarlet. His fat lips opened and closed as if he were trying to unloose the hook that would draw him into captivity. "You imbecile! You don't know what you're doing. You're signing your own death warrant. No one will believe an earl extorted money on the word of some simple country MP."

Stratham rolled his shoulders back. "That may be, but there are four of us 'simple country MPs' who have been at your mercy these past years. I'm sure Britt, Walker, and Dawson will be as relieved to be free of your tyranny as I am and will gladly confirm what I'm saying."

"Insolent half-wit!" Norris turned a darker shade—nearly purple. "That doesn't change Fox stealing from me last night."

"He didn't steal anything." Stratham looked to Saxton as the only objective party in the room. "Norris had me put the money in Fox's cloak, and I'll testify as such. Fox is innocent."

Norris's eyes nearly bulged out of his head. "But he climbed into my office with a mask! Clearly he had criminal intent!"

Fox had hoped to not have to use this, but didn't hesitate. "As I told Saxton last night, I had ulterior motives with the mask. Motives that do not involve thievery, and motives I prefer not to disclose."

Saxton pushed away from the fireplace, his eyes murderous. "Watch what you say, Foxcroft."

"A pathetic attempt at deflection, Fox!" Spittle dotted Norris's breeches. "I've sent for the mayor and Carmody, who will no doubt identify you as the highwayman who robbed him."

Fox avoided looking at Saxton. "He might, but Lady

Miranda will testify otherwise and with contradictory testimony, I doubt the charges will hold."

The butler appeared in the open doorway. "The mayor, sir."

A ruddy-faced gentleman past middle age entered the room. He pulled his hat from his head revealing a scruffy shock of white hair. "Good morning." He took in the odd assembly and settled a puzzling look on Norris, who still appeared as if he were about to succumb to a fit of apoplexy. "I received your note, my lord."

Fox stepped forward. "Yes, thank you for coming, Mr. Forth. Unfortunately, we have distressing news to report. Lord Norris has been found to be extorting money from several people within the district."

The mayor didn't move. He thrust his lips out in a pensive expression. "This is very surprising. You have evidence?"

Stratham took the papers from Fox and handed them to Forth. "This is a list of everyone we've demanded money from, and the dates on which we received it."

Forth took the papers and glanced briefly at the top sheet before frowning at Stratham. "You're involved in this as well?"

Stratham didn't flinch beneath the mayor's scrutiny. "I and my fellow MPs in the district believed we had no choice but to support this scheme."

Fox wanted to convey his appreciation to Stratham. "I'd like to note, Mr. Forth, that if not for Mr. Stratham's testimony and his keen records, we would not be aware of Lord Norris's crime. I should hope there might be some leniency shown."

The mayor tightened his grip on the documents. "It's not up to me, Fox."

Saxton's features had relaxed, but his eyes were as hard as the fireplace marble. "I will ask if my father can speak on Stratham's behalf when it comes to sentencing."

Satisfied he'd helped Stratham as best he could, Fox nodded.

Stratham's shoulders slouched and he seemed to shrink back to his normal height. "Thank you, Lord Saxton."

Forth tucked the list of tributes into his coat. "I'll just see these gentlemen out, though I'm confused as to why Norris sent for me in order to report his own crimes. Unless," he turned to the earl, vainly trying to propel himself out of the chair, "you wished to turn yourself in?"

Norris held up a hand. "Might I have some assistance? I'm afraid my strength's a bit leached, what with this morning's excitement. But yes, I reasoned it time to come forward in order to demonstrate to our constituents that we cannot be bought."

Fox made an inelegant noise, part disbelieving snort and part amused laugh. The earl had no shame at all. Forth shot Fox a questioning look, but he merely shook his head in response. Let Norris try to work himself out of this mess.

The mayor helped Norris out of his chair and Stratham accompanied them from the room. Fox didn't know where they were going, but neither did he care.

Saxton stepped into the center of the room and fixed an angry glare on Fox. Before he could launch into what would no doubt be a tirade, Miranda rushed into the office. She appeared breathless, but utterly captivating with her riding habit donned in the appropriate manner. The lightness he'd felt earlier threatened to carry him away altogether.

She didn't seem to notice Saxton as she moved toward Fox. "Have you been cleared of the charges?"

Fox smiled at her. He wanted to wrap her in his

arms and never let her go. "Norris didn't even make the charges. Stratham did his part."

She exhaled and then froze when Saxton grabbed her arm. He glowered down at his sister. "You've made an absolute mess of this. When Holborn learns what you've done—"

Fox broke in. "Lord Saxton, it doesn't signify since she's to be my wife."

Saxton gaped at Fox for a moment. "*Your wife?*" He looked back to Miranda whose eyes had widened.

Unease stirred with the emotions swirling through Fox's mind. "Yes, we are to be married."

Saxton pointed at Fox with a stabbing motion. "Did you agree to wed this man?"

Miranda's cheeks hollowed as she sucked in air. She darted a glance at Fox and in her eyes he saw...regret. The lightness turned to black. Weight as heavy as iron pulled at his body, threatened his very sanity.

"No," she said, shaking her head, "I didn't agree to marry him."

CHAPTER 20

*M*IRANDA'S knees quivered as she watched the happiness fade from Fox's eyes. His pulse beat a steady rhythm in his throat, a rhythm she still felt in her bones.

Jasper relaxed, shaking his shoulders out. "Since you claim he's not your lover, I couldn't imagine why you'd agree to wed him."

Fox pinned her with an incredulous glare and the burden of her lie nearly suffocated her. "You claim I'm not your lover? What the hell occurred between us in the stable then?"

Her vision blurred. Had he just said that out loud? As close as she'd come to disaster in the past, for the first time the walls seemed to close in around her.

Jasper lunged forward and grabbed Fox's lapel. "You ruined my sister?"

Fox threw him off, his eyes blazing. "No, I made love to my future wife. I've been asking your sister to marry me for months. Fool that I am, I rather fancied her seduction in my cell last night a tacit agreement to my proposal."

Jasper swung on his sister. "What have you to say for yourself? You don't shag a man and then expect to walk away. You're the daughter of a goddamned duke, Miranda, not some trollop!"

She flinched beneath his fury and coarse language. She'd never seen Jasper this angry. Her body began to shake, but words wouldn't come. She had no more excuses, no easy way to explain herself out of this. She'd been caught.

Miranda's anger flared and she turned to Fox. "You didn't ask me to marry you last night!"

The blue, green, and gold of his eyes burned into her. "The hell I didn't. I told you I still wanted to marry you."

Had he said that? She didn't remember. She spun to face Jasper. "I don't have to marry him. No one knows what happened last night."

Jasper's eyes widened. "You're mad."

Fox stepped into her line of sight and tugged her arm so that she had to look at him full on. "I will personally inform your parents that you might be carrying my child."

Miranda shrunk back and pulled herself from his grasp. She could scarcely believe he could be so cold. "You wouldn't dare."

"I would. We're marrying, whether you agree or I drag you to the altar with your family's blessing." He leaned toward her with a menacing, humorless smile. "And I'm certain they'll give it."

Miranda turned pleading eyes to Jasper. "Mother and Father will help me."

Jasper opened his mouth then closed it abruptly. His brows drew low over his pale blue eyes. "Holborn will be livid—as I am very nearly—which is why I shan't tell him of your indiscretion. Pray you are not with child, Miranda. You'll never be allowed to raise it."

Fox grabbed Jasper's forearm. "What the hell are you saying? I don't care how your father feels, I'm marrying her. Especially if she's with child."

Jasper threw his grasp off. "You can bloody well try, but Holborn won't want you in this family." He returned his attention to Miranda and frowned. His blond brows slanted low over his sharply piercing blue eyes. He'd never looked more like their father and she had to suppress a shiver. "What a godforsaken tangle you've made." He turned his attention to Fox. "Because I think it's the conscionable thing to do," he threw an icy glare at Miranda that practically froze her insides, "I'll do all I can to see you married, especially if she's with child. Be warned however—it may not be enough. Holborn's a right prick, and he always gets what he wants."

A bit of Fox's tension left his frame. "Thank you. All I've ever wanted is to marry Miranda."

Yes, that was all he'd wanted. Practically since she'd arrived. And now she may *have* to marry him. Regardless of what Jasper said, Miranda was certain her father would wed her to Fox if she carried his child. How neatly this had all turned out for him.

The frost of a moment ago melted beneath her hurt and outrage. "You've been hoping for this, haven't you?" As she asked the question, she knew it was true. They'd been alone so often, and any one of those occasions might have been construed as an intimate moment if they'd been interrupted by Beatrice or Mrs. Gates. She'd been foolish and so had he—or maybe he'd been incredibly shrewd, just waiting for the perfect scenario. And what about the brothel? He could have pushed her out of that closet instead of touching her, arousing her. "You've been trying to compromise me for some time."

His gaze didn't waver, his nostrils flared. He swallowed. "Somewhat." He looked as if he might say more, but only added, "Yes."

Her limbs stopped quivering, and the ice returned, taking away all sensation so that she was left with nothing but a void where her emotions should have been. "Well then, you shall be the most envied man in London to have finally captured my hand. My congratulations, for you lured me well. Bravo." She pivoted toward her brother, his face impassive. "Come Jasper, I'm in need of rest."

She took Jasper's arm and as they left, she tried to contemplate what to do next. For the first time, she had no idea.

~

*T*HE following evening Miranda couldn't discern what made the day drearier: the incessant rain pelting the carriage or her parents' persistent, chagrined glowers from the opposite seat. Jasper's presence beside her did little to calm her. He was still furious with her for lying to him and sneaking into the stable to see Fox.

"Stop fidgeting, Miranda." Her mother pursed her lips and frowned. The tiny lines around her mouth indicated she made this expression far too often. "My, but you've acquired atrocious habits this summer. I suppose it goes without saying if I had it to do over again, I would never have sent you here."

"Just so." Her father didn't bother looking in either of their directions. "If you recall, I preferred sending her to a convent."

Her mother exhaled a long-suffering sigh. "So you've said."

Indeed, this had been an ongoing conversation since they'd arrived that afternoon.

"Remind me why we're having dinner with this bumpkin?" Miranda's father asked no one in particular.

"Because Jasper persuaded us Mr. Foxcroft is a decent gentleman who's interested in marrying Miranda. And marrying her to someone is your primary goal, isn't it?" Mother blinked at him.

Father cast a dark look at Jasper, who stared mutely out the window. "Yes, but I doubt this Foxcroft fellow is up to scratch. No matter since Lord Walter is champing at the bit to declare himself, and he's an acceptable choice."

Miranda's temples throbbed. She didn't know what Jasper had said to induce them to come tonight, but it didn't matter. Jasper believed she ought to marry Fox because she was ruined. Her parents preferred she marry Lord Walter because of his social superiority. No one bothered to ask what she wanted.

At least her parents didn't know she'd spent the night with Fox. She hadn't even had to ask Jasper to keep the secret. As furious as her brother had been, he couldn't consign her to the excruciatingly bitter and eternal disappointment of their parents. And she refused to entertain the idea of a possible pregnancy. It simply couldn't be borne.

Miranda wanted to climb the walls of the coach. She began to clasp her fingers together again, but stopped herself lest her mother admonish her once more. She glanced at the duchess, who, naturally, managed to sit rock still, barely even swaying with the movement of the coach.

"Miranda, you lived in the area all summer, want to be *betrothed* to this man, and yet you haven't seen his home, this Bassett Manor?"

Fox never entertained, but she didn't enlighten her parents. He had enough marks against him without adding social recluse to the list. Although, if she truly wanted to avoid marrying him, she'd let them see precisely who he was.

What was she doing? Protecting him apparently. "I've been busy with the orphanage, and if you'll recall, I was banned from socializing." Mother didn't even flinch. "When you visit Stipple's End tomorrow, you will see how so much of my time has been spent." Miranda anticipated showing them her accomplishments. Because of the benefit, the roof would be fixed, and the girls were a glowing display of Miranda's commitment. At last, perhaps, her parents would bestow upon her the approval she craved.

"Shame we couldn't have talked Kersey into marrying you. He's making such an effort to restore the family name. Nice title, too. Lord Walter will have to do, however." Mother nodded, agreeing with herself.

Father leaned toward Mother. "Or—I never thought I'd say this—even Darleigh. A bounder to be sure, but at least he's the nephew of an earl with five thousand a year. How much did Saxton say this Foxcroft has?"

"I didn't," Jasper answered, though he didn't take his gaze from the window.

More pursed-lip frowning from Mother.

They'd allow her to marry Darleigh? They'd already judged him as completely unworthy. In fact, her kissing him was the reason they'd exiled her here in the first place. And now Fox was reprehensible enough to make Darleigh attractive?

Despite her residual anger toward Fox, Miranda found herself outraged on his behalf. "Fox is a good man. He may not be the wealthiest gentleman, and it's true he has no title, but he owns quite a bit of land, two estates, and dedicates himself to those who are less fortunate."

Her mother's frown tilted briefly upward. "A... charming defense, my dear, but an impoverished altruist is not a prime candidate for a husband. Will he even spend the Season in London? Come to court? Take holiday in Brighton? His *dedication* sounds unbearably dull."

Miranda gritted her teeth. Further discussion would prove pointless.

They turned into the drive, passing a deserted gatehouse whose age and disrepair were quite pronounced,

despite the darkness caused by both fading daylight and
the terrible rainstorm. Miranda hoped the rest of Bassett Manor didn't appear as shoddy, but she had a
sinking feeling it might be even worse.

After several moments, they came upon a large ram-
bling domicile, part medieval castle, part Tudor hall,
and part Restoration manor. Its myriad of architectural
designs didn't detract from the structure. On the contrary, whoever had overseen the enlargements had
done so with a keen eye and more than a bit of flair.
Tall, mullioned windows threw light onto the darkened
drive and lent a cheery glow.

Father peered out of the window and studied the
house. "Big enough, I suppose, but it's nothing if he
doesn't have the land to back it up." True to himself no
matter what, her father measured everything in land
and money. At least this earned a point in Fox's favor.

One of their grooms opened the door and assisted
the duchess and then Miranda from the carriage. Another groom held out a large umbrella. Miranda followed closely to seek protection from the downpour.

By the time they'd reached the stone stairs leading
to the great oaken entrance, Miranda's neck and back
had caught more than a few fat drops of rain, but her
discomfort evaporated when she stepped inside.

The massive entry gave Miranda the impression of a
cathedral. Soaring three stories high, the room split at a
wide staircase ascending the far wall. Mid-landing, the
stairs forked left and right, curling downward along a
thick wooden balustrade gorgeously carved with highly
polished oak leaves and acorns.

Large rooms led from each side of the foyer. Corridors disappeared to the sides and back of the house on
either side of the stairs. Though the structure screamed
importance, the appointments lacked everything except
age and use. An old, tattered carpet covered part of the
stone tile floor, but an array of chips and cracks were

still visible around the edges. Tallow candles, not beeswax, filled the overhead chandelier, further illuminating Fox's shallow coffers.

He strode into the entry hall from one of the back corridors. Miranda sucked in her breath. He wore the same clothing he'd worn to the benefit, elegant black perfectly offsetting the brilliant white shirt and emerald green waistcoat. His slippers looked a bit worn, but then he had dashed after her to the brothel, if memory served. He returned her perusal with equal interest, and she quickly thrust all thoughts of the benefit from her mind lest she betray she still wanted him. Coerced marriage or not, she desired him with a ferocity that sent a shiver up her spine.

Fox stopped in the center of the room and offered bows to the duke and duchess. "Good evening, Your Grace, Your Grace." He looked past them and inclined his head toward Saxton. "My lord." He stepped forward and took Miranda's hand. "My lady." Did anyone else hear the note of possession in his tone?

"Good evening, Foxcroft." Her father clasped his hands behind his back, likely to keep from having to touch Fox in greeting. "Quite a...house." His judgmental gaze traveled upwards and around before settling back on his host.

"Yes, it's been in my family since the twelfth century. Not in its entirety, however. There have been several additions over the ages." He smiled. "I'm sorry the daylight is gone, or I would show you the gardens. They're quite lovely. The maple trees around the lake are breathtaking this time of year."

He had a lake? Miranda realized there were still many things she didn't know about him. What did he eat for breakfast? How did he relax? What did the rest of his house look like? His bedchamber? She hoped no one noticed the heat rising in her cheeks.

"Dinner is nearly served. If you will just accompany

me." He presented his arm to Miranda, and she took it, trying to ignore the familiar jolt of excitement running up her arm. For months she'd disregarded the response as a mere aberration—the reaction of a lonely woman used to the attentions of dozens of men. Now she knew it to be different. Only he was capable of such provocation.

She walked with him toward the right side corridor, passing an enormous hall. Judging from its exposed, arching beams, it no doubt existed as part of the original building. Similar in form and shape to Stipple's End, this hall rose higher and swept longer. And, she noted, it didn't leak.

Turning right, they traipsed a shadowy hallway— the sconces were few and again lit with tallow—coming to a large doorway on the left. Dark, Tudor-era paneling arched high above the dining room. Carved deer and other woodland creatures decorated the focal point, a massive fireplace. A beautifully woven but worn cloth covered the long table. Embroidered foxes frolicked around the hem, declaring the piece a Foxcroft family heirloom. The silver and plate were also aged, but didn't appear overly abused. Overall, Miranda breathed a sigh of relief at the state of Fox's house.

A setting for five graced one end of the table, presumably so they could more easily converse. Fox gave Miranda the seat to his right and waited for her father to assist her mother into the chair opposite. The duke sat down beside her, while Jasper took the remaining chair next to Miranda. With everyone positioned, Fox took his own chair at the head.

Two footmen, oh Lord, only two footmen, came forward and poured wine. Mother acknowledged the deficit of servants with a frown. Miranda sipped her wine and fought to keep her face relaxed. Bleh! She nearly choked. How old was the vintage? Had it been stored properly?

Her gaze flicked to her father. As he took a drink, his eye twitched and he set the glass back on the table. "I think you might have a bad bottle there."

Miranda cringed, afraid all of the bottles were spoiled, or worse—Fox had no other bottles.

Fox lifted his lips, but didn't smile. "You may be right." He turned to beckon a footman. "Rufus, another bottle please."

"What an interesting motif above the fireplace, Mr. Foxcroft." Mother studied the animals cavorting amongst a wide-armed oak and other, lesser trees.

"Thank you, Your Grace." Fox turned to briefly glance at the carving. "A previous relative handcrafted the scene. Interestingly, the stag depicted there was later killed by the artist. In fact, the antlers were made into a lamp currently displayed in the great hall."

The duchess managed a brittle smile, but Miranda could well imagine what she thought of an antler lamp.

The footman finished opening the new bottle of wine and poured a sample into the duke's glass. Father wasted no time in tasting the replacement and, judging from the wrinkling of his nose, found it lacking.

"How much land do you have here, Foxcroft?." Father had apparently deemed further commentary on the wine to be pointless.

"Over two thousand acres." *That much?*

If her father was impressed, he didn't show it. "How badly did the weather affect you this year? The yields from my southernmost holdings will be down nearly a quarter."

Miranda darted a look at Fox. He appeared serene, completely unruffled, affable even. "I'm not yet certain how devastating our loss will be, but I'm certain it's significant. A shame, too, as I'd planned to expand my sheep population in the spring."

He had sheep?

Miranda picked up her spoon to taste the mock

turtle soup—she'd be surprised if Fox could afford real turtle soup—the footmen set before her. She'd never had the calf's head substitute, but it wasn't bad. In fact, the herbs used created a most delectable flavor.

"Must be difficult overseeing an orphanage. Likely takes away from time you'd rather be spending on your estate, making repairs, refurbishing." Father looked around the room, leaving no doubt as to his opinion that the dining room draperies needed replacement and the walls could use redecoration.

"Precisely why Miranda will be such a valuable helpmate." Fox smiled at her, but his eyes remained distant.

The duke narrowed his eyes. "Don't overestimate Miranda's skills, my boy."

Fox's jaw clenched just before he opened his mouth. Miranda clanked her spoon against her bowl to draw his attention then gave an infinitesimal head shake. Fox took a deep breath and looked away, but she could just detect color rising above the edge of his cravat. She appreciated his defense, but such heroics were pointless in her father's eyes.

The soup dishes were soon cleared and the footmen appeared with the next course, red mullet with a béchamel sauce. With only two footmen serving, it took considerably longer than it ought. The gentle clink of silver against plate and the footfalls of the servants against the wood floor punctuated the droning silence.

"Oh!" Mother took a bite of the mullet and dabbed at her mouth with her serviette again. "Are there bones in this fish?" Dear Lord, she hated bones in her food. She likely wouldn't be able to finish her dinner now.

Fox took a drink of his wine. "I'm certain at some point, yes, there were bones in this fish. I apologize if a stray one is still present."

Mother did not look mollified. She rested her fork

on the table and spent the rest of the course studying the room with an austere frown.

"So you've been to this orphanage, Saxton?" Father asked.

"Indeed. Massive undertaking what with the children, the building, and the land."

"From what little I've seen of your estate, Foxcroft, it looks as if your energies should be directed here, not on some charity project." Father took a bite of fish.

Fox set his utensils down. "My family founded that 'project' four hundred years ago. Just as you carry the titles of Holborn and Saxton and see to all of the requirements associated with such responsibility, I am committed to doing the same for my family's legacy. It may not be a title, but I find it equally important and wholly fulfilling."

Three sets of eyes stared at Fox. Had he just insulted them? Miranda bent her head over her fish.

"Humph. Spoken like a true provincial." Her father didn't bother lowering his voice. He never did.

More quiet while everyone ate, or in her mother's case, beleaguered the art of silent disfavor.

"How's your stable, Foxcroft?" The duke asked. Her father had one of the most successful breeding facilities in the whole of England. He lived and breathed horses.

Fox sent her father a bored glance, the gold in his eyes nearly impossible to detect tonight. "Dilapidated."

"Have you any decent horseflesh?" Her father's question made Miranda cringe inwardly. Phrased as such, it sounded as if he highly doubted the occupants of Fox's rundown stable could possibly be judged adequate.

"Yes, but that's subjective, isn't it?" Fox cocked his head to the side, never wavering under the duke's superior expression. "Perhaps you'd like to come back another day and provide your esteemed opinion."

Her father grunted. "I'm afraid our time here is

short, and we agreed to tour this infernal orphanage tomorrow."

"How magnanimous of you." Fox sliced his knife across his fish, splitting it in half. Miranda wondered if he imagined the duke's face in its stead.

Did her family's obvious condescension bother him? It had to, but he was doing a good job keeping his temper in check.

Miranda paused, her fork halfway to her mouth. When had she begun to notice their condescension? One could argue—and several had—she behaved as arrogantly as any of them. So why did she now feel so uncomfortable? She took the bite of fish and looked over at Fox. Was she more comfortable with him? Not now, while they were at odds. He'd barely registered her presence since the meal had started.

Her father winced after sipping his wine. "I suppose you'll be asking for a larger dowry?"

Miranda's mother turned narrowed eyes on her husband. "Surely this discussion can wait until after Miranda and I have left the table."

Fox barely looked up from his food. "I'm certain Miranda's dowry is sufficient."

Her father leaned toward Fox. "Do you even know how much it is? From the look of this place and from what I hear of this ramshackle orphanage, you need thousands and thousands of pounds. Doubtless why you're keen to marry her. Miranda's got four thousand."

Miranda set down her fork. "What about Grandmama's estate? She left it to me and my heirs."

Her mother's eyes narrowed. "Great-aunt Cecilia still lives there."

"And she may continue to do so, but the estate is to be mine." Miranda's heart thudded at an irregular pace. The evening was slipping toward catastrophe.

Her father inclined his head to one of the footman to indicate he'd finished his plate. "Yes, Turnbridge is yours." The derision in his tone was evident. Leaving property to women was, in his opinion, the height of lunacy.

"Enough of this vulgar conversation." Miranda's mother adopted a half-smile. "Mr. Foxcroft, tell us of your ancestors. You say they founded this orphanage. What other illustrious deeds might they lay claim to?"

The footmen removed the fish and brought out a roasted pheasant and several side dishes. Fox sat back in his chair. He was incredibly handsome presiding over his table, something Miranda had never seen him do before. "Henry VIII imprisoned some ancient relative in the Tower. Turned out to be mistaken identity, so not a terribly romantic story, I'm afraid. Wait, you may enjoy this. Sometime in the fourteenth century, an indirect female relative was arrested for witchcraft. She escaped, however. Don't know what happened to her."

The pathetic attempt at a smile on her mother's face disappeared, and again, her parents gaped at Fox as if he'd sprouted the antlers he'd mentioned earlier.

Miranda had heard quite enough. "Fox, I'm sure there are other relatives worth mentioning?" She pleaded with her eyes for him to stop. Now she was certain their condescension affected him.

He returned her steady gaze and the gold in his eyes seemed to flare. Finally, a bit of emotion. Miranda relaxed in her chair.

Suddenly two small girls burst into the dining room shouting at once.

"She did it!"

"No, she did it!"

"Fox!"

Then their voices died, and Miranda swore she *heard* her mother's shock. She chanced a glance at the duchess. Before she could register her mother's expression, a set of small arms hugged either side of her.

"Lady Miranda!"

"You're here!"

Miranda opened her arms and gave them each a pat on the back. She didn't dare look at her mother or her father or even Jasper. "Good evening, young *ladies*. I'm afraid you've burst into our formal dinner. Where are the manners I've taught you?"

They both pulled back and looked up at her with sheepish eyes. "Sorry, Lady Miranda," said Becky, the smaller girl on Miranda's left. "We weren't sure where to go. It's our first day here."

Miranda looked to Fox. "Why are they here?"

His gaze was inscrutable. "I'm moving the children here until the roof is repaired."

He was opening his home to them. Once, Miranda would've wrinkled her nose at such an intrusion, but now her heart warmed at his kindness and generosity. She'd never known anyone like him and likely never would again.

Mrs. Gates appeared, a bit breathless, in the doorway. "Girls! Come away with me now!" She held her hands out to them.

Becky and Emily clung to Miranda. Emily whispered, "Do we hafto?"

Miranda gave them each a squeeze. "Yes. But I shall see you tomorrow, all right?"

They both nodded, and after one more hug, joined Mrs. Gates who ushered them out of the dining room.

Now Miranda dared to look at her family. Her mother's brow was puckered, and her lips drawn tight. Her brother shook his head at her with the ghost of a smile.

Her father glowered at her and said, "If those are the manners you've instilled, I can see you're no better at overseeing those children than you are any of your other supposed skills."

Fox cleared his throat. "I beg your pardon, Your Grace, but you are quite mistaken. You saw two young girls whose manners are greatly improved. Three months ago, they would've dashed in here and probably jumped on the table and helped themselves to your plate. Miranda has done an excellent job with all of the children, and I demand you speak of her in a more respectful fashion."

Though his words were finely crafted, Miranda could see the ire burning deep in the gold rimming his pupils. She held her breath waiting to see how her father would respond.

The duke turned his frosty glare on Fox and leaned lightly forward. "You'll demand nothing of me. I'll speak to my daughter however I please, and you've nothing to say about it."

"I will when she's my wife."

Her father snorted. "A fate that has not yet been determined. Your current course isn't doing you any favors."

Fox wrapped his fingers around the stem of his wineglass, and Miranda wondered if he might snap it in two. He inclined his head slightly and then downed what was left in his glass.

The footmen brought out dessert, and with it the interminable meal limped to an uncomfortable end.

"An excellent syllabub, Mr. Foxcroft." Miranda could scarcely believe she'd bothered to compliment their host, but then Mother loved her sweets.

Father pushed his still half-full wine glass away. "Might you have some port for our after dinner discussion, Foxcroft?"

"Sadly, no." Fox didn't look at all sad. "But I've some French brandy."

"I suppose that must suffice." His tone clearly said it would not.

"Come, Miranda." Her mother stood from her chair with the aid of a footman. "Mr. Foxcroft, is there someone to direct us to the drawing room?"

Fox stood. "Certainly. Rufus will take you."

The footman bowed and preceded them from the dining room. Nervous, Miranda reluctantly left the men alone together. She walked slowly and looked back over her shoulder. Fox gazed intently at her brother and father as they all resumed their seats.

With an exhalation of pent-up breath, she turned to follow her mother and Rufus. He took them to the left and opened a door across the corridor. The large drawing room sported wide mullioned windows. Like the dining room, it appeared part of the Tudor addition. Unlike the dining room, it looked incredibly shabby. So much so, that her mother gasped. If not for the cheery fire burning in the enormous stone fireplace, the room would have been downright maudlin.

Her mother didn't wait for Rufus to depart before launching into her criticism. "He can't actually live in this room?" There were no draperies at all and the one rug—completely inadequate for such an expansive chamber—showed holes and had faded so much it appeared monochromatic. "Why, the carpet is brown on brown."

Miranda looked abysmally at the five meager pieces of furniture arranged before the fireplace. A decrepit settee with a sagging middle, two commanding wooden chairs from the Tudor period, and two mismatched tables, one oval and painted with ivy leaves, many of which were cracked and peeling off, and one square with a semi-circular divot along one edge.

The duchess turned to Miranda wide-eyed. "You can't live here. This is beyond awful."

Miranda couldn't disagree. How could he stand to inhabit such a place? Actually, he spent so much of his time at the orphanage, perhaps he didn't even notice how badly Bassett Manor needed his attention.

"Only imagine how horrid his bedchamber must be!" Her mother poked at the cushion on the settee and a cloud of dust rose. "He's either a miserly penny-pincher or a terrible spendthrift."

"He's neither, Mother."

"Well, then what is the problem? His estate is quite large enough to support an affluent lifestyle. There's no call for this level of degradation." She waved her hand about the room, her face pinched in distaste.

How could she explain someone like Fox to her mother? That he spent as much of his time and energy on Stipple's End as his own estate, probably more in all likelihood. "It's not as if he doesn't work, Mother."

"I don't care. I couldn't abide you living here." Her mother shuddered. "It's clear to me that a marriage with Foxcroft won't suffice. Perhaps you've forgotten what you're used to after being closeted up in this backwater all summer. We never should have left you here this long. When we return to London in a few days you won't want to come back. Mark my words."

London. Miranda had almost forgotten how badly she'd wanted to return. To shop on Bond Street, ride in Hyde Park, have an ice at Gunter's…but only for a short time. "I do miss London."

"Of course, you do. You're a sophisticated girl. A lifetime in the country would bore you to an early grave." Her mother came back to her and patted her hand, an atypical gesture for her general lack of sentimentality. "Your father will persuade Mr. Foxcroft that marriage to you is not what he wants." She glanced around the room to punctuate how easy the persuasion would be. "Come, wedding Foxcroft is a nonsensical idea."

Miranda couldn't disagree. Hadn't she gone to great pains—even hurting Fox—to refuse him before Jasper had demanded they marry?

What kind of marriage could they possibly hope to have anyway? He wanted her for her money and, presumably, her body. She wanted him for the same physical pleasures, but at what cost? She didn't expect love, an emotion her family skirted at the best of times and outright neglected at the worst. But she'd never expected, never wanted, to enter into marriage under these circumstances—feeling as if she had no choice. And now her mother insisted she not only had a choice, but that she was absolutely making the wrong one.

"Yes, Mother, you're right. As usual."

$\sim$

OX turned on his heel and stalked quietly from the drawing room door. He hadn't meant to eavesdrop, but the duchess's shrill tone carried into the hallway and he hadn't wanted to interrupt. Once he heard the topic of their conversation, he'd been rooted to the floor. However, upon hearing Miranda's statement, he couldn't get away fast enough.

Served him right for trying to personally attend to their comfort instead of sending one of his two footmen. He'd done so because Saxton had given him a silent communication to give him a moment with the duke. Seeing to Miranda and her mother had seemed a logical—and inviting—opportunity. How wrong he'd been.

He reentered the dining room and tried to forget what he'd just heard, but he feared it would be impossible. Miranda's words were engraved in his brain.

Saxton stood near the fireplace with his brandy. The duke, still seated at the table, frowned into his glass. Fox waited for the inevitable insult about the quality of the beverage.

The duke didn't disappoint. "You say this is French brandy? A damaged cask, perhaps?" He held it up and studied the amber liquid. "Reminds me of the bad batch Rothbury served last spring. Bloody hell, Foxcroft, but your cellar needs attention."

His demeaning observation eroded the last of Fox's tolerance. "I don't know if you've noticed, Your Grace, but I am rather low on funds."

Miranda's father tilted his silvery-blond head and pierced Fox with a glacial stare that should've sent him running. "And why is that?"

Rage exploded in Fox's chest. He'd been patient. He'd been kind—well, he'd tried to be kind. "I can assure you I manage Bassett Manor and Stipple's End quite well."

The duke snorted and set his glass on the table, apparently abandoning all pretense of drinking the noxious liquor. "It doesn't look like it to me. A ramshackle house. Insufficient servants. A dilapidated stable. And from what I can tell this orphanage of yours is in even worse shape, particularly if you're moving the urchins here. If this is running things 'quite well,' I'd despair to think if things were going poorly."

"Things *are* going poorly." Which didn't put him at fault. "I manage the best I can with what I have. And as you can tell, I don't have much."

The duke stood. "I understand your…dedication to the orphanage, but perhaps it's time to let it go. There's no shame in protecting your own interests and those of your tenants."

Fox didn't know their definition of shame, but it clearly didn't match his. "There is plenty of shame in turning out forty orphans and six staff members. Those people have nowhere else to go, and I won't consign the children to a workhouse."

Holborn shrugged. "There are other orphanages, and absent those, a workhouse is precisely where those brats should be."

Fox barely kept his rage in check. Brats? These people didn't understand. They'd never understand. How could he marry into a family of such self-absorbed, arrogant, egotists? Fox stalked to the other end of the table, as far away from the duke as he could get. "Is there really anything for us to discuss?"

Holborn tugged at his waistcoat and straightened his spine, accentuating his still-impressive frame. "No, you're quite right. You'll not do at all for Miranda." His lip curled. "For all I know you squandered your fortune at the gaming tables."

Fox slammed his fist on the table. "I've never gambled a penny. Not once. Not ever. My life carries enough risk without the added stupidity of games of chance." They couldn't know about his father's gambling habit, that it was the very reason Fox looked as if he were a complete failure.

"Wait." Saxton set his glass on the mantel and finally entered the conversation. He'd been noticeably quiet all night. Like the others, he'd seemed terribly uncomfortable, but now Fox wondered at the reasoning behind it. Was it Fox's house and offerings, or was it something else?

"Holborn, why don't you give him a chance to explain?"

He called his father by his title?

The duke glared at his son and Fox began to perhaps see the root of Saxton's discomfort. "What could he possibly explain? That if he could just marry my daughter, he'd turn all of this around? I can see the man's got no head for estate management."

Saxton's eyes frosted nearly as cool as his father's. It was a bit impressive, actually. "You don't know that. Look at his books."

Fox appreciated Saxton's interference, but thought it was likely pointless. If Fox had been a betting man, he'd wager Bassett Manor *and* Stipple's End that the duke would look at his books on a cold day in hell.

Holborn snorted. "As if I'd bother. This was a fool's errand. Don't know why I let you talk me into it." He spared Fox a meager glance. "Foxcroft." Then he turned and strode from the dining room.

Saxton came toward him. He kept his voice low. "Couldn't you have tried a bit harder? He's going to forbid Miranda from marrying you, and I'd just as soon not explain why she must."

Fox ran a hand through his hair. He *had* tried. Could he help it if her parents were completely insufferable? "Get him to Stipple's End tomorrow. Maybe I can change his mind."

Saxton shook his head. "I don't see how." Then he too quit the room.

Fox cut his fist through the air as if he were punching that supercilious ass, Holborn, in the face. God, but he wished he didn't want Miranda so badly. He'd tell the lot of them to go rot.

Including Miranda?

He plucked his brandy glass from the table and gulped down the sharp brew. The conversation he'd overheard in the drawing room filled his ears. Chances were, he wouldn't have to turn her away. She'd leave of her own accord.

CHAPTER 21

*F*OX'S head hurt. Too much lousy French brandy. He only prayed today went better than last night. Miranda and her parents were due at Stipple's End any moment.

He peered up the ladder to watch Rob descend from the roof. "How does it look?" They'd just barely covered the gaping hole with the canvas following the collapse, but water had begun seeping into the hall again.

His steward jumped to the ground. "Not too bad, just lost one corner and I re-nailed it. Your future in-laws here yet?"

Tension throbbed along Fox's shoulder blades. "No, but any moment. And they likely won't be my in-laws."

Rob looked Fox up and down. "Such optimism. Shouldn't you be inside getting ready?"

Yes, he should. He owed it to Saxton—and Miranda if she was still remotely interested in having him. But therein lay the question. She'd never actually said yes to any of his proposals, had just gone along with her brother's directive. Would changing his clothes make any difference?

"Last night I wore my best clothes, served my best food and wine, and donned my best behavior—and I came up short."

"Hell, you didn't give them that offensive brandy did you?"

Fox arched a brow at him. "They asked for port."

Rob grinned. "No wonder they don't like you."

Fox snorted. And then, though he tried to fight it, smiled. "You should have seen her mother. Well, I suppose you will, shortly."

A look of terror entered his friend's eyes. "Oh no, must I?"

Fox sighed. "Never mind. One can only hope they won't visit often once we're married." A tremor of unease skittered along his spine. *If* they married.

"Still can't quite believe you pulled it all off. Norris facing charges of corruption, Stratham as well, betrothed to Lady Miranda..." Rob shook his head.

But it wasn't as tidy as that. "Betrothed" was a bit of a stretch at this point. "I'd better go in." Fox strode toward the house.

Rob called after him, "Might smile about it now and again!"

He opened the door and stopped short. Miranda stood just inside. She looked refreshingly beautiful in a pale blue dress with tiny flowers and a pearl necklace. She'd started wearing jewelry after she'd returned from the house party. Today it accentuated the divide between them.

"There you are," she said. Her gaze flicked over his clothes.

He stiffened. "We had to adjust the covering over the roof."

She walked to him. "Yes, I noticed the wet floor."

They stood there at the threshold of the back door. Her inside, him outside. A perfect visual representation of their differences. She, of the parties and balls and London Society, and he, of the outdoors and country—a match doomed in hell.

Nevertheless he ached for her. She stood so close, he

could smell her citrus-spice scent, see the remarkable details of her beautiful skin. Faint shadows of purple colored the flesh beneath her eyes. Had she slept as little as he? If he took one step, he'd feel her breath, her heat...

She tore her gaze from his and turned. "My parents are here. Last night didn't go very well."

A colossal understatement. "No."

She turned back to face him, her forehead creased. "Fox, why didn't you tell me about Bassett Manor? I might've prepared them—"

"How? It's not as if I could have refurbished the place."

"You can if we marry." She eyed him uncertainly. "Turnbridge earns upwards of five thousand a year."

"Really?" Fox had no idea she had an estate worth so much money. That could mean the difference for him. For all of them.

Her nostrils flared. "All you care about is my money. That's the only reason you compromised me, isn't it?"

Unable to help himself, he did move closer then. "No." He leaned in and whispered against her ear, felt her shiver beneath his lips. "And you know it isn't." He pushed past her and made his way to the hall where her parents waited with Mrs. Gates.

"Good morning, Your Grace, Your Grace." He bowed to them.

"I begin to see why Bassett Manor looks as it does." Holborn stood near the leak and appeared to be studying the damage. "I'll give you the name of an architect in Town. You don't want a country bumpkin bumbling through this."

Fox swallowed an acerbic retort. "I've already hired Bleeker and Dench. Representatives are due from London in two days' time."

"Indeed?" The duke's eyebrows raised. "An excellent

firm. Used them myself when we added a conservatory to Holborn House."

"Would you care to see the rest of the building?" Fox asked.

"I suppose. We came all this bloody way."

Fox bit his tongue lest he tell the duke to bugger off.

Mrs. Gates went back to her duties, and Miranda led them on a tour of the downstairs. The duke commented on different aspects of the building and the duchess frowned without relief. In the library, Miranda showed her parents the girls' needlework. "Some of them are quite accomplished."

"More accomplished than you, I see." Miranda's mother looked at a particularly elaborate piece Delia had stitched. "What else do these orphans do? Watercolors? Play the pianoforte?"

Miranda stood near the fireplace, her hands clasped demurely before her. "I should like them to do both, but there hasn't been money for paint and we don't have a pianoforte."

We. Love warmed Fox's chest, though he tried to suppress it. Why did he have to love her?

Her mother inspected the room, her piercing gaze scrutinizing every detail. "So you're a glorified governess here?"

Fox hoped Her Grace tripped. Why would Miranda want to go back and live in London with these people? They had nothing pleasant to say about anything. Their disappointment and irritation couldn't be more obvious.

He studied Miranda closely, looking to see her reaction to her parents, but couldn't detect anything beyond her serene expression. What happened to the passionate girl he fell in love with?

"All of the children have benefited greatly from Miranda's presence," he said, aching to see something positive from her parents—for her. "Some of their backgrounds are quite tragic. She's given them a sense of purpose and self-esteem most of them would never have known. In fact, if not for Miranda, I never would've realized anything was missing at Stipple's End. It's one thing to provide food, clothing, and shelter, but quite another to give these children the means to really *live*."

Instead of praising their daughter or at least looking at her with something akin to admiration or approval, her parents glanced at each other and exchanged some sort of private communication. Miranda's lips pursed, but Fox couldn't determine if she was annoyed or hurt, or something else entirely.

Fox had had enough of this farce. "I'll leave you to complete your tour as I've things which require my attention." He bowed and took himself into the corridor.

He needed heavy work.

After a good half-hour of trimming a hedge, his mood improved. Sweat and dirt clung to his shirt, but exhilaration thrummed through his body. Were Miranda and her parents still here? What would the duchess say when she saw him in this state? Perversely, he rather hoped he could find out.

Detouring to the front of the house, he looked to see if their carriage remained. A tiny shard of disappointment pierced his chest when he saw the empty drive.

He circled back to the rear entrance and went directly to the small washroom off the corridor. A basin of fresh water sat on the dresser in which he kept spare items of clothing. Tossing his soiled shirt onto the single chair, he grabbed a cloth from the top drawer and worked at getting himself clean. The icy water refreshed his heated flesh.

As he finished, the door opened. Miranda stood on the threshold, her mouth open.

Too aware of his shirtlessness and her proximity, his body flared into arousal. "You're still here."

She stared at his bare flesh, her gaze traveling downward.

Fox turned his back to her and opened a drawer to find a clean shirt. "I'm done here."

"I'm just fetching the lice combs." Coming out in a rush, her words collided with his.

"That time again, is it?" He pulled the ivory linen shirt over his head and faced her. She hadn't moved. "Why didn't you leave with your parents?"

She shrugged. "They're going to pack for London. They wish to be on the road first thing tomorrow."

He noticed she avoided answering his question about whether she planned to leave. "I see."

She stepped into the room. Light from the small window over the sink filtered across her face, illuminating the aqua of her eyes, the perfect slope of her cheekbones, the luscious pink of her lips.

He had to know. "Are you going with them?"

"I…yes." She looked down.

Unspoken questions and admonitions collected between them until the small, dim space overwhelmed his ability to think. He needed air.

Fox made to leave, but as he drew near her, the need to touch her conquered all else. He grabbed her upper arms and pulled her against him, claimed her mouth in a blistering kiss. She angled her head and wrapped her arms around his neck. Standing on her toes, she pressed her body into his.

Savage lust took hold of his senses. He reached out with his left hand and slammed the door shut. She opened her mouth, inviting his tongue inside, and arched her neck back. Fox accepted her offering, supporting her head with one hand and gliding the other down the side of her face. He traced his finger down her neck until it settled against the satiny flesh above the bodice of her gown.

He closed his hand over the swell of her breast and

she gasped into his mouth. Desperate to touch her, he unfastened the front of her gown. The bodice dropped down to her waist. He ran his thumb over the top of first one breast and then the other.

Breaking the kiss, he pulled back. Their panting breaths filled the shadowed chamber. Fox guided her backward and lifted her onto the edge of the worktable.

He gazed hungrily at the ivory softness of her breasts pressing above her stays. With each shallow breath, the tantalizing flesh rose and fell. He pulled the laces open and the globes of her breasts tumbled free. Pushing her clothing to the sides, he cupped her in his hands. She closed her eyes and tipped her head back, small sounds of ecstasy escaping her lips.

Her nipples pebbled, and he squeezed each one between his thumb and forefinger, pulling on their tips. She cried out and pulled his mouth to her chest. He suckled her with ravenous need. This was no time for gentleness. Not when emotion thundered through him, and he wanted to make love to her until she didn't know her name.

She spread her legs, and he stepped between them, never taking his mouth from her breast. She leaned back with the force of his hunger and he eagerly devoured the other breast. All the while, she tugged at his head, her fingers twining in his hair. She could pull all of it out and he wouldn't care.

He reached one hand down her leg and found the hem of her dress. He shoved it up, running his fingertips over her stocking-glad calves. His finger tripped over the garter and he pulled it against her flesh, eliciting a sharp gasp from her mouth. She gripped his head even harder and he nipped at her breast.

Her breathing came even faster amidst her erotic cries. His cock raged in his breeches, screaming for its own release. Soon. But first, he would taste her, lick her, savor her.

Dewy softness greeted his fingers when he at last settled between her thighs. He slid his finger over her clitoris and she bucked up from the table. He grinned against her breast. Gliding his finger up and down, he didn't enter her. Her hips rotated, seeking his penetration.

Fox pulled away from her breasts, reluctant to leave them but so eager for the feast that awaited him. He pushed her skirts up to her waist and knelt between her legs.

"Fox?" She sat up and looked down at him.

His gaze connected with hers when he thrust his finger inside of her. She cried out. Immediately he replaced his finger with his mouth, licking the lips of her sex.

She fell back against the table with a moan, pressing up against his mouth. He sucked at her and gave her one finger, then two until she arched off the table in a steady rhythm with his mouth and hand. She felt so close.

So was he, but he would give this to her. He worked his fingers, feeling her muscles contract around him. She tightened, her hips lifted in sweet offering. For a breathless moment, he paused, delighting in her imminent release. And then he sucked hard on her clitoris, and she shattered against him. She shouted out, but then whimpered softly, as if she'd put her hand to her mouth.

Fox worked to keep his own orgasm at bay. Christ, but he'd never been close to coming before penetration. After a moment her breathing slowed and he managed to check his lust. He got to his feet and looked down at Miranda, her dress bunched up and wrinkled, her swollen nipples gorgeous and dark as red roses atop the white silk of her breasts.

She opened her eyes and met his gaze. Her face softened and relaxed with pleasure. Her eyes were dewy and dazed. She struggled to sit up. He took her hand and pulled. Facing him, her lips curved into a satisfied smile. She looked as if she might purr. "At least our marriage would have had that. I suppose that's more than most people enjoy."

Would have had. There would be no marriage. Fox's desire faded and was replaced with a frigid void. He could turn and walk away from her now, never see her again, but first he wanted to tell her what she was missing. What she denied them both. "I hoped we could have shared love. I love you, Miranda. I would have honored you and protected you. We could have built an incredible life together."

There were tears in her eyes, but she didn't shed them. "My father never would have allowed it."

Her family would always stand between them. "And if there's a child?" he asked.

She swiped at her eyes. "I don't know."

"I'll do whatever you want. All I ask is that if there is a child, and you still won't marry me, you give it to me to raise." His voice nearly broke, but he forced steel into his tone. He wouldn't give her a choice in this at least.

She raised her gaze to meet his. He saw fear and a torrent of other emotions. She didn't—maybe couldn't—respond. Time stretched and his heart crumbled.

He turned his back to her. "You should go. To London. Send me a letter and tell me if you're breeding."

He left without a backward glance, pulling the door shut behind him.

CHAPTER 22

*T*HAT night after dinner, Miranda folded the last item of clothing from her dresser at Birch House and placed it into the trunk. She shook her head at how she performed this task instead of allowing the maid to do it for her. How far she had come.

She looked down at her hands. She'd taken to wearing her nails short, but one of them had cracked. Her skin maintained its softness, but only because she applied lotion multiple times a day in an effort to keep it so. How long before they revealed her as a working woman?

Beatrice pushed into her room. "You left the door ajar. I hope I'm not interrupting."

"No, I've just finished packing."

Beatrice looked at the packed trunk and glanced about the room, now devoid of Miranda's effects. Her forehead creased. "It doesn't look as if you're coming back."

No, it didn't. Miranda had said tearful goodbyes to the children that afternoon but didn't tell them she might not return. Suddenly the dam burst, and she sank to the bed. "Oh, Beatrice. I don't know what to do!"

Beatrice closed the door and sat beside Miranda.

"Have you changed your mind about marrying Fox? And here I believed you'd made a love match."

She goggled at Beatrice in shock. "You did?"

Beatrice narrowed her eyes. "Why else would you marry him? His fabulous estate? His staggering income? The lure of running an orphanage?"

"Beatrice, I never knew you to be so sarcastic."

"I'm sorry." Beatrice patted Miranda's hand. "It's just that I'm worried about Donovan. I know he's going to lose his seat. I only pray he doesn't go to prison."

Miranda was glad to think of something else, if only for a moment. "You're first-naming Stratham? He knows how you feel, then?"

Beatrice nodded and a pretty pink colored her cheeks. "He's asked to court me. And since Father's tenure as MP may have been fraught with corruption, what could he say?" She smiled. "And unlike Father, I believe Donovan will be a good husband and father."

Husband and father. As Fox would have been. As he would still like to be. God, could she really just hand her child over to him? Would her father even let her? And why on earth, if she *was* pregnant, wouldn't she just marry him, regardless of what her parents said?

"There you go again, Miranda. All sad-faced. I thought you loved Fox."

"It doesn't matter. I'm not marrying him." Did she love him? She thought of his declaration of love that afternoon, how her heart had broken.

Beatrice frowned at her. "I'd begun to like you, Miranda, but I'm afraid I can't abide you throwing Fox over. He may not be rich, but with your money, who cares? Perhaps his need for money and your overabundance of the same is simply happy coincidence. Makes your love story rather destined, don't you think?"

"You've been reading too many novels." Miranda had read those same novels, and once upon a time she'd wanted to find such a love. What if she'd missed the only opportunity she'd ever have?

Beatrice stood, her eyes blazing. "Fine, wallow in your self-pity! When you get back to London with your fancy friends and your empty life, mayhap you'll realize what you're giving up. Pity your parents have never allowed you to make your own decisions."

"Yes, they do."

But they didn't. They dissected every decision she made and judged it poor and unworthy. Even her good work at the orphanage had been denigrated. And as soon as she returned to London, they would immerse her in her old life until her memories of Wiltshire were faded and worn, like an old pair of gloves. Until there was no way she would consider coming back here.

She didn't want that to happen. She didn't want to forget the children, Mrs. Gates, or Beatrice. And she certainly didn't want to forget Fox.

Her chest lightened, as if a weight had been pulled from her. She hugged Beatrice, who stiffened. "We're going to be hugging more, Beatrice. Both of us. We need it." She hugged her again and grinned.

Miranda turned and opened the door.

Beatrice's brows collected over her eyes. "Where are you going?"

"To make a decision."

~

*A*S soon as Miranda shut Beatrice's door, her parents stepped from their bedchamber in the middle of the hallway. They wore matching expressions of doom.

"Ah, there you are, Miranda." The duke clasped his hands behind his back, looking as if he planned to deliver an important speech.

Miranda had no intention of listening to it. "I'm staying. And I'm marrying Fox."

Her mother came forward, a sconce throwing light over her desperately tightened features. "No, you're returning to London with us where your father's solicitor will draw up the marriage settlements."

They were allowing her to marry Fox? She'd expected at least a small argument, if not a full-out battle. "Can't you conduct the business without me? I'd like to help Fox with overseeing the repairs."

Her father shook his head and Miranda knew she'd misunderstood. "The marriage contract will be with Lord Walter, not *Foxcroft*." He said Fox's name as if it carried the plague.

Miranda's heart hammered. Could they hear the racket it made in her ears? "I'm not marrying Lord Walter. I'm staying here with Fox."

The candlelight reflected in her father's ice-blue eyes. "You don't seem to understand, Miranda. Marriage to Foxcroft is too far beneath this family. You'll get over him, just as you did the diamond necklace we refused to buy when you were sixteen."

Miranda felt a bit dizzy. Fox wasn't a diamond necklace. He was a person. A man. *Her* man. They didn't really care what she wanted, would never approve of her choice. And right now she had to make the most important decision of her life. Could she suffer a future without their approval, possibly without *them*?

The weight of Mother's cold expression and Father's dispassionate gaze forced her eyes shut. In the blackness of her mind rose the smiling face of Fox as he danced with her, held her, *loved* her as no one ever had.

Opening her eyes, she saw things with a clarity she'd never experienced. "I'm marrying Fox because I love him. And because I could already be carrying his child. So, you see, I'm afraid the choice is all mine."

Her mother staggered back, her hand flying to her

throat and her eyes peeling so far open, Miranda feared they might pop from her head. Her father, on the other hand, glowered menacingly as if he wanted to commit some act of violence. Miranda instinctively stepped backward.

"Is this a ruse to win your way?" The duke sounded as if he'd chewed a mouthful of glass.

"No. Jasper will confirm it." She hated bringing her brother into this mess, but she wouldn't put it past her parents to insist she leave anyway. They still might.

Her father's eyes spat ice and fire. "He knew of this? No wonder he was pushing this infernal marriage." He grabbed Miranda's wrist. "I should've sent you to that goddamned convent. But this changes nothing. You'll still marry Lord Walter."

Miranda's knees went weak. "No," she breathed, then more firmly. "No. I'm going to marry Fox."

"The hell you will." The duke dropped her reddened wrist. "Get back to your room."

Her mother's face had drained of color, but now red bloomed in her cheeks as anger overcame her shock. After giving Miranda a thoroughly derisive stare, she turned to her husband. "You'd marry her to Lord Walter in this state?"

"Especially in this state. She needs a husband yesterday, and he's the only one who wants her."

Miranda felt like she was drowning, and her parents were simply standing by as she struggled to stay afloat. No assistance. No compassion. Certainly no love. "Fox wants me! And I want him. I *love* him."

The duke leaned forward and sneered in her face. "When are you going to realize it doesn't matter what you want? That's been your problem all along. I would've supported any number of suitors, allowed you to make a choice, but you only entertained substandard gentlemen. You and your brother are a bloody matched set."

What on earth did that mean? Miranda didn't know, but the duke's anger was also directed at Jasper, and she was now doubly sorry she'd pulled him into this.

Her father straightened. "I am your father, and I will see you do your duty. Now get to your chamber. We depart early." He turned and left her shaking in the corridor.

That hadn't turned out at all as she'd planned. She'd finally tried to take control of her own destiny, only to be forbidden. *Lord Walter*. No, she wouldn't marry him. She loved Fox. *Fox*.

She spun on her heel and hurried back to her bedchamber—not to sleep, but to fetch some things before she left. She wondered if her parents would ever forgive what she was about to do, but realized she didn't care anymore. She only hoped Fox forgave her for taking so long to see what was right in front of her upturned nose.

Three quarters of an hour later, she was pacing Stratham's ridiculous Gold Room, awaiting her brother.

When he entered, his brow creased as he regarded her agitated state. "Miranda, it's quite late."

She walked to him and took his hand. He looked down at her touch, reminding her how closed off they'd all kept themselves. But no more. At least not between them. If they were a matched set, or whatever the duke had said, they needed to stick together.

"Father is ordering me to marry Lord Walter, but I'm going to elope with Fox. If he'll have me." God, she hoped he'd have her. She just couldn't imagine a life without him anymore.

Jasper sucked in a breath. "You can't. Holborn will hunt you down. And it won't be that he simply drags you off and forces you to marry Lord Walter. He'll make Fox pay for his audacity. He'll ruin the man and his orphanage."

Miranda's knees went weak for the second time in the space of an hour. "He wouldn't."

"He would." He glanced away. "He's done it before."

She felt Jasper's pulse pounding in his wrist. "What is it? Father said you and I were a matched set. Something to do with substandard suitors."

Jasper withdrew his hand. His mouth compressed into a slim line and his eyes hardened. "I'll talk to him. You don't need to elope. Just tell Foxcroft to post the banns as soon as possible."

His demeanor worried her. "How can you do this? You've already tried—"

He shook his head. "It doesn't matter. He's never really cared if you make an advantageous match, just that you don't embarrass him. I'm the one who needs to marry well."

She took his hand again, firmly so he couldn't draw away. "Jasper, what are you saying? That you'll marry whomever he dictates? I can't let you do that."

He surprised her by squeezing her hand. "You can, and you will. I've always known what lay in my future. And it seems that future is now." He smiled softly at her. "It's all right. I want you to be happy. Please, for the love of Christ, let one of us be happy." He released her hand. "How did you get here at this hour?"

"Beatrice helped me borrow one of her father's coaching horses."

"You rode it here? Good thing you're such an excellent horsewoman." He put his hand at the small of her back and made to escort her from the room. "Come, I'll have a groom return it, and I'll see you to Bassett Manor in my coach."

Relief and gratitude poured through her. "Thank you." She paused to look up at her brother. "I love you, Jasper."

And then, because he clearly needed it, too, she wrapped him in a fierce hug.

∾

*F*OX tossed in his bed for the hundredth time, wondering if Miranda was leaving for London in the morning. Or maybe she'd been in such a hurry to get away from him and Wootton Bassett that she'd already departed that very afternoon.

He stared at the aged, woven canopy high over his head. He wanted her with everything he had—every heartbeat, every breath, every empty moment she wasn't by his side. He should be doing whatever necessary to persuade her to stay.

Instead, he'd all but shoved her away.

If he was lucky, she was carrying his child and would come back to him. Disgust rose his in throat. He didn't want her that way. He wanted her willing—nay, eager—to be his wife. He wanted her to love him.

A breeze from the open window ruffled the hangings around his bed. The heavy blue damask buffeted, and the lone candle sputtering near the bed blew out. Fox jolted upright. He hadn't left the window *that* open.

Then he heard it. A gentle shuffle against the wood of the floor. He strained to hear every sound. If there was someone in his chamber, they wouldn't know about the—

Creak.

—in the floorboard at the end of the bed. He glanced around for a weapon, but knew there were none. And he was naked. Where the bloody hell was his dressing gown?

Creak.

There was no help for it. Someone was clearly in the room, and he needed to move.

He pushed the covers back and leapt from the bed, ready to meet his attacker. A good fight might be just what he needed to erase a certain blond siren from his mind.

From the meager light of the dying fire, he made out the form of the intruder. Without pause, he jumped forward and knocked the figure onto his bed.

A feminine gasp rewarded him as he straddled her body.

"Miranda?"

The bed curtains weren't drawn tight enough to obscure the firelight. She wore a dark cloak, but the hood had fallen back when he'd tackled her beneath him, revealing her golden, upswept hair. A black kerchief covered the lower half of her face, but her aqua eyes sparkled.

She reached up and touched his chest. "Are you naked?"

"So it would seem." Hope surged within him as he reasoned why she might've stolen into his room in the dead of night. "Are you here to take something from me? My virtue, perhaps?"

She reached behind her head and untied the mask. "Actually, I thought I might give you something."

Fox nearly froze in disbelief, but he didn't want to lose the sheer ecstasy of this moment. "You're not supposed to remove your disguise. It quite ruins the whole idea of anonymity."

Her lips curved into an alluring smile. "I assure you I'm not here to commit a crime."

His cock surged against her waist. "Pity."

She arched a brow at him and laughter threatened to bubble up from his chest. "Are you going to continue sitting on me or help me get undressed?"

Doubt invaded, terrible and black. "Why such haste? Do you have somewhere to go? London perhaps?" If she'd come here for one last tup...he didn't know what he'd do. He inhaled her familiar scent and considered chaining her to the bed.

"You think I'm in a hurry to leave?" She wriggled beneath him and his desire flared. "You might have a deficit of money, Fox, but I never took you for lacking intelligence. I'd like to take my clothes off so that I may make love to my future husband." The exasperation in her tone was endearing, and the words flooded him with a dizzying mixture of joy and satisfaction and love. She'd come for him. She wanted *him*.

"I trust I demonstrated earlier that clothing needn't be a hindrance." Even so, he pulled her cloak apart. She wore a stunning gown the color of rich amethysts. He'd never seen it before. He traced his finger along the edge of the bodice, high on the crest of one perfect breast. She shivered and her tongue darted out to wet the pink softness of her lips.

He could scarcely believe she was actually in his bed. He'd dreamed of this moment since she'd first kissed him on the dark road.

She gazed up at him. "Do you plan to keep me imprisoned?"

"I just might." He fingered the kerchief she'd tossed to the side of her head. "I could easily lash you to the bed frame with this for instance." Fox hardened at the thought. Later, he would do it. And a thousand other things.

Her eyes widened and then narrowed provocatively. "If I'm to be your wife, I suppose I must submit to you." She spread her arms wide in open invitation.

With an inward groan, Fox lowered his head and ran his tongue along the outline of her ear, then tugged on the lobe with his teeth. He murmured against her, "Are you sure?"

She clasped her arms around him, holding him close. "Oh, yes."

Fox devoured her neck with lush kisses and teasing bites. She arched up into him and cast her head back against the bed.

"It's unfair for you to be naked and me to be clothed. Will you please take off my dress at least?"

In record time, Fox flipped her onto her stomach and unhooked the sumptuous gown. He roughly pulled it down her back.

"Careful! I may need to sell this."

Fox slowed. "Indeed?"

She turned her head to the side so he could see half of her face. "I'm afraid my parents aren't in favor of this marriage. I doubt they'll provide a dowry. Never fear, for I've my belongings—which are vast and expensive— and Turnbridge, of course."

"I don't give a damn about your material offerings." Fox purposefully rent the fabric away from her body. "I've managed this long, and we'll continue to do so. All I want, all I need is you." He pulled her shift apart, exposing the ivory flesh of her back.

With far more gentleness than he'd shown her garments, he ran his palms over her satiny skin. "Are you really here? With me?" His hands trembled. "What did I do to deserve you?"

She twisted to face him. "Oh, Fox. I'm the one who needs to deserve you. Today at Stipple's End, you told my parents that I'd given the children a reason to truly live, but it's you who've given that to me. You make me...happy." Her eyes glistened, as if she held back tears.

He crushed her lips beneath his, wanting to draw the happiness from her and coat his soul. In turn, he gave her the bliss racing through him. She kicked her ruined clothing away and reached down to strip off her boots. When she tried to remove her stockings, he pulled her hands up and pinned them on either side of her head. "Hang the rest of whatever you're wearing." He kissed her again, brutal in his need to consume her and be consumed.

She thrust her hips against his and pressed her breasts to his chest. God, his body was still aroused from that afternoon. He couldn't wait. He released one of her wrists and put his hand between her legs. She was hot and wet and completely ready for him.

With a tilt of his pelvis, he slid into her wet heat. She moaned, low and deep, and he was lost. Blindly, he drove into her. She wrapped her legs around his waist and he pushed her across the bed with the force of his thrusts. Her cries grew louder, more frenzied. She was so close. He wanted to see her face in this moment before the storm overtook him. Her eyes were closed in ecstasy, her lips parted. With a final stroke he dove over the edge into sweet oblivion.

He rolled to his side, taking her with him and holding her close to his chest. He never planned to let her go. "If your parents aren't in favor of our marriage, do we need to leave for Gretna Green immediately?"

She drew her finger around the back of his shoulder in wide circles. "No. Jasper's arranged things so that my father won't intercede. Furthermore, I told them the truth."

His breath nearly caught. "The truth?"

"That I love you, that I could already be carrying your child—"

Fox kissed her, quickly but thoroughly. "*Miranda.* I have loved you for so long. I can barely remember a time when I didn't. Not for your money. Or your beauty. For you."

She clutched at his neck. "I know. I don't know why it took me so long to realize this is where I belong. I wanted so badly for my parents to be proud of me, their approval means—meant—everything. Now..."

He nuzzled her cheek. "Now?"

"Now, I crave only your approval."

As much as he loved hearing her say it, fear curled along the edges of his mind. "Won't you miss your life in London? And all of the trappings that go with it?"

She flung an arm to the side. "What trappings? You ruined my clothes. And now that I have nothing to wear, I shall have to be your prisoner. Just promise you'll keep me locked here, in our bedroom."

Her words enflamed him. He hardened inside of her. "I can promise that."

She looked around the bed, her hair abandoning the last of its pins in wild, gorgeous disarray. "Where's the kerchief? Didn't you have a plan for that?"

Fox laughed, reveling in the love threatening to burst from his chest. "You're quite shameless, did you know that?

She looked up at him with a flirtatious quirk to her lips. "If I wasn't, I'd never have met you."

His lips found hers in a fiery kiss while his hand found the makeshift mask. With surprising agility, Miranda plucked the fabric from his hand and pushed him over onto his back. "Actually, perhaps I'll employ this. I've a mind to try what that woman was doing to that man at the brothel."

Lust poured through him, clarifying his emotions even more vividly. "As you wish, my lady."

She shook her head. "Oh no, that's Mrs. Foxcroft. I'm no lady."

Fox grinned and gave himself over to her ministrations, profoundly grateful for her wicked, wicked ways.

EPILOGUE

MARCH, 1817

MIRANDA stood atop a ladder holding one edge of the gorgeous tapestries they'd regained from Lord Norris. Felicity Knott, who'd become a dear friend in the months since Miranda's marriage to Fox, was on another ladder holding the other corner of the tapestry.

"What the devil are you doing up there?" Fox demanded as he strode into the great hall at Bassett Manor.

Miranda threw him an exasperated look before dropping the rod onto the hook Rob had affixed into the wall the week before. "What does it look like?"

"Endangering your life," he said, coming to stand at the base of her ladder.

"Have you no care for Felicity's life? She's equally in peril." Satisfied with her work, Miranda climbed down the ladder. When she was very near the bottom, Fox's hands came around her waist and set her on the floor.

He scowled down at her. "That was very foolish." He shot a glance at Felicity. "Rob would agree if he'd seen you up there."

Felicity waved her hand. "Oh, piddle."

"Yes, piddle," Miranda agreed. "It wasn't foolish; it was necessary. I asked you to hang these last week."

Felicity tiptoed from the room wearing a wide grin.

"I've been busy," Fox said defensively.

"You're always busy." Miranda brushed a speck of dust from his shoulder.

"As if you're ever idle." His gaze swept the completely refurbished great hall, a project she'd attacked with vigor as soon as they'd married in October.

"There's plenty to do, as you know. Besides, you like me this way. If you hadn't married me, only think of how atrocious this would still look." She wrinkled her nose.

"Yes, I married you entirely for your decorating skills." His hands brushed over her backside, giving lie to his words.

"I knew it." She pressed closer to him, thinking it might be nice to christen the settee that had just arrived from London two days ago.

His hands caressed her back. "Stratham and Beatrice have returned."

After losing his seat in Parliament, Stratham had become a hermit. Beatrice had spent months laying a romantic siege until she'd ultimately won his heart. They'd married in February and had spent the last fortnight in Yorkshire on an extended wedding trip.

"Lovely. We should invite them for dinner."

Fox arched a brow. Though he appreciated Stratham's help in saving his neck, the two men still hadn't formed a friendship as Miranda and Beatrice had.

She laid a placating hand against her husband's chest. "I'll invite Rob and Felicity as well, that way you won't have to put up with Stratham alone, all right? Besides, it's good practice for when we go to London next month. You're going to meet a lot of people you'd as soon never speak to."

Fox rolled his spectacular eyes. "Yes, and how delightful that sounds. It's really no wonder you don't miss it."

And she didn't. To her mother's complete and utter horror, Miranda hadn't returned to London or Benfield or any of her father's properties since marrying Fox. She'd only agreed to visit London in April to spend time with Jasper and their Aunt Louisa, who was keen to fund a finishing school for the girls at Stipple's End. Miranda could scarcely wait to get started on the project.

"I appreciate you coming with me," she said, stroking the lapel of his new coat. He hadn't wanted to spend a lot of money on a new wardrobe, but he'd indulged Miranda's desire to see his exceptionally attractive form well-turned out. "I promise you'll love my aunt. She's nothing like her brother."

"She wants to provide a better future for our girls. She couldn't possibly be like your father. Is there any chance we can avoid seeing him?"

Miranda curled her hand around Fox's neck. "No. But I guarantee he'll want to keep our association to a minimum." He'd begrudgingly attended their wedding at the church in Wootton Bassett, but they hadn't seen him since.

"Excellent." He gave her a provocative look that sparked the copper centers of his eyes into a smolder. "I have to admit I'm looking forward to seeing you in your element."

She could almost feel his male pride. She felt the same way when she thought of the envious stares she'd get from other women in Town. Title or no, Fox was undeniably handsome, and when they saw how he danced...well, they'd gape at Miranda with green-eyed jealousy.

She smiled up at him, so grateful for their fortune and their love. Not everyone had fared so well. Norris had suffered a fit of apoplexy in November and died. Cosgrove sat empty like a forgotten museum, waiting for his wayward heir—a distant cousin who'd traveled to some far off place—to claim his inheritance.

Though Fox's eyes had lit with desire, he stepped back. Miranda frowned as he went to the first of three sets of doors into the hall. He closed them and proceeded to the next set.

"What are you doing?" she asked.

"Ensuring some privacy."

"I see." Her frown instantly curled upward, and she made her way toward the new settee. "Mr. Foxcroft, when did you become so wicked?"

He finished securing the last door and strode toward her with seductive purpose. "It just so happens I had a very good teacher." He wrapped his hand around her waist and drew her tight against his chest. "And I do believe it's time for another lesson."

He lowered his lips to hers, and Miranda kissed him with thoroughly wicked intent.

THE END

Don't miss the next book un the *Secrets and Scandals* series, *His Wicked Heart*
featuring Miranda's brother, Jasper, Lord Saxton!

Need more Regency romance? Check out my other historical series:

The Untouchables
Twelve of Society's most elite bachelors and the

wallflowers, bluestockings, and widows who bring them to their knees!

The Spitfire Society
Meet the smart, independent women who've decided they don't need Society's rules, their families' expectations, or, most importantly, a husband. But just because they don't need a man doesn't mean they might not want one...

Wicked Dukes Club
Six books written by me and my BFF, NYT Bestselling Author Erica Ridley. Meet the unforgettable men of London's most notorious tavern, The Wicked Duke. Seductively handsome, with charm and wit to spare, one night with these rakes and rogues will never be enough...

Secrets and Scandals
Six epic stories set in London's glittering ballrooms and England's lush countryside, and the first one, Her Wicked Ways, is free!

Legendary Rogues
Four intrepid heroines and adventurous heroes embark on exciting quests across Regency England and Wales!

Would you like to know when my next book is available? Sign up for my reader club at http://www.darcyburke.com/readerclub, follow me on social media:

Facebook: http://facebook.com/DarcyBurkeFans
Twitter at @darcyburke
Instagram at darcyburkeauthor
Pinterest at darcyburkewrite

and on BookBub to be notified of deals and new releases.

Let's keep in touch! I have two fun Facebook groups:

Darcy's Duchesses for historical readers
Burke's Book Lovers for contemporary readers

I'm also a member of the Jewels of Historical Romance. I hope you'll visit our Facebook group, the Jewels Salon. Read on for links to our Fabulous Firsts collections, two six book anthologies featuring starters for our most beloved series—each set is just 99c!

I hope you'll consider leaving a review at your favorite online vendor or networking site!

If you like contemporary romance, I hope you'll check out my Ribbon Ridge series available from Avon Impulse, and the continuation of Ribbon Ridge in So Hot.

Thank you again for reading and for your support.

xoxox,
Darcy

One Night to Remember by Erica Ridley

One Night of Temptation by Darcy Burke

Secrets and Scandals

Her Wicked Ways

His Wicked Heart

To Seduce a Scoundrel

To Love a Thief (a novella)

Never Love a Scoundrel

Scoundrel Ever After

Legendary Rogues

Lady of Desire

Romancing the Earl

Lord of Fortune

Captivating the Scoundrel

Contemporary Romance

Ribbon Ridge

Where the Heart Is (a prequel novella)

Only in My Dreams

Yours to Hold

When Love Happens

The Idea of You

When We Kiss

You're Still the One

Ribbon Ridge: So Hot

So Good

So Right
So Wrong

The Untouchables Series

THE FORBIDDEN DUKE

"I LOVED this story!!" 5 Stars

-Historical Romance Lover

"This is a wonderful read and I can't wait to see what comes next in this amazing series..." 5 Stars

-Teatime and Books

THE DUKE of DARING

"You will not be able to put it down once you start. Such a good read."

-Books Need TLC

"An unconventional beauty set on life as a spinster meets the one man who might change her mind, only to find his painful past makes it impossible to love. A wonderfully emotional journey from attraction, to friendship, to a love that conquers all."

-Bronwen Evans, *USA Today* Bestselling Author

THE DUKE of DECEPTION

"...an enjoyable, well-paced story ... Ned and Aquilla are an engaging, well-matched couple – strong, caring and compassionate; and ...it's easy to believe that they will continue to be happy together long after the book is ended."

-All About Romance

"This is my favorite so far in the series! They had chemistry from the moment they met...their passion leaps off the pages."

-Sassy Book Lover

THE DUKE of DESIRE

"Masterfully written with great characterization...with a flourish toward characters, secrets, and romance... Must read addition to "The Untouchables" series!"

-My Book Addiction and More

"If you are looking for a truly endearing story about two people who take the path least travelled to find the other, with a side of 'YAH THAT'S HOT!' then this book is absolutely for you!"

-The Reading Café

THE DUKE of DEFIANCE

"This story was so beautifully written, and it hooked me from page one. I couldn't put the book down and just had to read it in one sitting even though it meant reading into the wee hours of the morning."

-Buried Under Romance

"I loved the Duke of Defiance! This is the kind of book

you hate when it is over and I had to make myself stop reading just so I wouldn't have to leave the fun of Knighton's (aka Bran) and Joanna's story!"

-Behind Closed Doors Book Review

THE DUKE of DANGER

"The sparks fly between them right from the start... the HEA is certainly very hard-won, and well-deserved."

-All About Romance

"Another book hangover by Darcy! Every time I pick a favorite in this series, she tops it. The ending was perfect and made me want more."

-Sassy Book Lover

THE DUKE of ICE

"Each book gets better and better, and this novel was no exception. I think this one may be my fave yet! 5 out 5 for this reader!"

-Front Porch Romance

"An incredibly emotional story...I dare anyone to stop reading once the second half gets under way because this is intense!"

-Buried Under Romance

THE DUKE of RUIN

"This is a fast paced novel that held me until the last page."

" ...everything I could ask for in a historical romance... impossible to stop reading."

THE DUKE of LIES

"THE DUKE OF LIES is a work of genius! The characters are wonderfully complex, engaging; there is much mystery, and so many, many lies from so many people; I couldn't wait to see it all uncovered."

"..the epitome of romantic [with]...a bit of danger/action. The main characters are mature, fierce, passionate, and full of surprises. If you are a hopeless romantic and you love reading stories that'll leave you feeling like you're walking on clouds then you need to read this book or maybe even this entire series."

THE DUKE of SEDUCTION

"There were tears in my eyes for much of the last 10% of this book. So good!"

"An absolute joy to read... I always recommend Darcy!"

THE DUKE of KISSES

"Don't miss this magnificent read. It has some comedic fun, heartfelt relationships, heartbreaking moments, and horrifying danger."

-The Reading Café

"...my favorite story in the series. Fans of Regency romances will definitely enjoy this book."

-Two Ends of the Pen

THE DUKE of DISTRACTION

"Count on Burke to break a heart as only she can. This couple will get under the skin before they steal your heart."

-Hopeless Romantic

"Darcy Burke never disappoints. Her storytelling is just so magical and filled with passion. You will fall in love with the characters and the world she creates!"

-Teatime and Books

Secrets & Scandals Series

HER WICKED WAYS

"A bad girl heroine steals both the show and a highwayman's heart in Darcy Burke's deliciously wicked debut."

–Courtney Milan, *NYT* Bestselling Author

"…fast paced, very sexy, with engaging characters."

–Smexybooks

HIS WICKED HEART

"Intense and intriguing. Cinderella meets *Fight Club* in a historical romance packed with passion, action and secrets."

–Anna Campbell, Seven Nights in a Rogue's Bed

"A romance…to make you smile and sigh…a wonderful read!"

–Rogues Under the Covers

TO SEDUCE A SCOUNDREL

"Darcy Burke pulls no punches with this sexy, romantic page-turner. Sevrin and Philippa's story grabs you from the first scene and doesn't let go. *To Seduce a Scoundrel* is simply delicious!"

–Tessa Dare, NYT Bestselling Author

"I was captivated on the first page and didn't let go until this glorious book was finished!"

–Romancing the Book

TO LOVE A THIEF

"With refreshing circumstances surrounding both the hero and the heroine, a nice little mystery, and a touch of heat, this novella was a perfect way to pass the day."

Legendary Rogues Series

LADY of DESIRE

"A fast-paced mixture of adventure and romance, very much in the mould of *Romancing the Stone* or *Indiana Jones*."

-All About Romance

"...gave me such a book hangover! ...addictive...one of the most entertaining stories I've read this year!"

-Adria's Romance Reviews

ROMANCING the EARL

"Once again Darcy Burke takes an interesting story and...turns it into magic. An exceptionally well-written book."

-Bodice Rippers, Femme Fatale, and Fantasy

"...A fast paced story that was exciting and interesting. This is a definite must add to your book lists!"

-Kilts and Swords

LORD of FORTUNE

"I don't think I know enough superlatives to describe this book! It is wonderfully, magically delicious. It sucked me in from the very first sentence and didn't turn me loose—not even at the end ..."

-Flippin Pages

"If you love a deep, passionate romance with a bit of mystery, then this is the book for you!"

CAPTIVATING the SCOUNDREL

"I am in absolute awe of this story. Gideon and Daphne stole all of my heart and then some. This book was such a delight to read."

"Darcy knows how to end a series with a bang! Daphne and Gideon are a mix of enemies and allies turned lovers that will have you on the edge of your seat at every turn."

Contemporary Romance

Ribbon Ridge Series

A contemporary family saga featuring the Archer family of sextuplets who return to their small Oregon wine country town to confront tragedy and find love...

The "multilayered plot keeps readers invested in the story line, and the explicit sensuality adds to the excitement that will have readers craving the next Ribbon Ridge offering."

"Darcy Burke writes a uniquely touching and heart-warming series about the love, pain, and joys of family as well as the love that feeds your soul when you meet "the one.""

I can't tell you how much I love this series. Each book gets better and better.

"Darcy Burke's Ribbon Ridge series is one of my all-time favorites. Fall in love with the Archer family, I know I did."

Ribbon Ridge: So Hot

SO GOOD

" ...worth the read with its well-written words, beautiful descriptions, and likeable characters...they are flirty, sexy and a match made in wine heaven."

"I absolutely love the characters in this book and the families. I honestly could not put it down and finished it in a day."

SO RIGHT

"This is another great story by Darcy Burke. Painting pictures with her words that make you want to sit and stare at them for hours. I love the banter between the characters and the general sense of fun and friendliness."

ACKNOWLEDGMENTS

I can't convey the tremendous gratitude and love I have for my dear friends and critique partners Erica Ridley, Lacey Kaye, and Janice Goodfellow. I would not be the writer—or the person—I am today without your unflinching support and assistance. The ways in which you've helped are too great to count and the effect immeasurable. So many people have encouraged and guided me and none more than Jackie Barbosa, Courtney Milan, Kristina McMorris, Rachel Grant, Elisabeth Naughton, Leigh LaValle, Elyssa Papa, and Inara Scott. I am indebted and can only hope to give you a fraction of what you've given me. Thank you also to Sara Ramsey, who has been a wealth of information. And thank you to my spectacular beta reader, Kayla MacAfee, who shares my deep love of historical romance novels by Judith McNaught. Knowing I have you to read my draft makes me write that much faster. I also want to thank the Pixies. I've learned so much from your wealth of knowledge and experience, and you're all so incredibly generous.

Mom, thank you for being my number one fan—not just in this but in everything. I love you so much.

Finally, I want to thank my agent, the wonderful Jim

McCarthy of Dystel & Goderich Literary Management. Your optimism in this crazy, ever-changing publishing industry and unwavering faith in me has made all the difference. Thank you.

ABOUT THE AUTHOR

Darcy Burke is the USA Today Bestselling Author of sexy, emotional historical and contemporary romance. Darcy wrote her first book at age 11, a happily ever after about a swan addicted to magic and the female swan who loved him, with exceedingly poor illustrations. Join her Reader Club at http://www.darcyburke.com/readerclub.

A native Oregonian, Darcy lives on the edge of wine country with her guitar-strumming husband, their two hilarious kids who seem to have inherited the writing gene. They're a crazy cat family with two Bengal cats, a small, fame-seeking cat named after a fruit, and an older rescue Maine Coon who is the master of chill and five a.m. serenading. In her "spare" time Darcy is a serial volunteer enrolled in a 12-step program where one learns to say "no," but she keeps having to start over. Her happy places are Disneyland and Labor Day weekend at the Gorge. Visit Darcy online at http://www.darcyburke.com and follow her social media: Facebook at http://www.facebook.com/darcyburkefans, Twitter @darcyburke at http://www.twitter.com/darcyburke, Instagram at http://www.

instagram/darcyburkeauthor, and Pinterest at http://
www.pinterest.com/darcyburkewrite.